WHY

MEGAN MITCHAM

Published by MM Publishing LLC
Edited by Jenny Sims
Proofread by Tina Rucci & Lynn Mullan
Cover Design by Shayne Leighton of Shayne Leighton Designs

A STALKER SERIES NOVEL

WHY

To all you true crime "weirdos" and the ladies of My Favorite Murder. Thank you for the sense of community and acceptance for our curious obsession. I can't tell you how many quaint circles I've busted up with the story of my favorite murder. When you find your Karen or Georgia, it's worth all the wide eyes and odd looks.

WARNING:
This novel, while 100% fiction, deals with the difficult topics of death by suicide and sexual assault. It is my hope that by bringing these topics into the forefront, we can deal with them with better awareness in our own lives; however, it may not be suitable for all audiences.

PROLOGE

Dispatch: 911. What is the address of your emergency?
Caller: I need help! (Labored breathing.)
Dispatch: What kind of help, sir?
Caller: I need an ambulance and the police. Get the police here, now!
Dispatch: Sir, what is the address of your emergency?
Caller: <address redacted> (Coughing. Crying.)
Dispatch: Sir, tell me what's wrong, so I can get you help.
Caller: My family … Please, no! (A scream.)
Dispatch: Sir, are you hurt?
Caller: No. (Sobs.) My family! They're dead! They're all dead. Someone killed my family!
Dispatch: Sir, what is your name?
Caller: Perry Carter Jr.
Dispatch: Mr. Carter, I need you to hold on the

line while I send help your way. Do not hang up.
Hold the line.
Caller: Please hurry!
Dispatch: (Off call dispatcher requests police
to address.) Mr. Carter, who is dead?
Caller: Everyone! They're all dead! (Short,
erratic breathing.)
Dispatch: Are you hurt, Mr. Carter?
Caller: No! I told you, my family is dead.
Dispatch: What are their names, Mr. Carter?
Caller: Pamela Carter, Claire Carter, and Perry
Carter III.
Dispatch: Have you seen each of them?
Caller: Yes! (Scream.) They're all in the par-
lor.
Dispatch: Are they breathing?
Caller: Noooo! (Huff.) I told you, they're dead.
Dispatch: Mr. Carter, you requested an ambu-
lance. You're also saying they're dead. How do
you know they're dead?
Caller: There's blood everywhere.

ONE

"OKAY. LADIES. GLASSES UP." Libby lifted her froth-topped mug into the air. Her friend hadn't needed to tell Larkin or Marlis, who'd nearly beaten her to the punch by sloshing their beer high.

Genevieve clutched her mug to her chest and groaned. She'd picked this hole-in-the-wall bar to keep away from the spotlight. How had her dearest friends in the world, women who understood her better than she knew herself, not gotten the hint?

"This is not about me," Gen warned.

"Like hell, it isn't." Larkin leaned over and grabbed Genevieve's arm.

"Jesus, it's Indian summer out there, and your hands are icicles. How are you going to make it when the real cold sinks in?" Gen pulled her arm from Larkin's hold and lifted her beer toward the other ones suspended above their small high-top table.

"Hibernation." Larkin winked. "I know my hands are cold. It's ten degrees in this place." She whirled her frozen hand around the neon lit space.

On the little bit of wrist that peeked out from Larkin's perfectly tailored business suit, gooseflesh prickled her porcelain skin. Gen, on the other hand, had shucked her suit jacket as soon as she'd elbowed the last reporter out of the way in front of the courthouse and opened her Uber's door. Even in the dark, cool pub, perspiration collected between her breasts and dampened the fabric of the dress pulled tight across her belly.

Libby lifted her chin and surveyed them one at a time with her signature sultry smile. "To our Gen, the best attorney in all of New York. May the jury realize your majesty or have nary another orgasm as long as they live."

Surprise laughter snorted from Gen's nostrils, drawing with it a hint of the dread she'd carried around since the closing arguments. Her shoulders bobbed. The worry forcing her to walk like a hunchback lifted, and for the first time since jury selection, her spine uncoiled. She shouldn't have put her friends off for so long. They knew what was best for her. Always had. Always would.

Marlis choked on her giggles.

"That's a steep penalty, don't you think?" Gen asked.

Libby shrugged.

Gen wiped the tears from the corners of her eyes. "If we could enforce it, maybe we wouldn't have the burden of crime or the overflowing prison population."

"To Genevieve, her success, and having more time to help her horny friends get laid." Libby shoved her glass toward the center of the circled mugs with a hurrah.

Marlis's choking suspended, replaced by a whooping battle cry that drew the attention of every man in the room.

"To everything except the last." Larkin clanked her

mug into the middle.

"To Judge Faraday, the man who changed my life." Gen thrust her glass against her friends'.

"You did all the work." Larkin scoffed.

"But her family couldn't have afforded Harvard." Libby lifted her hand palm up. "No offense. Mine couldn't have either. Brooklyn babes." She offered Gen her hand.

She smacked her palm to Libby's. They shared that connection while Mar and Larkin shared more monied backgrounds. No matter how much money Larkin's dad had blown, they had more than her family. And she didn't hold their money, past nor present, against them.

"To you." Mar lifted her glass. "The baddest bitch attorney in all of NYC."

They all drew long swigs, Genevieve a little longer than the rest. She had some catching up to do. Since the trial started, she'd limited herself to one glass of wine on Saturday evenings and no men. Zero. Which meant she was starved to the point that her libido had cannibalized itself over the past three months. It was the saddest part of the whole affair besides having to watch a police officer cart her friend off in handcuffs at the end of every day.

"Some of us don't have a fine piece of ass warming our bed every night." Libby slammed down her glass and waggled her brows at Larkin.

"Not every night," Larkin defended.

"Right." Marlis's eyes rolled toward the back of her skull. "And anyway, I take offense to that."

"Take offense to what?" Gen had lost the thread of the conversation. She hadn't knitted any conversations without elements of timelines, evidence, and lines of questioning for so long. It took practice to keep up with this crew.

"He's been on an op for the last week," Larkin blurted. "I don't know where he is, what he's doing, or when he'll be home." She didn't state the obvious worry. What if he didn't come home?

Gen and the others had worried the same thing from the moment they'd learned exactly who Calder Beckett was and what he did for a living ... now that his last set of life-threatening injuries sustained on the job were behind him.

No one said a word. The sounds of the various sports games poured from the television screens and filtered between them. The Mets were up by one.

Genevieve hated the quiet tension leeching into their usual harmony. She looked Larkin in the eyes. "I don't understand how you do it. Especially after your mom."

"Gen," Marlis scolded.

"It's what we're all thinking about right now, so why not talk about it?" She hated the pit of worry in her stomach. Over the years, she'd crossed the proverbial line a time or two, but it beat silence.

Silence ruined lives.

Libby's upper lip curled, and her gaze narrowed. Her beautiful friend turned menacing when coming to the aid of another. "Well Christ, Genevieve, you—"

"She's right." Every heavily mascaraed eye shifted to Larkin. "In the beginning, it was in his past. It was something we didn't have to deal with. Then when they realized his capabilities, that he'd recovered one hundred percent, they wanted him back in the field. I knew it was a part of him. Helping people and restoring balance drive him, and I will never take that away from him." Her head hung, and Larkin picked at her perfectly manicured nails.

"But?" Gen prodded.

"The thought of losing him keeps me up, and it makes eating nearly impossible." Her friend dabbed at the corners of her eyes and sucked in a breath.

Marlis grabbed Larkin's hand and held it tight.

"I'm sorry, Lar." Libby rubbed the handle of her mug.

Gen downed half her beer in three gulps and then set it down with a thud. "Talk to him about it."

Again, they gave her the wide eyes.

"I can't." Larkin's head shook, flipping her low ponytail from side to side. "I'm not going to make him choose—"

"I'm not suggesting you make him pick only one of the two things that makes the blood pump through his veins." Gen liked cutting people off. It was a character flaw, but in this case, it was warranted. "I'm saying tell him how scared you are."

"What good will that do?" Larkin begged.

"It won't change the way he operates. It won't change your fear." Across from her, Larkin drew a breath to argue, but she wasn't the interrupting type. Gen smiled. "But he'll know how you feel. He'll reassure you, explain their capabilities and tactics so you'll understand it all a little better, and then you'll find a peace about it." She took another sip. "Ultimately, you don't want to lose him. Not in combat and not in a failure to communicate. If you hold it inside, you'll lose him."

They all stared at her with loose jaws and wide eyes. It wasn't a first. She said crazy shit all the time, usually to get a rise out of them, but this was the first time she'd ever used her powers for good. It fit like a department store bra. Uncomfortable, but it got the job done.

The rest of her beer burned its way along her esophagus. It'd been too long if beer hurt going down. "Now"— she turned her hiked brow to Marlis—"why were you offended?"

"Um, wait." Libby raised her hand as though they were in kindergarten and Gen were the teacher.

Gen shivered the thought away and glared at Libby. "What?"

"Who are you and what have you done with our hyper-sexual, over-the-top friend Genevieve Holst?" Libby grabbed her and pulled her close. The green of her friend's big eyes studied her intently.

"She's still in here, but she's trapped under case files, a pounding gavel, and an old bailiff's slow, shuffling steps." Genevieve wanted to wave the waiter over for another round, but she still had to appear in court. She didn't know when the old broad would sing. It could be tomorrow or fifteen days from now, depending on how well she'd done her job. This was no time to fuck it up. A life was on the line. Her friend's life.

When she shoved her glass to the center of the table, their gawking intensified. In the background, Javier Baez knocked one over the ivy with two runners on, giving the Cubs a two-run lead. Libby released her hold and muttered a curse. Brooklyn babes cared about ball even when it wasn't an American League game.

"You just made so much sense," Marlis awed.

"Don't act like I've never added two and two and gotten four. Christ!" Gen threw her hands up and let them smack the table. "Marlis, what were you offended about?" Anything to get the focus off her.

"Um …" Mar's cute nose crinkled. "I forgot." She looked from one of them to the other but stopped on Libby for a beat. "Oh, I remember. I'm offended Libby implied I'm not as good of a wingman as you are."

"You're not." Gen shrugged.

Marlis flounced and folded her arms.

Libby flashed Mar a sweet smile but couldn't quite hide her wince.

"Think about it," Gen offered. "How many times in the past year have I told you which one to pick and what to say? Think about your success rate. Now, think about the ones you've picked and your success rate."

Her friend's lips waggled from side to side.

"Did you pick that married yuppie?" Larkin asked Gen.

"What do you think?" Gen lifted Mar's mug and syphoned off a gulp of her barely touched brew.

"Hey," Marlis whined.

"You don't even like beer," Libby interjected. "I don't know why you insist on ordering it."

"When in Rome ..." Mar discreetly pointed toward the other, mostly male patrons. Pints and mugs littered their tables.

A jeer from the far corner yanked Gen's attention from the abundance of beer to a table of construction workers. On any normal night, the sight of thick biceps, sweat-matted hair, and worn jeans would have incited a lady boner so insistent she'd have ended the evening sharing the three pints on their table. Probably more, if she was being honest. Something about callused hands and work-hardened muscles got her going. But this trial had dampened her drive like none before. Damn the grueling subject matter and her unique position in the case.

"Look." Libby pointed at the largest of the screens that hung across from the men's table. Minutes ago, it hosted a ball game she'd been discreetly following—Cubs vs. Mets—but now, in its place, was the last thing she wanted to see. The news.

Perry's mugshot filled the screen. Of all the hurdles she'd had to overcome in the case, that goddamned mugshot might have been the most difficult of all. The normally charismatic man had such a blank expression that a ream of office paper boasted more character. His eyes held no life. They were dead. Like his family. That was the only way Gen had rationalized it in the media and in her own head. How was a man who'd lost his entire world in the most brutal way possible only days before supposed to look when he was arrested for their murders, especially when all the evidence pointed at another man?

"Shit," Larkin groaned. "Sorry, Gen."

"You can't control the networks, can you?" Genevieve joked, but her eyes remained glued to the screen.

The construction workers' jeers turned into mute, undivided attention.

A somber journalist spoke. "The second longest criminal trial in New York City's history nears its end as both sides offered summation this afternoon. Now, Perry Carter Jr.'s life is in the hands of the jury. If convicted of the grisly murders, the prosecution will push for the death penalty. While New York State maintains a memorandum on the death penalty, it can be sought in the Federal Court hearing the case. For more on this, we go to our legal correspondent, Trisha Moyer."

"The death penalty?" Marlis squeaked. "But ..."

"Thank you, Nancy. Good evening, everyone." Genevieve's once upon a time best friend, Trisha Moyer, stood with her forearm propped on the edge of a news station desk. Gen's headshot filled the background, misshaping her head and making her look like the girl from Willy Wonka, only she'd eaten a strawberry.

Thank you, red hair.

"After one hundred eight days of testimony, many questions remain to be answered. First and foremost in my mind, though, is why prosecutor Genevieve Holst was allowed to defend her employer and friend, Perry Carter Jr. Legally, the conflict of interest in this pairing is off the charts."

"Motherfucking, cock-sucking bitch," Gen growled.

"I'll buy the network." Larkin nodded, looking around the table. "Who has time to run it?"

The group of friends, her truest and best, looked from one to the other. None of them had time to finish their drinks these days, much less run another business. Marlis and Larkin each had their own multimillion-dollar endeavors respectively while Libby was trying her damnedest to make her mark at the Bureau. She'd been tirelessly chasing the same small arms hoarder for more than a year. And Gen, well, she was in the midst of her own hell.

Trashy Trish, as the other girls in their law classes often called her, blathered on about the case, but the first jab pierced too deep for her to care about anything else.

Truly, why had Gen agreed to take the job, and why hadn't the judge called her off the case? She and Perry had worked together for years, and they had a friendship outside the office. Family barbecues and after-hours drinks with the partners had been a monthly occurrence. Technically, they broke no rules because it wasn't like she was part of the jury. But had she been objective enough to perform to the best of her ability? Trish certainly wasn't worried about that angle, but it kept Gen up at least once a week.

"Hey, you okay?" Marlis grabbed her hand.

Gen held tight. She needed the support. She also needed another drink. "May I?" She pointed at Mar's mug.

"Of course. You know I don't even like the stuff." Mar winked and shoved the glass toward her. Before it made its way to her mouth, Trish's sardonic tone cut through the girl's chitchat.

"My final issue with this lengthy trial is the evidence. The scene was clean, wiped down, leaving no trace that the family ever stepped foot into that room except for the perfectly placed DNA of an Edger Sanchez. The DNA of a man Perry Carter defended and got off on two counts of rape in two thousand sixteen. DNA Perry Carter had access to days before the murders."

"She's not a practicing attorney." Libby flipped off the screen. "What does she know?"

"She knows enough to punch holes in my case." Gen

drained the rest of Mar's beer.

"Trashy Trish has been doing it since day one. You haven't let her get to you yet." Libby raised her glass, nodded, and then finished off the liquid.

"She's not really trashy. I was way trashier." Gen let a smirk take over her face to camouflage her worry.

"Forgive me, but isn't it trashy to steal your best friend's report and pass it off as your own?" The smack of Libby's mug on the table punctuated her point.

"True." Gen had almost failed the class because of Trish's little stunt.

"How do you keep the faith after reports like that?" Mar asked.

The sincerity in her friend's voice wiggled something long hidden under the fortress that was her bosom. She drew a deep breath and did what she did best. "Multiple orgasms."

Whooping laughter warmed the temperature of the table ten degrees. Only it didn't last long enough.

"Gen?" Libby eyed Larkin's beer but didn't grab it.

"Lib," she sang.

"I hate to bring down the party, but you know, it's always the husband." Libby bit her lip and then shrugged. "Every murderino knows that."

"It is always the husband," Gen agreed. "Until it's not."

"Why would Sanchez clean up everything except his DNA?" Libby grabbed the air and shook it as though it would reveal the answer.

"Because ... it's always the husband." Gen winked. "Sanchez is scary, not dumb. Rape. Aggregated assault. Extortion. The FBI knows his father is Amigo Ruez Sanchez, the head of one of Mexico's up-and-coming cartels, and they know he's laying the groundwork for his father in the States."

"Why isn't he locked up already?" Larkin asked.

"Because he's smart, and he had a good attorney." Gen lifted a finger. "But there are two things. One, Sanchez didn't get off scot-free. He was assigned hours of group therapy and community service."

"Excuse me? He got community service and therapy for rape?" Marlis's eyes were as big as two moons.

"He pled to simple assault. It sucks, but it happens every day," Gen said.

"What's the second thing?" Larkin asked.

"Oh, Edger Sanchez is now in Manhattan Detention Complex awaiting trial."

"What?" Libby gasped.

"Yep." Genevieve couldn't contain her grin. "He stabbed a woman in the middle of a public park in broad daylight, and Perry refused to defend him on that charge because there was indisputable video evidence."

"I don't understand how Perry could do that." Marlis's nose crinkled. "I know everyone deserves a fair trial and all that, but I don't see how he could defend a guy like Sanchez. A guy who has a record of terrible crimes."

"He's never been convicted. To Perry, no conviction meant no crime." Gen looked at the men who'd fallen back into the pace of the baseball game and the rest of the crowd engrossed in their own conversations and games who'd never noticed the interrupting report. Her gaze returned to her friends.

"I know Perry isn't a saint. It's like Trashy Trish said, I was friends with Perry, and I was friends with Pamela. I saw them through the trials of a new practice and infertility and the triumphs of success, both business and personal. I loved their children, and you all know I don't like kids." She couldn't fight the smile that drew her cheeks. Nor could she fend off the sorrow that clouded those memories. "I know how much Perry loved his family. I know how much of himself he gave them. He shifted his schedule and hired more help to make himself available for them. Above all, I know there is no way he could have hurt them, much less do to them what was done that night."

TWO

THE RAPID FIRE OF CAMERA SHUTTERS overwhelmed the questions hurled like grenades from every direction. Shoulders bumped her back, threatening to throw her off the thin heels of her pumps. Elbows grazed her arms. One jabbed sharp, jarring her ribs and jerking a gasp from her lungs. She'd been on high-profile cases before, but nothing compared to this madness. Everywhere she looked, faces pressed toward hers. Rage bubbled beneath the surface of her perfectly composed façade.

Vultures.

"How can you defend a monster?" someone in the throng shouted, proving her point.

At least she didn't need to worry about the sunshine baking her shoulders on the walk from the car to the courthouse lobby. Outstretched arms, video cameras, mini recorders, microphones, and a hundred jockeying bodies created a musty shade grove. She adjusted the suit jacket draped across her hand and briefcase and made certain not to hurry her steps. Sweat, even in the unseasonably warm spell of late autumn, didn't lend itself to innocence.

"You pursue the death penalty in cases you prosecute. Have your feelings on the death penalty changed now that your friend's life is on the line?" The question came from over her shoulder.

Genevieve tuned out the shouts, kept her head high, and aimed for the freedom of the steps. A cameraman stumbled on his backward tread, teetering for a beat before a fellow tradesman grabbed the back of his shirt and righted him. It wasn't an act of kindness but self-preservation at its finest. If one tumbled, they all collapsed like jittery little dominos.

What a shame.

Despite her better judgment, she picked up her pace. She needed some oxygen before her fuming rage combusted. Barricades and metal handrails funneled foot traffic into a narrow swath unwelcome to reporters without a special pass, and those scavengers were already seated in the courtroom with their pencils at the ready.

Genevieve stepped on a toe or two before she reached the steps. Freedom met her in the form of fresh air and searing sunshine. It struck the back of her ultra-white legs and the top of her shoulders with a ferocity matched only by her desire to get inside the courtroom and hear the verdict read aloud.

Innocent. Innocent. Innocent.

It opposed her usual wishes by 180 degrees. It went against everything she'd lived and worked for over the past two and a half decades. It was a once-in-a-lifetime event, and it was almost over.

She swallowed and shoved through the doors of the Thurgood Marshall United States Courthouse. It was a bit like coming home. She hadn't spent her childhood here, but her profession had grown up in walls like these. Echoes of the past hugged her in a warm embrace, stretching out arms from every direction. Intricately patterned marble covered the floors. Vaulted and etched archways adorned with bold murals hung overhead, perennial reminders of how far they'd come. The sheer number of proceedings that had taken place inside this historical location boggled the mind. It offered Genevieve a peace she'd never felt in any other place.

Justice was served inside these walls. And justice separated humanity from the animal world. Justice was life.

"How does it feel, counselor?"

Genevieve couldn't see the owner of the voice, but she recognized the deep baritone. In the past six months, it'd become heavily laced with sarcastically mocking undertones. More so with each lobbed insult and veiled threat. She slapped on a sultry smile, begged her body to cooperate, and turned.

Damn her, but her breath caught.

Detective Owen Graham strode from a dimly lit catacomb. There were so many darkened hallways in this massive expanse of concrete. Were it not for the open pack of peanuts he shook into his thick palm and the extra pack hanging from his pocket, she'd think him a vengeful wraith on a mission to steal her soul. Though wraiths didn't possess the faces of angels. Seriously, the thing was too perfectly formed.

"Winning?" Gen cocked her head to the side. "It feels great."

He stopped several feet away. His thick brows narrowed, turning his fiery blue eyes into quick shooting lasers. "You haven't won yet."

He popped a handful of nuts into his mouth. The pronounced muscles in his jaw went to work, drawing attention to the carved structure of his neck. Gen followed the line to the pointed collar of his gray button-up. For the first time ever, she'd caught him less than camera ready. The buttons on his sleeves were unfastened, and the wide cuffs flipped up. Under the smooth fabric, a hint of deep color marked the taut skin covering his forearms. She'd never expected the always-on-his-game, always-on-duty detective with an angel's face to sport ink. Then again, knowing they existed made his haircut make sense. The buzzed on the sides, long on the top, and slicked back do didn't match his all-business persona either.

Most people could be marked from twenty paces. Wall Street asshole. Yuppie. Detective asshole. Jock asshole. Lawyer asshole. It seemed there was more to Detective Graham than he let on.

"Sure, I have." She winked. "They've deliberated for five days. A quick turnaround and Perry would've been facing a lifetime of appeals. Now, I'm just waiting to pop my cork." Gen let the innuendo hang in the humid air that snuck in from the entryway and condensed between them.

He strangled the top of his open peanut bag and straightened. His stature in a slight slouch dwarfed her, so at his full height and breadth, forget about level playing fields. She banked the urge to stomp his toe with the stiletto of her pump and bring him down to her level.

"How does it feel to trade your high and mighty morals?" He licked his lips, seemingly satisfied with himself.

Maybe she'd rethink the stiletto to toe decision. The things she could do with lips like those. A low and sultry laugh rumbled up Gen's throat. "My morals have always been questionable, and my record squeaky clean." She lifted her arms. Damn, her briefcase was heavy. "Search me, officer."

"Detective." His voice was even, unaffected. "And I have."

"What a shame. I don't remember it." Genevieve let her hands fall to her sides.

Detective Graham gulped the distance between them and leaned his head down from the great mountain that was his shoulders. Lord, the handles those things would make. A nice anchor for a wild ride. Heat radiated through her chest and swirled low.

"You think you can throw me off the scent of a murderer with your provocative mouth and cheap bedroom banter?"

What she could do with her provocative mouth. Several scenes took turns playing through her indecent mind. Of all the men she'd come into contact with since the beginning of this trial, for the love of God, why was this the one her body responded to?

Gen bit her lower lip and leaned in, leaving only a scant inch between them. "I know I can." She let her gaze drop to the bulge in the front of his slacks. "But, officer, I don't need to. The evidence exonerates my client."

"Detective." When he growled, his perfectly aligned white teeth gnashed together. "The evidence was placed. Perry defended Edger Sanchez two years ago and got him off."

"Are you upset because no one is getting you off, detective?" Gen tilted her head.

Graham's nostrils flared. "Perry had access to Edger Sanchez's DNA, and Sanchez had no motive for an attack. Perry got him off."

This man was persistent. He had been on the stand, adding things to cross examination that she hadn't prepared for. Things that made her client look bad. Gen was nothing if not more dogged. She drew a deep breath and blasted him.

"Sanchez couldn't pay his bill. Perry put the collectors on his tail, and he foreclosed on his house. His family ended up in shelters on good nights and on the streets on the bad while Perry and his family lived in a house so big they didn't use half of it."

His head shook before she finished. "Bull. If you know anything about crime scenes, and from your record of prosecuting pieces of shit for eight years, I'd bet my pathetic salary you do, you know it's too clean. Too perfect."

Did the man never look in the mirror? Things that were too perfect existed, and they wreaked havoc on those around them.

Genevieve abandoned the innuendos and games and went with the only thing she had left. The truth. "I know Perry didn't murder his family in cold blood. I know he couldn't have looked into his son's eyes and carved out his heart while it still beat inside his chest."

"Which is why he cut them out."

Imagining that poor child and the hellish horror he endured rose the tide on her barricaded emotions. The only solace she'd found was that the boy's eyes had been removed post-mortem. She didn't blink. No way would she give Graham the satisfaction.

He straightened and stepped back. "Huh." The plastic wrapper crinkled in his hand. He tipped the package and poured another heap into his palm.

She shifted her briefcase and jacket into her other hand and glared at him. "Huh, what?"

"You really believe he's innocent." His head shook, but it didn't stop him from tossing back the handful of nuts. There weren't many left in the package.

"Because he is. Attorneys make enemies all the time."

"Do you have enemies, counselor?"

"If you want to make a list, I hope you have unlimited storage on your phone." She grinned.

He grinned right back. "And how many of those enemies actually seek retribution?"

She'd walked right into that one.

The doors to the courtroom opened behind them. "Genevieve!" She recognized the panicked voice of her assistant. "They're starting!"

"I'm on my way." Gen waved a staying hand to the frantic woman and then turned back to Graham. "A very dangerous few, detective. A very dangerous few."

THREE

"ANOTHER BOTTLE. PLEASE. JEFF. WE'RE CELEBRATING." Larkin beamed at the server.

"Larkin." Genevieve kicked her friend's leg under the table, drawing her gaze from the smiling man in a stiff white coat and obnoxiously large black bow tie. "No, it's too expensive," she mouthed.

"Congratulations, Miss Ashford." He bowed.

"Oh, it's not for me." Larkin's neatly manicured finger hinged in Gen's direction. "It's my treat for my fabulous friend. She won a hard-fought victory today."

"In that case, miss, congratulations to you." He bowed once more and flourished a hand as though she was royalty.

In truth, she felt it. With the weight of the trial off her shoulders, they rose a good three inches. Breaths filled the cobwebbed corners of her lungs. Food regained its taste just in time for the most exquisite food Larkin's money could buy. Gen made good money. Plenty enough for Daniel's Tavern a few blocks down, sure, but not for Daniel's—spoken with a French accent and costing more than her rent and clothing budget for the month.

"Thank you." Genevieve nodded at the man, and then he left. Her gaze traveled to each of her friends in turn around the table. "Thank you for putting up with me during this process. I know I've missed so many events and so much time with you, but I'll make up for it. I promise."

"Gen." Marlis grabbed her hand. "We're just happy it's behind us." Her smile grew. "And that you won. It's pretty awesome to have a famous kickass attorney on our side."

"Always," Gen assured her.

A phone chirped *at their table*. Larkin froze, and Marlis's eyes bugged out of her head. Gen choked on a laugh because after years of telling them that they didn't belong in swanky, slightly snobby places like this, no matter how heartbreakingly delicious each artfully designed bite was, they didn't listen. Libby's hand slapped across the O her beautiful lips formed, giving herself away.

"They're supposed to be off," Marlis whisper-screamed across the small table.

"You rushed me inside." Libby jabbed a finger back in Mar's direction.

Gen scanned the surrounding area. Since it was Wednesday, there weren't as many people as there would've been on a Thursday or Friday evening. The ones who gathered around the fine white linen and fresh flowers seemed more interested in their own conversations than in the interruption of the girls. "For goodness' sake, it's not like we're in a courtroom or a church—"

"Wouldn't want it to spontaneously catch fire." Libby chuckled.

They shared a quiet laugh.

"While Gen is right"—Mar nodded—"we all agreed …"

"I know. I know. I'm turning it off." Libby reached into her sweet pink clutch, covered her phone with her hand, and pulled it quickly under the table. The edges of her full lips kicked up, and a squeal resonated from the back of her throat.

"What?" Larkin stretched out an arm and did the give-me fingers.

"Stop encouraging her." Marlis grabbed Larkin's extended hand. "She's not supposed to read it. She's supposed to turn it off."

Rebellion reared its ugly head, forcing Genevieve to lean over and peer at her friend's phone. It was a *New York Times* news alert. The headline read "The Golden Lawyer Wins Again."

"They're talking about you." Libby giggled.

"Who's talking about whom?" Marlis released her hold on Larkin's hand, hiked both elbows on the table, and leaned closer.

"Wait a minute." Libby patted her upper lip with her index finger. "The phone police wants to know what the New York Times report on my phone says about our friend?"

Marlis grimaced. "Yes. Yes, she does."

Genevieve straightened. It didn't matter what anyone said about the case or her. The law and its effect on her career and her clients were all that mattered. Public opinion belonged in the toilet. She syphoned off the last of her champagne, ignoring Libby, her click happy fingers, and her phone. Someone had to maintain decorum. The other two leaned so far over the table that it just might upend and get them permanently banished from the most delectable foie gras—sorry, little duckies—that'd ever passed her lips.

"Okay. Okay," Libby began. "The seemingly unbeatable Golden Lawyer, Genevieve Holst, pulled out another astounding win against the city's toughest prosecution team. A team on which Holst usually bats first. The usual prosecutor held her own against the city's new lead investigator, Detective Owen Graham, and the evidence he and his team had meticulously cured from the most gruesome—" Libby waved her hand. "Never mind the rest. That's amazing."

"The Golden Lawyer? Hell yes, she is." Larkin lifted her glass and tilted it toward Gen.

"That's incredible." Marlis's cheeks reddened, as they tended to when she was tipsy and trying her best not to show it.

They all stopped and looked at her, awaiting her reaction. She thought about it for a moment. The newspaper didn't take it easy on anyone, and they'd given her props for a job well done.

"Hell yeah, it is." Genevieve grabbed her glass and realized it was empty. Not a second later, the server appeared, presenting them with yet another bottle of champagne more expensive than her shoes. And that said something. He filled each of their glasses and vacated the area.

They did a classy, no noise cheer and drank deeply.

Libby's eyes were still downcast on her phone screen. Her thumb scrolled, and Marlis was so entranced in her own tasty libation that she didn't notice … right up until champagne threatened to spew from Libby's mouth. She choked and convulsed as silently as she could manage.

"Shit, Lib, are you okay?" Genevieve leaned over and patted her back.

"No." She gaped and slid her phone across the table toward Gen.

Owen Graham's fine frame filled the screen. The picture must have been while he was at a crime scene because a stunning scowl screwed up his handsome face. Arms encased in a long-sleeve cotton T-shirt crossed over a chest that tested the fabric's tensile strength. Jeans held up by a thick leather belt hung low on his hips. Stomp-your-face-in black boots completed the look she'd never seen in person. Thank the heavens for small favors. This picture had her overheating. In person, her lady bits would spontaneously combust.

Marlis grabbed the phone and yanked it to her side of the table. Her eyes bugged, and her jaw nearly hit the table. "Who is he, and why isn't he on the menu tonight?"

If only Libby had been a good friend and choked to death before revealing the picture …

"Because he's the opposition," Genevieve offered. "Detective for the prosecution."

"I'd murder someone just to get him to frisk me." Marlis fanned her face.

"Mar," Larkin chided.

"What?" Marlis grabbed her napkin and dabbed her mouth as though she were actually salivating.

Larkin's eyes darted in Gen's direction.

"Shit. I'm sorry." Mar placed the phone onto the table.

"It's fine." Gen rolled her eyes. "Let's just drop it, okay?"

Marlis nodded and shifted to slide the phone back to Libby, but Larkin's hand clamped around Mar's wrist.

Larkin blinked. "That's not a city investigator. That's a cover model for *Cycle World.*"

"*Cycle World?*" Libby asked.

"It's a magazine for motorcycle enthusiasts that has badass men on the cover on their equally badass bikes." Larkin's shoulders bobbed. "What?" No one spoke. Their gazes bounced around the table in confusion. "Beckett likes the articles. He learns about maintenance tricks and the best bike routes." Again, she shrugged.

The table got so quiet the sounds of the bustling kitchen and staff settled between them. Larkin fiddled with the dessert fork lying off the side of her plate. Her cheeks turned a bright shade of pink.

"You've got it bad." Genevieve couldn't hide her grin. The woman who peddled weddings and babies, the same woman who swore a thousand times she wasn't the relationship type, was in over her head, drowning in love.

Larkin dragged in a deep breath. "I do." She covered her cheeks with her hands and giggled like she was a twelve-year-old. "He called yesterday. They're en route to the States. You were right, Gen."

"Naturally," Genevieve agreed. Libby and Mar rolled their eyes. "Envious much?" She lifted her chin and turned to Larkin. "What was I right about?"

"You're hopeless. All of you children." Larkin chuckled. "Anyway, he immediately picked up on my mood, so we talked for close to two hours. I've never talked to anyone on the phone for two hours, ever. And you were right. I explained my concerns. He salved my nerves, and I'm ready to do this. Long term. Long distance. We can make it work."

"That's great." Gen breathed a sigh of relief for her friend's relationship and for her own hide. She'd subverted the majority of a conversation surrounding the hunky, high and mighty detective.

"Yeah." Marlis swatted the air. "That's all great, but can we talk about Detective Hotness some more?"

Larkin clapped and leaned toward Genevieve. "Yes, Gen, tell us more."

"I have to pee." Gen grinned. "How's that for more?"

"Terrible." Larkin glared.

None of the girls rose to join her in the restroom. They were all too independent for co-peeing unless there was a real emergency. Then they were teens again all cramming into a single stall.

Gen grabbed her clutch and headed through the maze of linen-covered tables toward the back of the restaurant when his face stopped her cold. He sat on the same side of the sleek booth as his companion. His suit covered shoulder nestled so close to the bare, younger one that not a molecule separated them. Their arms were similarly melded one to another and disappeared under the cool white linen. The woman, girl really, waggled her brows and giggled. If she was half Gen's forty-three years, she'd be shocked. And he ... he was ... staring at her.

Neither of them moved, not outwardly. Inwardly, Genevieve steeled herself. She drew a calculated breath and smiled. "Judge Faraday?"

The man, older than Gen's father by nearly two decades and his date by about five decades, detangled his hands from who knew where under the table and stood. He approached her with arms wide. "If it isn't the Golden Lawyer of New York." When he smiled, his white veneers threatened to blind her.

She stepped forward and embraced the devil she'd nearly lost her soul to. Nearly. He was smaller than she remembered. Fragile between her arms. The fear he'd once wielded over her seemed a product of childhood imagination, but it had been reality. Too much reality. Too quickly. But not as quickly as it had been for her sister. Because Gen was still here, choking in the scent of expensive cologne and decay. "If it isn't my unwitting benefactor."

"Glad to see my investment turned a profit." He hugged her tightly to his chest, surprising her with his strength.

Genevieve was strong too. More so now than she'd been as a teen. Physically and psychologically. She clapped his back, grabbed his neck, and pulled his ear to her lips. "I have a safe deposit box that has reached maturity if your date hasn't."

He pulled back. She held tight.

It was his choice. Make a scene or stay put and answer her.

"She's legal," he growled quietly. It didn't have the effect it used to.

"I hope so because our agreement lasts right up until I spit on your grave."

"She's painfully legal."

"You're disgusting." Gen relaxed her arm but kept her grip on his neck as she eased him away from her.

"Maybe I'll spit on yours, first."

"Oh, Faraday." She grinned and shook her head. "I've told you time and again. Worry about my health more than your own. If I go first, you're ruined for certain. My copies of the tape are digital now, plentiful, and have contingencies in place in the event of my death."

"Bitch."

"Good evening to you too." She released him and headed to the bathroom without a backward glance. Her heart thundered in victory, not fear.

Gen handled her business, washed her hands, and grinned at the slick, smart, and sexy woman in the mirror. "You did it." It hadn't been the conventional nor easy way, but by God—or in this case, the Devil—she'd done it. She smoothed a hand over her vibrant red hair and headed to the front to find her friends. They stood at the entrance waiting for her, unaware that she'd had a run-in with Faraday.

Judge Delaney Faraday had changed her life. Gen had told the girls the family-friendly version of her upbringing on one of their first girls' nights in. She met the esteemed judge at a low point of her life when she was to be tried at sixteen as an adult for aggravated assault and battery.

He'd seen potential in her and had endowed her to the best law school in the country. He'd written her glowing recommendations and set her career on its trajectory. The night had been a chance for all the girls to dig deeper and explore the growing respect and camaraderie between them. After all these years, she still hadn't told them, nor anyone else, the no-holds-barred truth about why that powerful man had changed her life.

When they emerged from the building, Douglas, Larkin's driver and newly-found-out biological father, stood at the ready with the door open to usher them in the limousine one at a time. Her friend had tried firing him or transferring him to a cushier office job, but he wouldn't hear of it. He liked protecting her on the ground level just as he had for years.

Genevieve kissed the dashing old man's cheek. "Thank you, Daddy D."

He slapped a hand over the kiss and rubbed it in, as he always did. "My pleasure, darling." God love him and she did too, because it was as innocent as it could be. If she'd ever really tried to plant one on him, he'd run screaming.

She slipped inside the car next to Libby, and Douglas shut the door.

"You keep that up, and one day, you'll give him a heart attack," Libby warned.

"I've told him as much." Larkin's head shook. "He said, 'What a way to go.' Can you believe that?"

"Yes." Gen chuckled. The car pulled away from the curb and blended seamlessly with traffic.

"So"—Marlis grinned—"what do you know about Detective Owen Graham?"

"Gah!" Genevieve collapsed back onto the seat. "I thought we'd moved past this." It was better than talking about Faraday but not by much.

"You wish we had," Libby countered. "We were just

waiting until we had you cornered."

"I'm not above a tuck and roll," Gen threatened.

"In those clothes, you aren't." Larkin pointed at the pricey ensemble she'd bought especially for the victory. She really loved the bold red body-hugging Armani dress. It plunged low, revealing the perfect amount of cleavage. The pencil skirt accentuated her curvy bottom, completing the killer look. No pun intended.

"Fine," she caved. "He's the enemy. That's all I know."

"He wasn't always the enemy." Mar's head shook. "You are a prosecutor by trade. You've been on the same team."

"No." Gen thought about the man and his barely veiled disdain. She hated that he looked at her as though she'd had a hand in orchestrating the murders. "He wasn't always in the department. He came in after Miller retired, just in time to catch Perry's case." Just in time to paint her as the villain. She had no problem wearing horns, but usually, she'd earned them fair and square.

"Where from?" Larkin asked.

"Brooklyn." She'd hoped on a daily basis that traffic across the bridge would keep him from showing up in court. It hadn't.

"Hot," Libby purred.

"You only think that because he could be your neighbor," Gen countered.

Libby leaned across to the small bar and poured herself a shot of whiskey. "I already have a hot neighbor who won't bone me. I don't need another."

"He's gay, for sure." Gen nodded.

"Your detective?" Marlis gasped.

"No. Her neighbor. And he's not my detective." She motioned to Libby. "Hand me that."

Libby added some more liquor to the glass, pulled a large gulp, and then passed it over. "I don't think so.

My neighbor bangs the same chick once every couple of weeks."

"Girlfriend?" Larkin asked.

"Again, I don't think so." Libby's upper lip crinkled. "No Hallmark moments. Only screaming orgasms."

"Sounds fantastic." Genevieve let another swig of whiskey burn its way down her throat.

"Tell me about it." Libby flicked her fingers, demanding the whiskey.

Gen lifted the glass. "To screaming orgasms for all."

FOUR

GENEVIEVE SHOVED OPEN THE DOOR to Carter, Cleary & Mc-Mellon Law Firm Inc. on the tenth floor of The Ashford Building. The eerie pitch of night greeted her as it had every morning for the past four days. Technically, it wasn't nighttime, but no one else was behind enough on their caseload to show up at this ungodly hour. Apparently, she was the only one behind on anything. She'd been the only sorry soul in the place over the weekend. Good thing too. No one had been there to see her dust-covered gym shorts and oversized T-shirt. Better yet, no one had been there to find out about her secret hiding space for the cases she'd shoved to the side for Perry's.

The door clanked behind her. She didn't bother locking it. Surely, the lazy sons of bitches she worked with, all Ivy League overachievers, would trickle in soon enough. She was an Ivy League overachiever, too, but in an entirely different way than the rest. A smile curved her lips.

Stiletto pumps carried her tired body through the dark down the corridors she knew better than her own body. And that was saying something. She passed the receptionist's desk and waiting room, passed some of the Ivy's bests' offices, passed the conference and break rooms, until she finally reached her dungeon door.

She placed her hand on the knob, drew a deep breath to summon all the go get 'em she could muster, and then stepped inside. With a flick of the switch, the mountain range that'd become her office came into view. There was nothing scenic about the jagged rise and fall of boxes filling her floor and visitor's chairs, nor the piles of folders bulging with papers covering her desk.

Too bad she couldn't get away with wearing gym clothes in the office on a weekday. There was still so much muck to shovel through. She smoothed a hand down her skirt. It provided little wiggle room, as did the goat path she'd left herself. One heel after the other, Genevieve teetered her way to her desk and eased into the chair, careful not to create a gust. A tantrum yesterday had left her with a landslide of epic proportions and a crick in her neck after fishing them from under the desk. She really should get back to yoga and men. Both helped with her flexibility. Despite the literal mountain of work in front of her, a chuckle started low in her throat.

That buoyancy carried Genevieve through three case files. Sheer determination saw her through four more. Her stomach growled so loudly she braced for an earthquake of paper-slide proportions. When nothing fell, her gaze found the clock on the wall. 8:32 a.m. People would begin arriving soon. If she worked diligently, she could get through another small file. Maybe even two. She ignored the dent she'd yet to make in the mountain, pulled the two thinnest files from her for-today heap, and opened the first.

Halfway through her third file, the door to her office burst wide open. The edge of the thick wood hit a stack of boxes five tall. They were files for Perry's case but not all of them. Many still littered her house. Each box held so many papers with heavy, horror-ridden shit on them that the stack didn't budge. It deflected the door like an enemy.

"Look—" Genevieve didn't have time to finish the warning before the door bounced off the wall of boxes and careened toward her assistant's face.

"Ugh! Ow! Gosh. Damn." Luckily, Janney turned just in time to be rubbing her elbow instead of cradling a bruised jaw or a broken nose.

"Janney, I'm sorry." Gen stood, scrambled around her new to-be-shredded pile and shimmied toward the sweet older woman. "Are you okay?"

Janney's teeth gritted. "Jesus, Mary, and Joseph. What kind of mess have you made?" Her words carried the barest hint of an Irish accent.

"It's organized. It looks like a mess, but it's—"

"Forget about it." The woman hugged her elbow to her body.

"How bad is it?" Genevieve reached for Janney's arm.

"Forget that too." Janney swatted her hands away. "We have real problems, girl."

"How many times do I have to tell you? Don't call me girl, you cranky old hag."

Janney's cold uninjured hand wrapped tightly around Gen's wrist. "There's no time for ball bustin'."

It was what they did. Her beautiful assistant gave as good as she got. Day in. Day out. It kept them sane in the midst of insanity.

Dread bubbled in Gen's belly as thick and as vast as the La Brea Tar Pits had been in the days when it had slowly and inexorably sucked the life from ten-ton beasts. Had the trial been hung because they'd found evidence of jury tampering? Had someone killed Perry? Had the media scrutiny driven Perry to commit suicide?

Guilt added noxious fumes to the cauldron of decay that was her stomach. She should have booked a room at the hotel he stayed in immediately following his release. She should have spent more time making certain he was stable before she'd hightailed it. Work had been a legitimate reason for leaving. There wasn't a single thing in her life that didn't require attention. She was weeks behind on a cut and style. Her nails needed a new coat of polish. Hell, her vagina needed a proper penis inside it. And work—there was enough of it to keep her busy for the next thousand hours straight. In reality, though, it had been an excuse.

Seeing the shattered remnants of Perry's life had almost dropped her where she'd stood. Everything he'd known for the past fifteen years was erased from existence. During the trial, she'd been able to block out the horror of his loss because getting Perry off for the murder of his family had been more important. Once she'd done it, the walls protecting her from the thoughts of how impossible the next few days, weeks, months were going to be for her friend and mentor vanished. And she'd run.

Gen stared in agony at her assistant's bright green eyes. "What is it, Janney?"

"Perry …" Janney's gaze bounced around the room.

Fear turned to dirt in Gen's mouth.

"I don't know how to say this …" Her thick shoulders bobbed, and she searched the ceiling for the answer.

"Just say it!"

The edges of Janney's mouth crinkled as though she was about to tear into Genevieve for speaking to her that way, but it eased too soon. "Lisa saw Perry pull into the garage when she was waiting for the elevator."

Gen blinked at her assistant for several beats. Of all the things she could have said, that would've been last on her list. She and Perry had talked about him taking time to acclimate to the outside world, his new world, before he worried about the practice. Yet the receptionist's report contradicted that.

"Why?" The question was out before Gen could recall it.

"I don't know. She said he wore a suit and was gathering his briefcase from the back seat. What would he be doing at the office this soon after his release?"

It was Genevieve's turn not to know, and she shook her head. Janney released her hold, and Gen turned toward her desk. She fished her phone from her purse and checked the screen for messages. There was a text string of mischief from the girls but nothing from Perry. She checked her inbox on the office phone. Nothing.

"I hate to tell you this," Janney whispered, "but Deanne nearly hyperventilated when she heard he was on his way up."

Genevieve's mouth opened, but no words came. Their researcher wasn't one to overreact. After all, she lived in the same world they all did, raw and aware of the terrors that happened in it every single day.

"Rosalyn practically ran to her office and slammed the door."

"Maybe she had a conference call," Gen hedged. Damn Perry, but this was another reason she'd urged him to take his time before coming into the office. He'd been cleared of any wrongdoing, but people still needed time to get used to the idea he was out of the state's custody and moving forward with his life one small step at a time. Hell, she'd interacted with him nearly every day since the murders, and she wasn't ready to do it in the context of the real world.

"He needs normalcy. As much as we can give him. So go act busy and slyly watch YouTube baking tutorials."

"Hey, now." Janney crossed her arms over her ample bosom and cocked a hip to the side.

"Are you really trying to argue the point?" Gen hiked a brow.

Janney's hands dropped to her sides. "I only watch them when my work is done."

"Usually. Not only."

"So fire me." She propped a hand on a full hip and flashed her green eyes at Gen.

"Work harder and I won't have to."

The women engaged in a fierce stare off. Immediately, the urge to blink clawed at Gen's eyeballs, and every ounce of moisture evaporated from their surface. The confident tilt of Janney's mouth said the fight was futile. Her teeth ground together. Her breathing labored. She opened her eyes as wide as they would go and willed the older woman to blink.

Loss tainted the sweet relief that came from closing her eyes.

"Ha," Janney celebrated.

"That's fine." She blinked her opponent into view. "How about a drinking contest this evening?"

Her assistant placed her index fingers together, formed a cross, and held it up to Gen. Janney warded her off as if she were a demon. The first and last time they'd tried that contest, the poor lady had ended up expelling some demons of her own ... all over the mahogany bar.

Janney backed out of the office and reached for the door handle.

"Leave it open."

"Okay." Janney winced. "We're acting normal, right?"

"Right."

"If you need me, I'll be out here, acting normal." Her

assistant's too wide, too fake smile didn't bode well for the interactions about to unfold inside the firm. The middle-aged auburn beauty swiveled in the doorway, drew a breath that lifted her shoulders and cinched her waist, and marched from view.

Gen stared at the vacant space, willing inspiration to strike, but a vast desert made itself at home in her frontal lobe. The grit of wind-swept dirt and dehydrated air gridlocked every movement, every thought. At least it kept her from running out through the fire escape and down the stairwell to avoid the discomfort.

Too soon, Perry's usual jovial voice filled the front office and filtered down the long corridor. "Good morning, all."

If anyone responded, it wasn't loud enough for Gen's strained ears to hear. In fact, the hum of the office turned mute. Gone was the shuffling of papers, the singing of the copy machine, and the flap of gossiping gums in the break room. The phones didn't ring. Even the espresso machine called in sick.

Perry's heavy tread heralded his entrance into the hallway.

Saliva pooled in Gen's mouth, but the fluid refused to travel down her paralyzed esophagus. She tried to clear her throat, to prepare to speak, but the spit tried its best to cut off her airway. This wasn't her. All her life, she'd handled situations head on. It was what made her successful. Determination. That, and Perry. He was the man who'd leveraged everything to take a chance on a wet-behind-the-ears, smart-mouthed attorney from a family with no greenery nor prestige behind its name.

She snapped her shoulders to attention, plucked her shirt, and waited for her mentor to stop in the doorway of her office, the office he'd given her when no one else would even give her the courtesy of a callback. The saliva still stuck in her throat, but if she had to, she'd talk around it.

Perry's steps drew nearer, each one a tiny earthquake that shook the plaques of law firm accolades and pictures of partnerships forged that hung on the walls. Being a curvaceous, petite woman, she scarcely had to worry about the force of her footfalls. Her boss never worried about it either but not because his didn't have an effect. He'd always liked the effect his larger-than-life presence had on legal proceedings and business dealings. In his personal life, though, everyone who'd really known him called him the gentle giant. Right up until the day the police manacled his wrists, wedged his massive frame into the back of the police cruiser, and carted him off to prison.

"Another day, another scale to balance, hey Holst?" The all-too-familiar words rolled from Perry's mouth while his booming steps carried his hulking frame past her office and on to his own.

In response, Gen usually gave a whoop, a groan, or an expletive, depending on the day's caseload, but this was no ordinary day. She gagged down the spit that had pooled inside her mouth far too long and gaped at the once again empty space of her doorway. Utter bafflement unspooled her nerves and invited a herd of kittens to toy with them, leaving her tangled in a knot of irritation.

A fire grew in her belly. Where Genevieve was concerned, there was never a smolder or a slow burn of anger. She went from spark to evacuate the town in seconds. Some cited it as a character flaw, but it allowed her to attack a situation head on and snuff it out before it became a problem.

Through the walls and open doorways, she heard the thunk as Perry set his briefcase atop his desk and the squeak of his office chair as he rolled it back from his desk.

Call the fire department.

Gen placed one heel in front of the other and tried her best to stomp down the hallway toward her client's, her boss's, her mentor's, her friend's office.

He lowered himself into the cushy leather chair with a strength in his legs she hadn't noticed until that very moment. How had she not noticed the blatant change during the trial?

The last time she'd watched him sit at his desk—before the murders—he'd only squatted a quarter of the way before gravity had taken over and dumped him into the seat. Before the murders, what had once been an athletic physique had given way to a bulging middle and drooping ass. Years of overindulgence in the finer things and hours spent under the stress of a law firm's leadership roll had taken their toll. But now …

Now he wore a freshly tailored suit that accentuated the reduction of his middle and the newfound definition of his ass. Now the buttons were clasped at his waist, a feat not seen in years. Now his shoulders stood at the ready. Now he looked less the gentile giant and more the capable killer nearly half of Manhattan thought him to be—because of the sensational media coverage and an overzealous population thirsty for the next Gary Ridgway or John Wayne Gacy.

Thank all the fucks in the world the trial was over before the reveal of his new and improved physique. Any hint of his physical changes had been hidden under thick woolen suits or oversized prison garb. How had she not noticed? Why hadn't he mentioned the development?

Call the fire department, indeed. Maybe an ambulance too.

Gen stepped inside Perry's office and slammed the door behind her.

Instead of appearing startled, which had been her aim, his still thick jowl turned toward her and offered a penitent quirk of his lips. "Genevieve." The smile didn't reach the tops of his cheeks, much less his shifting gaze.

There wasn't shit else to look at in the office. The police had taken almost everything into their custody, though no crimes had taken place here. She stomped to his desk and braced her fingertips on the uncluttered top.

"What are you doing here?"

"Looking at my star prosecutor and now, star defender." His smile brightened a touch.

"Don't do that," she snarled.

"Do what? Compliment you?"

"Try to derail me."

He reclined in his chair. "Give me some credit, Genevieve. I've known you for nearly your entire career, and I've never known you to lose course." His thickly veined hand lifted in the air. "Shoot, give yourself some credit. Your closing arguments moved mountains."

Her fingers relaxed, easing her palms onto the desktop. Unlike any before, her closing had come from her heart. "It was pretty damn great."

Perry's head bobbed. The overhead light glinted off the gray hair that had multiplied and migrated up from his sideburns over the course of the trial. He was more salt than pepper. Somehow, the lack of color smoothed the harshness of the wrinkles on his brow and around his eyes, taking five years off his appearance.

People who went through hell were supposed to look worse, not better.

"You know, as a defender, you could name your price, and people would pay it."

Gen straightened. "And you know this is a conversation we'll waste our breath having."

"I thought maybe—"

"No, Perry."

"You're so hardheaded sometimes." He snapped forward and slapped both fists on the arms of his chair.

"My hardheadedness saved your life."

"Mine, yes. Why not others?" He stood. The breadth of his shoulders towered over her. He was actually smaller than he'd been six months ago, but a strength in his stance wedged her rebuke inside her lungs.

"Before, I wouldn't push you into something you didn't want to do. But now I've seen what good you can do for people like me. Think of all the people who are caught up in circumstance. In the wrong place at the wrong time. Who have the wrong associations." He pointed at himself. "Who need someone to fight for them." He pointed at her.

"Are you finished?"

"No. Because of you, I'm not finished." He offered her a smirk.

Gen made a show of shoving her finger down her throat. She gagged and simultaneously glared at him.

"Ugh! I hate when you do that." Perry wiggled his shoulders and shook his hands.

"I know." She grinned.

"You're not even going to hear me out?"

"I'd have left already, but you still haven't answered my question."

His brows hiked.

"You were supposed to give it some time before you came back to work."

"That's not a question."

"God, I don't know how the police kept from bashing your head into the interrogation table." Her hands formed impotent fists.

"I had a great defense attorney." This was the first smile that reached his eyes.

"Perry." Her voice shrilled in the near empty confines. His smile fell.

"You were supposed to hang low until the firestorm died down. It's been less than a week since they read the verdict. Six days, to be precise." She shook her head. "We were supposed to warn people and warm them to the idea of your presence around here. They're freaking out, Janney among them, and she doesn't let much upset her."

"Look around, Holst." He motioned to the empty office. "It's past time I get back to work. There's a lot to do, and I'm ready to tackle it. I'm ready to move on with my life."

Ready to get on with his life … like he'd gotten a traffic ticket. Genevieve stared at him with no words.

"I ripped the Band-Aid off this morning. It was uncomfortable, but people will forget the sting by lunch."

"You give people too much credit. Me, most of all."

"You deserve all the credit. What you get is more work." His even shoulders shrugged. "Make people okay with me being back because I'll be here tomorrow, and the next day, and the next."

"And when the reporters show up?"

"My spectacular defense attorney will give a statement."

"We came up with this plan to keep you safe and out of the public eye."

"You came up with it. Not me." He sat and rolled his chair to his desk, effectively dismissing her.

"Goddamn you, Perry."

He was being so pigheaded. Her hardheadedness didn't endanger her safety nor her livelihood or the livelihood of those around her. Genevieve turned and stalked to the door.

"He already did."

She stopped with a death grip on the doorframe and looked over her shoulder. Perry's eyes held none of the jubilee she'd heard in his greetings. None of the pizzazz he'd used in his arguments.

"I hired people to replace some things in the house.

They were coming today, and I didn't want to be there."

Gen's lips gaped. Sorrow dashed all irritation. Compassion seeped through her pores. "You're back at the house already? I thought we agreed that the hotel—"

"The security was good, but it didn't stop reporters from finding ways around it."

Her heart dropped. "Perry, I'm sorry."

"You're not the sorry type. Don't start now. Just do what you have to do to soothe people's consciences or tell me who I need to fire. Because I'm not going anywhere."

A nod was all she could offer. When she didn't move, he shooed her with a wave of his hand. But her feet remained rooted until she asked the question gnawing at her.

"You're staying in the house?" The words squeaked between her collapsed throat.

"This is my practice. I'm not going anywhere. That is my home. I'm not going anywhere."

No matter that someone slaughtered his family inside it.

A knot formed in Genevieve's stomach. She carried it with her throughout the day and into the evening. It embedded there as a new, unwelcome companion.

FIVE

HER SHOES STUTTERED. The underside of royal red caught the gritty sidewalk twice, nearly tipping her over onto her head before coming to rest. A wince crinkled her cheeks. Could she have nothing nice? An image of red trailing behind her on the ground caused her brain to stagger. That image. Blood. Red.

Gen's gaze scaled the smooth and ornately carved concrete façade of Perry Carter's home. She blinked away the pictures. All 397 crime scene photos were burned into her memory, creating smokescreens in her dreams and haunting her. And here she was at the origin of her nightmares.

Well, not the origin, per se. The epicenter of her disquiet began long ago. Her unbalance was deeply rooted … in the past. This was her present. This was her life. And she had a duty to live it.

She'd attended about a hundred parties in this finely

appointed home through the years, so one more was nothing. A series of rehearsed motions in a familiar setting.

"What a bunch of bullshit," she grumbled.

"Pardon me?"

Orienting to the world around her, Genevieve noticed the Town Car parked at the curb. Its rear passenger door yawned onto the sidewalk, very near where her Uber had dropped her off. In the mouth of the door, a woman with slender fingers covered in paper-fine opaque skin clung to the sleeve of her driver. Not because she needed to. But because—the woman had told her once—she liked the feel of a man in her arms. Even better if they were young and in her employ.

"Mrs. Carter?" She nearly choked on the woman's name. It didn't matter that she'd likely heard Gen's expletive. She'd learned a few from the salty broad, and that said something. No, that didn't matter. Of all the people in the city, she hadn't expected to see her this evening.

"Genevieve, dear girl, I thought that was you." Perry Carter's mother lifted elegant French tips and beckoned her forward. Her feet complied without seeking permission. While she approached, the driver stepped with Mrs. Carter onto the curb and closed the car door behind him.

"Hello." She held the woman's outstretched hand and stepped in close, placing a chaste kiss on her medically enhanced, ultra-smooth cheek. One day, she hoped to have skin so well doctored. Only her bank account, while robust, didn't come close to rivaling the accounts of Perry Carter Sr.'s widow. "You look devastating, as ever."

"No harm in trying." Beena Carter winked.

"So long as you succeed." Genevieve chorused the woman's famous words along with her.

"Damn right." Beena smacked her cheek with a hand on one side and her full lips on the other. "Now, tell me why on earth you're standing out here looking like you've seen a ghost."

"Because I'm afraid I might." She straightened and flicked her gaze toward the house for a second to solidify her meaning. If there was anyone she could talk straight to, besides her girls, it was this woman. Over the course of the trial, Beena had become more of a mother to her than her own had ever been.

"Dear, you know they are long gone from this cruel world. No chain rattling here." She pointed at her son's gorgeous home and then swung the sharp finger to her escort's other suit-clad arm. "Now, grab hold and let Roderick do his job."

Of all the things she didn't understand when it came to Perry's mother, her ability to take the brutal murders of her daughter-in-law and grandchildren like a chuck on the chin baffled her the most. Maybe the loss of her husband to food poisoning after her son had graduated college shut down an integral part of her emotional availability.

Sublimate much? Yes, yes, I do. So what if Beena does too?

Then again, maybe Genevieve's shrink was a dolt with no inkling of what she spouted. Her emotions were readily available to those for whom they were deserved.

Genevieve slid her fingers around Roderick's bulging bicep. His tanned hand smoothed over top, warming her skin on contact. He offered her a hint of his unique blue eyes and a flash of the vibrantly white teeth he kept hidden behind full caramel lips. While supporting both of their hands with his sleek, strong arms, he ushered them toward the cascade of concrete steps.

"Such a good boy." Beena rubbed his shoulder with her free hand.

"Roderick, how long have you worked for Mrs. Carter?" And by worked, she meant fucked, and they all knew it.

His gaze skittered to the older woman, seeking guidance. She nodded and gave a suggestive hike of her brow.

"Twelve years." His voice was deep, thicker than she'd expected for his fine facial features.

"Wow, that's the deepest voice I've ever heard." The surprise timbre of his voice was the only thing that kept her from focusing solely on the electrical shock of his words. As it was, the man couldn't have been more than a quarter of a century.

"It's certainly become full-bodied over the years," Beena purred and walked so proudly beside him.

Him, the child she'd molded into her personal sex slave.

Gone were the overt jokes Gen had been teeing up for when they parted at the door. Gone was the far-off idea of being invited into a three-way with Beena and Roderick. Gone was all the respect she'd had for the spicy woman in a world that didn't understand her. Who in their right fucking mind could understand her? Certainly not Genevieve.

She'd had no problem with the disparity in their age. She still wouldn't had Beena courted him when he was old enough to drink legally. Hell, she might even be okay with voting age, but this? No.

Gen pulled her hand from the boy's arm, slipped it into her clutch, and withdrew her phone. "Excuse me just a second." Her fingers flew over the keys, typing into the girls' group text the universal signal for just needed something to do in an awkward situation.

Genevieve: What the actual fuck?

The two continued their ascent.

Libby: Ooh! Can't wait to hear this one.

Larkin: Seriously! Gen is NEVER in an awkward situation.

She dropped the device into her clutch and managed to shuffle up the rest of the stairs without falling on her face or vomiting over the wide concrete railing. Knowing she'd make an even bigger fool of herself if she made a scene kept her focused. At this point, Roderick was a brainwashed man without a thought of his own. Where had Perry been when this guy was a kid? Why had no one spoken up about Beena's inappropriate and most likely illegal relationship with a minor?

The longer she lived in this world, the more she hated it and everyone in it. Except her girlfriends.

A woman Genevieve had never seen before answered Roderick's knock. She wore black pants, a starched white shirt, and a tiny bow tie. He hardly needed a full catering service for a dinner party with associates. Then again, Beena was here, which meant it wasn't just associates like he'd promised.

Anita, the family's housekeeper and nanny, had been let go after Perry's arrest. The woman at the door ushered the odd couple inside. Gen hung back until Beena dislodged herself from Roderick and sent him on his way. Now, she couldn't look at the man without pitying him. How had his family not protected him from this predator?

Good looks and money made the best camouflage.

The prey didn't know they were trapped until it was too late. And sometimes, the trap was so comfortable it didn't feel like one at all.

Time had a way of revealing the bars and barbs.

Genevieve thanked the stranger and stepped inside, allowing her to close the door. She turned to the right toward the coat closet before realizing she hadn't worn one. Nine times out of ten she covered her arms because nine times out of ten, she was in a business setting. Revealing too much arm along with too much cleavage and too much leg was frowned upon. But tonight was a casual gathering; a re-building of camaraderie after a frightful storm.

Habits. Gen dismissed the closet, and her gaze drifted up to the ornate archway that led to the parlor. Her eyes locked on the banister, and she swore under her breath. She wouldn't look into that room. She wouldn't look for the children because they weren't here. They were … away at boarding school. Could she make herself believe that? Her eyes opened, and Beena stepped into her path.

"I startled you with my answer." She raised a hand and stopped Gen's response. "It's okay."

No, it was most certainly not okay. Rage bubbled deep in her past and in the present standing in front of her, creating so much heat her hair might just spontaneously ignite.

"The key happiness is to get them young and train them right."

"For pedophiles, maybe." She spat the retort when all she wanted to do was scream it at the top of her lungs and add a prison yard's worth of expletives.

"Dear girl, were that the case, I'd be on my twentieth by now. I'm not. It's only Roderick. And he is only for me." Beena flicked the air between them. "Besides, he was legal. Barely, but legal all the same. Though, certainly not everything I've done in my life has been legal." The woman leaned in, exposing a hint of a facelift scar at her bottle-blonde hairline. "I'm quite sure you can say the same."

The words weren't threatening, but her tone and the glint in her eyes said differently. As though Beena knew something Gen didn't know … or knew something Gen didn't want to know.

A roar of laughter filtered in from the banquet room. It was loud, forced, and brittle as though the slightest gust could shatter the sound. It spoke of fear and discomfort but decorum above both. What a load. The more people expressed truth, the better the world. The volume also spoke of a crowd. One much larger than Perry had promised.

Gen pulled her gaze from the hallway off the foyer,

from the fake laughter, and aimed it at Beena. "I was told the party was just associates and partners."

"I bet you were." Veneers glinted in the light of the foyer's decadent chandelier. Beena moved past her and headed toward the noise.

"Meaning?" Gen caught up to her.

"Perry says what he needs to get people to do what he wants." Her smile didn't falter. In fact, it hiked to sharp peaks. "Why do you think I'm here when I could have spent my night otherwise entangled?" The woman didn't wait for a response. Instead, she borrowed a deeply masculine affect and shook her fists. "Be here or else."

"Or else?" Her voice was a reed.

"Wouldn't you like to know." Beena chuckled. Her arms outstretched, framing Genevieve without touching her along with the width of the room. "My darling son, look who I've brought you."

Her gaze slung from the old woman to the formal living room that brimmed with people. Perry stood in the center. To his left and right stood the ever-present and rarely seen Cleary and McMellon, who made up the law firm of Carter, Cleary & McMellon. In near slow motion, Perry's right hand formed a fist. It shot straight into the air, almost triumphantly. Her brain was still working on the calculations of what the hell was going on when the room erupted into cheers and whoops.

The word, "Congratulations," rang above the din followed by, "Partner."

Air vanished from the room, gobbled up by the swarm of people who suddenly surrounded her. Perry Carter was first and the most enthusiastic. Then it was McMellon. Then Cleary. The oldest partner's wrinkles were so defined they seemed drawn on and highlighted like Beena's eyebrows. Their arms clung. Their hands patted. Their mouths formed words of well wishes that sounded like shrieks in the desolation of night.

They passed her around the room from one person to another. Maybe her feet moved, but she couldn't be sure. Maybe she said something in return. Again, she couldn't be sure. A dizzying buzz started at her ponytail. Slowly and methodically, it worked its way around to her gaping sinus cavities. Someone placed a glass of champagne in her hand. She gulped it as though it were air. Air that refused to feed her lungs.

Surprises. Of all the people who knew her, Perry knew she didn't do surprises, and she sure as shit didn't do ambushes either. She worked with facts and figures. Odds and outcomes. He should have told her about a partnership. More than that, he should have asked her. Proposed terms. Confirmed details. Given her time to decide.

This was too much.

Someone brushed past her, knocking her sideways.

"Pardon me." The words were cast her direction, but she didn't catch them. She didn't even know from which way they'd come.

The room spun in a tight circle.

One flute of champagne wasn't enough to put her on her ass. A case of wine wasn't enough to do the job.

"Earth to Genevieve Holst." Cold hands around her upper arms accompanied her assistant's firm, chiding voice. The gruff and kind woman shuffled her backward. Something brushed her calves. "Sit and don't you move." Janney tapped her knee. "You need some water."

"I needed fair warning," Gen croaked.

"Well, I had about as much as you." The woman huffed and shifted to walk away.

Genevieve grabbed her hand, needing an anchor in the madness more than she realized.

"What now?" Janney snapped. The rebuff lacked the teeth of her usual indignation.

For the first time since Wrinkles Cleary, Genevieve focused. The woman's scowl gave more comfort than it should have. "Aren't you going to tell me congratulations?"

"No." A smile cracked the sullen façade. Janney's hand squeezed back. She leaned in. "I might, after you decide whether you're going to accept the position."

Genevieve let her gaze slip around the room. The crowd had divided up into small groups categorized to dispatch the most in personal gratification. Some hovered quite close, so she dropped her voice. "Oh, you think I have a choice."

"You always have a choice, and you always make it known." Janney winked. "It's the main reason I tolerate your filthy mouth." She released Gen's hand. "Now, let me get you that water."

She blinked her response to keep her head from swimming once more.

Janney scurried off. In her absence was a direct view of the staircase.

The staircase.

Her gaze honed in on the eighth and eleventh slats in the railing. They'd been removed and replaced with new, perfectly varnished wood. The grooves that'd been clawed into them were gone.

The temperature in the room dropped twenty degrees. At least it did to her. She stared at the spot as though the ties remained knotted in place even though they'd been removed and analyzed months ago. How the fabric was pulled so tightly over on itself had confirmed the coroner's and her worst fear.

Pamela had been forced to watch the killer work on her children.

Inside Genevieve's brain, the fabric knotted over on itself in an effort to get away from the facts. Her gaze dropped, and there was no escape. She sat on the sofa where the madman had brutalized young Perry Carter. Her fingers gripped the same linty fibers they'd found under his tiny fingernails. When she looked, she still saw dark merlot stains from the crime scene photos.

Genevieve jumped to her feet.

She should've run.

Her gaze slipped behind her. The stains weren't there, but sweet Perry's lifeless, eyeless face stared up at her.

At least he'd taken the heart first.

That was what she'd told herself throughout the trial. Now, staring into the face of the dead, no amount of rationalization could help.

She should've run.

Her gaze skittered left, past the heels and skirts, suits and wing tips and landed on the other sofa. To Claire.

Unlike her brother, the tiny girl had fought. There had been no neat puddle under her. Blood had spurted from the slice across her neck. It had been slung from wall to window to floor to ceiling. It dripped there now, setting Genevieve to quake.

Any oxygen Gen had managed to find in the house of horrors vanished. Her fingertips turned numb. Every place she looked, blood and the faces of those she loved haunted her. She looked left, past the dissected portions of Pamela's gagged and bound body to the hallway and nearest exit, and then right past the sea of people who'd celebrated and dismissed her in equal measure.

Genevieve tottered on unsteady ankles away from Claire and Perry. A man called her name from the huddle of people in the threshold between the banquet room and parlor. She offered a curt wave but couldn't bring herself to look in his direction. Her gaze locked on the makeshift torture chamber of the staircase, and for an instant, she was there, tied and gagged, forced to witness. Sorrow clawed at her ribs, seeking escape. The world would not see her cry. Long ago, she'd locked away tears. The useless things. If she didn't get out now, the world might see her faint.

She unhinged her arm, pried her clutch from under it, and fumbled for her phone; her lifeline.

SIX

THE SOS HAD BEEN SENT. EAST 42ND. STAT!

Marlis and Larkin were out of town. They were co-hosting a social media convention in sun-soaked Cali. She would have known that if she were a better friend. Both girls texted that they were devastated they couldn't be there for her in her hour of need. After all, this was only the second time she'd ever tossed out the white flag, sent up the flares, and all the other dramatic life-in-the balance colloquialisms. This was the only time she'd ever truly meant it. The first time, she'd had a legitimate excuse, but she'd handled a similar situation on her own before. Before, when she'd been much younger, much less experienced, and much less equipped to handle the fallout.

Genevieve had thrown down the gauntlet as a test. Would they still love her if they knew …?

Yes. Yes, they would. And they did.

Libby was on her way and would be there in thirty. At nineteen after, she shoved the exorbitant cab fare through the slot, peeled herself from the worn leather seat, and slammed the door. The car pulled away from the curb, leaving her on the sidewalk with the dim and unassuming lights of her haven. It wasn't her apartment. She kept that place only to hold her wardrobe and a place to sleep. It wasn't a friend's home. They were all too upscale to offer much comfort—except for Libby's, but who had time to go to Brooklyn these days. It wasn't even a place she frequented.

Hot, grease-laden air syphoned up her nostrils and filled her lungs. Somewhere between 52nd and 50th, the need to sob subsided. The clawing turned to pawing. Still insistent, but not nearly as painful. Staring at the silver exterior and pale neon lights, she eased up on the grip of her phone. Something about the curved edges of the walls and windows, counters and chairs settled her most manic edges.

She hurried into the no frills 40s-style diner. A couple huddled into the same side of the first booth while a scornful group of older men traded war stories in the largest booth across from the lovebirds. Beyond them, a sporadic few hunched over the counter on swiveling stools.

Thankful for the minimal crowd, Gen kept her head down and snagged the last booth in the corner. She placed her clutch and phone on the table in front of her and tried her best to refrain from texting Libby to find out where she was exactly.

"Evening." A menu sailed through the air and smacked onto the table, jarring every bone in Gen's neck as it snapped up to a twentysomething waitress wearing black pants and a black long-sleeve shirt. "I'm Lulu, and I'll be taking care of you tonight. Will you be dining solo, or are you waiting for someone?"

Genevieve stared at her as though she'd asked her to solve the world's hunger crisis. Words refused to come.

Lulu plucked a pencil from her bun and pulled a pad from her apron. A smile softened her sharp cheekbones. She propped a hip onto the seat opposite Gen and leaned in, revealing a silhouette of bountiful cleavage on her tiny frame. Pencil to pad, she waited for words that refused to flow.

"How about I get you started with something to drink? Coffee?" Lulu offered a sweet smile.

A nod took the place of proper words.

The girl twisted around and hustled for the counter. Within seconds, she was back with a mug and a carafe of dark roast.

"This should help." Steam curled off the stream of coffee she poured into the mug. The nutty, rich aroma wrapped around Genevieve's shoulders like a blanket, easing the tightness in her jaw.

"So much. Thank you." Her voice sounded steadier than she felt.

"My pleasure." Lulu winked. "Drink that. I'll come check on you in a few minutes. Okay?"

She nodded again, and the young woman trundled off to help the men near the entrance. Her phone screen offered no hint as to Libby's location. If her friend's traffic estimation had been accurate, she had fifteen more minutes to hold herself together. Fifteen minutes seemed like an eternity. Her eyes caught a glimpse of herself in the dark brew, and she stared at the harried reflection. This wasn't her. She wasn't a sniveling waif. She was a woman about the world. About business. She got shit done. All day and all night. Holiday or none.

Genevieve hugged the mug between both hands. Warmth radiated up her fingers and seeped into her palms, chasing away a cold no one else in the city noticed.

Slowly lifting the cup to her lips, she blew and then carefully took a sip. When the liquid didn't scald, she sipped again. Comfort in a cup rolled across her tongue, heated her cheeks, and cascaded down her throat. As though the trip through Perry's house and the cab ride here had been a lucid dream, the world around her snapped back into view. A light above the register hummed. The tread of the cook's shoes squeaked with each step he took. Beyond the window, a sporadic viewing of pedestrians rushed past. And from the counter, a man stared.

On any other night, Genevieve would snap her ghoulish green gaze on him and tell him exactly where he could fuck, but not tonight. Everything was raw and exposed, so she just kept her head down.

Long, heavy jeans-covered legs hung casually off the stool. One propped on the bar's metal footrest, but the other one … It was nearly in her direct line of sight. A big, black boot sat at the base of the leg that propped him more on the ground than in the chair. One thick arm hooked over the stool's back, obscuring its existence. A network of tattoos made an already imposing thing downright menacing.

"Your hands are shaking because you did the devil's work." His voice rumbled over her like storm clouds. Terrifying and powerful while soothing and familiar at the same time.

She'd dealt with storms before as well as Detective Owen Graham. But he was a devastating storm for which she had warning to prepare.

"Go away." Her gaze remained on the coffee mug. It was safer than Owen.

"I will as soon as Lulu gets my order ready." He swiveled the chair to face her and spread his legs out wide, consuming the walkway.

Genevieve braced her right hand on her chin to still its

shaking and placed the other in her lap because they were, in fact, quaking rather aggressively. So what if her hands shook. They weren't, and she wasn't, any of his concern.

"How was the party?"

Her head snapped up so quickly she nearly pulled a muscle. His grin was as wide as his extended legs. His eyes were as blue as the canton of the American flag inked into his right arm. Blue also popped out at the top of the collar of his T-shirt on the arch of his trap. On his left arm and collar, the colors of the fly end of his flag were muted black and skin white.

The instinct to fight and flight warred. Any other night, she'd fight, no question, but right now, she might lose. Unbuttoned from the day job as he was, her mouth watered for a taste. He was so much more complex than she ever realized, and she was so stripped.

"How'd you know about that?" She didn't have anything to hide, yet she sounded defensive.

"Ah, I hit a nerve." He dragged a palm over the thigh of his pants. "I'm good at that." The smug grin remained.

Gen straightened, rising to the bait. But then, a lion must hunt. "The women you associate yourself with must have pathetic expectations."

"Man." The detective's smile skidded, and he clutched his chest over his heart. "You don't pull any punches. Not in court. Not in life."

"Not in the bedroom either," she growled. It felt good. This back and forth made her feel more like herself than she had all evening.

"Fair enough." The detective nodded and used the back of his hand to wipe the hint of moisture away from one eye. He cleared his throat. "I was just shooting in the dark. I mean, a stunning woman in a sexy outfit too sophisticated for my diner, and all alone ..." One bulging shoulder bobbed. "I didn't make detective off my looks alone."

"Screwed your way to the top?"

His laughter was rich. It created creases around his stunning eyes and carved a groove out on either side of his mouth. The sound sang over her skin, shifting every unpleasant thought along the way.

"Low standards," he reminded her.

"Oh, yeah." She tapped her forehead with her index finger and found that her hands operated normally.

He gestured to the seat across from her. "May I?"

Genevieve didn't answer right away. While she loved their banter, it didn't need to escalate to anything more. She didn't want to hate him for the interrogation that was sure to come.

"No, Detective Graham, you may not."

Those intense blue eyes studied her for several seconds, and for the first time, she cared—if for no more than a fleeting second—about what he didn't see when he looked at her more than what he did. When he looked at her, he didn't see the "marrying kind." When he looked at her, he didn't see maternal instinct. When he looked at her, he didn't see any standards; high or low.

"I'm sorry you've had a shitty night, counselor. I hope it gets better." He turned back to the counter.

She stared after him, shocked at the kindness of his words and sincerity in his tone. Muscles bulged and contracted under his T-shirt, giving a tantalizing preview of what was beneath. His ass filled out the well-worn blue jeans like a piece of art. A hint of another tattoo design peeked out of the back of his collar. Her throat worked on a large gulp. When her interest became too acute, she tore her gaze away and focused on the safety of her cup.

Her eyes struggled to stay in the safe zone. They flickered toward the door, looking for her friend. They skittered toward Graham's fine backside. Then they locked on to the smaller, sweeter, kinder, younger, and less irritating Lulu. The woman placed an order slip in the clip of the small window into the kitchen and then headed for Graham.

Lulu's steps were long and exaggerated, almost childlike. Her head canted to the side, and her brown gaze pinned him. Too soon, she was in front of him. Gen couldn't see her face nor Graham's. The two spoke softly and quietly as though the conversation was intimate. He propped his tatted arms on the bar and leaned in, highly interested in what the woman was talking about.

Did Lulu inform for the detective?

Graham's forearm pressed onto the bar, bringing his face closer to Lulu's. The gesture was so personable, she pulled her gaze away.

Maybe Lulu was one of his low standards lovers?

But it wasn't that overt. They didn't touch. She didn't flaunt her largest assets. He didn't ogle, which made the exchange even more intimate.

Gen grabbed her mug and gulped while she scrambled for her phone.

"I'm here." Libby shoved the rest of the way through the door and ran toward her, long legs eating up the tile. "I'm sorry it took me so long. I parked on the curb three blocks away and had to pull my badge on a cop." Her friend's green eyes rolled skyward.

Genevieve was so thrilled to see those vibrant eyes she didn't care that every eye in the diner centered on Libby and would soon be on both of them.

"I mean, girl trouble is an emergency. Am I right?" Lib reached the booth, unwound the purse that crossed her body, slung it in the open seat, and grabbed her hand. Her friend pulled with a might the slight woman shouldn't possess. Willingly or not, Gen stood, and Libby's arms encircled her.

"Thank you for coming." Despite the crowd and her usual reserve, Genevieve sank into the affection, allowing herself to be hugged, and clung to her friend in return.

"He should've never had the party at that house. Christ, he doesn't pay you so much that he couldn't afford a venue." Libby's fast talk had the words in the air before Gen had time to stop them.

"Libby," Gen gritted.

"What?" Lib eased back and followed her gaze toward the bar. "Oh, shit." She pulled her into the booth, and whispered, "What's he doing here?"

Genevieve shrugged, tossed up a hand, and bulged her eyes. "Eating, I guess." Less than whispering, she mouthed the words.

Her friend scrutinized the detective, who'd turned back to his conversation with Lulu. Gen didn't think for one second he wouldn't have an ear turned toward her table. He may have presented her with a genial manner tonight, but one hint of a scoop on Perry, and he'd pounce.

"Who's she?" Lib covered the side of her mouth with a hand, but Gen would swear it amplified the question. "She's cute." Her friend's lower lip pouted. "She's young."

"You're young." Gen jabbed her shin with the toe of her Choo.

"Ouch."

In their little friend group, Genevieve was the senior by five to seven years. College and paying dues in some pretty shitty post-law school jobs had taken a while. When she'd finally made something of herself, all the other girls her age had been strapped with a husband or divorced with a kid or two. Their friendships fell into place because they were all on the same wavelength, no matter their age.

"Stop talking so loudly," Genevieve whisper-screamed.

"Well, you start talking." Libby leaned forward and rubbed her leg. "I didn't run here, literally run here, to get abused. Spill."

She looked at Libby, then at Detective Graham's fine ass, and then back at her friend. Her thoughts drifted back to the party, back to the images, back to her whatever it was—a freak-out, a panic attack—and her chest tightened once more. Desperation to expel her thoughts and feelings bashed against her tongue.

Gen shook her head.

Graham stood, handed Lulu two bills, told her to keep the change, and headed for the door with his takeout as though he knew she wouldn't talk with him in the diner. He gave her what peace he could, and a small well of respect puddled for the man. She watched him leave, staring at the door even after his frame disappeared from view.

Libby leaned over and grabbed her hand. "It was pretty bad, huh?"

"I probably overreacted."

Her dear friend glared at her so hard Gen feared her face would freeze in that expression. But the tactic coupled with her silence helped her admit the truth.

"It was the fucking worst."

SEVEN

"EH, SWEET TITS, WAGGLE THOSE THINGS THIS WAY!" **A fair look-**ing, if not supremely archaic male specimen with a shaved head leaned out the window of a delivery truck parked on the curb. His 'roid bloated bicep flapped in the air, begging for her attention.

Should've wore the damn suit jacket instead of draping it over my arm. Where the hell are the promised autumn temps?

The moment the thought crossed Genevieve's mind, she placed it in the crosshairs and shot it down. Hell no, she shouldn't have to smother in sleeves to ward off unwanted advances. He should've learned some fucking manners, and she was just the girl to teach him some. It didn't matter what a woman wore, nor how much she drank, nor her career path. Consent mattered.

On any other morning, she'd engage in a bit of warfare. Depending on her mood, she'd spout off, shouting over the crush of pedestrians about how she wasn't interested because his dick was the disappointing size of a basic ballpark wiener. Or she'd lure him in with false interest, get his number, and post it on an ad for gay escorts. Sure, she felt bad about the men who took up the offer. They'd done nothing wrong. They didn't deserve to deal with the archaic, most certainly homophobic asshole with the ad, but it was justice being served. Justice was no victimless game.

As of late, her favorite thing to do with their number was submit it to every call service she could get her hands on. The sex addicts hotline. The gender identity crisis hotline. The erectile dysfunction hotline. To name a few.

Genevieve battened down her inner warrior and marched on with the crowd. The man yelled out a few more suggestive offers, but these were professional New Yorkers with which she migrated, and nothing got in the way of their morning commute. Not traffic, not snow, and certainly not limp-dick hecklers. She noted the place and time. If the mood struck her, she could battle another day.

This morning, however, she needed to get in the building before Perry and barricade herself inside her office once more. She had no time to waste thanks to the emotional hangover that beat all actual hangovers. Her gaze locked on the front of The Ashford Building, which housed the Carter, Cleary & McMellon Law Firm Inc. among many other companies. One more block and she'd reach her destination.

Yesterday on her first day back to work after the surprise partnership party, her subsequent breakdown, and escape, she'd used a side entrance and a service elevator to avoid Perry. She hadn't been ready to explain herself. She still wasn't ready, which was why she ignored the asshat. Gen broke from the crowd headed for the main entrance, scrambled through a side door, and rode one of the ugly but operable service elevators up. The car lifted her to the small rectangular foyer of the law firm's rear entrance. It was bare and undecorated with the exception of an end table with absolutely nothing on top of it on her left and an oversized, very fake tree in a planter in the corner to the right of the door.

Hand extended, she was ready to shove through the single door until the sharp edges of a hushed and heated conversation hit her ears and stopped her cold.

Perry was already here. She'd know that voice any-where, though she wasn't accustomed to his whisper. He was a confident, assertive man with no cause for appease-ment.

Gen's heart dropped into her stomach, adding some-thing inedible to an already putrid situation. Her hand fell from its journey to the door and smacked over her belly. With a shuffle, she sidestepped the door. Perry in a great mood would be bad enough, so she certainly didn't want to see him while he was agitated. Her shoulders met fabric leaves that crackled and groaned against her. She winced and stilled, hoping beyond hope that Perry hadn't heard.

Through the small window of the metal door, Gen saw Perry and the quarter profile of a blonde woman whose stature exceeded her boss by two inches in her high-rise heels. She wore a knee-length dress that accentuated her long legs, an ample backside, a tiny waist, and nice breasts. Uniformly straight hair hung well below her shoulders, and long bangs hid most of her face from this angle.

In a flash, Perry drew down on the woman. His new and imposing physique dwarfed her thin frame. His fin-ger stabbed the air inches from the woman's nose. His face followed close behind the accusing digit. Thin lips moved in a strict line. The words, though, refused to reach her ears.

Had she ever seen him like this before? She'd known

him long enough to have witnessed a range of his character traits. The majority of them were variations of jovial and determined. On occasion, his voice hit a boom that commanded a room. He lived in a jostling city, owned a business, and headed a family. *Had*. He had headed a family. Those tasks sometimes called for a firm hand. This quiet menace left her mouth gaping and her eyes wide.

"Go." Perry's finger swung toward the door, demanding the woman leave.

Luckily, their gazes remained deadlocked. Gen jerked back from the window, causing a leaf to poke her ear. Her gaze jumped to the elevator. There wasn't time to call the car and flee. She scanned the sparsely decorated room. It left no place for her to hide except where she cowered. Cold sweat broke out over her skin. She was completely exposed with no explanation as to why she hadn't simply stridden through the door. Damn Perry's meeting, heated or not.

What she found interesting was that Perry never met clients without another lawyer present. Lawyers were occasionally hit with suits from their own clients, much like physicians. Everything was fine when you were healthy and winning, but the moment either of those things changed, the accusations flew. To her knowledge, Perry never conducted a meeting in anything but the nicest of their offices. Clutter, the likes of which her office currently boasted, and subpar décor, the like of which the rear entrance always boasted because no one ever used it, were forbidden to clients' eyes at Carter, Cleary & McMellon.

Image was everything to Perry. At least, it had been. It wasn't like he'd asked for his family to be murdered. It wasn't like he'd asked for the media scrutiny. Some things were outside of anyone's control, even Perry Carter's.

This lady wasn't one of them.

The door swung wide, pinning Genevieve on three

sides. Wall. Door. Plant. Her mouth clamped shut, silencing her breaths. A flash of blonde and blue sailed past the window, and then a smack reverberated in the anteroom. She'd called for an elevator. Slowly, the door eased toward its frame, exposing Gen inch by mortifying inch. There wasn't even a fucking magazine in which she could feign interest. Maybe she should retrieve her phone and pretend to be on an important call.

Too soon, the woman was in her view, hands fisted at her sides at the large bank of elevators. A small black purse hung at her hip with the fine strap perched on her shoulder. It swayed left and right, bumping into her arm with each diminishing sway. If the woman offered Perry a backward glance, she'd get quite a shock.

Gen would too, so she held perfectly still. Even her breaths stalled.

White metal careened toward Genevieve's face. Trapped again. Her gaze shot wide, searching for some hint from the world beyond. The little window revealed nothing, but the small crack between the door and its frame showed a tall column of charcoal gray fabric. The expensive stuff.

Perry stood six inches from her. She'd recognize that aftershave anywhere.

"I'll be down in a moment. We'll take my car. Jeff will know you're coming." Perry's voice was so genial he might have been speaking to a dear friend. Gen hadn't gotten a good look at the woman's face, but nothing about the rest of her was familiar.

"That's all I wanted."

The door began to close once more, revealing Genevieve in a slow curtain pull. A ding rang in her ears. She watched one side of the elevator's door open. The audience was about to see what was behind door number one. Long Legs stepped into the car and turned, her fingers extended toward the bank of buttons.

Her face was a stunning sculpture of sharp lines that Genevieve was certain she'd never before seen. No one forgot a face like that. She was very near Perry's age but hadn't let one thing slip. Amazing. Gen was on the front-side of forty and already her ass and thighs held the extra drink she enjoyed here and there.

Long Legs shifted toward the corner of the small space and made her selection, sending a wave of relief through Gen's stilted body. Then the woman stepped back to the center of the car.

Every muscle in Genevieve's body locked in place. One move and the woman's gaze would lift from the floor and zero in on her.

Excruciatingly slow, the doors drew to a close with a gentle thud. Metal groaned. The hum of cable sliding through their pulleys filled the room.

Gen sagged against the wall, crushing the tree in an obnoxious series of crunches. The suit jacket she'd held in the crook of her arm that held her suitcase since she exited the subway slipped to the ground. Pants rocked her chest as though she'd run to the tenth floor. With the infiltration of fresh air came the barrage of what-the-fucks. The interaction she'd witnessed wouldn't compute. None of it. Perry. The woman. The clandestine meeting.

And it wasn't finished.

He'd been so close and hadn't known she was there. It seemed a breach of contract. Trust went both ways, and it seemed Perry wasn't ready to explain something either.

The one double-edged question that repeated in her head like a megaphone blasted once more.

Why is he hiding this woman, and who the hell is she?

Even as she shoved off the wall and ran for the bank of elevators, Genevieve knew she shouldn't follow. Whoever the woman was to Perry, there was a 99.9% chance that the relationship was benign. She smacked the call button in rapid succession, causing her finger to sting. That 0.1% would haunt her along with the images of Perry's family.

The gears of her mind squeaked from the struggle of comprehension. Perry planned to meet Long Legs downstairs to share his car with her, but he hadn't joined her on the elevator.

Why?

Perhaps he needed to grab something or tell Lisa, the receptionist, that he was headed out. Sweat beaded on Genevieve's upper lip. He could push through the rear entrance door at any moment. She strangled the handle of her small briefcase and danced from one foot to the other, willing one of the damn cars to stop on her floor, open, and take her away. Like the woman before her, Gen dared not look back terrified of what she might see.

What excuse could she give Perry for being here? None sprang to mind.

Gen jabbed the button as though it were a doorbell and the increased racket would get someone's attention. Seconds ticked past. They piled into half of a minute. A full one past. Doubt nagged. She could, no, she should turn around, march through the doors, go straight to her office where a thousand case files begged for her attention, and forget everything that'd happened in the past five minutes.

Her hand dropped from the button, and a huff of air rushed from her lungs. She turned back to the door. If Perry entered at this point, she'd just tell him, "Good morning," and be on her way. No harm done. It wasn't like this was the first conversation she'd eavesdropped upon, accidental or otherwise.

She reached for the door's handle, and a ding rang in her ears. Behind her, the car cables squeaked to a stop, and the doors rumbled as they rolled open. Her 0.01% stopped her. Curiosity turned her. Determination carried her onto the open elevator car, down ten stories, and out onto the street. Gucci pumps reminded her that they were only two block heels and that the side trip around to the front of the building was past their limit.

Jeff, Perry's driver, stood on the curb near the back-passenger door, arms folded across his middle. The mystery woman was nowhere in sight. Gen guessed she'd already gotten into the vehicle. She scanned the main entrance. No sign of Perry.

Genevieve maneuvered through the flowing crowd. Eye rolls, elbows, and shoulders hit her without apology. Normally, she'd walk with the current and ease to the street like a native, but there wasn't time. Her briefcase caught on someone's knee and propelled her sideways. Only the crush of hot bodies heading to work kept her upright. A vicious hand shoved her off. She careened forward and teetered headfirst toward the edge of the sidewalk and the surprisingly steady rush of traffic.

At least she made it to the damn road. She waved her arm and steadied herself on the edge of a garbage receptacle. Desperate times. In short order, a yellow fish parted from the sea. The car jerked to a stop, rocking on its frame. She jumped inside, slammed the door, and scanned the building front. Suits and slacks, briefcases and handbags obscured her view of the main entrance.

No wonder Jeff waited outside the car. Otherwise, he wouldn't see Perry's approach.

"Where to?" a gruff and most likely cigarette worn voice demanded.

"Um ... just a minute." Genevieve slung her briefcase onto the seat and searched for Perry once more. Again, she couldn't see anyone entering or exiting The Ashford Building. Her gaze swung toward Perry's car.

"Lady, where you wanna go?"

The top of Jeff's hat and a snippet of his face stood out from the line of cars in front of them.

"I just want to sit here for a minute." She pushed up to the edge of the seat and craned her neck toward Perry's Town Car. The top was all she could see, but it was enough.

"Look, this ain't no bench. I drive or you get gone."

She spared the man a glance for the first time. Younger than she'd expected by a lot, considering the frayed voice and crotchety attitude.

"What's it gonna be? The meter's runnin'." His gaze narrowed, and a sneer maimed what could've been a sweet face.

Gen rifled through her briefcase and then wallet. She snagged a twenty and shoved it through the slit in the partition.

"On top of the meter. Okay?" she asked.

He plucked the bill from the front seat and inspected it. While he wasted time ensuring its authenticity, Gen checked on Jeff. Still there.

"You bought yourself five minutes."

"No. Ten minutes or I'll take my twenty and find a cabbie with some sense."

"I got sense," he whined.

"Ten minutes?" She bartered but didn't take her eyes off the Town Car.

"Fine."

"Then yes, you have some sense." Ten seconds—not minutes—later, the crowd parted, and Perry strode toward his car. "Clearly, I don't."

"What?"

Perry disappeared into the car. A blink later, Jeff did too.

"Never mind." Gen pointed at the traffic. "Let's go."

"Nah, you agreed. I agreed." The driver shoved the

twenty in his pocket.

"Keep the twenty. Just go."

"Crazy bitch." He growled the insult under his breath. Did he really think she couldn't hear him?

He eased his front wheel into traffic but not as aggressively as Jeff. The car lurched away from the curb and zipped into the flow.

"Go!" She banged on the partition.

"Wait a minute." His gaze followed hers to the black Town Car pulling away from the curb. "You trying to follow that car? Are you serious?"

Gen lunged for her wallet again, grabbed a president he'd recognize on sight, and slapped it face first against the clear plexiglass. "I am."

While he went bug-eyed at the money, she found Perry's car sandwiched between two delivery trucks.

"Look, I don't want in the middle of no domestic thing."

Was this guy serious? Just drive the fucking car.

"There's no domestic thing. Not mine, anyway." Genevieve reached into her briefcase a third time. She hated what she was about to do. She lambasted dumbasses who let this go to their heads and cursed those who used it in an effort to get out of tickets or into exclusive nightclubs. Yet she slapped the prosecutor's badge against the glass on the far side of the hundred. "Follow that car or I'll haul you in for impeding an investigation and I'll keep my money."

The cab thrust itself into traffic, tossing her back onto the seat on purpose, no doubt. She shoved the badge into its pocket, crumpled the money in her fist, and tried to shelve her self-loathing.

Apparently, all the cabbie needed was the proper motivation. He zipped and jibed through traffic like a professional NASCAR driver until he was two vehicles behind

Perry. They followed the flow, clearing two more blocks, four in total so far.

The driver had implied that she was a wife—ha— spying on her cheating husband. A knot formed in Genevieve's stomach and didn't sit well. Had Perry been having an affair before the murders? Had he not told her to minimize the blowback? Was she a new romance, only a week and a half after being released from police custody? She clung to the oh-shit handle, breathed deeply through her nose, and let it out slowly several times.

Her head shook, rejecting the possibilities. Perry loved his family more than his career, and he loved that a hell of a lot. The sacrifices she'd seen him make for the firm paled in comparison to those he'd made for his precious baby girl. When she'd spent two weeks in the hospital with a bout of the flu, not once did he leave her side. She'd brought Perry and Pamela clothes, food, and toys to help keep up morale.

The Town Car shifted to the right. Without her having to say a word, the cabbie followed suit. The car parked in front of the World Mutual Bank's largest branch, housed in the first fifty floors of the WMB Building. They pulled to the curb more than 200 yards back, and Gen kept her face glued to the window, watching and waiting.

In no time, the pair exited the Town Car and headed for the bank's main entrance. The pedestrian flow was more sporadic, so Genevieve watched as Perry cordially ushered Long Legs into the revolving door and disappeared inside.

She propped her elbow on the door and rested her chin on her fist.

"You were hoping for more?" the cabbie asked.

Gen didn't answer right away. She took a moment and thought about what she'd hoped to accomplish. It was successful. By their demeanor, it was clear those two had no sexual relationship. She'd witnessed a business or possibly, a personal business transaction. Nothing more. Her 0.01% was appeased. Now to grab that healthy heaping of self-loathing off the shelf and guzzle. Forget a hangover. She felt run over.

"I wasn't hoping for it. Just expecting it."

"You wanna wait?" He was so amiable that she suspected he'd had trouble with the law in the past and didn't want to make waves. Then again, the last time she suspected something, she ended up $120 plus the cab fare poorer.

"No. Just take me back to The Ashford, please."

"You got it."

Gen slumped back against the seat.

A familiar chime tickled her ear. Her phone? It rang from inside the briefcase. She retrieved it and saw Janney's office number on the screen.

"What do you want?" she answered.

"Your disrespectful butt in the office five minutes ago."

"What now?" Gen's head pounded as her queasiness returned.

"The Carnegie Deposition."

"Shit. I'll be there in ten." She ended the call, drew a deep breath, and exhaled in a gust. A hundred and twenty bucks poorer and late to work. *Fabulous.*

EIGHT

FIVE P.M. CAME AND WENT. By seven p.m., the light shining through the crack under her office door dimmed, marking the last of the firm's employees heading out for the night. Finally alone. Gen threw down the pen, shoved away the legal pad, and stretched her cramped fingers. Two massive stacks of files created uneven pillars on her desk. One-third of them had shifted from the deal-with pile to the you're-a-rock star pile, so at least she'd made progress. A yawn arched her mouth wide. Coffee had been put off too long already.

Genevieve rose from her desk, released herself from the prison of her office, and strolled toward the break room.

Coffee.

She'd have sworn just the thought of it made angels part the clouds and sing.

Midway down the hall, it grew as dark as the backs of her eyelids. As many times as she'd made the middle of the night trek, she didn't stutter a step. Light from the break room filtered down the hallway and directed her in the path to heaven. Heaven wasn't a place, it was a thing or three; coffee, chocolate cake, and really great sex. She licked her lips. It'd been so long.

A fresh pot would have to hold her over. It would also get her through a few more files. All those damn files kept her from getting good and laid. She rounded the corner into the break room.

He sat at the table. A wicked grin animated his features.

Genevieve gasped so hard she nearly swallowed her goddamned tongue. Choking on her tongue kept a concussive scream lodged in her throat. She lurched back toward the door, and her hands scrambled for the knob. The left side of her body crashed into the uneven doorframe.

"Christ, Genevieve." Perry stood gently and offered his palms. "I didn't mean to scare you."

She blinked at him while she dislodged her tongue and tried to remember how to operate it.

"I just needed to talk to you. You've been avoiding me like every other person in this cursed city."

"For fuck's sake, Perry, knock on my door. Hell, pick up the phone and call me." She clung to the frame that had most likely given her a fabulous bruise. Blood still vibrated in her veins. Once it settled, she'd know.

"You're right. And you were right. Maybe one day, I'll learn to listen to you." His head shook. He gestured to the chair across from him. "Sit with me for a minute?"

He looked like a beaten dog. Gone was the chipper affect and world tackling attitude. His newly thickened shoulders hunched, and the lines on his face that had seemed near youthful two weeks ago now looked like deep crevices on an ancient mountain. Sympathy, something she'd thought but not felt for him in a while, welled. Maybe the eagerness to reenter the free world had taken its toll. Maybe the world had proven to be a place he no longer recognized. Maybe he'd known that all along and created a front to hide his pain.

"Not as my lawyer," he added when she didn't move right away. "As my friend?"

"That sounds good." It too had been a long time since they'd been able to act as friends. It might take some fine-tuning to get that part of their relationship back, but he needed a friend now more than ever.

Gen sat at the circular oak table next to Perry not across from him and shoved his left shoulder. He made an act of tipping to the far side of his chair. "Don't ever scare me like that again."

"Promise." He crossed his heart.

They exchanged knowing smiles.

"Is your office still an obstacle course?"

"Dodging boxes is my cardio. Don't judge me." She winked, but it was too late to recapture the words. There were so many hot button topics they needed to discuss. More than anything, she wanted to approach them without hurting him.

"I'm hardly in a position to judge anyone."

"About that." She drew a circle on the table with her finger. "I'd like to circle back to the 'I was right' portion of this conversation and wallow there for as long as possible."

"Of course you would." He chuckled. The pitiful laughter didn't reach his shoulders, much less his eyes or heart. "You were right about me not returning to work right away. You were also right about me not hosting the party."

It had been more than a week since that damn party.

The law conference in DC kept McMellon out of the office and her hair. Perry had been scheduled to present on a panel and even give one of the keynote speeches, but the conference organizers had kindly revoked the invitation the moment they'd learned of Perry's arrest. If only his family hadn't been murdered, he hadn't been a suspect, and they hadn't traded partners for the speech, she wouldn't have had to hole up in her office from morning until night.

"Would it help to say that in these instances I hate being right?"

His head shook slightly.

"Didn't think so." Gen rubbed her palms on the edge of the table. The angle of the wood against her skin distracted from Perry's raw pain and her own discomfort. She'd acted like a spoiled child by hiding in her room when things didn't go her way.

"It was too soon. You knew it. Hell, I knew it. I was so ready for a fresh start that I didn't realize it would mean leaving them behind." Perry gnawed the inside of his cheek. Moisture glimmered in his eyes. He buried his face in his hands, drew a deep breath, and then smoothed the lines out of his features for a beat.

"Where to begin?" He shrugged. "I had no business hosting a party." His head shook. "I thought that … if I … if I could make a new memory in that house, a happy memory, then all the rest wouldn't seem so goddamned overwhelming."

During the trial, he'd shown emotion. When the medical examiner took the stand, he'd hardly been able to look in the direction of the exhibits. The strong, commanding man she'd known for years had sobbed quietly beside her. He'd shaken his arms out like a boxer about to enter the ring in the pre-trial discovery and on the day of closing arguments. He'd prayed quietly to himself for the souls of his children and wife, and that he might see them again soon.

Genevieve had worried about the possibility of Perry committing suicide in those first few days and when he'd been released.

"I should've made you come to my condo."

"You've done enough." He patted her shoulder when really, she should be the one providing comfort. "The media would have fornicated on that bit of news for days. Our relationship would have been called into question, and your career would have stalled."

She wasn't ready to discuss her career, so she placed her now tingling hands in her lap and kept her mouth shut.

"Genevieve?"

"Yeah?" There was such question in his voice that she looked him straight in the eyes. The tears were gone but not the concern.

"Why have you been hiding from me?"

"I didn't want to ask you what the fuck you were thinking by offering me partner because I know it means a lot to you. There's been so much disappointment and upheaval in your life over the past six months that I didn't want to cause you anymore." She covered her mouth to keep from saying more, but now that the cork was popped … Her fingers slipped to her chin. "Why did you do it?"

"You deserve it."

"The liability? More responsibility? The capital investment? Less court time?"

"I thought you always wanted to be partner."

He also apparently thought she liked surprises. Did he not know her at all?

"*You* always wanted to be partner." She pointed her finger gun at him for a flash. "You always wanted me to become a partner. I only want, and have only ever wanted, to practice law."

Perry drew an empty money clip from his pocket and absently slipped it over and over in his hand. The silence grew, but she kept her lips pinned together.

"Is that a no?"

"It's an I'm not ready to think about it."

"That's a relief." He grinned. It was bigger than his earlier attempt, but still hollow. "I assumed you were turning on me like the rest of the office."

"Turning on you?"

"Sideways glances when I walk by. Questioning my innocence even after I've been acquitted." His upper lip quivered as though he banked the need to snarl.

Maybe a good old-fashioned roar would give him some relief, if only fleeting. Her shrink suggested it once. She'd never seen that shrink again. He'd suggested yoga and meditation also. Of the three, screaming was something she probably should've tried.

She leaned in and placed her hand atop his. "People always want to believe the best and worst about people. Mediocre is boring."

"You're not boring." He held her hand and placed his other atop it.

"I'm not mediocre. Sometimes I'd like to be," she whispered.

"But you can't. A star does its job and so do you."

Genevieve couldn't help herself. She rolled her eyes at him.

"Seriously, Genevieve—"

"If you thank me again, I'm going to break your hand—" She shifted her hold as though she would actually hurt him. It positioned them palm to palm.

"Thank you for standing by my side." He smoothed a thumb over her wrist. "You're the reason I'm not locked away for eternity."

A tingle pricked her skin in the path his warm finger traced. She hiccupped on her thought, and warning bells rang in her ear. "The evidence spoke for itself."

"It did, but you backed it, and that made all the difference. Because everyone knows you don't defend." His index finger tapped the back of her hand.

His large hands bracketed hers. She couldn't pull her hand away without making her discomfort with the situation obvious. What the hell happened to her fuck politeness policy?

"Victims need me because defendants are mostly guilty," she explained.

A massive smile grew from one corner of this mouth to the other. It lit his eyes from the inside and perked his slouched shoulders. "Yes, they are."

Genevieve's heart skittered to a stop. There was something there in his features. A nuance hidden for days, months, years. It didn't have a name or a convenient tick box. She didn't know what it was, but it was there in his eyes, and it flash froze her to the seat. In stark contrast, her palm slicked with sweat. The need to retrieve it from his grip shrieked.

"I need coffee before I fall over." She patted his hand with her free one, pulled them both away, and stood. "Want some?"

She made for the counter without falling over and without his answer.

Some asshat had left the dregs of this afternoon's brew in the carafe. They'd also left it on the warming plate. No respect. It was nothing new. Nearly every time she wanted coffee, she had to first wash the pot. Focusing her irritation on some unknown perpetrator was easier than trying to catalog what she'd just experienced. So she yanked the glass container from the machine and turned toward the sink with a flourish of grumbled expletives.

Rushing water soon filled the silence. The silence unsettled her more. Almost as much as that eerie look on Perry's face. She set the carafe in the stream of water and turned to find him standing only a few feet away. His relocation hadn't made a sound, but that was only the third most disturbing thing. Beyond his expression and before the too quiet movement, the item hanging from Perry's grip stilled the oxygen molecules in her bloodstream, muscles, and brain.

"I found this last week." He turned an emerald green jacket over in his hand, examining it.

Gen knew the silky material well. It had a slight snag on the inside collar where the clasp of her gold ivy necklace had grabbed hold and refused to let go. It'd taken her three minutes, her bathroom mirror, and the full range flexibility to free herself from the debacle. He must have had it on his lap or on the chair next to him. She hadn't seen it before.

"It could only fit three women in the office, and I—"

"It's mine." Her steady voice belied the unease contorting her mind.

She hadn't thought about the accessory since tossing it over her arm and heading for the subway more than a week ago. It had been the same morning she'd played detective, following Perry and the long-legged blonde from The Ashford to the bank. The same morning she'd locked herself inside her office and buried herself in work in an effort to forget what she'd witnessed that morning.

Perry made no move to extend his hand to exchange the jacket for her thanks.

All for the best. Genevieve's limbs weighed a thousand pounds as did the apprehension sitting on her chest.

"I found it near the firm's back entrance." His gaze narrowed slightly.

The intense examination incited a chill. It flourished

at her nape and unfurled tendrils down her spine, freeing her from shock. She extended her hand and leaned forward.

"Oh my goodness, thank you! I hadn't been able to find the thing anywhere." Her cheeks hurt from forcing a smile.

He extended it toward her so slowly it seemed he didn't move at all. "Any idea how it got behind the door of the back entrance?"

"It probably slipped off my arm when I opened the door. You know, last week it was too hot to wear the thing on the commute." Gen snagged the jacket and inspected it, for lack of anything better to do with her frantic self.

"I wasn't aware you used that door." His arms hung limply by his sides. If he'd shove them into his pockets, she'd feel more comfortable. He was being awkward and almost provoking with his stance. Where was the happy, slightly pudgy guy she'd known for years?

"Don't usually, but I've been hiding from you, remember?" Genevieve winked and turned away from him. "How about that coffee?" Her hand trembled as she raised the jacket and set it on the counter. She moved fast, snagging the dish soap and sponge from the cabinet, and set to work on the carafe.

"If you've been using that entrance, why didn't you see your jacket?" His breath heated her neck.

She swallowed a lump of you're caught the size of Riker's Island, clamped her eyes shut, and scrubbed at the burnt-on grounds. "Focused on minimizing my obstacle course, I guess."

"You know ... caffeine in the evening will make you jittery and keep you up all night."

"Yep." Her eyes popped open. Was that a threat? She stared at the water rushing over her fingers and forced a genial tone. "But I have work to do. You don't want a lazy partner, do you?"

"No. I already have two." Perry's palm wrapped around the back of her neck. His fingers sank into either side and swayed her gently. He'd done the same thing a hundred times before in her backyard or at an uptown party as a sign of celebration and camaraderie, yet tonight, it felt like a threat.

"Is that an agreement?" His words whispered into her ear.

"Nope." She reached back with her sopping wet hand and patted his. "Not yet." Water dripped over her arm, shoulder, and neck, and on Perry's hand and suit sleeve.

He released his grip and reached around her for the dish towel hanging on the hook. After meticulously rubbing the water from the fabric and his skin, he returned it, crowding her too much. Her gaze slipped to the drawer with all the knives. Could she get one in time? Could she even use it on anyone, much less her friend? Could he really hurt her?

"Soon," Perry said his demand and turned. Light footsteps marked his exit.

Genevieve clung to the countertop for support. The aftermath of adrenaline ravaged her body, making everything weak and shaky. If Detective Graham could see her hands now. She shut off the water and drew deep breaths, willing back her usually unwavering composure.

Was she losing a step, or was Perry Carter not the man she thought she knew?

NINE

WINE SLOSHED AND MOUNTED THE TOP of her glass. The table vibrated, jittering and clinking the silverware on Genevieve's plate. In turn, she squeaked and jerked. The red liquid spilled over the edge, drizzling down her fingers and onto the starched white tablecloth. Three red-purple circles grew as the fabric soaked it up.

Her phone vibrated several more times in rapid succession, chiming on her dishes.

"Damnit." She released the whispered curse before she remembered exactly where she was. Two sneers from the neighboring table of perfectly posh Upper East Siders reminded her that she sat at an upscale eatery, outdoor seating or not.

A neatly quartered Focaccia Robiola sat untouched on her plate. The brick-oven toasted sandwich brimming with spinach, tomato, cheese, and truffle oil was the Amaranth's specialty. Since the phone call informing her that Perry had been taken into custody and his family murdered, Genevieve had been hit or mostly miss on her low carb diet. Yet her stomach revolted against even the thought of food. Drink, on the other hand—literally—was all she'd done since the end of the trial.

Last night's encounter with Perry had set her on edge, and she'd teetered there all day. Only the idea of action had soothed her. However, stalking your boss and dear friend who may or may not be hiding something wasn't the place to keep them ironed out. She'd braided her red hair and looped it into a tight, low bun in an effort to hide in plain sight. In any other city, a muted pink boatneck top and pleated black leather skirt might have outed her from a mile off, but in her city, she blended in like a pro.

Gen dabbed at the tablecloth with her napkin, but it was too late. The evidence of her slow spiral into premature alcoholism remained. She wasn't an alcoholic yet, though she had the jitters and current drinking habits of one. It was only a matter of time.

The phone vibrated once more.

Using the napkin, she wiped off her fingers and ignored the couple dining next to her. If they wanted finery, they should've dined inside. The sidewalk dining could be a crapshoot. One time, Gen had dined next to a woman wearing $2,000 blue jeans. That would likely send their snooty asses to therapy. She took a long drink of wine—without spilling a drop—placed the napkin in her lap, and swiped the screen on her phone. She'd shoved it under the edge of her plate at the beginning of the stakeout in case she needed to snag a photo. Not that an iPhone was made for long distance photography, but it was all she had. A group text from the girls lit her screen.

Marlis: When are we having our congratulatory dinner?
Larkin: I won't be back in town until Friday afternoon.

Marlis: We just left the conference, headed back to NYC. Your plane can't be delayed for two days!

Larkin: I know!! Since I was already out here, I decided to move up a meeting that I had scheduled with a tech company next month. They're thrilled about the schedule change. NOT!

Marlis: You can't miss spa day!!

Genevieve cast a glance up at the street. The movers worked steadily, loading large, extravagant pieces of furniture from Perry Carter's house onto a large truck occupying too much of the street for passing motorists. Several of them had voiced their opinions, which had ruffled the feathers of the couple next to her before they'd even sat.

No sign of Perry yet.

Her phone vibrated again. She scooped it off the table, set it in her lap, and read.

Libby: If they can't help your business now, they won't help it in a month.

Larkin: That's what I said. Don't worry. I'll be back in time for the board meeting. Just a touch more important than spa day.

Marlis: Depends on who you ask! Gen?!

Genevieve: I can't make the spa Friday either. Sorry! Good luck with the biz stuff!

Marlis: Not you too! Traitors, all of you!

There wasn't an event to get in the way of Friday's spa day ritual. Larkin's absence had given her an out, and she might need it. If she didn't have answers to what the hell was going on with Perry by then, her money would be wasted. No way could she relax and enjoy either Eric's practiced hands on her or his ample cock inside her. It was against every policy of the prestigious institution and every certified massage therapist, but that hadn't stopped them from enjoying each other before. Prepping for that fucking trial had.

Libby: I'm not a traitor. I'll be there with or without those two.

Larkin: How about we celebrate Saturday?
Libby: I'm in. What are we celebrating?
Marlis: Gen making partner, of course!
Genevieve: Only one of you is supposed to know about that!
Larkin: I'm a better interrogator than Libby is a criminal.
Libby: I should get her a job at the Bureau.
Libby: Gen, I'm sorry!!! I'm a terrible friend!!!
Genevieve: The worst!
Marlis: You know you can't keep anything from us for long.

Genevieve looked at the home Perry had shared with his wife and two precious children right up until the day they'd been ripped from the earth. Libby couldn't keep a secret. She and the girls had pried juicy gossip and FBI secrets from her without waterboarding. Perry, though, that man could gridlock and take a secret to his grave. She'd tried prying details from him on past cases. Not a peep. She'd entrusted things to him that she hadn't told a soul and entombed in him they remained.

So what was Perry hiding? Why was he moving? Why hadn't he mentioned it the other night?

Perhaps the memories in the house were too sweet and brutal to bear.

As though she'd conjured him, Perry stepped through the doorway onto one of the grandest front stoops New York City had to offer. He'd yet to change out of the suit she'd seen him in at the office. A meeting about a change in the tax law that affected them all necessitated her expedition into the fray, where again Perry had prodded her about the partnership. He'd lost his jacket somewhere along the way as well as his tie. Both hands perched on his hips, accentuating their narrowness. The folds of his sleeve exposed sinew she hadn't known existed on his frame. His mouth was moving, and she'd give up her swanky apartment and move back to Brooklyn to hear what he said. A man popped his head out the truck. They two exchanged words. Perry pointed from the guy to the house. His face contorted, and the pointing grew more intense.

"Miss?"

Genevieve jerked once more. This time, her glass swayed in her hand, but there was no more liquid to spill.

"I didn't mean to startle you." A server in black pants and a white button-down shirt bent at the waist. His hand was clasped wide over his tie.

Great, she was visibly startled. Again. The entire reason she'd come to the Amaranth was because stoop sitting on this street would get her jailed or, at the very least, shooed off like yesterday's garbage. Plus, she'd have stuck out like fake fur at fashion week. And this guy interrupted the show.

He smiled sweetly. "Is there something wrong with your entree?"

"Um, it's fine. I was enjoying the wine," she lied. Well, the glass was empty, and it had been a nice red. So, not a lie.

"Another glass?"

"Yes, please."

The server's gaze fixated on the stains. Genevieve glared at him, daring him to say anything.

"Very well." He gave a curt nod and headed into the restaurant.

When she looked back, Perry and the movers were gone, as though the house had swallowed them whole. She watched intently for the next two minutes, willing them to re-emerge. In the hour she'd been sitting here, scrutinizing every item or box they removed from the structure, she'd also been looking for any sign of Long Legs. There were none except perhaps for the move itself. Perry had been adamant about living in the house that had been his family's home.

There were so many questions and no answers. She

scrolled back through the text string to remember what they'd been talking about and then added her rebuttal.

Genevieve: I haven't said yes to partner.

Marlis: But you're going to, right?!

Genevieve: I don't know. It's complicated.

Larkin: We'll discuss the pros and cons and weigh them Saturday night! Fancy or fun food?

Libby: Fun

Marlis: Fun is fine.

Mar always preferred fancy. She put up with fun for them.

Genevieve: Fine!

Larkin: Great! See you then.

Libby: With the sexy details on your exotic international trip!

Larkin: A lady doesn't kiss and tell.

Genevieve: I don't know any ladies.

Libby: Lol

Gen knew she should take the partnership and run with it. What a boost for her already over-the-top career. Later, she could parlay both into a seat on an early morning talk show. She should leave the past in the past and claim her future.

The tall structure loomed like a dream turned nightmare. The dreams were fleeting, but the nightmares clung. They grew tentacles and burrowed deep. This was one nightmare she couldn't easily leave behind.

TEN

THE CORRECTIONS OFFICER INSIDE THE CONCRETE, STEEL, and bulletproof glass control room was new. He fumbled with the buttons on the dash that operated too damn much for him to be learning on the fly. Where was Henry when she needed him? Driving stupid transports when his place was here, cracking jokes with her. At this juncture, she'd take the shit-for-personality Ronny. At least he knew his ass from a hole in the ground. She shuffled back and forth on sedate black pumps, waiting for the new guy to notice her. The control room was ten feet from her behind a network of heavy steel doors and small holding cells. A scream would get his attention, which was probably why another officer yelled through the echo chamber from the corridor opposite her. He wanted out. She needed in, but she dared not holler. In a facility that housed upward of 800 men against their will, a woman's voice stood out.

This was not the place to demand attention.

"Come here often?" A deep, masculine voice poured over her. She knew its owner before she turned to see Detective Owen Graham's approach. He was back in business mode buttoned up in a suit and tie. Shame to hide such a magnificent body. Her hands, clasped in front of her, fidgeted among themselves. As much as she liked looking at him, as much as she liked their flirtatious or often contentious encounters, he needed to be anywhere else on the planet right now.

"Quite often actually." She nodded a hello and turned her gaze back to the control room and the still struggling guard. "I'm not going to let you buy me a drink, though. They ferment their hops in the john."

"I've heard that. Never seen it." Surprised, she slid her gaze to him and found him shivering. "The thought … disgusting."

"I'd expect you were a regular here."

"Only when I absolutely have to. I like easy access to freedom. Plus, I usually leave my patrons at the door."

Genevieve returned her gaze to the hub to find the grated metal door across the hallway from her finally yawn. The corrections officer walked through the gate and turned left away from them, demanding that another section be opened for him.

"Well, shit," she grumbled. "We might never get inside with this brainless freshman running the show."

"We could always go somewhere else and grab a drink until shift change."

She pinned him with a look. His shoulders were relaxed. He wore a small, sweet lopsided grin. The man was well respected on the force, among the law community, and even in political circles. He shot from the hip and didn't dick around. Everything about him made her want to say yes, which was exactly why she wouldn't.

"What's your angle, detective?"

His cheeks turned a rosy shade. It was the cutest damn thing she'd ever seen. The cutest damn thing she'd never seen until today. A grown-ass man with the eyes of an angel and the lips of a devil who blushed.

Despite herself, Gen smiled. "What was that thought?" She was dying to know that answer almost as much as she wanted this trip to answer questions about Perry.

He shook his head, and his neatly arranged hair escaped its confines, slipping onto his forehead. "It's inappropriate."

Gen thrived on inappropriate, but something in his tone told her he wouldn't cross that line. If the chivalry stuck, he'd be the first.

"Okay."

"Can't a guy just be interested in getting to know a beautiful woman?"

"If by getting to know, you mean getting acquainted with the holes between her legs and the bumps on her chest, then yes."

He choked.

"If you mean getting familiar with the inner workings of her personality, her passions in life, and the origin of the forces that drive her, then based on my vast experience, no." She shrugged. "Not that I can blame them. Us women are stunningly gorgeous and extraordinarily complex on our best days."

"Complex for sure." Graham sighed. He looked dazed.

Genevieve stole the opportunity and stepped forward. She banged on the columns of steel and called for the officer in her deepest voice. The guy turned and seemed stunned to see them standing there. He held up a finger. She had a finger for him. Two of them, in fact.

"I know from vast personal experience that if the woman is complex enough, he's interested in both."

"So if a man only wants in our pants, it's our fault for not being interesting enough?" Genevieve slapped her long hair back over her shoulder, quite pleased with herself for catching him.

"There is a certain carnal reality, proliferation of the species, that our bodies—male and female, alike—will never free us from. Often, interest can't move past that base level on either part because people aren't often compatible. Every once in a while, a person comes along who forces you past the fundamentals. And, Genevieve Holst, to me, you are that person."

He made no move forward. Even though his hands didn't touch her, heat plucked at her chest, plunged low, and licked at her core. Her body responded in the most unlikely of places, at the most inappropriate of times, as though he had laid her bare and attacked her most intimate parts. That was exactly what he'd done—seduced her brain first. It buzzed between her ears.

Gen licked her lips, trying her best to engineer words that would deflect the onslaught of thoughts and images of their bodies writhing together. But worse were the images of a lazy Saturday morning curled up together, talking, dreaming, sharing hopes for the future together. Over the years, her body had become a weapon wielded against men for her own pleasure, not theirs. Her mind, however, had become a fortress, forbidden to anyone with a cock and most of those without one.

The steel door rolled wide. Genevieve cooled the need to surge forward and leave Detective Graham behind. They could only approach the control room one at a time, and the last thing she wanted was for him to see the name of the prisoner she planned to question.

"Please." She motioned for him to precede her. When he stayed, she cast a glance over her shoulder. "Liar, liar, I need to see if your pants are on fire."

"I think you just want to stare at my ass, counselor."

"If I say no, then mine would be on fire." She shooed him along. "Now, let's go, I don't have all day."

His mouth quirked as though he wanted to say more, but he didn't elaborate. He grinned, nodded, and head-ed for the control room. She couldn't rip her gaze from him. The confident stride. The steady hands. The ass most certainly on fire, but for a whole different reason, even if mostly hidden by his suit. The slight bulge in the rear of his jacket from the ever-present and too damn endearing slim pack of peanuts shoved into his back pocket. Her gaze followed him from the sign-in sheet to the hallway one over from the one she needed. When he disappeared out of sight, relief and disappointment flooded, making thought next to impossible. The momentary break from her mind's incessant inquest eased the headache that had plagued her for days.

"Hey!" The officer's sharp voice penetrated her mo-mentary fog and yanked her forward.

The second her heels cleared the gate, it closed behind her, and it started. A communal roar of whoops and whis-tles so loud it dulled her thoughts once more. Inmates in cells on neighboring corridors hung their arms through gaps in the bars and angled small hand mirrors in her di-rection. Others without the privilege joined in blind sol-idarity an unspoken pact among criminals. Years ago, it had chilled her to the core, but now it hardly registered. Sad, really. Insulating dulled the other reactions, but it was Survival 101.

She signed in, appropriately flashed her badge, and waited for him to read the name of the prisoner she'd re-quested. He gave no outward reaction. After all, Edger Sanchez was no one to him, just one of the hundreds of men awaiting trial in the Tombs. Also known as the Man-hattan Detention Complex. Hopefully he wasn't one of the men catcalling her.

"Down that hallway, I think. First door on the …" He scratched at his chin.

"I've got it. Thanks." Gen hadn't lied to the detective. She came here too damn often for case discoveries. It was easier for her to come to see a prisoner than it was for them to come to her. There were no shackles or armed guards involved in her stroll down the hallway to the third door on the right. Well, there were corrections officers, but they were posted outside the rooms of the prisoner they escorted. She nodded at a man in the familiar black uniform two doors down and then shoved inside the small interview room.

Unlike an interrogation room, it didn't have a two-way mirror, thank goodness. Gen hated those things. Not knowing for certain who was behind them. Not knowing who was breaking her privilege by listening in. She moved around an anchored metal table and sat in the chair facing the door. The fluorescent lighting burned her eyes, but she didn't dare squint. When Sanchez was in there, she couldn't give away any hint of weakness, and it was always better to practice how you played. She staved the urge to check the time. In these blank confines, those numbers were the last kind that mattered. Besides, phones weren't allowed. So she placed her hands on her lap, engaged her best posture, stared at the painted steel door, and waited.

Less than ten minutes later, the small lever dipped and the door swung wide. A surprisingly short young man stood in the opening. Until now, she'd only seen him sitting in the back of a police cruiser or behind a table much like the one in front of her with guards flanking his sides. He wore a tan long-sleeve shirt and pants, and his dark hair was slicked back into a long ponytail. A silver chain encircled his waist and imprisoned his cuffed wrists with short leads at a loop in the front, leaving his hands to hang insolently in front of his hips.

Menacing, near black eyes narrowed on her. A smile cracked the hard line of his mouth. He grunted like an animal, a monster, and it spoke of excitement and approval. It scaled Genevieve's spine, digging sharp claws into cartilage between the vertebrae. She remained perfectly still. If she revealed any sign of weakness, he would win, and she was quite fond of winning.

He stepped inside the room. Shackles clanked.

The officer who stood sentry behind Sanchez also gave nothing away. Most of the corrections officers checked their captive's chains and made some sort of threat before leaving the room, but this one gave no effort beyond closing the door behind the detainee and turning to stand in front of it. Instead of getting angry, she focused on the man she needed to see.

"Edger Sanchez, do you realize you have the right to counsel, now or at any time during our discussion?"

Sanchez moved slowly toward the table as though deciding on whether to take a seat in the available chair or on her lap. He moved like a man who owned the room and had no reason to fear her. If he was stupid enough to think she posed no threat, her job would be ten times easier.

"Oh Roja, I don't plan on sharing you." He pulled the chair back from the table, pushed his thighs against the unmoving metal, and leaned across the table.

Let him underestimate you. Let him think he has the upper hand.

"No recorder? No notebook?" He grabbed a handful of his crotch, arched his hips, and shook it at her face. "Looks like you're here for a piece of me."

Adrenaline ran like wildfire through her veins. The familiar sensation of fight or flight warmed her like the arms of an old friend. Her gaze zeroed in on his handful of pants, cock, and balls.

"If you ask me, that's nothing to boast about." Gen deadpanned.

"Ha, ha, ha, ha!" His exaggerated laugh was forced through clenched teeth. He released his crotch, adjusted the chair, and sat hard. "You're funny. I always enjoy our talks. Haven't seen you since before the trial."

"It has been a while."

Sanchez reclined in the seat. "I liked those meetings better. The police have better snacks than these privatized hijo de perras."

Gen wasn't fluent in Spanish but understood enough to decipher the whispers from her informants and spoke enough to get her into trouble. Yes, lawyers—at least, the good ones—had people on the inside. They listened and reported pertinent information. They'd reported chilling accounts of Edger Botella Sanchez, and she'd expected nothing less from the son of a rising Mexican cartel leader.

"I alerted your lawyer to my visit. Why isn't he here?" There was a slim possibility that dear old dad had had enough of his son's blatant bullshit and left him to rot this time.

"Because I told him not to come." His brows waggled. "Like I said, you're mine, and I don't share."

She ignored the empty threat.

"I don't advise skipping counsel." Even though it would make the meeting easier, it went against the grain.

"Should I be afraid of you?" Sanchez used a bound hand to point at himself and then turn the finger on her. It was another scare tactic, but she wasn't afraid of the half skull tattooed on the back of his hand. In fact, it had the opposite effect. The etched nose, gnarled teeth, and jaw-bone almost made her laugh. Only when the tattoo was held to its owner's face did it read correctly, but his hands were imprisoned.

"Only if you're smart."

The cold-blooded murderer smiled. A simplistic, effective threat. Fear mounted Genevieve like a stud. She shoved it off and focused on the task ahead.

"The police turned their suspicions on Perry and released you months ago." She let her gaze dance around the room. "Seems you squandered your free pass."

"They won't get me on this. No witnesses."

"You stabbed Carlina Martinez in broad daylight at a public park at her own family's reunion. There's video."

"A bad angle."

"There are dozens of witnesses."

"Only two now." He shrugged. "We'll see if it goes to trial. You know parents will say anything to protect their children."

Ice crystals formed in Gen's fragile stomach. He'd scared off all the witnesses except the woman's parents.

"Parents will also do anything to protect their children. That whore threatened to take my son away. I was protecting Eddie." He smirked.

"Eddie is Carlina's son. You're not on the birth certificate. No way you're getting off, and if you do, I'll be next in line."

His sadistic smile fell.

"I'm sure you're aware that Perry Carter Jr. was acquitted on all charges against him."

"Have to be dead as that stuck-up gringa GeGe Carter not to know."

Gooseflesh rose all over Genevieve's body, and her legs shook. Only a close few knew Perry's nickname for his wife. In his mind, and then later hers, it had a dark origin. In the beginning, they'd laughed and called it love at the first lap dance. As the years wore on and Perry rose in esteem, made partner, and aspired to politics in the future, the joke became taboo along with the nickname. That tidbit soothed Gen's growing worries about Perry's behavior and his innocence. He was learning how to get on with his life. This man was learning how to eliminate lives.

Genevieve leaned forward. "Good. I want you to know I'm coming for you."

Sanchez's chains jerked taut. His hips jumped forward and banged against the table. Over and over, he thrust, fucking the table. "Yes, Roja, come for me." He simulated sex only feet from her face. "You come for me, but I don't hear you screaming. You'll scream … when I kill you."

For the first time, she let her controlled façade slip, and laughter rumbled up her throat. She braced her hands on the table. "Empty words for a cock-worn man in shackles."

His thrusting hips stilled, and he leaned in, leveling his eyes with hers only inches apart. "I'm no one's bitch."

She lifted her hands and shrugged one shoulder.

Again, his chains jerked and shook.

"Your DNA is at the scene. The DA went after the wrong guy, but don't think for a second they won't circle back. I'm going to make sure they put you in the ground. And I never lose. So sit down, answer my questions without another gesture to your crotch, and I may let you skip the death penalty."

He sat and wrestled with his restraints. His angry gaze never wavered.

"How did you know Pamela's nickname?"

The anger flowing from him didn't dissipate, yet a smile tickled one side of his mouth. His head tipped to the side. He wiped his nose with the back of his hand and licked his lips. When he spoke, his voice was quiet.

"I know about GeGe the same way I know that your best friends are Larkin Ashford, Marlis McCain, and Libby Irish. The same way I know your sister got fucked by the same court system you proudly represent." He hit his stomach and puffed his chest like a gorilla. "The same way

I know she OD'd on heroin trying to forget the pain and humiliation."

Bile flooded Genevieve's esophagus. She was going to throw up. His words were horrible enough. Terrifying. Heartbreaking. Incomprehensible. Even more unsettling was that Edger Botella Sanchez's hands were free.

In all the years she'd worked around violent offenders, only once had a guy slipped his cuffs, and he'd been a child really. At seventeen years old, the boy had looked twelve with long, gangly limbs and sunken cheeks. A genetic defect had made it extremely difficult for his body to absorb nutrients, but it hadn't kept him from bludgeoning his healthy little brother to death. She'd been asked to sit in on the interview by an associate, looking for weaknesses in their case against the boy, when he pulled one of his hands from a cuff. The kid had grabbed a pen from the table and attacked her co-worker. He'd stabbed the man twice before she, the opposing counsel, and a corrections officer were able to subdue him. Even now, she felt the strength in those thin arms and the rage they channeled.

Sanchez, while short, was no weakling. Sinew covered every inch of his arms. There was no way he'd slipped a cuff, which meant he picked the lock. He stared at her. The lion hunted the lamb. Malice radiated through his pores. And malice scared her far more than rage.

Gen scanned the tabletop for a pen. She didn't want to be stabbed by anything, but a pen left gaps a doctor couldn't easily stitch. Gaps left scars; raised, gnarled, and discolored skin. There wasn't a pen in sight. She hadn't brought anything with her. What had Sanchez brought to the party? The image of a roughly filed plastic spoon with a razor-sharp point flashed in her mind.

"Where's your mouthy cunt comeback, Roja?"

She had none. There were words she could speak. She could plead. It wouldn't help. She could bargain. But she wouldn't. Death would be easier than a promise that would slowly kill her to keep.

The eyes of the damned studied her. She stared back into the abyss.

Scream. Call the guard. Run for the door. Something! Now!

Fear paralyzed every muscle, nerve, and blood vessel.

"Ha! Nothing?" Sanchez spread his arms wide and tilted his head, listening. He drew a deep breath through his nose, then hissed it out between his teeth. "That's better."

His hands clapped together so fast and so loudly, Genevieve jumped. Everything inside her relinquished control to a bone-deep quiver. Suddenly, she was nine years old again, and Uncle LeRoy's massive hand connected with her cheek. Pain exploded behind her eyes.

Don't you know better? When a door is closed, you knock! You better not make me tell your father. That'll be big trouble, little lady. Big trouble for you and your sister.

Evangeline's sobs seeped through the crack in the bedroom door, past her uncle, tormenting Genevieve thirty-four years later.

"Now." Sanchez smacked his chest, reeling her back to the present. "Let me tell you how this is going to end."

Anger slowly bubbled around her stilted blood vessels and through her muscles.

He pointed a finger from his half-skull hand at her. "You're going to forget about that whore GeGe, and the bitchy little girl of hers, and that whiny little boy. You're going to put that fine ass and your magic lawyer skills to use to defend me against Carlina's family and get me my son."

Anger had gotten her through childhood. Cunning had gotten her through the teen years. This minute, she needed both.

"It's going to cost you." Genevieve shoved the chair as far back from the table as she could without being awkward and stood.

"Money, I have." Sanchez stood too.

She folded her arms over her chest, turned away from the door, and paced. "First, I'll have to find a judge who'll take your money. Believe it or not, some people have integrity in this world. I know quite a few of them."

"Ha! You only think you do."

With her gaze cast to the ceiling, Gen let her periphery catalog the man's movements. He kept to his side of the table but mimicked her pace, blocking her route to the door. The shackles remained in place around his ankles, but they didn't slow him down enough for her to make a run for the door.

"What does that mean?"

"You think that just because your people have fancy houses and big bank accounts that they're upstanding citizens? You think that just because Perry and Pamela were doe-eyed for each other that he couldn't kill her?" His laughter filled the small room. "Gringos."

She stopped and rounded on him. "I thought you killed GeGe and her bitchy little girl and whiny boy."

"Careful, Roja." He stopped too and squared to her, lifting his chin and glaring down his nose.

She didn't tower over him, but she won in both height and weight. It was something on which to hold a hope or two.

"I could have killed them, and you know it. Perry could have, yet you refuse to believe it. Love and hate are a heartbeat away. Remember that. A heartbeat away."

"Next, you'll have jury costs." She continued walking, unable or unwilling to analyze his words now. "I won't have you threatening hardworking people just trying to do their civic duty."

Why had the corrections officer not noticed them up and walking around the goddamned room? It broke policy. As did Sanchez's free fucking hands. Twice since she'd been pacing she had seen the back of his head in the small window. Did he not have peripheral vision or the dutiful sense to check in on his charge?

"And if they don't take the money?"

"I'll make sure they do. In jury selection, I'll pick people with financial woes; overdrawn accounts, medical bills, bankruptcies. There are more of them to choose from with every day that passes."

"What next?"

Genevieve walked past her chair as though making another lap but stopped and took one step backward. She placed her left hand on the back of it and turned toward Sanchez. As she'd hoped, he blocked her path to the door, putting him two steps to the right of the large metal exit.

"There's my fee." Gen forced a smile. "I'm not cheap on a regular day. Put me on the opposite side of the courtroom, and it's double. Put me there against my will, and we double that."

"Don't forget where you are, r—"

She heaved the chair up from the ground and used both hands to shove it through the thick air toward the door.

A freight train collided with her body. It knocked her off her heels, and the room tilted. Florescent brilliance filled her vision. She swam in nothingness, weightless for seconds. Gravity took hold and yanked her to the unyielding concrete. Every particle inside her lungs evaporated. Impact created a vacuum.

Then Sanchez consumed her gaze. His hands locked around her neck, and his fingers bit into her flesh. His forehead drove the back of her skull into the ground.

For several seconds, everything was okay. Nothing hurt. There was no shank arching toward her middle. She wasn't dead.

Just as quickly, Genevieve's body remembered the taste of oxygen. And those precious seconds without it translated into infinity. She was starved. Her body thrashed. Her fingers clawed. If she could've screamed, she surely would have, but nothing moved in or around her neck.

"If you ever threaten me again, Roja, I'll fuck you while I slowly cut your throat and take your head from your body. Then I'll have my friends do the same to your friends." He yanked her into a sitting position. He pulled her because someone was pulling him. "Do you hear me, Roja?" His hands slipped from her neck, and he grabbed at her. "Do you hear me?"

He moved farther away from her as an arm locked around his middle. Still, his fingers clawed at the doorframe. He no longer crushed her neck, but she couldn't breathe.

ELEVEN

"THE AMBULANCE ISN'T HERE YET." Ronny, the shit-for-personality corrections officer, huffed. His feet moved faster than they had in years in an effort to keep pace with her.

"That's fine because I don't need one." She rushed ahead toward the last checkpoint before she'd be free of the Tombs' confines.

"Protocol states that we summon an ambulance when an altercation occurs with any inmate and an outside service provider."

Since when did Ronny use big words? Was he trying to railroad her?

"And you have summoned it. That doesn't mean I have to use it."

"But—"

"Open the gate." Genevieve didn't scream. She didn't know if her throat would allow it, so she clung to composure with both shaking hands.

The closer she got to the outside, the looser her hold on control became. It weighed a thousand pounds and threatened to crush her, much like Edger Sanchez had. She swallowed, and it burned her throat. Liquid fire. The muscles holding up her head ached. A migraine took aim at the back of her skull.

"Like I said in the interview room, I can't let you leave without filling out an incident report."

Genevieve stopped because if she didn't, she'd run into the last steel hurdle to freedom. She turned and faced the man who should've hung up his nightstick and cuffs years ago. It was only a matter of time before a younger, thinner, faster man turned them on him.

"If I have to ask you to open this gate one more time, I will slap a lawsuit on you and your employer for holding me against my will without cause. I will bring a lawsuit down upon the negligent officer who allowed the attack and any other person who gets in my way from walking out of that door." She jabbed a finger at the opaque glass double doors beyond the gate. "And, Ronny, I will not lose. So please, open the fucking gate."

After Ronny's wide eyes adjusted, he waved to the officer inside the front-of-house control room. The metal lock gave way, and the door rolled open. She drew a shallow breath, prayed her ankles would hold, and stepped through the opening.

"Miss Holst, please. An incident report could keep the court from showing Sanchez leniency."

Genevieve ignored the corrections officer and headed for the exit. Too bad the freedom from this place meant the opposite of freedom from the trauma that'd unfolded inside it. The farther away from Sanchez she moved, the louder his words echoed, and the stronger his grip squeezed. She panted and pushed through the door. The muscles in her neck and back twinged. Hazy New York air filled her distressed lungs. To her right, cars zipped by on Centre Street. Self-preservation revolted at the sight of people and traffic. She scrambled down the steps and shuffled left past columns that held up absolutely nothing, under the secured detainee skywalk, and around a large van meant for hauling prisoners. She slowed at the next vehicle and stopped, unable to walk another step. Her hand gripped the last rung on a ladder protruding from the rear of a utility truck.

The streets and cars around her swayed, and Gen doubled over. She heaved once, twice, but nothing fled in the revolt. Hair slipped off her shoulders and created a messy curtain around her face behind which she hid her shame. Lancing pain radiated from her lower back. Her neck throbbed with the pass of each breath. Heaves turned to sobs. Moisture slipped from her eyes and slid down her nose in rapid succession. Imperfect circles splattered the gray stone pavers, turning them as dark as her thoughts.

In the courtroom, Genevieve had been next to invincible for so long, she'd forgotten how vulnerable she truly was. In the city, she walked among people so often, she'd forgotten how exposed she had been to attack. In her life, she'd fucked with so many people without repercussion, she'd forgotten her own mortality. One misstep refreshed reality. God, she hated the fear and insecurities it roused.

"Genevieve?"

Of all the people she didn't want to see, Detective Graham was second, right under Edger Sanchez, but she couldn't stop sobbing long enough to tell him as much. Despair hit her like ocean waves. One after another, her fears came, driving her down, stripping her of oxygen, and forcing her to fight to the surface only to be battered low once again.

Everything shook. Hands. Legs. Lips. Core. Complete

meltdown.

System failure.

Warmth covered the hand with which she clung to the ladder. That hold was the only thing keeping her from toppling to the ground. Gently, Owen Graham pried her fingers from the metal rung.

Indignation fought fear for control of her brain. She hadn't asked for his help. Why did all men think women needed their help? Gen yanked her hand away from his and pitched sideways. The ground came up fast and hard. A hiss rushed through her teeth as pain zinged her anew. She blinked up from the pavers past tears and blinding light to see Graham standing over her. His jacket was gone, and his sleeves were rolled once again, revealing a bit more of his inky artwork.

"Let's go ahead and get this out of the way right now." Both hands braced on his hips and a hiked brow exclaimed his irritation. He made no move to help her up. "I'm not helping you because you're a woman. I'm not helping you to get in your pants. I'm not helping you because I think you can't help yourself. I'm not helping you because I think you need it. I'm helping you because, for better or worse, it's who I am. I find joy in helping people. Fuck me sideways for caring." He gave a wide false grin. "And, for the record, caring has fucked me several times in several uncomfortable ways. I get it. Pushing people away keeps you safe. It also keeps you isolated."

He shoved out his hand. The expression of his blue eyes dared her not to take it.

Gen looked at his calloused palm and long, strong fingers. She could get off the ground without him, but it would hurt more, take longer, and embarrass her further. On any other day, she'd have rolled onto all fours and shoved herself off the ground. Today, however, the world reminded her how sensitive she was. If anyone was going to get it, it would be this hard-assed detective with a surprisingly disarming center. She slid her fingers over his rough palm and held on tight. He placed another hand under her other arm. Together, they transferred her from the ground to the concrete steps just a few feet away.

Back to the entrance with her feet on the lowest step, Genevieve braced her elbows on her knees and her head in her hands. She drew several deep breaths and waited for Graham's wing tips to disappear from view. They only shifted from in front of her to beside her.

They sat together in the chaos of the city. The rhythm of people moving about the world, completely uninterested in anything but their day's agenda, soothed the most jagged of her edges. It reminded her that life went on, no matter what.

"Thanks," she croaked.

"Christ, you sound like you snacked on a bag of rocks."

She shoved the hair back from her eyes and found him sitting there with a bag of peanuts in his hand. Tearing the plastic, he shuffled some into his palm, tossed them into his mouth, and then offered her the package. Her lips itched to smile, but her body didn't allow it. She gave the softest shake of her head, and he returned to feeding himself.

"I have friends." Why did she feel the need to emotionally defend herself against this man? Because she never let any of them get close enough to warrant a defense.

"I know you do." His jaw worked a bit more. "They're some of the most successful women in the city. Your little group is near famous." He swallowed. "How many boyfriends?"

A pause stretched several beats as she stared at him.

"I'm guessing too many to count or zero." He twisted the plastic around and around, and secured half of the peanuts in his rear pocket.

How the fuck did this guy get her? Normally, she'd spew rage all over his nice suit, but seeing how it already had detention center stairs all over its butt and she'd been wrung of all her rage …

"Both too many to count and zero." She swallowed past the pain and fear. "None of them matter."

He nodded like he understood, but he knew nothing.

"I don't need your pity."

"Good thing. I have exactly none to give you. People with actual problems get my pity. Addicts. The homeless. Abused and abandoned children."

This man, this good man, didn't deserve her snappy attitude, though he brought it on himself by staying.

"What happened in there?" His head crooked toward the building.

She drew a deep breath. The longer she sat here with Owen Graham, the easier breathing became. The less she focused on Sanchez's words, the less she felt his hand around her neck. The longer she sat next to Owen Graham, the longer she wanted to sit with him.

"Nothing."

"A ball breaker like you, who feasts on criminals for a living and can hold her own with the most gnarly of judges, doesn't cry over nothing."

Genevieve blotted her face with the back of her hand. As if removing the evidence could change what he'd seen. The man had witnessed her total breakdown.

"Everyone has an off day every now and again," she explained.

"My last off day led to a psychopathic, narcissistic murderer being released into the world. Would that about sum up your off day?"

And just like that, the magic was gone. He wasn't helping because it made him feel good inside. He helped because he hedged for information. What better way to squeeze the un-squeezable than when she was losing her shit?

Gen stood. The world tilted but didn't topple. Neither did she.

Graham sat with his forearms braced on thighs that stretched the width of his slacks wearing a relaxed and unapologetic expression. The shrewd blue gaze of his cataloged the crazy red hair crowding her face, the button missing from her blouse—news to her also—and her twisted and hiked a little too high skirt.

Both their mouths opened to speak.

Behind him, a detention center door groaned. Gen's gaze shot to it. Her brain paused all function. The secured panel swung wide, and the largest black man she'd ever seen, still to this day, trundled out. She didn't know how he kept from teetering over with the hulking torso, boulder-like shoulders, and arms the size of Graham's thighs.

"Genny Miss." He flagged one of those big arms in the air. "I didn't figure I'd catch you, but I had to try."

"Henry." A smile cracked the stone grimace her face had turned into.

He basically fell down the stairs with a hammy leg catching him on each step and stopped front and center. His gentle hands braced either side of her shoulders. She realized with a start that this was the first time he'd ever touched her. Inside the Tombs, it was against their beloved protocol. Also, he'd usually been behind control room fortress.

"You have to press charges." He crouched lower until they were eye to eye. "Don't argue with me, missy."

"Forget pressing charges." She placed a hand over his and ignored the cramp in her ribs. Sanchez had made threats, and she might have negotiated inside those walls to buy time, but he was in there and she was not. He might have friends on the outside, but so did she. Hers were more powerful and so was she. Before Henry could rebut, she made herself clear. "I'm going to watch that son-of-a-bitch draw his last breath and know that I put that needle in his vein."

"That's my girl." Henry patted her shoulders and released her. He turned to Graham, who stood. The two exchanged a handshake, the moves to which she lost after the third step in the elaborate sequence. How old were they? Twelve. Was this what men did in their spare time, practice secret handshakes?

It seemed the universe was against her. Of the 8.6 million people in the city, these two just had to know one another. Rather well, judging by the final bop-bop of their fists.

"What happened in there?" Graham posed the question to Henry.

Indignation filled Gen's mouth.

"Ah." Henry disengaged his hand from Graham's and stepped from between them. "You'll have to get that info from Genny Miss." He turned to her and smiled.

It turned to admiration for the big, sweet lug. "Thank you."

"I'll be in the courtroom cheering you on every day I can. That man is bad news."

Coming from a man who worked daily with the worst of humanity, that meant something. Something that shrank the certainty of her earlier proclamation. She shivered despite the heat.

"How's your neck?" Henry bobbed his head, trying to get an angle through or around the wild collar her hair had made.

"Fine." She offered him her widest gaze and looked toward the transport truck he drove.

Henry turned his back on Graham and dropped his massive head low. His caramel eyes were intent. "Of all the people to have in your corner, he's a good one. You should tell him," he whispered.

Gen pursed her lips.

He grinned, offered a take-it-or-leave-it shrug, and straightened.

"I'll check in on you soon, missy." He flashed her the old double thumbs up and headed for the building. It warmed her heart to know Henry really had come, trying to check on her. He threw a peace sign over his shoulder. "Later, Dick-tective."

"Later." Graham's voice was so close it brought her around.

A whiff of ranch and nuts toyed with her nose. It was a good enough reason as any to hate him. She loved ranch and wanted to snuggle into him and breathe deeply. He stood inches away with his arm outstretched toward her.

If this were her daydream, he'd step close and graze her ear with his full lips while telling her all the naughty things he'd like to do to her. There. In the street. Up against the Tomb's wall.

Too late, she realized what he was actually doing.

Graham brushed the mess of her hair back over her shoulder, and his gaze zeroed in on her neck. The sunny sky-blue eyes she'd grown to enjoy in her own masochistic way—hello, sunburns—turned a cloudy gray. His jaw flexed, and his nostrils flared.

"Fucking Christ, Genevieve."

It was the first time he'd used her name, second, but there was no tenderness in it. She'd been so stupid to allow herself the daydream. Still, there it had been. There he had been nagging her needy body for weeks, months. In it, during a witty and stinging back and forth, he'd whisper her name. The wit was gone. The daydream demolished. Reality returned, the cruel and very usual suspect.

"Who did this to you?" Hand still in her hair, he demanded the answer.

She closed the narrow gap between them, exposing her neck further. Then she looked him in the eyes.

"The same man who slaughtered Perry Carter's family."

TWELVE

Liza Piggot grabbed a handful of the gray curly bun atop her head and studied the bank of twenty or more filing cabinets that lined the wall of the file room at the Rape Crisis Center. "You need Brasher, Montgomery, and Travis?" She jibed left toward the B's. Her flowing black pants lagged behind.

"No, I was given Brasher, Montgomery, and Travis." Genevieve clutched the incorrect files to her chest and pointed at the Q's. "I need Quincy, Saunders, and Vorhalt."

"Vorhalt? I don't remember her?" The woman moved to the one cabinet that housed the Q's, S's, and T's, while the J's and M's had at least three to their letter.

"Him," she amended.

"Oh, then I'm doubly stumped. There are so few males who come forward. I usually remember every one of them."

"There are thousands of files in here, Liza. You shouldn't remember every one."

"I try to, though." Liza slipped the glasses from her head and adjusted them on her face.

"I know you do."

When a person left the police office just across the complex or the hospital across town after experiencing a sexual assault, they were always recommended to the Rape Crisis Center. These ladies were highly trained professionals who counseled on a range of topics survivors of trauma often faced. Denial. Guilt. Anger. Despair. Many times, their expertise was used in court cases.

"Vorhalt was probably one of Alexa's."

The mention of Perry's sister's name shot a bolt of lightning through Genevieve. She dropped her briefcase on a table in the center of the room and walked toward the wall of filing cabinets with a renewed sense of urgency.

"She in court?" Gen asked as casually as possible.

"Early session." Liza plucked a file from the Q's and eased down the line. "She should be back any minute."

Sweat gathered between Genevieve's breasts. She tugged at the collar of the sleeveless turtleneck dress she wore, willing the air conditioning to jump inside the itchy fabric. Only an intern at the office had joked about her hiding a hickey. If the guy had any idea what she hid under the fabric, he'd have pissed his preppy pants and dropped out of law school immediately.

"Can I put these away for you?" Gen flapped the files someone had messengered over months ago in the air. She wouldn't leave without the files being properly stored, and the only way to hurry that process along was to help. If she could get out without seeing Perry's sister today, it would make an already shitty day a little more tolerable.

"Please!" Liza waved her toward the cabinet. She

hadn't seemed to notice Gen was already by them and scanning for the proper drawer for the Brasher file. "I can't believe the wrong files were delivered. It makes me sick to my stomach. You know how important they are. You know how much paperwork is needed to request a single one. And don't get me started on the chain of custody." She sagged over the open drawer. "At least I'll be able to track back and figure out who screwed up."

Stiffness followed closely by bone-deep agony chased Gen down into a crouch. The bags of ice she'd slept on and the cool shower this morning had worn off hours ago. Each move compounded the pain, which was why it'd taken her all morning to work up the courage to walk the two blocks from the courthouse. The front door chimed, and Gen froze with her hand between Bosniac and Bruster.

"Alexa?" Liza called.

"I'm back from the pits of hell," Perry's sister huffed.

"Went that well, huh?" Liza plucked another file from a cabinet.

Gen slipped the first file inside the drawer, closed it, and clamped her lips together to keep in the scream that demanded release as she stood. She loved Alexa, admired her ethics, and had eagerly worked with her more times than she could count, despite Perry's disapproval. The siblings never got along, according to them both. She never pried, and it had never mattered until Alexa showed up at her office after the murders, begging her to deny Perry's plea to be his attorney.

"Ericson got on the stand and …"

"And?" Liza asked. She and Gen turned together to see Alexa Carter standing in the doorway with her mouth hanging open.

"Sorry." Gen waved the remaining files in her hand. "I'll be out of your way in just a minute."

"Oh, right." Liza smacked her forehead with her free

hand, turned back to the last cabinet, and pulled open the last drawer. She'd apparently forgotten upon what hostile terms the two women had last parted.

The dark expression on Alexa's thin face told Gen she hadn't forgotten or forgiven a thing. The glower didn't pair well with her bright floral print business suit. She cradled a stack of files in one arm. Her other was free except for the key chain wrapped around her wrist and what looked like a phone clutched in her hand. Gen knew better, though. That "phone" was really a 20-million-volt stun gun she'd used more than once on overzealous assholes in the city. If Gen didn't play this out just so, Alexa could turn the immobilizing electricity on her.

Genevieve turned toward the filing cabinet and shuffled toward the M's.

"What are you doing here, Holst?" Alexa's voice boomed across the room. It was stronger and deeper than Perry's. His could get loud, but unlike his sister, he had a quietly commanding presence. There was nothing quiet about Alexa. Not even her clothes.

"Calm down." Liza fanned away Alexa's attitude as though it were a pesky gnat. "There was a mix-up with the delivery of some files, and she was kind enough to come herself and get them sorted out."

"Well, isn't she a good Samaritan." Alexa's sneer deepened.

The fighter inside Gen, though battered and bruised, stretched and flexed in response.

"Yes, she is." The older of the women closed the drawer in which she'd rummaged, walked to Gen's side, and addressed Alexa. "You know another attorney who would have realized the mix-up in the first place? You know one who'd have hiked their ass over here in the heat, filled out the paperwork for the right ones a second time, and made certain the strays were put in their proper place? No, you don't. Because I don't." Liza plucked the remaining two incorrect files from Gen's arms and handed over the ones she'd requested. "I'll see to it that these get where they need to go."

"Thank you." Genevieve hated to cause trouble between the co-workers, but it seemed Liza was accustomed to dealing with Alexa and her boisterous personality.

"Hell, you saved my ass." Liza hugged the folders to her chest with both arms. "So thank you." She winked, and then returned her attention to the wall of filing cabinets.

Gen drew a bracing lungful. Paper had a unique smell that soothed. Locked away in metal coffins as it was, it went stale with a mineral bite that had her tongue folding over on itself. She stepped around the table and grabbed her briefcase. The pain was there, throbbing and dull, and Alexa's presence overpowered it. Years of practice allowed Gen to smile genially as she walked past a woman who despised her without a second thought. She turned right down a long corridor and headed for the main entrance.

Alexa's gaudy purple pumps followed with a heavy staccato. Maybe she'd moved offices. Maybe she'd forgotten something by the door.

"You think you did the state a service?"

Perry's sister was clearly spoiled for a fight.

Genevieve wheeled on her even though Alexa had a stun gun. Oh well. Gen had a bruised backside, a throbbing throat, and zero fucks left to give this woman. "I could give two shits about the state. I care about Brasher, Montgomery, and Travis, Quincy, Saunders, and Vorhalt. The latter three are top on my caseload right now. Getting them justice is what I care about."

"I thought you were a defense attorney now." Alexa squeezed the device in her hand so hard it might shatter.

Can stun guns explode?

"Like I told you before, it was a favor for a friend." Gen rolled her eyes and didn't care if the other woman saw. "Goodbye, Alexa." She turned and headed for the door. "I'd say it was a pleasure, but it wasn't."

"You shouldn't have represented him."

"It's over. Let it go, already." She didn't even bother looking back. The door was within her reach. Freedom from one headache, at least.

"He's done it before."

Her hand rested on the opaque glass of the entryway and exit. All she had to do was push. Push and walk. She'd done it a million times in her life. Push and walk. Leave and don't look back. Her body and mind gridlocked.

Alexa approached with the same heavy tread. "Give me five minutes and you never have to talk to me again."

"I don't want to hear what you have to say." Gen's voice quivered because it was the absolute truth. Over the past two weeks, she'd harbored enough doubt about Perry to unsettle even the most devout believer. Yesterday's visit to the Tombs and her attack by Edger Sanchez had cleared her conscience. 100% back on the prayer chain. Front pew. Bible in hand. Hymns on the tongue.

"Which is why you need to." Alexa retreated down the corridor, her shoes clomping and creating an aggravating echo in the empty and sparsely decorated waiting area.

A shiver pinged across Genevieve's skin. Her hand slipped from the glass, leaving an unsightly smear as she turned and walked to Alexa's office. The woman had discarded her files and weaponry on her desk but sat on one end of a long sofa opposite it.

"Are you going to try to counsel me?" Genevieve closed the door, chose a chair across from the sofa, and set her briefcase on her lap.

"You took the chair for that job." Alexa moved from her semi-reclined position to the edge of the sofa. "Besides, I've needed therapy more than you."

Assumptions. People made them every day about everything. Most of the time, as now, they were completely incorrect. Utter bullshit.

"Get to the point, or I'm leaving." Gen opened her briefcase, laid the files inside, snapped it shut, and placed it on the floor next to the chair.

"Fine," Alexa huffed. "Thirty years ago this summer, Perry killed Rita Ayers."

Genevieve's fingers fumbled on the handle. The briefcase fell over, and she expected her jaw to join it. Instead, everything inside her revolted against the thought. Her head jerked back as though the brusque woman had slung shit in her general direction.

"You're lying," Gen growled.

The woman hadn't been moving much, but it seemed her breaths and her microscopic fidgeting ground to a rusty stop. It was as if the breeze died on a hot spring day. Trees lost their happy sway. Oxygen became more difficult to cull from the environment. Birds fell from the sky. Fear became a heavy woolen blanket. It gathered over her, drew close around her face, and suffocated hope.

She willed Alexa to rebut the statement or even rebuke the attack, but she did neither. Her dark brown eyes were so familiar because they looked just like her brother's. Those haunting eyes simply stared.

"Say something." Gen's upper lip curled and shook.

Moisture gathered in Alexa's eyes. Any hope Gen had that this was some elaborate ruse or a convenient lie died like the poor little birds. They all dropped from the sky. The impact compounded yesterday's trauma and yanked a dry moan from Gen's lips. She placed her hand over her mouth.

Alexa, like her brother, seldom showed emotion. And the woman would never willingly reveal any to her. Tears slipped down her cheek in earnest but not a sound followed.

This was bullshit. People did things every day to suit their own whims. They played parts and manipulated others to get what they wanted. Gen needed to find her angle to restore balance to the world she knew and was quite fond of. She dropped the hand covering her mouth and leaned forward. Alexa's distant gaze honed on Gen's movement. She seized the opportunity.

"Why tell me this now? Why not mention it, oh, I don't know, before the trial?"

A foreign expression of helplessness contorted Alexa's features. The tears ran in tiny rivulets down her neck and stained her pink undershirt a darker shade.

"I didn't expect you to represent him. I certainly didn't expect you to win."

"Winning is what I do." It sounded bombastic and totally conceited, but Gen didn't give a fuck. If what Alexa was saying was true, there was an increased possibility that she had freed a murderer. "Did you not know my record? I mean, the media made sure I remembered details of my successes I'd long forgotten."

"I knew your record on the right side of the aisle." Alexa slapped at a tear, revealing the first weak sign of fight.

"The right side?" Genevieve gripped the arms of the chair. "Even though I love and live for prosecution, I know a small handful of people are wrongfully convicted every year. The defense is there to protect them. If anything, it's more the right side than the prosecution. It's easy to get people to believe the worst about another. It's harder to make them believe the good. So I'll ask you again, why not before? Why chance the proverbial roll of the dice?"

"Because I was ..." Alexa shook her head. "No, I am his accomplice."

Genevieve's jaw joined her briefcase on the floor. Her

hands loosened on the armrests. She fell back into the chair and stared.

Alexa absently picked at a place on her thumb. Slowly, almost as if she didn't realize she was doing it, she rocked forward to back. "It was out of state. The minute Perry was old enough, my parents sent him to Camp Caraway, an all-boys summer camp outside of New Haven, Connecticut. They did all the usual. Sports. Sailing. Clambakes." Her eyes glazed over as she completely immersed herself in the past. As though she was seeing it all again.

"I begged to go to a summer camp, but they always said it was too expensive." She laughed, and it seemed a sob. "In their eyes, Perry was an investment. I was a prize to be auctioned off. So the summers passed. Me in New York and him in Connecticut. The one weekend I looked forward to more than any other was family week. Every year, we visited for an extended weekend but not for the whole week, and every year, I got to bring a girlfriend along. Otherwise, I'd have no one to ride the inner tube with or talk to. Perry was always too busy showing off to worry with his little sister. Until the summer of eighty-seven."

"That would've made you ..." Gen tried to do the math in her head.

"Fourteen. Perry was eighteen on his second summer as a camp counselor." Her hands shook while toying with a button on her suit. "I swear to God, he'd been there for so many summers, and he was so bossy, he ran that place by the time he was fourteen. Of course, he'd had a chance to run the house the entire school year." Alexa blinked furiously.

"What do you mean he ran the house at fourteen?" Gen couldn't have been trusted with a crimping iron at fourteen, much less a multimillion-dollar household.

"My father died when I was eleven. When Mom

checked out completely, Perry didn't miss a beat. He took up the slack, orchestrating the help, overseeing the banker's reports, and making certain all the bills were paid. Dad's business partner sold the company for a massive profit, and we lived off the interest."

Alexa traded picking her button for chewing the edge of her thumb. Gen had never seen the bold woman so unraveled.

"I brought Tiffany Renly with me to camp that summer. She was gorgeous. All my friends were, but that was the first time Perry seemed to notice. He used me for Tiffany. I used her to gain a bit of my brother's attention." Alexa shrugged. "It was innocent enough. A little experimentation. Alcohol and heavy petting. No big deal." It was as if she were trying to convince herself.

"Where's Tiffany Renly now?"

The woman looked at Gen as though she'd asked her the meaning of life. "I don't know. We never really talked after the camp. I think she was scared of getting caught drinking and fooling around, but I wasn't. No one in my life set boundaries. She was only at Dalton a few days into the next school year before she moved. I never saw her again."

"When does Rita Ayers come into the picture?"

"The next summer. Eighty-eight. Rita Ayers was my best friend that year." Alexa paused for so long, Gen thought that was the end of the story. She hoped it was anyway.

"I went through them pretty quickly. I've always been... loud and outspoken. It was the only way my parents ever acknowledged my existence. They were so busy. My dad with his business. My mom with her parties, politely called philanthropic events. Then Dad died, and I became unbearably obnoxious." One of her flower-covered shoulders bobbed.

"During those past two summers, after Perry finished his head camper duties, we'd sneak over to the lighthouse. It wasn't far. Five minutes through the woods on a bike. The path was even from all the campers coming and going. He'd bring a friend. I'd bring mine."

"We'd race to the top every time, but I always lost. We always climbed out of the gallery. Perry loved heights. They scared the shit out of me, but hell if I'd whisper a word about it. After a lifetime of trying to be with my big brother, go where he went, and do what he did, I didn't say anything at all. Not the summer before. Not that one. We shimmied around the narrow catwalk, leaned our backs on the glass, dangled our feet between the bars, and shared bottles of hard liquor. The first summer on the lighthouse I was a rookie. Sure, I had snagged a bottle here and there. After all, what was an unattended fourteen-year-old supposed to do when her mother was at New York society social events? But I'd always carted it to parties and hadn't had more than a drink or two in a night."

Alexa pulled her finger from her mouth and stared it with wide eyes. Her head shook. She stuffed both hands under the edges of her thighs. A huff filled her lips and slowly bled out.

"At the end of that first summer, I'd puked off the lighthouse twice. Perry gave me shit for being a child, so I went back to the city with a mission. My brother would never see me weak like that again. When my mother went out, so did I. No one was there to stop me. By the time I made it back to the lighthouse at Camp Caraway, I was a professional underaged alcoholic."

The rape crisis counselor slipped a hand from under her leg and into the pocket of her slacks. She produced a large, goldish-bronze coin. "Twenty-one years sober."

"Are you going to make it to twenty-two?" Genevieve didn't mean to ask the question, but based on Alexa's behavior, she was concerned.

"Yes, because as soon as you leave, I'm calling my sponsor." Alexa stared at the coin. "She knows all of this. She's the only one, besides Perry, who knows all of it."

"Good." Genevieve rubber her hands together and recognized the bone-deep chill that'd taken hold. "I'm glad you have someone you can trust."

"Yeah, I'm sure you're deeply concerned," Alexa snarled.

She held her tongue. The woman's opinion of her didn't matter here. The story did. She wanted to hear it as much as she didn't want to hear another word.

"Sorry, I ..." Alexa stuffed the coin back into her pocket. "Perry and Rita had been an on-again, off-again item for six months before we went to the camp. Off more than on because Rita's parents didn't approve of their relationship. Perry was too old, too demanding of her time, and too controlling. He was all those things, but he worshiped the ground on which she walked. He'd vowed to wait for her as long as it took her parents to come around.

"Rita was a stunning brunette. She was funny and flirty. All the boys liked Rita. And she, unlike Tiffany, liked a lot of attention." Alexa's eyes rolled. "What girl doesn't at that age? I liked it. With Perry as my big brother and Rita as my friend, people who had never given a shit about me suddenly clamored for my ear.

"The night started all wrong. Some of the other counselors were in the bunk playing spin the bottle. Rita and I were buzzed enough that we joined in. They were innocent pecks. Fun among friends. Perry came in and didn't say a word. That's when I knew we were in trouble. If he yelled, you were good, but when he went cold, bad things happened."

The phone on the desk split the story in two. Genevieve nearly jumped out of the seat. As it was, she jerked.

A groan escaped her lips before she could recall it.

"Sorry. Voicemail will pick up in just a second."

"It's fine." She swallowed and waited for the ringing to stop. It didn't take long. Alexa adjusted on the sofa. She licked her lips and continued.

"I pulled Rita from the circle and followed Perry out the back door and into the woods. I thought he'd come around if I could make light of it. I gave him a bottle of his favorite Cognac; Remy Martin XO. I'd stolen it from one of my mother's many liquor cabinets and had saved it for our last night. He thanked me, cracked the top, and handed it back. 'You're the bartender tonight,' he'd said. And I was good at it. No one's mouth was dry for long. We passed the bottle and walked the path to the lighthouse, Perry guiding our way with his trusty flashlight. Every other time we raced bicycles, but that night, we meandered and drank. I didn't care that we left his friend in the circle of counselors. It was one less person I had to compete with for Perry's attention. And it was one less time I didn't have to worry about getting pregnant."

Sweet Christ. Whether willing or not, Alexa had been coerced into sexual encounters at a tender age. Gen hadn't been an old maid by any stretch, but compared to Alexa, she had. Compared to her sister, Evangeline, Alexa had been. Her stomach twisted and coiled like a snake in death's throes.

"Looking back, I only remember seeing Perry take the first shot. He held the bottle, but I don't recall the satisfied hiss he gave after every gulp of liquor."

Something inside Gen died. It exhaled the last breath and gave over to the reaper because she knew the exact sound Alexa talked about. Gen'd made fun of Perry about it for years. So much so, that he'd reined in the habit among clients and the New York elite.

"It seemed like we were walking forever, and I remember complaining about walking so much. At one point, I grabbed Rita's hand and told her we were going back. I told her we were too drunk to climb the metal ladder." Alexa used her hands to depict a long cylinder. "The first nine loops were a narrow spiral staircase. Hard enough to navigate sober. The steps were so close together. When you reached the watch room, a metal ladder with thin rungs led up to the gallery and the narrow deck."

"Perry hadn't said a word since we started the bottle of Remy Martin. The moment I mentioned leaving, he asked me about my day. I was all too excited to tell him about the horse-riding trail my cabin mates and I had taken. He grabbed my hand and towed me along the curving steps. In turn, I pulled Rita along." Alexa stared at her hands as if they were the perpetrators of a horrendous crime.

Were they?

According to her, a girl was dead.

"When we got to the watch room, Perry was done with me and my stories. He shoved me out of the way and yanked Rita to his chest. For a long time, he just looked at her. No emotions flickered across his face. No rage. No lust. Nothing. I knew I should have grabbed her and run. I felt so cold. Lost. All I wanted to do was climb into my bunk and stay there until it was time to leave. I was going to run and leave her behind."

Alexa sobbed openly. Tears dripped off the end of her nose and made more fuchsia circle over the chest of the bright pink shirt she wore under her floral jacket.

"Rita kept asking, 'What? What are you looking at? What? Is my makeup smeared?' I couldn't take it. Her babbling and his silence. Rita tried to touch her lips. He caught her hand and turn her toward the ladder. 'You first,' he said. I stepped back toward the spiral staircase. He looked at me and smiled. 'When we get to the top, we toast to your special day.'"

Genevieve could see the smile. Sweet and sly all at the same time.

"I can still hear Rita's voice. She called over her shoulder from the middle of the ladder, 'Mine too.' She sang it, loud and proud. Perry chuckled. 'Yes, yours too.'"

No one spoke for a while. Gen hardly breathed.

"Rita and I crawled out of the narrow deck on our hands and knees, knowing we couldn't make the walk to our usual positions. Feet through the railing, dangling into nothingness. Backs on the glass. Eyes to the sky." Alexa sighed. We toasted twice. My nerves had settled a little. I was asking Perry what was special about his day that we would toast when Rita leaned over the railing and puked. In an effort to save myself from the same fate, I looked away." Even now, Alexa's nose crinkled as though she could see and smell it.

"Perry grabbed the bottle from my hands. 'To the end of my relationship,' he said. Rita seemed not to have heard him. She gave no reaction, just continued expelling the alcohol I'd fed her. I didn't know what to say, so I just stared at him."

Alexa wiped a line of tears from her neck and shivered. She pulled her jacket more tightly around her narrow body. Red rimmed her brown eyes.

"He reached his hand over the edge into the nothingness. He studied the remaining liquor in the bottom of the bottle at an arm's length. There wasn't much left. A shot, maybe three. Then he said, 'Hey Rita, watch this.' His hand spread wide, and the bottle dropped. I grabbed the rail, leaned over, and watched it disappear into the dark. My breath caught in my lungs, and I waited. It took a long time, but finally, the crack and shatter found my ears. I don't remember whether I screamed. Rita shoved Perry's shoulder, and she yelled at him. 'You bastard. I needed that to wash my mouth out.'

"I held my breath. My fingers went numb from holding on to the railing. I knew he'd retaliate. I knew it, and I did nothing." Her head shook. "When he didn't push her, I was shocked. His voice was calm, almost caring. 'Sorry. We can go down and get you something.' Rita agreed, and Perry motioned for me to go, so I crawled. He said, 'If you two would stand and walk, this would go so much faster.' I didn't. I couldn't. I don't know if Rita did. I was watching the cracked paint under my hands and the darkness to my left when I heard it."

What?

Genevieve banked the urge to scream the question over and over. Sweat slicked the nape of her neck and the valley between her breasts. Her hands shook.

"It was the squeak of tennis shoes on a slick surface. The glass, I think. Rita gasped. I turned to see her tumbling backward over the rail. I lunged for her, but she was too far away, and Perry was between us. Her fingers reached for him. Perry just stood there, his hands by his side, watching her fall. I called her name as if that would help. He did nothing.

"I watched my friend kick and flail and fight to reach the railing, safety. I'm glad the night took her before I saw her realize she was seconds away from death."

A tear slipped down Genevieve's cheek. She wiped it away and swallowed the lump in her throat.

"Based on the laws of physics, I know she didn't fall any faster than that bottle, but it seemed like it. That sound. It came so fast and loud." Alexa bit her thumb. "I hear it every day. The railing had caught me in the throat. I laid there with my arms hanging over the rail, and I screamed. I screamed for so long my voice went hoarse. Perry just stood there, staring. When he finally turned, his features were blank. Nothing in his gaze. Nothing. I clutched the railing for my life, and that's when he smiled. He told me to stay put, and that he would check on her. I couldn't speak, not even if I'd had something worth saying." Alexa shivered.

"Before he left, he crouched low. He put his face an inch from mine, and said, 'It's a pity she slipped, isn't it?'"

THIRTEEN

GENEVIEVE LATCHED ALL THREE LOCKS inside her Midtown apartment and collapsed against the door as though holding the door closed would keep the thoughts trying to breach her sanity at bay. Her gaze swept left to the yawning living room. Past the curved white couch and mauve area rug, the short marble fireplace and two squared gray chairs on their fluffy white rug, light poured in the curved bank of windows. It glanced off the white wainscoted walls. The rich chocolate wood floors drank it in. It had been months, maybe six or better, since she'd seen the place with a "view of Central Park" in the daytime. On particularly trying days, she would pad through the wide-open space, sit on the narrow window seat that arched along the windows, look past the large, dull gray building across the street to the sliver of greenery and open blue sky.

The button to the left of the door clicked under her

fingertips. In unison, screens rolled down, shutting out the city she loved so much. Her gaze swept right. It didn't pause to acknowledge the tiny kitchen in front of her. She clicked on the small chandelier in the foyer, basically the only hallway in the apartment, and turned the dial for the lamps in the bedroom beyond to a dim glow. Sultry light warmed the metallic tiles that covered the wall opposite her. She toed off her shoes and let her feet soak into the foyer's rug. If anyone deserved an afternoon off, Gen did. There had been no appointments to cancel. Besides, she couldn't face Perry. Not yet. She needed time and distance to think. She needed objectivity before her mind sent her down a dark path. If he killed …

"Objectivity. Objectivity," Gen chanted. "Look at the facts." She held a trembling hand over her mouth. "Objectivity was not possible." Her voice echoed, leaving a hallowed chill at the base of her spine.

No one was objective. No matter how much they tried, life experiences and subconscious biases shaded their views, turning fact into a mutated form of fiction. Even the best judges, those required by law to remain impartial and rule based on law, were once children. Children were at the whim of everyone larger than them, be it their classmates or parents.

First and foremost, Alexa had been a child. A child under the influence of alcohol. A child lacking the influence of structure and boundaries. A child drunk with the need for attention.

Alexa hadn't told a soul that she suspected her brother shoved Rita Ayers to her death because Rita had kissed another boy. The woman had drowned her sorrows in bottle after bottle. She'd become a drunk, and a drunk wasn't permitted in the Carter family. When she refused to go to rehab, they shoved her out of the house, the will, and the family. The bottle had been Alexa's lifeline up until that bottle had made her incapable of protecting a friend from harm a second time. After witnessing a partying buddy's sexual assault, Alexa had gotten herself clean and vowed to help as many women as she could.

The fact remained, Alexa had not seen her brother push Rita Ayers off the lighthouse.

Gen dropped the hand covering her mouth and turned right, walking past the bathroom into the second largest space in the renovated prewar apartment, her bedroom. She sat on the edge of her bed and tossed her briefcase beside her. Normally, the downy softness of the white comforter soothed her frayed edges and invited her to relax and unwind. Most nights, it invited her to do other more illicit things. Apparently, its magic evaporated in the daylight hours. Her gaze lobbed around the room from the single window—of which she never drew the curtain because it faced a brick wall with no windows and she never slept in—to the wall of closets in front of her.

The same charcoal metal tiles covered the closet wall as well as the one to her right. They hid the glut of her shoe, handbag, and clothes collection so well, you'd have to know they were there to find them. Her reflection stared back in the patchwork. Her hair was wild and as unkept as her thoughts, which went directly to the far-right closet closest to the foyer. It housed a file box of copies she'd made of Perry's case files. Even her reflection shook her head no. There was no need to go down that road. Not yet, at least.

She turned and crawled to the head of the bed, propped her back against the ruched gray satin headboard, and pulled the thin laptop from her deep and crowded nightstand drawer. The 12-inch screen burned bright, ready for her eager fingers the moment she opened it. Her cursor eased down to the Safari icon. The letters practically typed themselves into the search engine. Rita Ayers 1988 death

Connecticut.

The pinwheel spun. Before she could blink, the results flooded the screen. As she gawked and scrolled, article after article offered their whitewashed, non-murderous version of the story. She tried the New York Times site, entered her subscription's access code, and searched. It offered quite a hit. "Rita Ayers of New York City, heiress to the Ayers Financial Investments empire, died tragically while visiting friends in Connecticut." The article doubled the other in both size and breadth. Their journalist was the only one, so far, who'd dug deep enough to find any details, but those tidbits were buried in the fold. "Ruled a tragic accident of teen partying gone wrong." Her teeth ground together. It should have said underaged drinking gone wrong. They had all been so young. The article also sighted two eyewitnesses to the unfortunate events but didn't name them. Alexa's and Perry's names were nowhere to be found in any article.

Genevieve had seen enough to recognize a Carter cleanup when she saw one. It must have been nice to have family money. The moment she thought it, she rejected the notion. Money wasn't nice. Too often, it equated to absentee parents. Squalor wasn't nice either. Neither was the lower-middle-class upbringing she'd had.

What was nice?

Parents who loved you, not just by saying the words every time they looked at you, but also by protecting you from predators, trusting you when you told the ugliest of truths, and fighting for your rights as a human. Sentiment didn't mean a goddamned thing. Not like actions did.

Gen's actions had been to defend her friend and mentor. What were the consequences? Had she released a murderer into the world, or had she kept free an innocent man?

The call of the case files was too great. Genevieve shoved the laptop to the side, eased off the bed, and hurried to the corner before she thought better of it. Behind the neatly hidden door sat a bulging box of everything she could copy from Perry's file without getting caught. Using every bit of ass and leg she had, she heaved the rectangular hunk of cardboard and looked at her bed. Too often, she'd needed sleep and found the thing buried under heaps of files, so she shuffled the box into the living room. The box smacked onto the carpet between the couch and coffee table, which was actually three tree trunks carved into teardrop shapes and positioned with their points facing the foyer. She sat on the edge of the couch's heavy white upholstery, peeled off the box's lid, and started dredging.

Depositions for the defense went on the left teardrop. Depositions for the prosecution went on the right. She paused the digging, ran to the bedroom for a legal pad and pen, and then hurried back. Notes were everything in a case, especially one as bloated with files and motions as this one had been.

Had been.

She had no business going through this again. Yet her hands moved to the box and gathered the next heap of files. The juror notes, selections, and their information went on the floor behind the box. Perry's pleading went with them. Circumstantial evidence sailed right and landed on the floor and slid just off the side of the carpet and onto the hardwood. Direct evidence she laid by her feet.

The next chunk of files stole a beat of her heart or three.

Gen stood, placing the crime scene photos and diagram folders on the floor on the other side of the coffee table. They were the last things she wanted to see. Every night when she put her head on the pillow and closed her eyes, she saw them as plainly as if the photos were pasted onto the backs of her eyelids.

"Eyelids." Genevieve closed her eyes and shook away the thought. It stuck. Thankfully, instead of the children's—no—the victims' hollowed-out eye sockets, her brain conjured an image of Detective Owen Graham. He had harped on the childrens' eyes, or lack thereof, during his time on the stand and again when he'd accosted her the morning of the ruling.

When the perpetrator of a crime knew a victim intimately or when the perpetrator showed some level of remorse for their actions, they often covered the victim's face or turned their head away. That wasn't the same thing as forcibly removing eyes with a knife. To Gen, the sheer horror of the act did not allude to remorse but a deep-seated hatred of the victims. It also spoke to disassociation of the perpetrator. They no longer saw the victim as a person.

Even if Perry had pushed Rita to her death, it was a crime removed from gore. The extent of the crimes inflicted on the Carter family, the torture, was up close and personal. The two were not mutually exclusive. If he'd killed Rita, it didn't automatically mean he'd killed his family.

"Right?" Gen asked the files as though they could answer. She peeled open the first file and prayed they would.

Time passed. The light peeking in the edges of the shades waned, and the room grew dim. She switched on the lamp and continued to pore over every line and note. The need for caffeine forced her off the sofa, but she brought a stack of files with her into the kitchen. Not all of them made it back. Pee breaks came and went. Thoughts zipped by, but none stayed for long. Her sense of dread grew roots.

Incessant, intermittent buzzing finally forced her to leave the case. The balls of her feet pounded on the floor. She ran to her bedroom and found the phone jittering in her briefcase against the hard metal of her badge.

A text string she didn't have time for, even if it was from the girls, lit her screen. Gen closed the screen with one click while she headed back to the scattered mess she'd made. She shoved the phone between two couch cushions and returned to the diagram of Perry's house. The whole of the crime had been contained in the formal living room, a room they never used as a family. Pamela and Perry used the space to entertain but not often. Only once or twice a year.

Genevieve slid from the couch to the floor and found the file with her closing arguments and notes. She had painted a picture of Edger Sanchez with her closing arguments as a man used to power and luxury, a man used to getting his way with anything. In Mexico, he got away with everything. He was the revered and feared son of Amigo Ruez Sanchez, a cartel leader fresh on the scene and making loads of noise. In Mexico, he lived the good life in fancy homes with servants. All that changed when Edger's father forced him to move to the States. He was sent to set the groundwork for his father's growing empire, but Amigo failed to send the resources he needed to succeed. Here, he shared a modest home with his mother and sister. The two women were sent with Edger for their own safety. No reigning cartel wanted a newcomer on the scene, and it became increasingly apparent to Edger that no up-and-coming cartel leader wanted a son to murder him and seize the organization he built.

She showed them proof of Edger's spiral from wealth and power. She also showed them his attempts to get it back. She used Perry's own case file, the pictures of the brutal attacks on a young Latin American woman, to help prove her points. She offered the crime scene, contained to Perry's formal living room, as evidence of Edger's hatred for Perry Carter and his family, who lived so well that an entire room in their home went largely untouched while he was forced to sleep on the couch most nights or share a room with his sister and her rotating door of Johns.

Edger Sanchez was a brutally horrible man.

That didn't mean Perry wasn't also a brutally horrible man.

It had taken Alexa's story for her to realize it.

Between the cushions, her phone buzzed one long, unbroken string. Again, she ignored the irritating electronic. She crawled across the landscape of mostly gaping files and their contents that spilled across the floor toward the heap she'd hoped to avoid altogether. Her hands shook as she reached for the first of the three victims. They weren't her friends. They weren't the people who treated her like family more so than her actual family. Those three humans no longer existed. Their souls had left their body and gone to a much better place than this brutal pile of rocks.

She disassociated as much as she could and flipped back the first tab. An eight-inch strip of professional-grade duct tape covered Pamela Carter's face from one side of her jawbone, across her lips, to the other side.

Genevieve clamped a hand over her own mouth, blocking the sob that poured out of her. She slammed the file shut and slung it away as though the paper itself had attacked her. It had. Necessity had forced her to study the gruesome scene time and again. The need to save the last remaining Carter who was so dear to her had allowed her to get through the horror to look at the message each nuance of it sent. Now, she couldn't look at them even to find the answer she so desperately needed.

What happened that night inside the Carter home?

Her search was too narrow and case focused. What she needed to determine was if Perry Carter had become a master at hiding the murderous side of himself. A side he let rule him more in his youth. Regardless of whether it was an accident or murder, Rita Ayers was dead. What she needed was to find Tiffany Renly, his summer of '87 girlfriend. Gen needed to find out why exactly she dropped Alexa as a friend right after that Camp Caraway trip and what she remembered about young Perry Carter.

Over the years, Genevieve had learned that using Google was not the best way to find someone. It took a lot of time and provided a ton of false leads. She'd been spoiled by the private investigator on retainer for Carter, Cleary & McMellon, but no way could she use him this time. Gen scrambled to the couch on hands and knees and fished her phone from the depths. Her screen lit with a missed call from Larkin, a voicemail, and again the text string between the girls. She cleared them away and hunted through her contacts.

"Detective Graham." His contact was in her phone just so. Months ago, before the Carter case and before he'd signed the papers to transfer to her precinct, she'd gotten his number from a detective in the department. She had intended to call the new detective, introduce herself, and begin courting him. It was one of only a few times that her wooing had nothing to do with sex. She needed him, as she'd needed the retiring detective with whom she'd worked with for five years, to know they were on the same team. If they worked together, they could successfully put away more criminals than he'd ever imagined.

She'd never made the call. Two days later, three of the people she loved most in the world were murdered, and she was called to defend the man charged with their murders.

Her finger hovered over his name. If she tipped her hand to him, he'd hate her more than he already did. If she didn't tip her hand, he wouldn't help her find Tiffany Renly. A smile, so foreign to her lips these days, re-emerged. She scrolled down her contacts to the name that conjured it and smashed the screen to call him. The line rang several times before coming to life. The light whoosh of car noise filled her ear.

"Miss Holst, how may I be of service?" Douglas's

crisp, deep voice was kind and so endearing.

"You'll find yourself in a heap of lady troubles by asking every woman how you can service them."

His quiet laughter filtered in through the line. "Not in many, many years have I had that sort of trouble, Miss Holst."

"Please, I know more than a few who'd happily take you up on the offer. And call me Genevieve or Gen. I swear, do you still call your daughter Miss Ashford?"

Yeah, that revelation had shocked them all. Larkin's kind, caring, totally badass driver for more than fifteen years had turned out to be her father.

"Yes, I do."

"When it's just the two of you?"

The older man's stubborn silence caused Gen's smile to grow. He probably didn't know that Larkin had told all the girls the big reveal. For Douglas's and Larkin's safety, they'd decided to keep the revelation under wraps. He had to have known under wraps didn't include her, Marlis, or Libby. Of course, those goodie-goodies surely never alluded to Douglas that they knew.

"No," he finally admitted.

"It took you long enough. Do I have to make you my daddy before you'll call me Gen?"

He quietly waited her out. No matter how inappropriate she'd been with Douglas over the years he'd driven Larkin, never once had he been inappropriate back. She tested him more than most men because, well, he was a hot older man, he never reacted, and he drove one of her best friends around. She'd had to be sure he wasn't going to take advantage of Larkin. These days, she messed with him for fun.

"Fine," she relented. "I need to find Tiffany Renly, forty-five years old, went to school with Alexa Carter, Perry's sister, until the beginning of the 1987-1988 school year."

Gen held her breath for an interrogation. Douglas, more than most, could chase down the information he sought with one or two well-placed questions.

"I'll get on it and let you know what I find."

"You're the best. I owe you one."

"One?" He chuckled. "You owe me two for tonight, alone. I haven't bothered to tally the past decade. You're welcome."

"Two for tonight?" Genevieve's heartbeat kicked up a notch. Her mind skittered to Larkin's missed call, and the text messages she'd ignored.

"You should know your friends better than to think they'd give up on you after no response to texts and a call. If anything, they think they're on their way to save your life from a deranged killer."

"On their way?" she squeaked.

"Oh, yes. They're all in the back. We're five, no, four blocks away, traffic is light, and you know as well as I do that they won't take no for an answer."

"How's traffic light on a Friday evening?" They couldn't be blocks away.

"Everyone's in the Bronx for the Yankees game," he explained.

"I owe you a million. Gotta go."

Genevieve ended the call and jumped to her feet to survey the living room. Files, legal papers, and notes littered one corner of the rug to the other. They were mounded on the couch, and some had spilled off onto the floor. When, she couldn't say. Pen marks and highlighter decorated her hands. Her feet were bare, and there were near permanent creases in the material that folded at her hips.

She hurried to the bathroom and nearly screamed at the reflection that stared back. Mascara and eyeliner sagged low, creating dark circles. Her hair went every which way except the one she wanted it to go. A shower would do wonders, along with a new outfit and a new face of makeup, but there was no time for it. She settled for a wipe of tissue under both eyes and across both lids, a couple of swipes of her brush, and a fresh swipe of deodorant. Her reflection glared at the hideous, sleeveless turtleneck dress. Too soon it was forgotten and the reason for it stepped into the forefront. She peeled the edges of the fabric down. Garish light-purple fingerprints marred the left and right sides of her neck, reminding her it would be at least two more days before makeup would come close to covering the evidence.

The buzzer announced her friends' arrival. It announced them four more times by the time she made it to the intercom and pressed the button. Two, no, three faces bobbed in the camera. Four, if she counted Douglas, standing sentry by the Larkin's extra-long Town Car, not to be confused for a limousine, which it totally was.

"Oh, thank goodness, you're okay." Marlis sighed before Gen had a chance to say a word.

"Of course, she's okay." Libby's hand shot into the frame in a thank-you-Lord gesture.

"Right, like you weren't nervous too," Larkin hissed.

"What, you three can't take a hint?" Gen groused. Though she gave them a hard time, just seeing their faces lightened the worrisome load on her shoulders.

"Told you she was ignoring us," Larkin offered.

"Hell no, we can't take a hint." Libby shoved Larkin to the side and pushed her—what looked massive from the angle—nose toward the camera. "You should know us Brooklyn girls don't give up easily."

Larkin grabbed a handful of Libby's hair and yanked her backward, reclaiming her space. "Us Manhattan girls don't either."

"Unless you ask nicely." Mar's head bounded with each jump she took in an effort to sweetly get screen time.

Libby and Larkin gagged in unison.

"Let us up," Libby demanded.

"Can we go to dinner?" Genevieve offered her most pitiful expression. "I'm starving and have exactly zero edible things in here."

"What about those strawberry panties you bought last time we went to The Pleasure Chest?" Libby quipped.

"Gross." Larkin bumped her out of the way. "If you'd bothered to return ten texts or a phone call, you'd know that's what we're doing."

"True." Gen winked. "I'm coming down."

"Good." Libby butted in again. "'Cause if you weren't, we were coming up."

Genevieve released the button, grabbed her purse and phone, and took one last look around her apartment. It was a few pushpins shy of a serial killer's lair. A chill slid down her arms. She locked up and rushed down the flights of stairs and out the front door where warm arms, cool kisses, cheers, and quips greeted her. They filed into the car one at a time while Douglas held open the door.

When it was her turn, she paused in the doorway, reached up on tiptoes, and pressed a kiss to Douglas's cheek. "Thank you," she whispered.

"You're welcome, Miss Holst." He winked.

FOURTEEN

THEY PARKED THEIR ASSES at a four-top across from the bar at a trendy little farm-to-table restaurant in Brooklyn that Libby had been raving about for months. Greenery hung in neatly lined copper pots fastened to the wall overhead. Dried herbs adorned the small open kitchen just down from the bar, and past that, through a door, more food sprouted from planters lining the back patio.

"So what's up with you?"

Larkin asked the question, but Genevieve had been so caught up in the ambiance, it took her a minute to realize she aimed it straight between Gen's eyes. Both Libby's and Marlis's gazes were locked on Gen, awaiting an apparently eagerly sought answer. If one of them at the table had the most interesting or exciting life, it certainly wasn't her.

"Uh ... work," Gen offered.

Larkin's eyes rolled around toward her brows. Marlis

pursed her lips.

"What?" She shrugged. "I got behind while working exclusively on Perry's case for so long. The people who said they would pitch in on my caseload did a pretty shitty job, if they did anything at all."

"You're a terrible liar." Libby shook her head. "Has that hot detective been harassing you?"

"No, and that's the problem." Gen gestured toward her breasts. "He's not harassing me, and I'd very much like him to." When things got hard, she made inappropriate jokes. Jokes kept her from crying or punching someone.

"What is it, really?" Marlis leaned forward and placed both her elbows on the table, an etiquette rule she wouldn't break without a compelling reason. "You're not acting like yourself. Lately, you've been brushing us off left and right. You missed a board meeting."

Genevieve's eyes bugged, and her gaze flew to Larkin. "I'm so sorry."

"Even in the middle of the trial, you didn't miss the quarterly board meeting," Mar continued.

Again, Gen repeated her apology.

"I'm not worried about the meeting, Gen." Larkin offered a small smile. "I'm worried about you."

"I'm fine." Gen's teeth ground and her mind hunted for a safe topic. "How was your business thing in LA?"

"Good evening, ladies. Welcome to Olsted. My name is Benji, and I'll be taking care of you. Would you like to start with some drinks?" The shaggy-haired man pointed at Gen.

She looked at Larkin and saw her sorry-but-we-need-a-few-minutes-with-the-menu expression blooming. So she jumped in, abhorring any more interrogate-Gen time. They'd been right not to do it in the car. She'd have demanded Douglas take her back home, and he would have.

Now, she was stuck against the brick wall, hemmed in by Libby, another dozen Brooklynites, and plants. Unless she wanted to make a scene. Which she wasn't opposed to.

"I'll take a shandy and a glass of water, please."

With Gen's drink order out in the open, the girls had no choice but to offer their own. They called them out in turn.

The cold brick absorbed some of the heat from Gen's irritation and embarrassment. She was used to having her shit together. By outward appearance, anyway. When her life had been the darkest, no one had known. Now she was like an open book with dog-eared pages, coffee stains, and a worn binding. Everyone saw her flaws first. Thank goodness they were book lovers who were only trying to help.

They finished their orders for drinks and an appetizer for Libby, always. Thank goodness. The rest of them lusted after an appetizer as much as the next person, but they didn't want to be the one to order it. Larkin didn't out of time sensitivity. If they worried about an appetizer, it wasted time they could be spending on the main course. Marlis didn't out of manners. She didn't want to be seen as greedy or overbearing. Gen never ordered an appetizer because her ass got big enough from the main course alone. One bite, though, especially from someone else's order, never hurt too much.

As soon as the server turned around, all the gazes at the table zeroed in on her. "Larkin, the tech company? LA?"

"A waste of everyone's time." Her friend grimaced and drew a deep breath to pelt her with questions.

Gen pelted first, aiming for a topic sure to divert the mass. "So, Libby, how's the case?"

Her friend's perky and eager shoulders fell. Yeah, that'd do the trick. Gen didn't even have to elaborate on what case. They'd both been dogged by one and only one case each. Hers had been—fucking still was—Perry's. For Libby, it had been and was still the gun collector case.

Libby drew a deep breath and then vomited words until their entrées arrived. Genevieve took turns hitting each of her friends in their high or low points. In turn, each took time revealing or lamenting the topics that lasted through the meal, which relieved her from having to venture into her own darkness. If she spoke about the possibility of Perry being a killer, they'd think her crazy. If she spoke about the threats from Edger Sanchez, they'd think her crazy. And she was afraid that they'd be right, and that she just might be a little bit crazy.

They dropped Libby off at her cute little Brooklyn house that actually had a hint of a side yard and a decent backyard that provided ample room for the spy-the-hot-neighbor party she hosted shortly after the hot neighbor had moved in next door. Before Libby ducked out of the car, Gen had to know.

"Hey Lib, how's your neighbor?"

"Still hot and uninterested in all I have to offer." Libby smacked her own butt, practically waving in their faces.

"Gay," Gen reasoned.

"Nope. Screaming orgasms, remember?" The smile slipped from Libby's lips. "He bangs a badass looking chick on the regular. Panting. Wall banging. The whole bit."

"Sounds like it's time for another backyard party." Gen could do with a screaming orgasm and some wall banging in her life.

"I'll be busy with wall banging of my own." Larkin chuckled.

Marlis chucked her small pink Givenchy tote at Larkin, and they all shared a laugh before Libby stepped onto the sidewalk and wished them a good night.

Gen looked at the house next to Libby's. All the lights were off. It was only nine p.m., so she wondered if the neighbor was home. They had spied him the night of the party. He was indeed hot and a little bit scary to Gen's taste. Okay, the one time they saw his fine ass walk from his house to his sexy as sin motorcycle. He'd moved as though nothing touched him and he'd been disconnected from the world around him. Selfish, but she wanted someone very kind and connected living next to her friend.

Next, they crossed the Brooklyn Bridge and weaved through the downtown streets. Douglas stopped at a swanky hotel she'd had a business lunch inside once, years ago.

"What are we doing here?" Gen asked.

"You really should check your texts." Marlis kissed her cheek. Douglas opened the door. Mar slipped out of the car and poked her head back inside. "I'm hosting a business luncheon tomorrow, and it just made sense not to fight traffic in the morning. Night, ladies."

They wished her luck on the luncheon. Soon, they were rolling again.

"You've been calculated and quiet this evening."

Gen pulled her gaze from the line of spectacular architecture and found Larkin studying her. Of course, she wouldn't get away from this night without a better explanation than overwork and exhaustion. They were all overworked and exhausted and had been for the past decade or more, but it had never stopped them from getting together or sharing their lives with one another.

"I remember not too long ago when someone was similarly calculated and quiet?" Genevieve offered her a raised eyebrow and a challenge.

"And I had something to hide."

"Yes, and you told us when you were good and ready."

Larkin's lips pressed into a thin line. She was silent for

a full two blocks. "You know I'm here for you? No judgment. No expectations. Right?"

Gen leaned over and grabbed her friend's hand. "Yes, I do, and it means the world to me. You three mean the world to me."

Her friend lifted her hand and pressed it to her cheek, which almost landed Gen on the floor when Douglas pulled to a stop. They both canted their heads to take in the city outside the car.

"That's The Ashford." Gen leaned across the small aisle, braced her hands on the minibar, and looked up at the shiny, well-lit letters atop the entrance just to double check.

"I figured he'd take you home first." Larkin's brows knitted.

The rear door opened, and Douglas offered his hand to his daughter.

Larkin reached for her father but stalled. "I ... I'd like to ride with Genevieve to her house."

"I know you would, but you have a surprise on the roof that's been waiting for quite some time already." The man's about-business face gave way to a bright smile. After years of pretending to be nothing more than an amazingly keen driver, Douglas was now able to act like the father he was to Larkin.

Her friend's lips stretched wide. Her gaze swung to Gen. "I don't want to leave you."

"Leave me." Gen grinned and shoved Larkin toward the open door. "Go bang some walls," she whispered.

Larkin wedged herself in the doorway. "But you're in a bad spot, and you shouldn't be alone."

"I'm never alone with you ladies in my life." Larkin's mouth opened to protest, but she shushed her by pointing at Douglas. "Besides, he'll keep me company until I get home."

Big blue eyes bugged, and it was her friend's turn to whisper. "Don't you dare put the moves on my dad. I love you, so I'd hate to have to hate you."

"I love you too. Now, quit stalling. Your man is waiting." Gen kissed her cheek, but the stubborn broad didn't move.

"Waiting for the person you love just one minute can seem like a lifetime." Douglas extended his hand and canted his head toward the sky as though he were looking at Calder Beckett on the roof. Gen had a notion he was looking toward the heavens at the lady he'd loved and tragically lost, Larkin's mother.

Larkin planted a kiss on Gen's cheek, jumped from the car, planted a kiss on Douglas's cheek, and wrapped him in her arms. "I love you, Dad."

He enveloped her in turn and buried his face in her hair. The gesture was so sweet Gen withdrew deep into the car. Tears pricked her eyes. She blinked furiously, hating herself just a little. She was happy for Larkin and Douglas. It'd taken decades and another near tragedy for them to truly find one another. A hint of jealousy rankled. Genevieve Holst knew exactly where her mother and father were. There were alive and as well as two humans could be who clung to denial like a life raft in the middle of the Atlantic. That raft had only room for two. Gen and her sister had been cast aside with a great big ocean to contend with. Like Larkin had told her, she hated that she hated her parents, but she did. She hated them and their shaking heads so much it hurt.

A tear slipped from her lid and landed in a splatted circle on her wrist. She slapped at it, smearing it across her skin. Douglas closed the car door, and Larkin practically ran for the building's entrance toward her man. A smile stretched her lips. It was as it should be.

After watching his daughter disappear into the building filled with a security staff and system he and Beckett had handpicked, Douglas didn't miss a beat. He slid into the driver's seat, and the car pulled away from the curb. A second later, the partition that separated the driver's and passengers' sections of the car descended.

"You know, you can leave that thing down when we're all back here?" Genevieve blinked away the last of her emotions and scurried to the seat nearest Douglas. Well, the one that didn't require crawling through to the opening to the front. She draped her arm across the back of the seat and peered out at the taillights of the neatly flowing traffic.

"So you and Larkin tell me, quite often."

"Yet you never do."

"Old habits, I suppose." Douglas depressed the blinker, checked the mirrors, and gently maneuvered the car into the next lane around a nightly tour bus. As a former CIA operative, the man was accustomed to separation from everyone and everything. Hell, Gen didn't have the training, and she did her best work alone.

"Besides, I don't want to hear most of the things you ladies discuss."

"Fair point." Gen rubbed her finger across the smooth woodgrain of the center console. Her cheeks didn't have the decency to blush. Then again, he'd probably heard, seen, and done worse than all four of them combined.

"Tell me, why do you want to know about a girl who died thirty-one years ago?"

Genevieve's finger stilled, and her mouth dropped open. Every bit of moisture in her entire body evaporated as though she sunned in the middle of the Sahara. Slowly, her gaze shifted to the older man's profile. She tried to swallow. She licked her lips, but her tongue stuck between them. Her head shook.

"No," she managed.

"I'm afraid so. My first sources came back with the results before we got to the restaurant. I double-checked while you ate. She confirmed."

"Tiffany Renly? Tiffany with two f's. R. E. N. L. Y."

"Tiffany is always spelled with two f's. And yes, Tiffany R. E. N. L. Y. Born at Lenox Hill Hospital in 1973. She was the youngest child and only daughter of Barbra and Hanover Renly, a dynamic duo of stock investors. They owned, and still do, several nice chunks of Upper East Side real estate. Both are still trading and investing, though their two living sons are being groomed to take over the family business."

"Two living sons? Did they have a son who died?" Gen's throat felt as though it shrank by the minute.

"Yes. Their oldest, Henson Renly, died with his sister."

Her heart constricted, and—selfishly—at the same time, the tension banding her middle eased. Two children at once was a horror story no parent should have to endure, but the son's involvement decreased the chances that Perry had anything to do with Tiffany's death. God, she was an evil bitch. She banked her own self-loathing in favor of more information.

"How?" Her finger traced the outline of rippled leather around the even woodgrain.

"Car accident." Douglas maneuvered the car safely down the street and also managed to grab his phone from the cup holder inches from her hand and input a long security code without looking. He handed it to her.

"Oh, shit." Genevieve didn't know what she'd expected to see, but the mangled knot of metal was more than she bargained for. It didn't look like a car. It looked like a Coke can crunched under the foot of a giant. She studied the photos. Different angles. Different lighting. Night to morning. Even in the grim light of day, Gen couldn't figure where bodies would've fit into the wreckage.

"That's …" Her head shook as she swiped the screen. The next set of pictures were taken from farther back. It allowed her to see what the car had careened headfirst into. "Oh, God." A solid cobblestone archway butted out five feet on the side of the road, the base of a small bridge. "Is that a transverse through the park?"

"85th Street Transverse. They ricocheted twenty feet in the opposite direction from the impact site."

"Why were they going so fast through the park?"

"Keep swiping."

Gen's fingers shook, but she ushered on more pictures. There were images overlaid with speeds, lines, angles, and calculations of the impact. They'd been going nearly 105 miles per hour. "Christ." The next picture showed a set of skid marks, four tires locked up in the center of the road ten feet back from the cobblestone archway. It came from a different angle than the one of the Renly's car, which revealed not a single skid mark to speak of. It was in the middle of the narrow passage.

"Was there a witness? The person who tried to avoid them?"

"There was a witness, but they were never able to identify."

"What?" Gen growled. "Why wouldn't you stop and help?" The moment the question was out of her mouth, she knew the heartbreaking answer.

"Because the witness is also the person who deliberately stopped, forcing Henson Renly into the embankment, then fled the scene."

Nope. Nope. Nope. That wasn't the heartbreaking answer she'd expected. She'd expected someone was involved in the accident. She had most certainly not expected that someone intentionally drove them to their death.

Then again, hadn't she? Wasn't that the whole reason she wanted to find Tiffany Renly in the first place? She'd wanted a character witness. Someone who knew Perry on an intimate level, as a girlfriend, near the time of Rita Ayers' death. Someone to tell her whether Perry was capable of such a crime. But that someone was also dead, suspiciously so.

"How do they know for sure?"

"There was paint from another vehicle on three sides of the Renly's car."

"Meaning?"

"Meaning there had been a cat and mouse game going for at least six blocks."

"Why?" Genevieve pinched the bridge of her nose and spread her fingers wide, grinding them into the skin below her eyes.

"They don't know. Henson Renly picked up his sister from Trinity School at 9:45 p.m. Thursday."

"Trinity?"

"Yes. After having attended The Dalton School since kindergarten, a school that was only three blocks from her house, Tiffany transferred to Trinity, a school across the park, in August of the 1987-'88 school year. She never told her parents why she wanted to transfer, but she was adamant about the move."

Genevieve's gut told her exactly why Tiffany Renly had been desperate to transfer schools. And she hated the glaringly obvious answer.

"9:45 Thursday ..." *Oh God.* The homegrown salad inside her stomach threatened to revolt. "Why so late?"

"Tiffany was on the homecoming committee." Douglas said homecoming committee as though he'd never heard of such a thing. "They were decorating for a dance on Friday."

A dance Tiffany never attended.

"In the eighties, security cameras were just beginning to pop up on the scene, so the footage was grainy shit and completely worthless, at best. The police tracked down a camera near an ATM with a blurry shot of two cars on the 88th block of Columbia Avenue and a security video from outside a bank on Central Park West. It showed a dark-colored sports car repeatedly butting into the rear of a light-colored sedan. There were no plates or other identifying marks visible. The case was ruled vehicular homicide, but no charges were ever filed. They canvassed the area from Trinity to the park, looking for anyone who saw something, but as you know, most people are off the streets by nine, getting ready to sleep, wake up, and do it all again the next day." Douglas shrugged. "The case went cold."

"Mother fuck." Gen scrolled back through the pictures and groaned. "I dig myself into such marvelous messes." Seriously, if she'd just stopped, if she'd just ignored everything, her life would be so much easier.

"Because you care." Douglas plucked the phone from her hands, darkened the screen with the press of a button, and returned it to the cupholder.

"Caring sucks."

"It brings with it a ton of pain." He nodded.

"Gee, thanks." Gen rolled her eyes.

"But ..." His strong hand wrapped around hers and squeezed. "One day, it'll bring with it joy you never imagined."

"Yeah?"

"Yeah." He offered her a half smile.

"I'll believe it when I see it."

FIFTEEN

FILES SURROUNDED GENEVIEVE, along with her laptop, and legal pads, and pens, and coffee mugs, and heaps and heaps of emotion, as they had for the past five hours. The hint of sunlight that had shone through the blinds when she first began that morning had turned into full-blown daylight. Her determination had turned to despair. There was no use in her culling through these files. She knew them forward and backward. Nothing in them would tell her whether Perry had killed his wife and children. Nothing she'd found online could tell her whether Perry had killed Rita Ayers or Tiffany and Henson Renly.

She stared at the phone screen as she had for the past ten minutes. Beena Carter's phone number was the touch of the screen away, and she'd yet to pull the trigger. If anyone remembered if Perry wrecked his car in 1987, his mother would. Beena was a more reliable source than Alexa. His sister had biases that might lend to overdramatic, if she was told of Tiffany's apparent murder, but a bone-deep unease kept her from calling the older woman.

Her phone vibrated.

Larkin: I'm boarding a plan to Morocco!

"Morocco? What the hell?"

Libby: Why?

Larkin: Beckett surprised me with tickets last night!

Marlis: Oooh! It's beautiful there! Maybe he's going to *engagement ring emoji*!!!!

Genevieve: *Eye-roll emoji*

Larkin: Don't know what it's about, but it's not THAT!

Libby: When will you be back?

Larkin: No idea. But we've been instructed to put our phones away.

Libby: Flight number?

Lakrin: *screenshot of ticket* Here you go, mom.

Genevieve: Have fun! We love you!

Larkin: Kisses! Love you ladies too!

Gen swiped the last of the text messages away and stared at Beena's contact information once more. *Maybe she really didn't want to know the answer. Maybe she didn't want to deal with Beena Carter, the child fucker.*

Genevieve chucked her pen across the room. It landed in her bedroom and slid nearly to the wall farthest from her in the apartment. She leaned forward to retrieve another closer pen. Her gaze landed on a name on one of six legal pads surrounding her.

The Windsor House.

It was the name on the side of the truck that had loaded up a majority of Perry's belongings and carted them away. She keyed the name into her well-worn search and followed the links to a website. The Windsor House was an upscale Goodwill. Donors got major tax write-offs for their contribution, and the company used the funds from the goods sold to fund scholarships at the city's private schools and colleges.

She typed the address into her phone and requested an Uber. Thirty minutes, a brimmed black hat, and pointy toed slides later, she stepped onto the cobblestone street in the center of the once harrowed, then hallowed, and now trendy facet of NYC. The Meatpacking District.

Between a basement bar with a speakeasy feel and a handmade furniture shop, Gen found The Windsor House. Inside, old-world New York enveloped her. A tiny bell above the door echoed in her ear. Massive grandfather clocks, heavy and carved oak furniture, and too many paintings to count strategically lined the walls, distracting her from the tinny sound. Ornate vases, rugs, and lamps decorated the space, giving the cavernous room a cozy, familiar feel.

"Hello." A spritely young woman decked head to toe in a designer ensemble a little too fancy for the daylight sprang out from behind a massive four-poster bed. "Welcome to The Windsor House. Have you ever shopped with us before?"

"No, I haven't." Genevieve adjusted the hobo sack on her shoulder and shoved back the hair tickling her slightly bruised, makeup-covered neck.

"We are the city's premier luxury home re-sale shop that gives as good as it gets." Her perfectly nude manicure swept around the room. "And, as you can see, we get breathtaking pieces. Our store has fostered more than one million dollars in scholarships to underprivileged youths in our city to attend our city's most prestigious private schools and universities. So shopping with The Windsor House helps your community in three ways. You help educate your fellow citizens, spur economic growth, and create the perfect aesthetic for your home."

The holier-than-thou sales pitch, coming from a girl

who'd never seen an underprivileged moment in her life, tempted Genevieve to roll her eyes, open her big mouth, and actually educate the child. Damn. She needed the girl on her side. Gen smiled.

"What a lovely concept."

"Yes. Yes, it is." The girl clutched her hands together and drew them to her heart. "We want to do everything we can for the city that does so much for us."

"You're the owner?"

"Uh, no." The glitter sparkling in the young woman's eyes stilled. She blinked, and the point of her tongue took a stroll around the inside her left cheek. "But everyone who works for The Windsor House feels as passionately about the cause as Annette."

Genevieve had known the answer. She'd done her research. Pour la Ville owned the entire street's worth of buildings. A French named non-profit started by Annette Dubois—a well-known patron of the city—whose husband's family's early gamble on the oil industry had paid off in spades. She shouldn't have asked. The sanctimonious show had worked on her last nerve.

"Of course." Gen turned right to stroll toward the first installation of good ole NYC nostalgia.

Judging by the clop of heels, Miss Prissy Pants scuttled across the floor. Before Gen could blink, she was there, in her face, cutting off her progress. "What are you looking for today?"

Answers. She hadn't a damn clue how she hoped to find them.

"A client's grandmother passed away. I was told she'd donat—"

"I'm sorry. We can't give out any information about our donors. Each gift to The Windsor House is unanimous."

"Anonymous?" Gen asked, not quite able to keep her facial expressions in check.

"We want to eliminate"—the girl's thin hand sliced through the air—"treasure seekers and weirdos as much as possible." Her muted brown gaze roved Genevieve. "You understand, I'm sure."

Gen hadn't been in a bitch-off with such catty undertones since high school. Even then, she didn't do well with undertones. Since her sister's death, Gen lived over-toned and full throttle. It was the only way she could honor Evangeline's memory. After all, she'd done so little for her in life. She mentally reached for the Lord, pulled him from the sky, and shoved him kicking and screaming inside her chest.

"Of course." Genevieve forced a grin. She couldn't give teeth because it would turn into a snarl. It took her a moment to think of a workaround.

"I'm looking for any impressionist paintings or drawings you may have in your collection of artwork."

"Uh." The sound was so guttural and fast that every time the woman did it, Gen thought she'd caught her toe on an oak dresser. "We're high-end, but we don't carry any Monet."

"He was not the only painter to influence impressionism. I'm sure you don't have any Renoir, Van Gogh, or Cézanne either. But you must have some impressionistic works in your vast collection."

Miss Prissy Pants's nose shot toward the sky. "I'll see what I can find." She stomped toward the back of the building, a far different picture than the springy one first portrayed.

Genevieve followed close behind. After all, turnabout was only fair.

The girl stopped at a sleek counter at the center of the store, rounded it, and stopped at an iPad propped on a neatly placed stack of books. Her fingers got to work until Gen rounded the corner of the marble topped space.

"You can't come back here." Her upper lip curled as though Gen had an insistent case of body odor.

"Okay." She stopped, but she didn't retreat. Instead, she propped a hip on the back counter, folded her arms, and waited. Technically, she wasn't back there. Her feet were still on the public side of the counter. Her ass and eyes, on the other hand, were 100% in the no-go zone.

They had a mild stare off. It wasn't even a challenge when she squared off with murderers, rapists, and Janney on a daily basis. Several seconds in, the girl turned back to the screen and continued typing. A full-size monitor would've been so much easier to see. The tiny words and numbers blurred just enough that she couldn't make them out.

Was it time for glasses?

She'd know the spinning search wheel anywhere at any stage of cataracts. It whirred and whirred and then spit out a column with two entries.

Win!

Prissy Pants cleared her throat. "We have a sketch by Frédéric Bazille."

"I'm not interested in sketches."

"I'm sorry. We can't help you today." Her triumphant smile disagreed.

"What about the other entry?"

Prissy's lips flattened and thinned. "It's waiting for appraisal and has not been cleared for sale."

"Is it a Johan Jongkind?"

The girl kept stubbornly silent.

"What if price wasn't an option?" It wasn't an option because she didn't plan on purchasing the piece. If it was the one she sought, she'd hated the thing for the past six years it hung in Pamela's closet. She'd seen nothing more than a bunch of plain blots and scribbles. Her friend had seen a beach with mounds of sand, flowing grasses, and a vast ocean.

"As I said before, we have a strict privacy policy for our customers. Until items are on the floor, they are not available." Prissy's gaze slanted to a set of large double doors, leading to what Gen guessed was a back of store warehouse. The entire area had once been a massive meat processing and packaging facility. Their warehouse probably had a loading dock on the back, one street over.

"Thanks"—Gen smiled—"for nothing." She waved and headed for the exit.

A string of griping grumbles punctuated by the unmistakable word BITCH filtered through the open door, along with Gen and the store's over-chilled air. It didn't slow her down. It brought a wholehearted smile to her face. Bitches got shit done, and this bitch was on a mission.

The sun seemed brighter than it had only minutes ago. Genevieve adjusted the brim of her hat and strode past the bar, thankful it was closed. Had it been open, her mission would've suffered its second detour of the day. She crossed in front of a florist shop bursting with colors and aromas, and then a frame shop. Finally, she made it to a cross street. One small block over, she found the back of the massive brick structure. The back of the frame shop was a high-end boutique for dogs, something she'd never understand as long as she lived. Hell, buying $500 shoes for herself was a stretch, a stretch she practiced too often, but a stretch nonetheless. A dog came equipped with its own nature-provided shoes. No one needed to spend that much on dog's shoes.

Her pace increased. If the building's back was entirely storefronts, she'd meet another dead-end and have to commit her own murder to find the answers she needed more desperately with the passing of each day. The back of the florist was a Mommy & Me boutique for owners to dress to match their dogs. Cue the gag reflex. She rushed past, half afraid to catch the doggie disease. The bar's back was a loading dock and rear exit, judging by the pedestrian door, dried remnants of week-old vomit, and the oaky smell of day-old beer.

"Thank you." Gen fist bumped the air.

"Anytime, doll."

Gen whirled to find a guy carting a dolly full of cases of beer through the large roll top door. He winked. She did not, but neither did she wish him dead with her glare. Progress. And success? She held her breath and hoped.

Sure enough, a stack of cardboard boxes, various blue blanket-wrapped monstrosities of furniture, and large dollies lined the edge of the loading dock of The Windsor House's rear warehouse. A Windsor House truck, very similar to the one she'd seen outside Perry's home, was parked across the street with the back door rolled up. There was no one inside … or outside it. Her gaze scanned every inch of it from the distance. She searched the massive, raised concrete deck and couldn't see anyone either. A set of steps led to a small back door.

One concrete chunk at a time brought her to the paint-chipped entrance.

"Hello?" Gen kept her voice low. The last thing she wanted was to alert Prissy Pants in the front of the store. Well, the last thing she wanted was to be hauled off to jail for trespassing. One led to the other, she'd guess, and the other led to the end of her career.

She shoved open the door and listened as it creaked horror-film style. Like any sane New Yorker, she ignored the sound and stepped inside. Sunlight crept in from the open bay door. Its rays created a cave of light in the otherwise dark cavern. Dust floated on a current of air she didn't feel shift inside the dank space. The smell of mildew and decades of bad decorating decisions haunted the place. Whether it wafted off the walls or the columns of boxes stacked around the parameter and in neat rows across the large floor, she couldn't be sure.

In the far corner of the space, very near the double doors she'd seen from the other side just moments ago, stood an office no bigger than her local theater's box office. Its height didn't reach the nearly twenty-foot ceiling of the warehouse. Light shined through the opaque window in the unusually narrow door. Otherwise, she'd have thought it a maintenance closet.

Genevieve scanned the parts of the open floor she could see for box, furniture, and literally any other human besides Miss Prissy Pants who worked for The Windsor House. None appeared. She strained her ears in an effort to block out the street noise and listen for any movement or voices inside. Again nothing. Nothing beyond the hum of an air-conditioning unit.

She eased farther into the space. If no one was here, she could look through the stacks for Perry's stuff and be out in five minutes. Ten max. Her gaze swung to the light in the tiny office. Just to be safe, she walked quietly to the door and lifted her hand to knock gently.

The door opened slightly.

A knot formed in Genevieve's throat, then the door swung wide. Genevieve grabbed her mouth to contain her scream.

A short guy with a bulldog's build jumped back from the door and volleyed his clipboard. He caught the clipboard in the crook of his arm, but the pen that'd been wedged between the metal springs slipped out and crashed to the floor. His gaze ignored it and pinned her. He offered her a puzzled expression.

"You all right, lady?"

Gen released the hand from her mouth and drew a deep breath. "You scared me."

"Christ, you scared me more."

"I'm sorry." She reached down, picked up his pen, and handed it over.

"Thanks." A snort of laughter filled the space between them.

"What?"

"Scared by a lady." His head shook. Green eyes glinted. "The guys'll never let me live it down."

"Then it's our little secret." Genevieve's gaze swept the office. There was only one filing cabinet, but there was a computer and security monitoring system taking up most of the space inside the small room.

"Sounds like a plan." He chuckled.

They shared a quiet laugh.

"So the store is on 15th. This is just the warehouse." He hiked a finger toward her left. "I'd let you go through, but Bianca'd birth a full-grown cow."

Wouldn't that be a sight?

Gen ignored his comment. "Could we have another little secret between us?"

He repositioned his pen between the springs of his clipboard and appraised her. Slowly, he raised his hands in surrender. "Look, I've got a lady, and I'm trying to be good to her."

"That's good." Gen barked a laugh. "I'm not trying to stain your virtue." She slipped her hand into her hobo bag, fished a bill out from her wallet, and offered it to him. "Well, maybe a little, but not in the way that'll get you in trouble with your lady." Her head shook. "I'm trying to find the Carter's donations. I don't want to steal anything. I just need to look at them for a few minutes, and Bianca doesn't need to know."

He stared at the hundred as though it might bite him. His gaze swung to the double doors of the store even though he couldn't see them from inside the office.

"There are cameras," he whispered.

"Cameras I'm sure you can adjust to see nothing at all … for a little while." She offered him her best smile and batted her lashes. "What's five minutes, after all? Besides, you'll be there, making sure I don't take anything."

He plucked the bill from her fingers, shoved it inside the breast pocket of his shirt, and eased back to the computer. His fingers flew over the keys, surprising her with his prowess on the instrument. A few seconds later, he straightened.

"Five minutes." He shooed her out of the office.

Gen scuttled back and took in the massive amount of stuff inside the warehouse. "Don't you need to look up what they donated and where it is?"

"Are you kidding me? We all know exactly where their stuff is. I mean, it belongs to the guy who slaughtered his family and got away with it."

A sound clicked behind Gen, but she was too dumbstruck to pay much attention to it. Seconds later, the bulbs inside low-hanging halogen lanterns glowed dimly at first and slowly gained intensity. The guy walked past her and disappeared behind a stack of boxes. She stood there, staring after him.

"Hey, lady? You comin'?" His voice came from faraway and echoed.

Her gaze swung to the double doors. The last thing she needed right now was manic Bianca, aka Miss Prissy Pants, storming the door. She turned and ran after the man. A strip of wide tan packing tape separated each pile of furniture and décor. He dipped right around a metal column and walked all the way to the back of the warehouse. His steps slowed until they finally stopped in front of a square of red tape, containing a mountain of home goods that rivaled the rest.

"Here you go. Perry Carter's donations." His arms opened, and he gestured toward the massive heap. "Most of it is his wife and kids' stuff, if you ask me."

Pamela's Johan Jongkind sat among the furniture wrapped in clear cellophane. Layer upon layer of thick foam mummified its edges. The simple painting had given her friend so much joy and hope.

Pain, sharp and insistent, jabbed at Genevieve's heart. She grabbed her chest and drew a long, deep breath. Then another. It didn't help. The pain burrowed deeper.

"Why the red tape?" Even though it was a different color, it reminded her of crime scene tape.

"The pieces are under appraisal and not cleared for sale on the floor."

"Oh."

She couldn't imagine people rummaging through the children's things and placing a value on something that had meant so much to them. Now that she was here, the irreverence of what she'd planned to do seemed outrageous. She didn't want to be one of those people scouring their things.

"So?" The man pointed at the pile, pivoted his head from side to side, and shook his hip in counterbalance.

Gen swallowed. "I'm going to need more time."

"You haven't even started," he scoffed.

"I know." She nodded.

"Look." He placed his hands on wide hips. "Before you popped up, I was shutting it down. I got a pickup in the city, then I'm headed home." One of his arms gestured toward the river. "It's my girl's birthday. We gotta celebrate. You know, flowers, dinner, wine. The whole nine."

She studied him for a moment, and then reached into her purse and grabbed two more bills from her wallet.

"This could help you celebrate."

His eyes bulged toward the bouquet of money. "No joke?"

"No joke." Gen took the slightest step forward.

"Say, why're you so interested in this stuff?" His gaze swung back toward the heap.

"My offer ends in five, four, three …" She eased the money back toward her purse."

"Whoa! Whoa! Whoa!"

"So do you want it, no more questions?" The money hung in the crimp of her fingers and dangled in the air between them.

"I …" He shifted on his feet. One hand shoved inside his pocket. The other grabbed the green. "Yeah, okay."

"Okay."

"Don't let Bianca catch you back here. She'll freak out."

"I won't." If she never interacted with that special form of crazy ever again, it'd be fine by her.

"If she does, I don't know you." He offered a perfect impression of a surrender while he simultaneously walked backward.

"You don't know me. And I don't know you." They had not exchanged names, and she knew nothing about him except he had a lady and today was her birthday.

"Good." He shoved the money in his front pocket, turned, and hurried through the maze of forgotten belongings. She heard the scuffs of his shoes hook a right and fade through the large bay door. A moment later, the truck's engine roared. Thirty seconds more and it mingled with the city sounds before dissolving altogether.

Genevieve slid the hobo sack from her arm. It hit the ground with a thud that mimicked her heart. She turned to the stacks and stepped across the threshold of the red tape. The scent of plastic and the chemical aroma of foam brought her back to an innocent time when she'd moved to the big city. She was running from the past, sure, but at the same time, she was full of hope for the future. A future where she dictated her path. No one else. And here she was, dictating her path through heaps of emotional and physical baggage.

She grabbed the Jongkind with both hands and brought it to eye level. The unruly lines, swaths of color, and random scribbles weren't the man's best work. In fact, this was nothing like his other works. Despite it, and maybe because of its unkept nature, Pamela had adored the piece. It'd reminded her of freedom and had always made her want to break free from the city. It'd made her yearn for the beach. For the Hamptons. Time and again, she'd begged Perry to move there, and time and time again, he'd dismissed her desire for the practicality of the city.

How had Perry dismissed his wife's hopes and dreams after her death? Discarding this painting was doing just that. By the same token, it was possible those hopes and dreams were too hard to live with after her death. She set the painting to the side, grabbed a handful of the navy blue moving blanket, and yanked. Tape snagged in the middle, forcing her to brace a hand on the center of the piece of furniture and heave. The tape finally ripped, and the blanket gave way. It revealed the TV hutch that'd sat in the corner of their den and hidden a sizable collection of *Paw Patrol*, *Wild Kratts*, and *Barbie* DVDs. She pulled back the doors. The constriction of the blanket allowed it to open only two inches, but it was enough. Gone were all the things that made it personal.

A stack of boxes to the right caught her eye. Gen shifted over, pulled up the edge of the packing tape, and freed the lid. Stacks upon stacks of newspapered rectangles filled the box. She yanked the first one from its nook and unwrapped it with more fervor than she had a birthday present from the girls the prior year.

The high-pitched whine of sheer terror seeped from her throat. She shoved it back and aside and pulled out another. Then another.

"No." Her voice was angry and stronger than she expected.

Gen stared at the rough pewter edges of a picture that'd hung on the wall in the hallway between the kids' bedrooms. Then glared at the glass that revealed the felt back of the frame instead of the candid photographs of the children Pamela had filled them with. Every one of them. Empty.

She shoved the box to the side and ripped into the one underneath. Her elbow caught the edge of the stack behind her, and it wobbled. The oddly shaped cellophane wrapped package atop it rolled to the side and gained speed. It slid off the side of the stack and bounced down to a lower stack next to it, and then bounced back and forth between the two columns.

The entire ride down, Gen's breath lodged in her stomach, awaiting the inevitable crash. It never came. As the pillowy parcel came to rest with only a whisper, air whooshed from her lungs. She swallowed, and then yanked the hat from her head, suddenly too hot to deal with the wide-brimmed suffocation. Her hair fell around her shoulders. After tossing the hat toward her purse, she reached down and grabbed the ... pillow? She unwound the packaging loop after loop after loop until the hint of fabric appeared.

Her heart took another blow. A direct hit. She unraveled faster as though Little Perry's antique stuffed tiger suffocated inside. The creature's smiling face greeted her, blissfully unaware of the horror endured by the boy who'd loved him. Gen crushed the large, pillowy animal to her chest, buried her face in its worn tuft, and sobbed like she hadn't in years. Of course, she'd cried at the funerals, but even then, she'd had something dividing her attention. Perry. Now it was just her and the memories of Claire, Little Perry, and Pamela. Her knees buckled, and she crumpled to the floor.

Breaths and cries rocketed through her lips, but she muffled them in the tiger's neck. As the happy times assaulted her, her sorrow mounted. If the warehouse guy knew that Perry had murdered his family, how in the hell had she been so easily deceived? She had been too close to the case and to the family. Why was she here now, rummaging through their things? Crying over dead people's things wouldn't help solve the mystery of their murders.

She reached deep and searched for her backbone. It didn't reveal itself. Instead, she found a new fount of sorrow. Memories she'd thought she'd banished a thousand years ago reared high and imposing. Her body rocked of its own accord, and desperation took hold. Like every sad sack before her, one thought taunted uselessly and on repeat.

"Why? Why? Why?"

No answers came, but her anger did. It burned a hole through her chest and ceased the flow of her tears. As she crawled toward her purse, the pointed slides she wore slipped from her feet, but she didn't stop to collect them. Instead, she gently set the tiger next to it. No way in hell would that sweet animal be abandoned to the back of a warehouse forever. Fuck that. And fuck Perry Carter for getting rid of all their things. Yet the moment she thought it, she hated herself. She'd gotten rid of so many painful memories over the years. There wasn't a photo in her apartment nor a family heirloom. Not that they were fancy enough to have things called heirlooms, but the closest thing to the one she had was her face. Even her red hair went against the brunette grain of her genes.

Rampage seeped from her veins as Gen stood. The concrete cooled her feet but did little to soothe the heated anger inside. She walked to the stacks of their things and released the rampage. She unraveled cellophane. She snatched away moving blankets. She ripped boxes wide open.

Sweat slicked her brow. Her hair fell widely around her shoulders. Trash littered their floor, along with the remnants of their partial lives lived. Claire's red secretary's desk and the skeleton of her red bed frame stood side by side. Famed New York designer Nick Olsen had chosen the bold set, a gift for the precious girl's sixth birthday. Then there was Pamela's jewelry collection. It'd taken up three large boxes, and the jewelry box itself rivaled that of the television hutch. Gen opened it wide and stared inside the empty hollow of black satin. How many times had Pam stood in front of the thing, puzzling over which pieces of her extensive collection to wear? How many times had she let Gen borrow a piece or five for a special occasion?

Genevieve crouched and let her hand smooth over the interior, searching for some part of her friend's spirit. When her hand hit the bottom of the jewelry box, it shifted under her fingertips. Afraid she'd broken the lowest shelf, she jerked her hand back. A small gap remained between the side and the bottom. White was visible in the space. She reached back, prepared to fix it no matter the trouble.

Then a hint of blond curled hair came into focus.

Hand above the gap, she paused. She grabbed the thin board covered in black fabric and lifted it high.

Nothing prepared her for Pamela's sweet, smiling face staring back at her. Nor that of Claire's jubilantly balled cheeks. Nor Little Perry's wide-eyed grin. The three of them clung to one another in the midst of a fantastic laugh. Gen knew the picture well because she'd taken it three years ago at a restaurant in the city. They'd been in hysterics over Claire's unladylike burp. It'd been the soda Gen had ordered for her before Pam had arrived. She'd pick them up and taken them to Central Park. They'd walked around the lake, and then hit the zoo before she realized that children didn't have as much energy as everyone thought. Lunch had been key to keeping them going, and when Pam had shown up late from her meeting, the kids hadn't held it against her. They'd been overjoyed to share their experience.

Gen grabbed the picture and then realized that there were more. Several more.

"You!" a woman screamed. It seemed to come from far away. "You're trespassing. I'm going to call the police." Gen couldn't care about the threat. Not now.

The small compartment held a thin stack of pictures. She flipped to one with Little Perry swaddled as tightly as a burrito. The next was Claire toddling down a path in the park with a tiny teddy clutched in her hand. The next …

Her hands quivered.

In the center of the picture stood a couple nestled so closely their faces nearly melded into one. Their smiles brimmed almost into the other's. She'd never seen the nondescript white man with a kind smile and tawny hair. She had most certainly seen the blond woman with bright eyes and a jewelry fetish before.

She turned to the next picture.

It was the same couple in a hotel bed. The bright white linens and dim lighting were unmistakable. Pamela's hair spread across the stranger's chest. A thin strap slipped off the edge of her shoulder. Her breasts bulged at the top of her nighty. Despite the overt tone in the picture, there was also a hint of innocence in their expressions. An innocence Gen had never known. An innocence she'd envy were it not for her friend cheating on her husband with this stranger.

Had there been any doubt of Pamela's faithfulness to Perry, the distinct wedding band and massive rock on her hand that hovered over the man's bare chest dispelled it.

If she had a paint scraper, she still might not be able to pry her jaw from the floor.

Gen flipped through the pictures again and again. They didn't change shape or exposure. The characters didn't morph into something she understood better.

She set the pictures to the side, dropped to her knees, and ran her hands over the other edges of the jewelry box. High and low. Left and right. She tugged and shoved. But found nothing further.

Her mind flew to the Jongkind painting, and her body followed. She stepped over trash and moments, furniture and façades. The painting might have been the only thing in the space she hadn't ripped from its confines. So she did, peeling and yanking until it was free. She flipped the frame to the back and searched for a place to pry it apart, but there was nothing she could grab with her bare fingers. She scrambled to her purse, desperate for a nail file or keys. Something to reveal anything the picture might be hiding.

"Back there." Bianca's voice rammed into her conscious.

"What?" Gen growled. She was ready to rip this woman limb from limb.

This woman turned out to be with two police officers, beat cops no less. They rounded the corner with their hands on their weapons and then stopped cold. Their gazes jumped from her to the mess behind her. They didn't look familiar.

Dammit.

"Miss, slowly remove your hands from your purse and place them in the air," the stockier of the two said.

"I know this looks bad, but I can explain." Right! She couldn't even explain this to herself.

"Lady." The taller of the two lifted his side arm from its holster. "Hands up. Slowly, now."

Gen's heart lurched. She eased her hands from the inside of her purse, grabbed the tip of the strap, and placed it gently on the floor. "This is all a big misunderstanding."

"Hands up." Stocky stepped closer, but his hand remained on his weapon. His partner held a line on her feet, threatening to raise it to her chest at a moment's notice.

"Okay." She lifted her hands in the air. It'd been so long since she'd been on the perp end of the cop relationship.

The big one grabbed her wrist and snapped her around so quickly, she didn't have time to react to the feel of the pain. When he cinched down the second handcuff, it came in a burning, aching rush.

"Holy hell." She tried to pull away.

"Stop moving, or it'll hurt worse," one of them barked.

No shit.

Her wrists screamed.

"Let's go." Stocky turned her around and shoved her toward the exit, away from her purse, the stuffed tiger, and those pictures.

"Go where?" Gen attempted to apply the brakes. Stocky was all go. He manhandled her with ease.

"The station, Red. The station," the other officer answered.

"No. I …" She couldn't go to the station. They'd book her and end her career. "Please, call Detective Owen Graham. He can vouch for me! Please! Detective Owen Graham."

SIXTEEN

HERPES. CHLAMYDIA. GONORRHEA. Cocaine and methamphet-amine residue. Those were some things Genevieve should be worrying about with her forehead pressed to the grated metal partition of the police car. She knew the exact cast of characters these vehicles transported, yet she leaned her weight into the barrier and even rocked it in a slow side to side, gathering all the filth with her face. Or, maybe, just maybe, she should be concerned with losing her job, her license, and being made a pariah in the law community. But, no. She wrung her cuffed hands, making the skin on her wrists raw over the pictures she hadn't had time to grab or even capture a photo of with her phone. That and the poor child's toy left abandoned on the cold floor.

What did those images mean? The logical answer was Pamela Carter, her dear friend, had been eagerly partici-pating in an extramarital relationship.

That didn't compute. Pamela had confided so much in her through the years. Her desire to be a mother. Their struggles with infertility. Her perceived shortcomings as a mom. The strained relationship she had with Perry's mother. Above all, the adoration she had for her children. Never once had Pamela alluded to any bitterness in her marriage. Never once had she suggested a desire for other men. Never once would she have gambled with her children's happiness that way.

Of course, Gen once thought she'd never gamble with her career this way.

They'd been here, idling in front of the warehouse for nearly an hour. How fucking long did it take to record a statement? Every time she thought about them taking that little bitch's whiny, faux words, Gen wanted to scream. It didn't help. She'd tried. Neither did beating on the window. She had the sore shoulder to prove it. The beat cops left her with no choice but to wrestle with her thoughts. They'd left her unattended long enough that her brain turned itself into a goddamned pretzel. She sighed, sank deeper against the grating, and pulled in a long breath. It smelled of stale ass.

The cruiser's front door creaked open.

Genevieve braced for the questions sure to come. Unlike the intelligent, professional, well-respected woman she was, she kept her head hunkered and closed her eyes. No way would she answer a single question without her lawyer present. Too fucking bad she couldn't call Perry to return a quarter of the favor he owed her. He'd have his own questions. She needed hers answered first.

"If you wanted to see me again, you could've just called."

That voice would be her conscience, if she had one. Gen lifted her head and stared into the bright blue eyes and salty smirk of Detective Owen Graham. He leaned into the car and stared down through the plexiglass and grating at her.

"I didn't figure you for the grand gesture type." He lifted a hand to his chest and covered his heart. "I'm flattered." His heavy biceps bulged, inciting the first feeling that didn't have anything to do with despair and paranoia in days. She couldn't even enjoy the reprieve because there was no relief to be had. He was the last man she needed to have feelings about.

Gen swallowed. Owen Graham looked good enough to eat in worn jeans and a T-shirt perfectly molded to the striking topography of his upper body. And she looked … Her gaze dropped to the dirt on her arms, the dust covering her knees, and the sweat suctioning her jean shorts to her thick legs and her shirt to her less than flat belly. The top of her hair was flat from the hat they hadn't let her retrieve before stuffing her into the hot car. The usually neatly curled ends were frizzy with the moisture steaming from her body.

"Don't be," she snapped.

His eyebrows hiked. The corner of his mouth not turned up to the sky joined the other side in a full-blown grin.

Gen incited men. It kept her in control of the game. She wasn't used to men reacting to her with such a laid-back manner. It was unsettling. "What?"

"Nothing." He bit the sides of his cheek and shook his head.

She glared with every angry, hurt, and annoyed fiber in her body.

Graham gave her the sit-tight gesture and retreated from the cruiser. Gen readied to scream when he waved someone over. Seconds later, the two officers who'd shoved her into the back of the car appeared. They exchanged words she couldn't make out and gestures she didn't understand. Their smiles gave her hope that her career might get out of this day intact.

The men shook hands, and then the beat cops headed back toward the building. Graham opened the back door. Fresh air, as unpolluted as the Meatpacking District could offer, sailed into the back seat. She breathed deeply and scooted toward the edge. Her bare legs stuck to the worn leather. Shame and disgust threatened to turn her cheeks red. She jutted her chin and doubled her effort to scramble for freedom.

To his credit, Graham didn't offer her a hand. Not that he would. Her hands were cuffed behind her back like a perp. She ignored the fact that she was one, and very nearly could have been a booked one, found her footing, and stood face to chest with the too handsome detective.

She cleared her throat. "How often do cops clean their backseats?"

"Some, daily. Others ..." His lips pursed. "You don't want to know."

"I'm hoping for the former today." The guys who'd stuffed her into the back looked well-kept enough.

Graham's grin was back in full force, nearly knocking her on her ass. She liked it too much.

"What?" she hissed again.

His right hand lifted. The pad of his thumb rubbed over the center of her forehead. "You would've never lived down your mugshot with this."

Breath caught in her throat. Irritation bloomed in her chest. Charisma, a bit of charm, and a face meant to be adored wouldn't throw her off balance. She shifted to figure out exactly why she wouldn't have been able to live down this particular mugshot, but the cuffs stopped her cold. That stalled breath moved quickly through her teeth.

"Turn around." The command should've doused her irritation in gasoline, but heat built in her belly. She did as he said.

"What's on my forehead?" Maybe if she talked, she could regain control of the situation.

"Just a perfect etching of the cage on your skin."

Metal scraped metal. Clicks sang. The biting cuffs loosened. Freedom never felt so good. Gen felt the center of her forehead, and sure enough, the metal partition had made a perfect weave of indentions on her skin.

"Shit. I have scales."

"They'll be gone in a few hours."

"Hours?!" She turned to face him.

"I've seen it last an entire night, but I figure you're better hydrated than a junkie."

"Maybe." She traced the outline of the pattern that reached her hairline and stretched from one brow to the other. When was the last time she'd had a drink or eaten anything? She'd been so busy overdosing on the Carter family drama that she didn't remember.

"Christ." Graham grabbed her hand, pulled it from her forehead, and studied vibrant red rings around her wrist. A knit of concern formed at the center of his forehead.

"It's fine." Gen jerked her hand back, a protective instinct she might never outgrow.

"Like hell it is." His gaze jerked toward the large bay doors where the officers stood talking to the crazy bitch, Bianca. He stepped back, away from her and toward the building.

"It is. I'm a redhead." She reached for him. Her fingers wrapped around the top of his forearm over an intricate ink artwork of the American flag. The smooth, warm skin invited her to snuggle in and stay a while.

"That fact hasn't escaped me, ever." He stopped moving and stared at her hand for a second before meeting her gaze. "What does that have to do with the marks on your wrists?"

"I'm fair skinned. I mark easily, especially when I'm trying to break out of cuffs."

"Do you find yourself in them often?"

"Nope."

His gaze shifted back to the police cruiser, the cuffs on its roof, and then her wrists.

"Look, I owe you one."

"One," he scoffed. "Holst, you already owe me one. A big fucking one." His blue eyes zeroed in on hers, and she knew exactly the one to which he referred. Perry. "This is peanuts to that one."

"All the same. Thank you." Gen squeezed his arm. None of the steely muscle under her grip gave. She released her hold and stepped away. Her gaze searched the areas for her purse, phone, and hat, but found none. It honed on the warehouse.

"Don't even think about going back in there."

"I need my purse."

"It's in my car, along with your phone and hat." Graham headed toward a blacked-out SUV that looked too sleek and signature to be police issue.

Not wanting to be near the cruiser for another second, she followed in the wake of his booted tread. They rounded the back of the police car and to the passenger door of the Land Rover. He opened it and stepped aside.

"I'll drive you home."

Trapped in a confined space with him for twenty minutes minimum. "Thank you, but I'll grab a cab."

"Get in the car, Holst."

Her brows shot up.

His expression didn't waver. He didn't speak.

"I'm not leaving a tip," she warned.

"I'm not one that warrants tip-worthy services, remember?"

"Right." Gen tapped her forehead and remembered

the fabulous state of her appearance. She stepped between him and the door and slipped inside to keep him from seeing her grimace.

He waited for her to situate her belongings from the seat to the floorboard around her feet before closing her door. Had any man, besides Douglas, ever helped her into a car and closed the door? Not a single one that she could recall.

Stupid chivalry. It'd be tolerable if it didn't feel so nice.

Despite herself, Gen grabbed a hair tie from her purse, scraped the untamed mess of her mane to one side, and folded it in a quick braid. Then she swiped at the make-up below her eyes. She wiped the hint of black that came away on her fingers onto her dark shorts and pulled at the fabric clinging to her belly. Not a chance would she assess herself in a mirror. Feeling the pattern on her forehead was bad enough. She didn't want to see it.

Graham opened the door, slid in, closed himself inside, and gave her a sinister smile. The desire to climb on his lap warred with the urge to bail out the door. The opposing forces tore and gnashed at her insides.

"Buckle up." He turned on the engine with the push of a button.

She stared at him, rebellious to her core.

"Over four hundred thousand people died as a result of car crashes last year alone."

"I know."

"Then why the hell are you fighting me on this?"

"I don't know." Fighting let her know she was still alive, still pushing forward when all she wanted to do was fall apart. Fighting let her think she had some sort of control in this chaos called life. Fighting was what she'd done for so long it bled from her pores. But she couldn't tell him that.

"Strap yourself in, or I'll do it for you." There was no

suggestive wiggle of his brow. Gone was his smile. This was business for him, the business of helping people.

Gen reached back, pulled the belt across her body, and snapped it in place.

Graham put the vehicle in gear, whipped the car in a tight one-eighty, and pulled into the street so quickly that if she hadn't been wearing the stupid seat belt, she'd have been cheek to window with the SUV. He could have said, "Buckle up, I drive like a maniac." She wouldn't have given a shit about that. His caring nature put her on edge. It'd taken her long enough to get used to the girls caring. A man, though? They'd let her down time and again.

"Why'd you trespass to rummage through junk?" His grip on the wheel tightened, making the muscles in his hands bulge. "They were going to take you to the station and book you, Genevieve. That's your career and everything you've worked for down the drain. Have you lost what's left of your mind?"

Had she? So often she didn't play by society's rules, but they'd only landed her in the back of a police car once before. Right after her sister's trial. Right after her sister's suicide. She clamped her eyes shut to block out the past. When it didn't work, she flung her lids wide and stared at the buildings flying by.

"It's for a case I'm working on."

"Looking to get another monster back on the streets?"

His question ripped a layer of her armor off and delivered a blow that caught her off guard. Her head snapped around, and she glared at him. "I prosecute."

"Until you don't." There was no malice in his tone. That didn't stop the accuracy of its impact. His grip had relaxed on the wheel. Their pace grew more leisurely.

"Until I didn't." No denying it.

"What's your deal? A smart lady like you could have done anything. Why the law?"

She just stared at him. No one had ever asked her why. It just was what she did, a part of who she'd become. The best part of her, really. The SUV slowed to a stop as the herd of traffic paused for a red light. His gaze met hers. He didn't push, just studied her and waited.

"Because I wanted to protect those who couldn't protect themselves."

His eyes lifted as though surprised by her answer. Then his gaze narrowed. "Until you didn't?"

Genevieve had given him a small part of her soul with that answer. With it, he'd stripped the last of her defense away and cut deep. So deep that something inside her ruptured.

"He did it," she shrilled. "I set a sadistic murderer free. Is that what you want to hear?" Her hands balled into fists and slammed into her thighs. The emptiness of her gaze landed on the sky outside, barely visible for the buildings. "I fucked up. I completely fucked up." She squeezed her hands too tightly that her nails dug into her flesh. "Those sweet children. Pamela." Her head shook back and forth. Tears bombarded the backs of her eyelids. Waves crashing into a levee. She heaved. Her brain pressurized and pushed against her skull.

She lunged for the door, needing air, needing out, needing ... she didn't know what she needed.

Graham's large hand captured both of hers in his and pulled them back to the center of the car. Behind them, a car honked. Someone screamed. The traffic trudged on, but they remained still except for the rushing horror of her thoughts.

"Breathe." He placed his other hand under hers, trapping her. Only it didn't feel like a trap. The contact, his touch, quieted the demons. It was what she needed, and exactly what she didn't want to need.

"Let me out."

"I will. When I get you home. Now, breathe. In through your nose. Out through your mouth."

The inhale quaked inside her lungs and quivered out between her lips.

"Again," he demanded.

Someone else honked, long and mean.

"Good. Again." Graham ignored them and focused on her. She'd never been more terrified. The admission of suspecting Perry's guilt was haunting, but she gripped Graham back and held on for dear life, and that scared her more.

Another honk joined the chorus.

"You can drive."

"They can wait or go around."

"I won't jump."

A deep breath left his chest. He released her with his left hand but held tight with the right. His thumb flipped a button on the dash and blue lights danced in the front windshield. They must have shown in the back too. The honks immediately died, and the traffic poured around them.

"You sure?" he asked.

She nodded, which ignited a throbbing in her skull near the hideous pattern on her forehead.

Graham drove. A minute later, he turned off the lights and continued maneuvering them through the city. Gen closed her eyes and breathed. She held on to Graham's hand as though it were an anchor. When she opened her eyes, they were near the park.

"Perry never told you he did it, did he?"

Genevieve didn't speak. She didn't know how to play this. They turned onto her road. "What I said, it wasn't a proclamation of Perry's guilt. It was what you wanted to hear."

"You're a shit liar." Graham laughed a soft chuckle

that shook his shoulders and, in turn, her hands.

"It was worth a try." She shrugged. "I don't usually bother with it. People say the truth hurts, but lies, lies hurt worse than the truth." They get people killed, apparently.

He drove next to the stunning green grass and vibrant fall foliage of Central Park and then turned expertly into the parking garage of her building. She didn't ask how he knew where she lived. He was a cop and had access to all kinds of information. Information she'd love to be able to access. The car wheeled into a visitor's parking space, and he placed the car in park all while still holding her hands.

"You must think I'm a monster."

"Actually"—he turned toward her—"I think you're pretty fucking amazing. You've prosecuted over forty cases and won them all. You work with victims of sexual assault and—"

"I got him acquitted." Her near scream sucked the oxygen from the car.

Owen Graham's stunning blue gaze nipped low. "Anyone else could have."

She rolled her eyes. "You're a shit liar."

"Worth a try." He winked.

Gen cataloged his face. Every angle was perfectly formed. A hint of a five o'clock shadow tinged his smooth complexion. All those dummies who said eyes were the windows to the soul hadn't met Owen Graham. His eyes were lasers into her soul, not windows into his own. Those lasers and those plush lips were surprisingly close.

"You're the farthest thing from a monster."

Tears threatened to breach her tender eyes. She closed them, and her head shook. His anchoring warmth left her hand, telling her what she already knew. She was as guilty as the man she'd freed. Gen drew her hands into her lap and opened her eyes in time to see Graham's hands bracket her face and stop the shake of her head. The tenderness forced tears over her lids and over his fingers.

"We've seen the work of monsters, Genevieve. You're not in their orbit."

But she was. Perry had killed his family, and she'd gotten him off. There was no redo because double jeopardy was in play. He could never be charged for their murders, no matter what kind of evidence she found to back her gut feeling.

Graham leaned in. His gaze was locked on her mouth. Hers was on his. She loved the feel of him, the strength and the heat he radiated. Leaning in felt so right that she pulled back. Her shaking hand found the door handle, and she leaped from the vehicle and turned, grabbing her things in a rush.

"I didn't mean to frighten you." The sincerity in his voice drew her gaze.

"You didn't," she breathed.

"Says the woman standing ten feet away from me with a car between us."

She shrugged because she didn't know what to say. The truth that she'd wanted to kiss him more than she'd wanted anything in a long time would only hurt them both. She could hardly juggle the knives she tossed now. He was a machete.

"I'm sorry." He flashed her a smile that incited her libido.

"Why on earth are you sorry?" She gestured to herself. "I'm the one digging in literal dirt, nearly getting arrested, screaming at you, and crying like a maniac."

"I know, if Perry had told you the truth, you would have submitted a motion to withdraw from the case."

She nodded. "And I would have done anything in my power to put him away forever."

She still would.

SEVENTEEN

THIS WASN'T SCARY. Gen rolled her eyes. Marlis, the pampered New York City debutant, had never set foot in East Harlem, now known as Spanish Harlem or El Barrio. So why did she feel the need to spread falsehoods about the place? They didn't have doormen or multimillion-dollar condos, but it was nice. It looked like Gen's old neighborhood. Only Brooklyn in the 80s didn't have vibrant, artful murals on the sides of its buildings. It had straight-up graffiti. Ugly, rag-tag graffiti at that.

The Uber had carried her past small community gardens and cultural centers, delis and a handful of museums. Fifth-generation Puerto Rican immigrants and a growing segment of Latin Americans populated the area. She hadn't intended for anyone to know she planned on coming to this part of town, but a reminder flashed on her phone when she and Mar had been at lunch Monday. Not that she'd been likely to forget the trip. It had been foremost in her mind since nearly getting arrested Saturday. A day in court at the first of the week and prepping for it Sunday hadn't left her with time to go until after work today.

Genevieve hurried through the grassy courtyard of the low-rent complex. A freshly painted gray metal door stood slightly ajar at the top of three short steps. She didn't look left or right but opened the door as though she was meant to be there. Gen bolted inside the east wing of the building, letting the heavy door catch on a wedge of gnarled wood. As nice as the neighborhood was, she didn't want to be here past dusk.

The dim interior was quiet except for the low hum of old florescent fixtures and a Spanish music station behind the first apartment's door. Her phone burst into song. The Clash's "I Fought the Law." It'd been her ringtone forever, and it'd never made her jump until now. She jerked the phone from the pocket of her olive slacks. After unfastening the small wallet case with a single credit card and driver's license she hadn't used in nearly a decade, Gen silenced the call and stared at Owen Graham's name for a beat. Her gaze slid around the building's dank interior. This wasn't the place for a talk with her conscience, much less his. He was nearly the only man she knew who actually had an operational one.

She shoved the phone into the pocket of her slacks and turned right up the stairs. Gen ignored the blatant WTF stare of a full-figured woman with long, dark hair descending the last flight, found the second floor, and stopped in front of the door she sought.

The metal placard on door 2C had long since vanished. Several layers of paint had been slathered over and chipped off the space where it'd been. Black permanent marker announced the number. The unmistakable mumble of a soap opera drama filtered through the door. Gen drew a deep breath. She flapped the front of her ivory sweater and wished for a breeze. Heat radiated inside her crisp collared shirt, despite the cooler temperatures outside. She adjusted the floral printed cuffs, ignored the yearning for Owen Graham's hands on her, and knocked.

A string of Spanish lambasted her from the other side. Not her, exactly, but the lazy ass who'd forgotten their keys again. Maria Baheya Sanchez wrenched the door wide without so much as a glance and stalked away through a small living room toward what Gen suspected was the kitchen. Maria further cursed her daughter, Rubia, for not showing up to bring Carlo to his other grandmother's house like she said she would.

On the floor at the center of the living room sat a chubby-cheeked baby, kicking furiously at a pot lid. Each time he succeeded, the metal lid tilted and struck the empty pot. Carlo, Gen guessed, slobbered on a large wooden spoon. The baby caught sight of her before Maria and stopped mid-kick. Gen waved and offered the kid a smile. He screamed at the top of his lungs and broke into a string of sobs.

Kids. Ugh!

Maria rushed into the room with her arms wide for the child and a glare set for her daughter. The glare turned to wide-eyed shock.

Gen put her hands up and explained in stilted Spanish that she hadn't intended to startle the child or her, and that she was just here to talk.

"Talk?" Maria snarled in plain English. She scooped the baby off the floor, held him to her full chest, and bounced him gently. "You people don't talk. You tell me how horrible are my children. You want to take my children away from their children. You want to take them into prison forever."

Honestly, her son belonged in prison forever or six feet under. The man was a monster. A mother's love distorted views enough to blind a woman. From Maria's own complaining, her daughter wasn't doing a great job of caring for young Carlo either. But that wasn't why she was here.

"I'm not here to bring trouble or take anyone away. I just want to find out the truth about where Edger was the night of the Carter murders."

"The truth, you don't believe." She shook her head. Salted more than peppered hair swayed around Maria's face. "Edger was home with me watching TV until midnight, and then he went to sleep."

"We had testimony from Carlo's other grandmother, stating that when she came by at 9:00 pm to drop him off, she stayed for approximately ten minutes, and never saw Edger or Rubia." Gen pointed at the flat screen where a suave looking man and a beautiful woman stared intently at one another.

What bullshit.

"Do you have another television?"

"No, but we have a bathroom." Maria glared. "And two bedrooms."

"Was Edger in the bathroom when Carlo was being dropped off?"

"I don't remember." Maria patted the baby's diapered bottom, set him back on the floor, and scooted his pot close. "That was months ago. Near to a year."

"The next week, your son was brought in for questioning."

"Yes, and then he was released." Maria walked toward her. "And your boss was arrested for the murders." The older woman grabbed the door and pushed it toward Gen's face.

"Please wait!" She stuck out her arm and planted her

hand. "I—" Sharp pain cut off her plea. The door struck with shocking force, jarring her fingers backward and rattling every bone in her hand. Gen hissed an expletive. "I don't think your son committed the murders. I just need proof." She shook her hand and held her breath. When nothing happened, she knocked on the door with her uninjured hand. "Please. I need your help."

The rattle of a chain lock slid into place, punctuating Maria Sanchez's answer.

Go fuck yourself, Genevieve.

She'd certainly have more success at it.

If Maria knew something that could save her son, why wouldn't she say so? Maybe she had no idea where he'd been that night. Maybe she'd been telling the truth. Maybe she knew where he'd been and what he'd been doing, and maybe that would save him from one crime but incriminate him in another.

Gen scrolled through the possibilities as she shuffled down the steps toward the exit, shaking the sting out of her hand. A lady with a newborn and three toddlers spread out like unruly nesting dolls just outside the door. She wrestled with a large stroller, a diaper bag, two bags of groceries, and the door. Gen hurried forward and held the door wide. The woman sailed past with the baby and stroller without so much as a nod for Gen's efforts. Two of the kids, the girls, tottered past in her wake, each carrying a juice pouch as big as their heads and screaming, "Abierto! Abierto!"

The biggest of the kids, who hardly reached Gen's mid-thigh, the only boy, stalled at the threshold. His eyes were as big as balloons, and his gaze locked on her. She smiled and waved. He took a step back. When his mom hollered for him to come on, he slid along the far wall into the building as though she were a demon sent to reclaim his soul.

His tiny, well-worn shoe caught on the piece of wood holding the door open. His little arms pinwheeled. His brown eyes bloated in fear. Whether from her or the fall, she didn't know.

The chunk of wood skittered down the hallway. His fat little legs churned in double time in an effort to catch himself. Gen reached out to catch his fall, and he shrieked high and loud. He pivoted his shoulder away from her. The move gave him the footing he needed to stabilize. His mother yelled again, and he ran past her and into a first-floor apartment in the middle of the hall.

Kids. Ugh!

Apparently, she was the first stark white redhead he'd ever seen. She should've said, "Boo!" A smile had just arched her lips when she stepped outside.

Movement caught her attention a second before something hard connected with her cheek.

Her eyes clamped shut. Light flashed behind her lids. Stars burst and danced in a chorus line. She staggered back and lifted her hands to protect her head and face. Unyielding brick caught her shoulders and stopped her from running. Not that she could. The unseen world whirred at Mach speed, even behind the darkness of her eyelids. Hair held tightly in a bobby-pinned knot atop her head shifted from the impact.

An angry, garbled string of Spanish assaulted her. It was a woman's voice. The spicy Latina demanded to know what Gen was doing here. Only she didn't call her by her name. She used words Gen didn't know, and she thought she knew all the good curse words.

She needed to open her eyes. She needed to see her attacker. She needed to get the hell away from the crazy bitch. Gen pried her lids apart by force of will, the will to live. Tears flooded her vision.

"You're in the wrong neighborhood, Roja," the woman hissed. It wasn't the tone, but the nickname she used that clawed its way up Gen's spine. It lashed its way into her brain and nested in her amygdala, overwhelming her flight instinct.

The outline of a rail thin woman with tangled raven hair slowly focused in her field of vision. She stood with one foot on the stoop and the other on the top step of the entryway.

"I thought my brother schooled you." Rubia Sanchez spread her hands wide and bobbed her head. "Looks like you need a new lesson." She jabbed a sharp, acrylic nail at the building at Gen's back. "This ain't your turf, Roja. This is mine." Rubia slapped her talon against her chest.

Christ. As soon as the world stopped spinning, she could run. Until then, she needed to buy time. It was the first rule of self-defense. Actually, there were some things to remember before that, but the rules were all scrambled at the back of her brain. She swallowed, and a sob quaked her throat. This wild-eyed broad was scarier than her brother.

Buy time.

"I came to help."

"Help?" Rubia laughed. She rushed forward and raised her fist.

Gen formed a shield with her left arm and hunkered down against the building.

Rubia's fist connected to Gen's shoulder with a smack. It radiated through her body, shaking her ribs and rocking her lungs. Breath froze inside her chest. Still, it had nothing on the first blow.

The woman stepped backward and laughed a maniacal chuckle. Three steps she'd seemingly forgotten tripped her, and she staggered back. Her thin arms hung limply by her side. Her hands weighed a thousand pounds. She shuffled to the side, clearly, now that Genevieve could see,

—

high on something. But the woman didn't fall.

Dread welled inside Gen's chest. There were no guards here. No friends.

Gen's gaze shot right. A dozen yards away, a six-foot-tall wrought-iron fence blocked her escape. Through its thin bars, she could see people strolling along the sidewalk on the opposite side of the street. Too far away to help. Besides, she was an outsider. If she screamed, would anyone help? More than likely, they'd gather around and cheer on Rubia.

Her gaze shot left. The door was two feet away. Rubia huffed and sneered maybe six, maybe seven feet in front of her. There was little chance she could make it inside before the woman caught her.

Talking had gotten her out of so many precarious situations. It was what she did best. She had no idea how to fight, so talking was her only option.

"I don't think your brother killed Perry Carter's family."

"We told you that the first time you came nosing around. You and the cops. But you don't listen. Nobody listens. You all want to talk, talk, talk." The woman spread her thin arms wide. "Again, you're here to talk. So what do you have to say, Roja?"

Gen's back pocket vibrated. She couldn't think enough to answer it or the question before Rubia barreled toward her. Both skeletal arms stretched toward the sky. An animalistic scream rumbled from the woman's throat.

Anger and frustration that Gen stowed inside for days and weeks—hell, years—sprang free. Her own scream lit the sky, giving blood-red hues to the setting sunlight. Instinct took hold. Her arms cocked close to her body. She crouched low. Thick legs and her full ass churned slowly but fiercely, propelling her away from Rubia Sanchez.

Gen hurled toward the door. Her gaze locked on the

silver handle. She reached for the only lifeline she had. The cold metal had never felt so good in her grip. Her thumb pressed the small flat lever and nothing. It didn't budge.

She yanked.

The door remained. It might as well have been a castle wall. The metal barrier blocked the path of her only escape.

Her other hand formed a fist and banged furiously.

Once. Twice.

Hot tearing seared her scalp. Her hands immediately left the door and grabbed her skull.

Gen heard ripping a second before her head was jerked so hard it felt as though it was being disconnected from her body. The world upended. Red brick and gray sky filled her vision. Then everything turned to B-rated action flick with enough shaky cam to evacuate a theater. She hadn't liked it in her twenties on the terrible excuse for a date. Now it incited a riot inside her.

Bile rose, stunning her nostrils. Pain and terror battled for top billing as she lay on her back at the bottom of the steps.

Gen watched helplessly as Rubia Sanchez stalked toward her.

The woman's smile didn't reach her sunken, hollow eyes.

Before today, Genevieve Holst considered herself a badass. A woman about the world. A woman ready to take on anything and everyone in the name of justice.

Today under attack, in imminent danger, she curled her legs to her chest, covered her face with her arms, and cowered like the wimp she was.

The blows came fast but not remarkably hard. They sounded like dull thuds as though they were far away and not impacting her ribs, arms, and head. The ugly Spanish Rubia showered upon her didn't incite indignation or rage. Fear soaked her ego in kerosene and lit a match.

Somewhere a woman screamed. It had a horror movie quality. Non-human.

It took several seconds before Gen realized it was her screaming. She opened her eyes a crack and saw angry, bony fists flying at her time and again.

In that instant, she knew that if she stayed here cowering, she would die today.

She didn't want to die.

She wanted answers. She wanted the truth. She wanted justice.

Gen cocked her stilettos toward the sky and shot her legs toward heaven with all the strength she possessed.

A gust of wind hit her in the face. The hot and rotten breath being kicked from Rubia's lungs made her gag. The woman gurgled a second before she was launched backward. Her eyes filled with uncertainty. She flew through the air and landed hard against the brick exterior. Cartoon-like, she slumped into a heap on the concrete stoop.

Any thought of celebration washed away in the woman's frantic scramble for her purse. The vibrantly woven sack hung across Rubia's body. The thing hadn't registered to Gen until this second. One bloody hand plunged inside the deep recesses.

A gun. A gun.

Of course, the daughter of a Mexican cartel leader would carry a weapon. Why hadn't Gen thought of it until now? Why had she come here? What had she expected to accomplish?

It wasn't a gun.

A gun would have been better. Quicker.

Rubia pulled a fixed-blade knife from her purse. Her scraped knuckles wrapped around the matte black handle. She yanked it from its sheath and threw the plastic to the ground. The small silver bevel of the three-inch blade sent shards of fear slashing through Gen's soul, ribboning all hope.

The maniacal woman staggered to her feet.

Run. Run. Run.

She ordered her body to move, but nothing happened. Her gaze remained on the knife and the woman who would end her life without remorse. She shoved up to her elbows and wormed back mere inches, but the woman steadied her footing with each passing inch.

"Get up!"

The demand came from over Gen's shoulder. The voice was deep and so familiar she wanted to cry.

"Get up!"

Heavy footfalls came hard and fast through the grass. The urgency in his voice and speed bolstered her.

Gen rolled onto her belly and shoved onto her hands and knees in time to see Owen Graham grab the top of the wrought-iron fence. He tossed his legs high and cleared it as though it required no effort. Heavy boots hit the ground. His legs barreled toward her. Lines of determination creased his brow and deepened a frown she'd seen only once before on the day the verdict was read in Perry's favor.

Now that he was here, he could question Maria and Rubia Sanchez. Shit, he could take Rubia into custody for assault.

Owen's eyes widened.

"Run!" His demands turned into a singular plea.

No. That wasn't right. Everything was okay. He was here. He was the police. The enforcer of the law. He was the help she needed to find the truth.

The panic in his eyes forced her from the ground. Her slick bottomed shoes churned on the concrete several times before gaining traction. Finally, they propelled her forward. She gained speed and ran, not toward Owen, but toward the open gate at the end of the sidewalk.

His gaze lifted over her. His right hand dropped to his side. Not his side, but a side arm concealed beneath an army green T-shirt. The uncertainty vanished in his eyes. Determination and intent filled the void. His head shook.

Gen ran past him. Her heart hammered against her chest. She neared the gate and slowed, unsure of where to go.

"Right." Owen's arm wrapped around her and swept her into the fast pace of his jog. They rounded the fence. He didn't slow as they headed down the block across the street.

"Keep going," he urged.

Her lungs burned. The muscles in her legs turned to veal. Still, she pushed.

Three cars down, she saw Owen's black Land Rover. The lights blinked, and a few seconds later, he opened the passenger door and shoved her inside. He slammed the door in her face and nearly jumped the hood in his haste to get behind the wheel. Not a moment later, they were weaving in and out of 3rd Avenue traffic.

"Genevieve." He growled her name.

She couldn't tear her gaze from the road to look at him. They were going so fast. It was dangerous.

"If you ever set foot in this neighborhood again, I'll arrest you myself."

"You can't threaten me." Her mind reacted with her usual bravado, but her voice sounded small, broken.

"So help me God, it's not a threat. I'll see you in jail before I see you get yourself killed."

"I'm not—"

His fists connected with the steering wheel, jerking her attention from the road. "Look around you. Goddammit. Look in the mirror!" He didn't look at her. His gaze, his reflexes were intent on the cars around them and the streets he zipped past.

"If I hadn't found you …" His head shook. "If Douglas hadn't called me … If Marlis hadn't known you were planning to come down here, you'd be dead or dying on a fucking sidewalk." The tops of his thick knuckles turned white from his grip on the wheel.

"You live in a bubble of fancy restaurants and cushy condos where people don't go hungry, where people don't sell themselves for a few dollars, where law and order rule. Well, princess, Rubia Sanchez is entrenched with TMG." The muscles in his jaw flexed, sharpening his profile. "Any one of the two hundred plus gang members that live on these blocks could have turned that courtyard into a war zone neither of us would have escaped. Do you understand that? Badges. Law. They mean nothing good to those kinds of people."

The cramps started in Gen's back. They cinched so tightly that they straightened her and pinned her to the seat. Her arms had been firmly wrapped around her middle. Now they seized. Everything inside her went rigid, including her breaths. They wheezed slowly through her swollen esophagus.

"Shit," Owen gruffed.

Over half a dozen blocks from the Sanchez's building, he whipped the car into a loading zone next to a corner market.

"It's the crash. Adrenaline flooded your body. It helped you stay alive, but now it's gone. This is the aftermath. Part of it." He reached into the back.

Gen sat helplessly pinned to the spot with zero control over her muscles. Some quivered while others turned to stone.

"Here." Owen pulled a thick leather jacket from the back seat. "It'll help a little, but mostly you just have to ride it out. Like a hangover."

He wrapped the jacket around her torso and tucked the corners between her shoulders and the seat. Next, he grabbed the seat belt, secured it in the buckle, and pulled it taut across her chest as though she were a helpless child. She was helpless, and hopeless, and too tired to care about or compute anything.

EIGHTEEN

THIN WHITE RIBBONS SPLIT AND SWIRLED. danced and faded in the black marble of the fireplace. It hypnotized her and had for the past ten minutes or so. She'd seen the carved rock a thousand times or more, daily for the past six years, but it had never entranced her like it did now. The designs were complex and almost rhythmic. As though nature knew what the hell it was doing.

A year ago, so had she.

At least, that was what she'd thought.

Gen's gaze lifted to the stark white wall above the fireplace. It was the most prominent wall in her apartment. The mantle and the space above the fireplace were the galleries, the front windows into peoples' lives, but hers was void. There were no pictures of family or friends. Not even an overpriced piece of artwork that she identified with filled the space. It was empty.

She was empty.

"You don't have much." Owen read her mind while foraging in her kitchen. He headed toward her with a dishrag and a bag of frozen broccoli from a failed attempt at that keto bullshit. The vegetables had to have freezer burn or be petrified by now. "But this should work."

Would it?

It had before, but now it was exposed and raw. Everything was electrified, and every movement, every thought amplified the deficits in her life. She was rich in career. Rich in material. Rich in friends. After all, they'd saved her today as much as Owen had. But her ability to trust was third-world poor. And had been for a long time. Any bit of it she'd gained through the years shattered the moment she'd begun suspecting Perry killed his family.

Owen crouched in front of her and peered into her eyes as though looking for her retinas or retinal detachment.

"I salvaged enough coffee from a holiday tin in the back of the freezer that we might get you a full mug." One corner of his mouth kicked up. "No promises on the taste."

He wrapped the wet rag around the vegetables and slowly placed it on her right cheek. Contact amplified the throb, but it didn't rouse her to any movement or emotion. Since the crash, as he'd called it, she'd been near catatonic, relying on this man for everything from the use of her feet to entry into her own apartment.

She should be indignant with herself for relying on him, but that took too much effort. Holding her head up was almost too much. He wouldn't let her sleep, not for hours, he'd said.

"The pain will get worse over the next minute, but it'll numb soon, and the cold will keep it from swelling." He grabbed her hand, shifted her elbow onto the armrest, and wedged her hand against the makeshift icepack. "Hold that. I need to examine your skull."

"Are you a doctor or something?"

Why couldn't the first full sentence she'd uttered since he'd saved her ass have been something like *Thank you so much, Detective Graham. I owe you my life, and that scares the shit out of me?*

"Or something." His chuckle incited a small ember of warmth in her bones. He stood. Thick thighs pulled the fabric of his loose cut jeans taut. He rounded the end of the couch, and his quiet footfalls stopped behind her. Anticipation pulled her from the post-fight haze, and her heartbeat ticked up a notch. His fingers eased slowly, gently over the edge of her hairline.

"That laughter says there's a story."

"Several hundred, really." He pulled the bobby pins from her lopsided updo and unwound the spiral holder.

When he eased the thick mass onto her shoulder, she held her breath to keep from screaming. Not that her voice could effectively execute the sound.

"She went for the hair?"

"Yes," she croaked.

The breath he exhaled was heavy and vengeful. She'd never before heard it from him.

"I've never wanted to deck a woman until today."

"Really? I usually elicit that response. We've had more than a handful of conversations." Slowly, she was beginning to feel one with her body, her battered body. Focusing on Owen dulled the acuteness of the pain.

"You're starting to get your feet under you again." He laughed. "I'm glad."

His fingers sifted through her hair and over her scalp. It burned like fire at her roots.

"Tell me one of those stories," she hissed.

"Okay." His boot tapped on the floor for a beat. "So it's my first real deployment. Norway doesn't count. I was a highly trained Navy Corpsman, dealing with sprained ankles and mild frostbite from winter training. But Syria, that was a hot zone with live rounds buzzing past your head on a good day. On a bad day, they found their target. And that's when I went to work."

Gen's mouth fell open in full disregard of the cut on her inner cheek.

"We'd been there five months. We were all ready to go home. We were talking about the first meal back Stateside. The first, well, everything Stateside that we've been missing for so long it hurt."

Her scalp hurt, but Owen's fingers in her hair and the heat they emitted eased the ache.

"The night before a multi-pronged operation, probably the biggest and most dangerous one we'd all been a part of, the platoon commander was feeling exceptionally nostalgic. He bribed one of the guys from the mess hall to cook him up a Syrian version of a chili dog."

"Disgusting."

"Exactly." Owen's thumb rubbed over the back of her skull. The soreness faded there, and she was able to enjoy his touch more. A little too much more. Her eyes closed, and the sound of his voice lulled her.

"A few hours later, go-time rolls around. The guys are chomping on gum as though it were their lifeline. They're tapping and singing their favorite tunes as if it'll ward off the hell about to unleash around them. I'm ready with my pack of supplies, knowing it won't be enough to save everyone. And the commander is nowhere to be found." His touch trailed down her neck. It found a sore spot on her left shoulder.

"We can't go without him. So I go looking. The moment I enter his barracks, I smell it."

"What?"

"Shit. I mean, we lived in the middle of the desert with

concrete walls around us that kept out insurgents but also the wind. I'd smelled it before. I'd smelled death, and it had nothing on this guy. The chili dog did such a number on him; it was on his bed and the floor."

"Disgusting."

"Beyond." He flattened his hand on her back. "Sit up for me." She repositioned, and his fingers studied the topography of her shoulders and spine. He hit on a spot at the center of her back, near the bottom.

"Oh, gah." She nearly jumped off the seat. It was reassuring to know her body was back under her control.

"That's going to bruise." His touch eased. "Do you have any Epsom salt?"

"Yes."

"You'll need it." He continued his search. "So I have to stabilize his condition, find another officer, and relay the message that we're without command. By the time we're ready to move out, we get a cease and desist order from higher-up."

Owen lightly touched her shoulder. "You can sit back."

When she did, he returned to his squatted position in front of her.

"So?" she urged.

"Contusions and possibly a bone bruise on your cheekbone. You'll hurt like hell for the next couple of days, but with some over-the-counter meds, you'll function like normal."

She breathed him in and reveled in his masculine scent that had nothing to do with cologne and everything to do with action and pheromones. "I didn't mean me. I meant, what happened to the mission."

"Oh." He leaned forward, dropping to his knees. His abdomen brushed the outside of her thigh.

Gen's breath caught between her open lips. Her pulse revved, beating hard and insistently between her legs. Just like that, she forgot the ass kicking she'd sustained. Her breasts felt heavy, eager. And at the same time, heat filled her cheeks embarrassed at her reaction. A first. She held completely still.

He reached behind her, pulled the light pink throw from the back of the couch, and draped it over her shoulders.

"Come to find out, the building we were supposed to be clearing exploded exactly two minutes after we would have all been inside. It was false intel. A setup." He licked his lips. Nice lips. Lips that mesmerized. "They were able to find the leak and the cell that perpetrated the bombing."

"Incredible." It was, but so was he, and her reaction to him. Incredibly baffling.

She wielded her body as a weapon. She used men for her own pleasure with little regard for anyone involved, herself included. When she needed it most, her confidence fled the scene. Another hit and run with which she couldn't deal.

"Yeah, incredible." Owen nodded. "The moral of the story. Sometimes life hands you shit. Dealing with it can save your ass."

A laugh erupted from her throat, surprising her. She eyed him. "That didn't really happen."

"It did." He placed his hand over his heart and lifted the other in the air. "I swear to tell the truth, the whole truth, and nothing but the truth, so help me."

So help her. Owen Graham's kind eyes, his full heart, and his tender smile loosened something inside her long hidden by invisible scars.

Gen stared at him in amazement. He was all about helping people, his own safety be damned. "You know about the aftermath." When he'd spoken about it in his car, she hadn't really paid attention.

"I do."

"What's the other part of the aftermath?"

"It's different for different people. It all sucks." His wide shoulders bobbed. "It could be seeing your attacker when they aren't there. Like on a subway car. Could be feeling the punches steal your breath in the middle of a business meeting as though the attack is happening all over again. There's the super fun, unexplainable sense of dread that hits you out of nowhere for no apparent reason."

"Super." She stared at the vacant space above the mantle. Through the years, she'd experienced the inexplicable feeling of dread, only she knew exactly from where it sprung. Now she got to add death blows and the maniacal face of Rubia Sanchez. Freaking fabulous.

"Genevieve?"

"Huh?" She found the most beautiful, kind electric blue gaze searching her own.

Warmth radiating from his hand touched her cheek a second before his rough fingers glided across her skin. They slipped into her hair, and his palm cupped her face. His other hand slid along her jawline under the ice pack and held her neck. He tilted her chin up ever so gently.

"You have to let it go."

Defeat would have kicked her into the cushion was he not holding on. She knew he was right, had known it since she was flat on her back staring up at the sky. Fearing for her own life crystallized that message. Still, she didn't want to hear it, much less admit it.

Her eyes closed. She shook her head. The frozen vegetables wobbled. The packaging crunched.

"Yes."

A tear slipped from her lashes.

Owen slanted her head. Hot skin met the moisture at her cheek. His lips kissed it away, then slowly grazed up to her hairline. He placed another kiss on her temple.

Gen clutched her eyes tighter, soaking in the contact, savoring it. She was scared to open her eyes, afraid it might flit away, a forgotten dream.

"Look at me, Genevieve."

She drew a deep breath, swallowed, and looked into his devastating eyes. Shards of navy and a light gray splintered the blue spheres. Her tear glistened on his lips for a moment before he scraped it into his mouth with his teeth.

"Please, let it go."

Genevieve grabbed his forearm with her free hand, ready to pull it away and flee. Instead, she held firm and pulled him closer. "Even if he killed them?"

He exhaled. The heat of his breath bathed her chest. His lids closed for only a second before his gaze was back on her and as intense as ever. "Even if."

"You're the one who wanted him behind bars first."

"That hasn't changed, but …" His gaze centered on hers for several beats and then dropped to her mouth. "What's done is done. It's not worth you getting hurt."

Owen leaned in excruciatingly slowly, giving her every opportunity to bail. Anticipation batted her heart clean out of her chest.

Home run.

She parted her lips and pulled him to within an inch of her face. Her lids lowered.

He pressed his mouth to hers in a tender embrace. The expression was almost chaste. Not almost. It was … for a moment, and then his teeth glided across her bottom lip before pulling it into his mouth. His tongue skimmed the edge, revving her pulse. He released the bite, but his tongue traced her upper lip, coaxing her mouth to open wider.

Eagerly, she obliged.

His grip firmed and pulled her close.

Gen's hand slid up his bicep, grappling for more.

Owen's tongue delved into her mouth. Hers greeted it in an illicit mating dance she knew all too well. Their tongues coiled and undulated while their mouths battled. An animalistic grumble rattled in his chest. He pulled the ice pack from her cheek, freeing her other hand. It sought heat and found it in a handful of Owen's lats. He shifted, rising higher and pressing her back into the couch. Primally, her legs spread, preparing to wrap around his ass and pull him near.

The next instant, Owen retreated. Suddenly, there was a gap between them. He grabbed her hands and pulled them from his body. He held them together in front of him. His massive hands dwarfed her own.

Gen's chest rose and fell as though she'd just run a marathon. Only the finish line was unattainable.

"I'm sorry," he gasped.

"Sorry?" She rested her head on the back of the couch and stared up at him. "Sorry you started, or sorry you stopped?"

"Yes. I mean, no." His gaze narrowed, and his mouth scrunched. "Christ, Genevieve. I tasted blood. I don't want to hurt you."

Her laughter was one of relief and amazement.

"Contrary to what you think, a kiss isn't going to break me." She slipped her hands from his grip and straightened.

"No, but it might break me." He winked and stood. "I'm going to draw you a bath. Put the veggies back until it's ready."

"If I had all my faculties about me, I'd tell you to fuck off." She glared.

"If you had all your faculties about you, we'd be fucking off, and on, for the next twelve hours." There wasn't a smile or brow waggle to tamp the declaration.

"Well, damn."

"Tell me about it." He pointed at the veggies on the

couch. "On your cheek."

She stuck her tongue out at him but did as he demanded. And good Lord, she'd like to do more, much more.

NINETEEN

IF THE BATH WAS SUPPOSED TO HELP, it hadn't. While she'd reclined in the warm, salted water, she'd frothed, replaying
the day's events. The pains in her back had turned to pure
agony. Dressed in an oversized sweater and cotton pants
with no patience for even a scrap of product on her body,
Gen shoved out of the bathroom ready to fight. Only,
Owen wasn't in the living room. It was empty. As was the
bedroom.

She hadn't known what to expect after that kiss and
retreat, but a goodbye would've been—

A rattle to her right pulled her gaze toward the kitch-
en. The edge of a gold breakfast tray, which she used mostly for working in bed, peeked around the corner. Owen
carried the tray waiter style. On it sat a full mug of coffee,
a bowl of soup, and a freshly pressed panini.

"Where'd you get all that?" Gen's mouth watered. Ten minutes ago, she'd thought about puking. Now she wanted to sit and scarf. The food. The man. All of it.

"Not from your kitchen, that's for sure." He grabbed her hand, twirled her toward the bedroom, and dragged her behind him. The covers had been pulled back. Her phone sat beside her bed, next to a bottle of over-the-counter pain meds and a glass of water, all lit by her bedside lamp. "In you go." His grip gently propelled her in the direction of pure comfort.

She crawled into the center of the bed, careful not to hiss at the pain in her lower back, and eased against the headboard and the pile of pillows he'd strategically placed for her. Her mouth once again dropped open. "You're married."

Owen's thick brows lifted toward the sky. "Nope."

"Why aren't you married?"

"You're not seriously asking me that?"

"Why not? You're kind and thoughtful and hot as the goddamned surface of the sun."

The corners of his mouth turned up, and she'd swear horns sprouted from his skull. Cute, nearly innocent horns that made him all the more handsome.

"Don't do that." She shook her finger at him. "Don't change the subject with a sexy smirk."

"I can do that?"

She glared at him. "Why aren't you married?"

"I haven't found anyone who challenges me." Owen leaned in, shooting her a pointed look. "Hadn't." He flipped the comforter over her legs and set the tray's legs on either side of them. "Why aren't you married?"

"Because I'm deeply scarred, emotionally broken, and incapable of true intimacy." She smiled sweetly. "That's what my shrink told me in college. So why bother?"

"Because you've found someone kind and thoughtful

and hot as the goddamned surface of the sun." His teeth were too straight and nearly too white. The barest hint of coffee addiction dulled the shine from blinding to manageable.

"Smartass."

"I figured soup because of the cut in your mouth." He pointed at the warm, pressed sandwich. "I got some starches too. Fighting leaves you weak even if you win. I always carb-load after a fight."

What was this? He was such a badass and equally as much of a caregiver. And she was a loner. No man had ever been inside her apartment for longer than it took her to come.

"Yeah, me too." She rolled her eyes.

As Owen laughed, he toed off his boots and slid onto the bed on top of the comforter. He grabbed two pills from the bottle on the nightstand and held them out for her. When she opened her hand, he traced her lifeline and its parallel fork before plunking the pills in the middle of her palm. She dutifully swallowed the medicine and then chased it down with several bites of soup. The liquid soothed her from the inside out far less than Owen's presence did. He watched on calmly, content, as though waiting to help with something else.

"I'm not a princess," she said as she lie on her bed being served and coddled in her Midtown condo with a view of the park. "I didn't come from money. All this, everything I have, I've worked my ass off to get."

"I know you're not a princess."

"Says the man who called me princess."

"I was scared and trying to make a point."

She snorted. "You were scared?"

"Yeah." His head shook slowly. The depth of his gaze revealed yet another layer to Detective Owen Graham. "I'd circled the block twice, looking for a place to park.

You weren't answering your phone. I thought I was too late. I almost was." His gaze dropped to her sore cheek.

Gen placed her fingers on the hot, aching spot. "It could have been worse, much worse. Thank you, Owen."

"Thank me by promising never to go back there."

"I promise." After all, she hadn't gotten any useful information from the Sanchez family, not one of them. For better or worse, they stood up for one another. She lowered her hand and continued to slowly eat the wholesome soup.

"Princesses don't get their hands dirty."

"Oh? And are mine dirty?" She snagged the sandwich, ravenous for a taste.

"Grimy, even before today." His thumb traced the outline of her toes, poking up from the covers. "I watched you in court. You scrapped and fought every day to save your friend."

"Don't remind me." Gen set the panini back on the plate without taking a bite.

Owen grabbed the sandwich and lifted it to her mouth. "We're just talking off the record. Not a cop and not a lawyer. Just two people who like each other, taking time to get to know one another."

"You think I like you?"

"Take a bite, stubborn woman."

She did as he demanded and smiled around the hunk of bread.

"I know you do. Otherwise, you would've kicked me out two hours ago."

Gen nearly choked on the cheesy goodness. "It's been that long already."

"Time flies when you're having fun or knocked loopy."

"No kidding." She swallowed the bite, took a sip, and stared at the beautiful man on her bed not trying to screw her but seducing her all the same.

"What makes you think he did it?" There was no malice in his question. No calculated angle, that she could see, and she was used to looking for them all.

"It's a lot of things and nothing … that I can't prove. Yet."

"Genevieve," he warned.

"I'm not going back there. I promised, and I won't."

"Good."

"You care about people, for people. It's your nature. Why do you care about me so much?"

"Somewhere in those long months of the trial, in the sparring of our opposition…" He lifted her hand in his. "You worked those vicious claws into my skin, and I can't shake them. About a month ago, I realized that fighting with you was the best part of my day."

She blinked at him in amazement. Men typically hated confrontation, especially from a woman. They wanted a meek and tender woman who didn't threaten their authority.

What could she say to that? Amazing. Astounding. A once-in-a-lifetime find. You've got to be shitting me.

Instead of saying anything, she shoveled food into her mouth as though she'd been deprived of food for the past three days. They ate in silence. Well, she did, until she realized she was eating alone.

"Aren't you hungry?"

"Nope. I demolished my own Italian pressed sub while you were in the bath."

"Oh." Goodness, she was shit with small talk, and she'd run out of food and a place to put any more.

"Want some more?"

"No, thank you. I'm stuffed, and, honestly, I'm surprised I ate it all."

"The shock is wearing off." He grabbed her bowl, stacked it atop the plate, grabbed the utensils, and carted them off.

Was it? The longer she spent with this man, the more in shock and awe she became. And she wasn't that type of girl.

Owen returned with a legal pad and two pens. Was he about to take her statement? She should press charges against that bitch, Rubia Sanchez, but she wouldn't.

He sat on the bed and placed the pad on the tray between them before offering her the pen.

"Thank you?"

"Don't thank me yet." He drew two parallel lines, running up and down the sheet, and then drew another set of parallel lines bisecting the first two. "If I beat you like I beat most, you won't be thanking me." His brilliant blues were shrouded by his long lashes in a mischievous, hot look.

"Tic-tac-toe?"

"You bet."

"How old are we?"

"Never too old for some good ole fashioned fun." He placed his X in the center of the grid. "Your turn."

"What if I wanted to go first?" A laugh surprised her, along with her willingness to play a child's game. There was something innocent about it. Innocence had been ripped from her at an early age, and that experience shaped so much of her existence.

"Then you should've moved first."

She drew her O in the bottom left corner and smiled at him. He moved quickly, not lunging for her mouth, but slashing his X in the most strategic position. They battled it out through four games with no apparent victor.

"So you're supposed to be some kind of tic-tac-toe whiz, are you?"

"Seems I've met my match." He chuckled.

How exactly did he mean that?

She offered him a sassy wink and wished like hell her body wasn't so battered. Without the ability to screw her way out of the emotional experience, she was forced to experience this connection with Owen that would leave her feeling hollow when he exited her orbit. And he would. All men did. Usually by her request. She'd never before invested time and vulnerability on a man, so even this little bit had her insides quaking.

"What is it?"

Her first impulse told her to make a joke, but she tamped it. "You seem so well adjusted."

He snorted. "Is that a compliment?"

"No, really. I mean, yes, it is. You have seen so much horror and still do, but you're not completely shut down. How do you do that? How do you deal with the shit and still function normally?"

"I don't know how normal I am. But I help people. I catch the bad guys. I try to, at least."

"Until some stupid lawyer gets in your way."

"It's checks and balances. The last thing I want to do is put away the wrong person for the crime. It demolishes an innocent person and their family while leaving the real perpetrator free. That's the opposite of helping. Talking about it helps. My war buddies and I didn't talk about it for a long time. Not until one of our best friends died by suicide."

Had he stabbed the pen through her heart? She glanced down. Nothing was sticking out of her chest, but it felt as though there was. Pain more acute than her throbbing cheek and twinging back clutched her heart. Tears filled her eyes. "How?"

"Overdose."

Gen scrambled away from him. Her back hit the pile of pillows and ground to a halt at the headboard. She stared at him in bewilderment. "Did you pull a background check on me?"

His brow furrowed. "No, should I?"

"I just." She shook her head, willing the images away. "You don't know?"

"Know what?"

"About my sister?" Gen slapped at her tears.

"I'm sorry." His head shook. His hand rose in a gesture of surrender. "I don't."

She bit her lips, hoping the words would stay inside, hoping she could shove the question away. It was so inappropriate.

"Gen, don't bottle it up. Say it. Whatever it is."

That was what she advocated, so why was it so hard to practice?

Owen pushed the legal pad to the side, eased closer, and grabbed her hand. He kept quiet, yet his touch said so much. She clung to that anchor. Her emotions steadied with each passing breath.

"Do you hate him, your friend who committed suicide?"

Owen rocked back as though her question had shoved him. He sighed. His lips smacked as they parted.

"I hate that he's not here. I hate that I didn't recognize the signs for what they were. I hate that I didn't do something to help. I don't hate him. He didn't mean to hurt anyone. He just wanted his hurt to stop, and that's the only way he saw to accomplish it."

Her tears came in earnest. There was no way to hide them from him, not this time, so she didn't try. She let all the sorrow flow through her, and then it poured out.

"I hate my sister," she choked.

"She died by suicide?" His voice was so quiet, yet the words echoed so loudly in her mind.

"Evangeline killed herself. She left me all alone ... because I left her all alone."

"Your sister, she's the reason you practice law? You told me you practice law to protect those who couldn't protect themselves. Evangeline was your younger sister?"

"She was my only sister. Older. Two years older."

"What happened to her to make her believe that was her only option?" He flipped her hand over and snuggled his palm to hers.

"She shot and killed our uncle LeRoy."

If her answer shocked him, he did a great job of hiding it. He simply sat and waited. A first-rate interrogation tactic.

"That was only the tip of the proverbial iceberg," she explained.

"Usually is."

"LeRoy had been molesting Evangeline since she was nine. He scared her enough that she didn't tell anyone, but …" She drew a deep breath and blinked through her tears. "But … when I was nine …"

She stopped, unable to continue for a moment.

Owen's other hand met the back of hers, and his grip tightened.

"I caught him. I didn't know until years later what I'd actually caught him doing, but it doesn't make me feel any less guilty. Evangeline was there. She was crying, and I didn't help her. LeRoy had a way of putting things. I didn't want to get in trouble," she scoffed.

"You were a child. So was your sister."

"I know. Rationally."

"Emotions aren't rational."

"Tell me about it." She wiped away the tears from her chin and stared into his intense gaze. Something swelled inside her chest.

He pulled her hand to his mouth and grazed her knuckles with a kiss. "You have to forgive yourself. After that, forgiving Evangeline will be easy."

TWENTY

HE KISSED HER ON THE CHEEK in the dark and slipped from the bed. Talk about a series of firsts. He didn't have to scrounge on the floor for his clothes because he hadn't taken off a single article. In fact, he'd cuddled her through the layers of bedding. The memory of his warm body against hers along with a double dose of over-the-counter painkillers staved off the worst of her aches. High-dollar concealer and the right tone of blush had minimized her bruise. Like any good liar, she had a backup story in case someone—Janney—noticed.

Gen shoved open the door to the office. Lisa, the receptionist, had the receiver clutched between her head and shoulder, jotting notes on a legal pad. The woman looked up only enough to see who had entered. Lisa tossed her a wave and then pointed toward the back. Her eyes were wide, and her head shook. She gave a thumbs down. Thumbs up indicated that the boss was out. Thumbs neutral meant she didn't know. Thumbs down said the boss was in. Gen didn't know exactly what the wide eyes and headshake indicated, but she'd guess it meant he was in a shitty mood.

Perfect.

She offered a nod of thanks for the warning and aimed for her office, hoping to avoid Janney until she had a good excuse to avoid eye contact with the woman. The first two offices were closed. Rosalyn was in court today, and most days, Craig took his time getting into the office. Must be nice. This was her first time to be late, maybe ever, and guilt weighed on her.

A hand grabbed her upper arm and yanked her from the modestly lit hallway into the blinding lights of the break room. Her right hand balled to bury a fist deep. Two days ago, the reaction would've seemed out of place. Now it was ingrained.

"Whoa there." Janney threw her free hand up and blocked her face. "It's me," she whispered.

"Christ, woman. I could've killed you."

"Child, please. You could've given me a black eye like the one you're trying to hide."

"How do you …? What are you …?" Gen's gaze scanned the otherwise unoccupied room. "What's going on?"

Janney yanked Gen's briefcase from her shoulder and shoved a stack of files into her hands.

"He's in a tizzy, he is. Stormed through thirty minutes ago, raising hell. Go act like you have a question about one of these cases and find out what's going on with that man because his demeanor ran Craig out of the office. Lisa tried to leave, but I caught her just in time."

"And you want me to—"

"Go." Her assistant grabbed her shoulders, turned her around, and pushed her back from where she came. Janney's short, Irish frame gave her the advantage of leverage.

Gen walked to keep from being tipped onto her face and to assuage her own curiosity. She passed her own office, the storage closet, and slowed in front of Perry's closed door. Her hand rose to knock but stalled at the sound of his voice rumbling through the door.

"I haven't called you back sooner because I've been busy preparing things on my end."

"I'm getting anxious, Perry.It's been too long." The woman's voice was ardent, insistent, and familiar.

Gen's raised hand trembled and dropped to her side. Where had she heard that voice before? Where? Where? It hit her like a flash, nearly knocking her over. The rear exit of the office near the elevator when she'd hidden like a coward behind the door.

"I know. I know. Soon." Perry must have sensed it too. His response coddled and cajoled but had no hint of the irritation Janney and Lisa had referred to.

She inched closer to the door.

"You haven't called in days. I need to see you." The woman's voice leaned toward desperation.

"We'll be face to face before you know it," Perry reassured.

"I hope you're right, for both our sakes." The edge of a threat speared the air and stabbed Gen in the heart.

"Now, Millie, don't be foolish." His voice firmed. "I need you to be patient. We're already rushing things. We have to be careful, remember?"

A scream ratcheted up Gen's throat and threatened to spew all over the door. She lifted her hand to cover her mouth, but it hit the edge of the stack of files in her arms. A heap of papers created a fast-flowing avalanche. They hit the floor and crashed into Perry's office door as loudly as one.

Gen dropped to her knees and shoveled the heaps toward her as quickly as she could. Before she blinked, Perry's door swung wide. His wing tips were inches from her face. Her gaze traveled up his long legs, past his wide chest, to his glower.

"Guess I should have opted for that second cup of coffee this morning." She grinned. "I was going to ask you a question about one of these cases, but"—her hands executed the perfect Vanna White at the cascade—"I doubt I'll be able to find it before lunch." She scooped the papers into an uneven pile, cradled them awkwardly, and stood. "Sorry to bother you." Her left foot turned toward her office in retreat.

"Gen." Perry stepped back and motioned her into his office with a Vanna gesture of his own. "Inside."

It wasn't a request.

She drew herself taut and stepped into the clutches of a cold-blooded killer. Sweat created a fine sheen over her chest, but she still smiled. This wasn't the first monster she'd dealt with, but it was the first to wholeheartedly fool her into thinking he was something else. Shame on her for allowing it.

Perry closed the door behind her, and then stood there like a wall, imposing and so close. She'd expected him to move toward his desk. "It sounds bad, I know."

Gen opened her mouth to rebut.

He raised a hand. "Your fair skin gives you away every time." His hands disappeared into his pants pockets, and he shrugged. "We were together a few times before ..."

They both knew what it was before.

Her heart turned to concrete in her chest and dropped to the ground. It didn't shatter but bounced along awkwardly between them and rolled under a leather chair.

"I didn't know her name, not until later. It was a meaningless fling. I didn't say anything because—"

It was Gen's turn to raise her hand. "I know why."

"You do?" His eyes were blank. Dark and more terrifying than if they had revealed rage.

"Sure, any indiscretions would have raised suspicion higher than it was already."

"I couldn't chance it."

"You should have told me."

"Would you have defended me?"

She met his dead eyes. "No."

"I knew it."

"Why'd you do it in the first place?"

She wanted to see if he knew about Pamela's indiscretions. If so, it would provide more motive than him cheating unless Pamela had found out about the affair and threatened to leave Perry.

"It's what men do." He shrugged as though he'd forgotten to put the correct amount of postage on an envelope. "We're genetically predisposed to spread the seed."

"Give me a fucking break." Gen turned away and grabbed the doorknob.

Perry's hand shot out and landed flat and wide on the door just above her head. "Now Gen—"

Gen turned on him and jabbed a finger at his face. "Don't you dare patronize me like I'm one of your two-bit whores. Remove your hand."

His arm remained outstretched above her, but his features softened. "You can't say anything. It'll ruin me."

"You're already ruined, Perry." Her head shook. "You just don't realize it."

"Are you threatening me?" His voice boomed.

"I'm stating facts. Everything you had is tainted with the blood of your wife and children."

"Which is why I'm trying to start over."

"Whatever you need to do, Perry. It's your life. Your wife and children's lives are over."

"I know that. I think about it every day."

But did he think about it with sorrow or pride?

Gen held the question as tightly as she clutched the heap of papers in her arms. She turned, grabbed the knob, and twisted. His hand moved slowly, limiting the speed of her retreat to maintain as much control over the situation as he could. It took all the strength she possessed, but she walked out of the office and held her head high, all without revealing the quiver in her steps.

His gaze followed her all the way to her office. She couldn't see it, but she felt it.

TWENTY-ONE

"IS THE BUILDING ON FIRE?"

A tall, young cop in his patrol uniform made a show of jumping out of her way. He gave her a smile to accompany the comment as she ran past him down the hallway of the NYPD Headquarters. The mop of dark hair that barely fit under his cap matched his playful gaze.

"If it is, I'm running the wrong way."

That cop was just her type. Cute. Playful. Easy. Well, maybe he had been her type. Given the current speed with which she ran toward a man 180 degrees from that description, her type had changed. Though, she wasn't running to him for any of the right reasons. Sex. Commitment. Love.

Were things supposed to go in that order?

Gen continued through the corridor and slowed at the

counter. The usual clerk worked the desk and buzzed her through to the sea of desks, cops, and perps without acknowledgment. He had his hands full with an irate woman wanting her neighbor arrested because of his wind chimes. Please, if wind chimes were the worst she dealt with, she needed to grab some perspective and some earplugs.

The moment she was through the door, her gaze locked on Owen. He stood at his desk near the back of the room. One hand clutched a pen while the other held a cell phone to his ear. His mouth moved, and he stabbed the pen at something on his desk.

"Hoowee. Please say she's my lawyer." A man cuffed to the desk nearest them clutched a hand to his chest and pointed at her with the other.

She rushed past him without a word. Owen's gaze locked on hers. His shoulders perked, and his eyes narrowed in a deep study to which she might never become accustomed. His lips moved faster, but she couldn't make out a word over the din.

"The Red Devil returns." This came from a familiar and not exactly friendly detective she'd only had the poor fortune to work with twice.

Gen offered him a curt wave and hooked a left toward Owen.

Detective Eric Hallard rolled back his chair, blocking her path. Of any of the detectives, she'd worked with him the most. At one time, she'd considered him a friend, but when she decided to take Perry's case, Hallard had taken it harder than most. So hard that she'd told him exactly where he could shove his badge.

"If it isn't the Red Devil herself." Hallard reclined in the seat and stretched his legs wide.

Of all the people to say, "I told you so," his would be the loudest and most obnoxious.

He was just the person she did not want to see, especially when she was still trying to catch her breath from the bombshell that'd detonated in her face this morning and the run over here.

"I didn't think you'd have the balls to show your face in here again."

"Shows what you know because I knew you'd be a pussy about it when I did." She smiled sweetly.

He harrumphed.

Behind them, someone laughed.

Hallard dragged a hand over his face and crossed his arms over his chest. "So, Holst, are you here with us or against us?"

Owen stepped around the desk between them and grabbed her hand. "She's with me." He turned away from his co-worker and towed her in his tracks.

It was as close to a caveman-white knight situation as she'd ever come. It was a thousand yards closer than she'd ever wanted to be to that kind of situation. He'd defended her and made a claim on her all in one simple sentence and with one swift act. The warmth that belied the cool breeze that'd returned to the city worked its way up her body, pooling in her chest and cheeks. A flutter captured her heart and toyed with her mind. It felt better than sex.

He pulled her past his desk and into a dark room she knew without sight. It had gray walls, no windows, two cameras in either corner, one metal table, and two chairs.

"How are you feeling?" he asked as he pushed the door closed, shutting out any hint of light. His fingertips grazed her cheek. His other hand glided down the center of her back, where he'd helped her place the refrozen pack of veggies later in the night.

"Fine." Physically, she was fine. Mentally and emotionally, she was a wreck.

His hot hands cupped her cheek. He tilted her head

so very slightly and pulled her mouth to his. She went willingly, near desperately, grabbing his collar and holding him tight. His lips were tender but fierce. Little noises of pleasure rumbled from his chest. Her fingers roamed higher, sliding against the heat of his neck and then over the prickly crop of his hair.

The kiss was unhurried and sweet. It stopped the world. Hers, at least, for the best moment of the day and maybe her life. In that small room, in that small chunk of space, everything was good and right.

It went on and on until someone shouted in the bullpen. She jumped and broke the kiss. Owen released her slowly.

"Watch your eyes." He flipped on the light and seeing him was almost as good as the kiss. His smile was for her and her alone. "I gave you a hell of a time yesterday. I thought for sure I'd never see you again."

Gen shrugged and surprised herself by lurching forward, burying her head against his chest, and wrapping her arms around his middle. His arms draped her like a security blanket. She'd never had one of those, not even as a kid. It felt too good.

He held tight.

When she was ready, she straightened. "Sorry. I—"

"No more sorry. Especially not for making my freaking day."

"You don't know why I'm here."

"It doesn't matter. You're here. Whatever it is, you came to me with it. That's big."

"It's huge." She grimaced.

He held her hands in his. "What's going on?"

She stared at his large, callused hands and wished she could let it go—Perry, the murders, her past, all of it. If she could, just maybe this surprising, amazing thing between them would have a chance.

But she couldn't let it go. She'd buried the dread she'd felt when she'd caught her uncle hurting her sister. Never again could she let it go.

"This morning, I eavesdropped on a conversation between Perry and a woman named Millie." Gen paused, waiting for his huffed breath or scolding, but neither came. His demeanor remained open and intent. "She's his lover, has been since before the murders."

"What was their conversation and where? I can't believe that they would have a talk out in the open that could implicate him or her."

"Her?"

"Yeah, you women are capable of all sorts of misdeeds."

She wiggled from his grip and placed her hands on her hips.

"Are you not?" he asked. "You know better than most."

It was her turn to huff.

"Where, how, and what did you hear, exactly?" He propped a hip on the interrogation table and clasped his hands on his lap.

Her hands fell to her sides. "I'm usually the first one in, but today, I was moving slower than normal, and I got in late. Lisa, the receptionist, was on high alert because Perry was in a mood. He'd apparently yelled at Craig, another attorney in our office, and Craig left. I walk into the madness of Janney, my assistant, shoving me down the hall with files—fake reasons for me to be in his office and an edict to find out what was going on with him." Her lungs filled with air, and she continued. "I stopped short outside his door when I heard him talking. He was apologizing for not calling back sooner. He said that he's been busy preparing things on his end.

"A woman's voice responded that she's getting anxious. She used his name in a familiar sense. Then she said it's been too long. By this point, I'm getting mad, but I can't make myself leave. He cajoles her, promising it'll be soon. Whatever it is."

Gen paced. "She's insistent. Again, he assures her that they'll be face to face before she knows it, and then she says, 'I hope you're right, for both our sakes.'"

"A threat," Owen noted.

She stopped and faced him. "Yeah, and Perry noticed. His voice hardened. He told her not to be foolish. He said that he needed her to be patient. That they were already rushing things. That they have to be careful."

"Then?" he urged.

"Then I dropped the damned files against the door." She threw her arms into the air.

Owen stood. Every muscle in his etched frame tensed.

"He didn't hurt me."

"What happened?" His voice was low and unbreakable.

"I tried to play it off like I didn't hear anything."

His lips pursed. "But he knows you and knows you're a shit liar."

"Yeah." She nodded. "I thought he'd take the out, but he didn't try to hide it. He admitted to the relationship. I mean, he tried to say it didn't mean anything, but that doesn't match their conversation. He's making plans. I think he moved all of Pamela's and the children's things out to move the girlfriend in."

He sighed heavily and sat back on the edge of the table. "Wouldn't be the first to do it."

"I need a favor."

Owen craned his neck left and then right. His gaze landed on her. "I mean, I don't think we'll get caught." He winked. "If we do, it's worth losing my job."

The laughter caught her off guard. Dread and misery had taunted her run over here, and he'd cast them to the side like meaningless pawns. She hadn't known it was possible to feel so many conflicting emotions in such a short amount of time. That's what Owen was—a conflict. He was nothing she'd ever needed, but now that she'd experienced him, he was all she wanted.

Gen nuzzled her face into the crook of his neck and breathed deeply.

Her phone chirped, shattering the intimacy.

She jumped back and pulled it from the pocket of her slacks. A text from Janney lit the screen.

Janney: Perry wanted to know where you were. I told him you'd gone to retrieve files from the shelter. Until he asked, I thought you were here! Where the hell are you?

"You need to stay away from him, Gen."

She scoffed.

"Seriously. You know something that no one else does. If he really mutilated and murdered the mother of his children and his own flesh and blood, you'd be just another notch."

"If he really killed them?"

"You said it yourself, you don't have proof. I didn't either. If I had, he'd be in jail right now. There was too much circumstance. Still is." He grabbed her right hand and caressed her knuckles. "I know he's your boss, and you have to be around him but not alone."

"Can you have someone follow him?"

"To what end? He knows there's nothing anyone can do. That's the only reason he copped to the relationship with you; that and he knew he was caught. Otherwise, he'd have told you about the relationship before the trial. And based on the conversation, it is a relationship that's lasted longer than the murder trial, which makes me want to look at the woman. Because it's always the husband until it's the new girlfriend."

That thought hadn't occurred to her.

Her phone rang, making the startling chirp a moment ago seem like a sweet whisper. She silenced the phone immediately and looked at the incoming call. "Larkin?"

"You can get it if you need to."

"No, it's fine. I just …" Gen cleared her throat and focused. "The girlfriend gives him motive. It was the only thing the DA's case was missing. A motive."

"Not the only thing. But I still can't have him followed. He's been cleared of the murders, and no one will okay the waste of those man-hours. We're short-handed as it is."

"What about his phone records?" Gen threw her hands wide, breaking contact with him. "If we could just—"

"Let it go, Gen."

"We need to get current phone records, track the girlfriend, and then look at old records for comparison. We can track exactly how long ago this started and …" The look on his face ripped her heart wide, and disappointment drew his lips into a tight frown.

Her phone chirped.

Larkin: I just wanted to check on you. It's been a while. Love you!

She shoved the phone back in her pocket and crossed her arms over her chest.

"I know you feel guilty, but it wasn't your fault. No matter what you find, Perry can't be tried again for their murders. If you keep running down this path, you're going to destroy your career, the one thing you've worked your ass off for. You've already nearly been arrested and beaten. You're pushing your friends away. It's not worth it."

"Guilty?" Gen glared at the man she liked more than any other person on the face of this earth. "You have no idea what guilt has done to me. I won't let it destroy me anymore."

"Then let this go."

"Letting it go didn't help my sister. I have some phone records from the day of the murders. I'll do it without you." Gen turned and shoved out of the interrogation room, leaving part of her heart on the table.

TWENTY-TWO

HER PHONE VIBRATED FOR THE FIFTH TIME since she'd left the police station. If she was smart, she'd stuff that thing between her legs and put the irritation to good use.

Janney, Owen, and now Douglas took turns sending her phone into fits. She tossed the thing onto a decorative sofa pillow to minimize the noise and yanked another file from the box on her living room floor. They'd been neatly organized until she'd lost her mind the other day and strewn them all over her home. Now she was back at it. Madness.

Owen's warning played in her head again and again. Her heart ached to forget all this and be with the man she … actually cared for. There were no better words to describe the indescribable feelings tossing her emotions like a freshly cut salad. They were like none she'd experienced before. That was as good of a reason as any to run head-long into the sticky depths of foolishness. It was safer than being vulnerable to a man.

If she could just find the phone records, then she could, what? She wasn't an investigator. She didn't have a database to cross-reference the phone numbers. She could use the freaking internet and the process of elimination, though.

Gen shoveled through three more files, ignored another phone call, and still no luck. They were here somewhere. Had to be.

A soft rapping sounded on the door. She froze. Her gaze went to the mess, scattered across her floor and couch. Her shoes lie like fallen soldiers in the mire. Her place looked much as it had been the other night.

"Gen?" Owen's hardline baritone had vanished, revealing quiet concern.

It tugged at her chest and pulled her to her bare feet. She dropped a handful of papers onto the sofa and hurried to the door. As much as she could ignore his calls, she couldn't escape the draw of his presence.

She stalled with her hand on the lock and looked back at the evidence of her mania strewn about the living room. Pride wouldn't allow her to let the girls see it. Yet she unbound the door and opened it wide for him.

Owen stood in the hallway with his hands by his side. She was struck by how much taller he was than her when she didn't have three inches of stylish heels helping her out. Red colored his cheeks, and his chest rose and fell as though he'd run all the way here from the station. It wasn't possible, or maybe it was ... for him.

Muscles in his neck and jaw flexed. Unlike the previous weeks, the weather had turned cold and biting. The jacket that'd been lying over the back of his chair at the station, the one that should be wrapped tightly around him, was nowhere to be seen. Gooseflesh prickled the intricate tattoos coloring his arms.

When she reached for him, the rigidity in his shoulders eased. His skin chilled her fingers. She wrapped her hand around his wrist, pulled him inside, closed and locked the door, and then turned to face him. His gaze roamed the living room for a long quiet minute.

The boyish blondness of his hair glinted in the daylight that streamed in through the large windows. Her fingers itched to thread through the windblown top and scrape across the prickly sides. The back of a man had never intrigued her as much as the front, but she studied every inch of Owen's neck, his shoulders. His T-shirt clung to the dip and sway of lats, and his jeans hugged his glutes. She longed to wrap him in her arms, rest her head on his back, and forget about everything but him.

"I've always led with logic." He braced his hands on his hips. His body spread wider. She hadn't thought it possible. He consumed her little foyer. The imposing breadth comforted her in a way no man's had done before.

Logic. Gen rarely used the skill. Knowledge and impulse ran her life ... just not where Owen Graham was concerned.

"It's kept me safe." Owen turned to face her. "It's kept me detached too."

"Impulse has always done the same for me ... because there was never any emotion driving it."

"Two different approaches. Same outcomes."

"Outcomes we're destined to repeat."

"No." His head shook as vehemently as his rebuttal in the small space. He stepped forward, crowding her.

"No?" Her chin jutted.

"We don't have to." His gaze locked on her mouth. "You could trust me."

She licked her lips and arched a brow.

"I trust you, Gen." He pinned her with his electric gaze. "If you say Perry did it, I know you'd never say that unless you had serious ammo backing it. You're holding back. Tell me what makes you think he did it. I'll do everything in my power to haul him in, acquittal or not. We'll get justice for Pamela and the children."

Her heart exploded with pure joy. He trusted her. He was here for her. What if she couldn't open up to him? What if she drove him away? Fear and doubt hit her like shrapnel. Its sharp edges carving holes in her happiness.

So she did what she did best.

Gen slipped her right hand in the back of his collar, wrapped her palm around his nape, and dropped her gaze to his mouth. "Kiss me and don't stop."

Mere inches separated their faces. Desire filled the gap.

"Gen." His teeth dragged over his bottom lip, then clenched tightly. Indecision battled in his bright blues. He knew this was a tactic.

She leaned forward onto tiptoes and dragged her tongue from the corner of his mouth to the crest of his upper lip.

He held perfectly still.

Challenge accepted.

Her head dropped to his chin. Unyielding teeth grazed his jawline and snagged on the meaty hinge of his jaw. He released a low groan. It rumbled from his throat and tickled its way through her lips, down her throat, and caressed her breasts. Just like that, it changed from a challenge to pleasure, her pleasure.

She touched her left hand to the center of his chest and pressed him back. He walked willingly until his shoulder blades met the small strip of wall between the kitchen and bathroom. His throat worked on a deep swallow. She licked her lips.

"Don't do this, Gen."

"Owen," she scolded while her fingers made a meal of his shoulders and chest. "Don't do what?" The ridges of his abdomen created a ripple under her touch. Her fingers stopped at the edge of his shirt and hooked on to the material. She lifted the edge, worked the fabric up an inch, and lowered her mouth to his hot skin. With each inch revealed, she traced the light and shadows of his stunning torso. His breaths grew heavy.

Gen straightened and peeled the shirt over his head. She dropped it on the floor. Her gaze drank him in. Ruddy cheeks. Wide chest. Thick, inked arms. Half-lidded gaze.

"Talk to me," he begged.

She dropped to her knees in front of him. "That'll be hard." The leather of his belt loosened under her diligent hands. "A lady isn't supposed to speak with something in her mouth."

"You're no lady, vixen."

"I've been called by many names but never vixen." His zipper gave way under her touch. She dragged the front of his pants down and groaned. Of all the penises she'd seen in her day, this was by far the prettiest. Not a freckle. Not a wrinkle out of place. Not too big. Not anywhere near small. It stood at perfect attention. It looked pristine, almost untouched.

God, please let him know how to use this thing.

Any other day, with any other dick, she'd have taken it to the back of her throat in one deft stroke. It was her signature move. It let them know exactly who they were dealing with, and it got them going. As ridiculous as it sounded even in her own head, this was a dick to savor.

She started with a taste, a simple slip of her tongue around the smooth tip. The heady flavor drew her lids closed and elicited a moan. Her lips arranged kisses in its wake and down the shaft to the base. She used the flat of her tongue and relished in his full flavor from bottom to top.

When she glanced up, he was watching her intently. His eyes were drunk with lust. His cheeks flushed. The desire to take him past climax pooled in her belly and dipped devilishly low. She would take him all the way but slowly. After licking her lips and lavishing the tip of his cock, she tortured them inch by delicious inch. The slow bob, suck, lick, and swallow drove her own desire. Her hips rocked in pace with the seduction. Her breasts shimmied with every withdrawal. Before long, they both panted.

At any moment, she expected Owen, the consummate gentleman, to try to pull her up and spare her from the mess for which she longed. But with each stroke, he surprised her, sinking deeper into the rhythm, thrusting with greater abandon. She scooted closer, slid her hands from the front of his pants to the firm globes of his ass, and grabbed hold. It ramped the tempo.

The flesh between Gen's legs slicked and swelled with each pass. She wanted his touch, needed it in her aching center, but this wasn't about her. A first, for certain. She focused on the feel of him, stretching her throat, abrading her swollen lips, swelling inside her mouth.

"Gen." His fists clenched at his sides. He groaned her name and tensed.

Heat shot into the back of her throat. She held him deep and tight, drawing out his climax. His body tightened. He shivered around her and then collapsed against the wall. His chest rose and fell. Triumph danced over her, plumping her breasts and stroking her clit. She popped him out of her mouth, licked her lips, and grinned like a vixen.

Owen's expression stalled her celebration. His brow was pinched and his gaze narrow. The muscles in his jaw worked as though she'd told him off, not gotten him off.

She stood, ready to defend herself.

He kicked off his boots and pants, yanked her loose silk blouse from her torso, and turned her to face the wall before she could form a single word. His fingers splayed across her back and roamed up her shoulders, sweeping the straps of her bra off with them. Hot, insistent hands plunged into the cups of her bra. The touch forced her back against his chest where she melted.

The expression had not been anger but hunger. A yearning she felt all too acutely. It hollowed her out in anticipation of him filling her up.

"Gen," he growled. She'd never heard her name said in so many different ways with so many different meanings.

His lips nibbled a trail from her earlobe down her neck. He pinched and worked her nipples so precisely her knees quivered.

"Yes." She arched against him. Her question turned into a sigh punctuated with a moan.

"You frustrate and satisfy me all at once." He gripped her shoulders and walked her forward.

"I know the feeling," she panted. The more swollen her sex became, the emptier and achier she felt.

"Not yet, you don't." His breath was hot on her cheek. The timbre rumbled from his chest and vibrated against her back. He pulled her bra down to her waist.

"I do," she groaned.

His laughter filled the intimate space between them. In a flash, he plastered her hands to the wall, shoved her shoulders down, and tilted her hips up, poking her ass into the air.

"I'm not into that dominant, submissive stuff." There, splayed out and not in control, vulnerability caught her breath.

"Your hands are up, so you don't fall over."

"Sure of yourself, aren't you?"

He nipped and dragged his teeth down the center of her back. Gen's mouth fell open on a sigh, proving he had every right to be.

Owen reached around, unfastened her pants, and dragged them down her hips inch by tormenting inch. His hands, lips, teeth, and tongue took turns ramping her lust. She swayed and wiggled her ass, trying in vain to rush the pace. His palms pressed her cheeks together. He buried his face in the cleavage he created. Her nipples brushed against the uneven wallpaper. Hot, fast breaths created dew across her lips.

Finally, he released her slacks. They cascaded to the ground in a puddle along with the slight confection of lace she called panties. She kicked them to the side and focused on his touch. Fingers that had been cold only minutes ago warmed the curving planes of her thighs. His nails bit in just so, and he spread her legs unnaturally wide. When those sinewy shoulders burrowed between her thighs, her breath caught. Silky hair tickled the crown of her cheeks a moment before they were spread. The wet, firm tip of his tongue caressed the length of her swollen clit.

He worked her as slowly and maddeningly as she had him. Taking his time, he sampled each intimate part enough that her legs shook. She hovered on the crest of an all-encompassing orgasm, but each time she threatened to crash into the maelstrom, he changed the tempo or location.

Gen panted with her lips against the wall. She clawed at the wallpaper in search of a handle to keep her upright. Her moans ricocheted into her ears, nudging her that much closer to climax.

"If you want it, you'll have to beg," he growled.

"Beg?" She managed to sound appalled, though she was a quivering mess.

"Or"—his lips grazed hers as he spoke—"you could

trust me."

"We're not just talking orgasms anymore, are we?"

"You wish." He pressed the flat of his tongue to the front of her clit. His rhythm and tempo, his groans of pleasure and determination to master her body shoved her over the edge of oblivion.

Worries evaporated in the heat of explosions ignited one by one throughout her body. They started in her toes and shot upward. They stole her breath. They stole her thoughts.

TWENTY-THREE

THE MOMENT HER BODY QUIT CONVULSING, he grabbed her shoulders and turned her to face him. She stood on shaky legs by sheer force of will. If she fell, Owen would have won. He'd given as good as he'd gotten, but no angels were singing. What could she say? Forget the block, she'd been around the world, and she'd had great orgasms before. Better even. She stared at the slightly uneven etching his well-formed muscles created just above his heart and found herself not unable but certainly unwilling to look him in the eyes.

With every passing breath, fear rushed in, polluting the freshly cleansed parts of her brain. Desire had been a part of her life for decades, but she'd never desired something that scared her. And now, she wanted to trust Owen Graham.

His fingers laced around her neck, and his thumb lifted her chin. She met his knowing gaze. The self-satisfied smile she'd anticipated was a heart-wrenchingly tender smile, if not a little devilish.

"Are you ready?" His voice was husky.

"For what?" Hers quaked as though he was asking her in which manner she wanted to die. She knew exactly what, and she wasn't ready, not even a little bit.

He grabbed her waist and lifted her high. His arms hugged her tightly, securing her to the warmth of his chest.

Gen encircled his hips with her legs and wrapped her arms around his neck. Their naked bodies pressed together. Hell, they'd shared bodily fluids, but that was far from the most intimate thing that passed between them. She didn't know what it was. She was wise enough, though, and experienced enough to know it was rare.

Owen walked them into her bedroom. Midday light filled the room with a hallowed glow. Or maybe it was just the man—the unsuspecting, caring, beautifully sharp-edged man. She smoothed a hand over the back of his head. A thousand hairs pricked her palm, rough and rigid, the exterior he shows the world. Then she reached the supple and soft top. Her fingers luxuriated in the feel, in the man she tried her best not to love.

His eyes closed. He whispered her name. His lips toyed with hers. A cascade of slick skin on skin. The tender touch of his mouth continued across her cheek, and then he buried his face in her hair. His arms tightened around her in an embrace. It was more shocking than any sex toy or maneuver she'd tried. It was her first true, real, deep, feel-everything hug maybe ever.

Her legs, arms, fingers, and eyes clamped tight. She clung to him, hugging him with all she had. And just like that, the tumult inside her drifted away, a heavy fog obliterated by the intense light of the sun. Owen wasn't the sun, but his intensity cleared her head.

When he levered back, she braced his hard, handsome face in her hands.

"I'm ready."

"What is it you think you're ready for, vixen?"

"To beg."

Any smugness that had quirked his mouth melted away. He stopped in front of the bed. His arms released her, more than that, they shrugged her off like a bad outfit. She fell and flailed. The plush white duvet caught her, puffing around her ass and elbows. Her mouth fell open.

He stood rigid and angry at the end of the bed. His hands were loose at his sides, but his chest expanded on a deep breath. It clearly wasn't the answer he'd wanted.

"What the hell?" Gen scrambled to her knees and stretched her arms wide. "You gave me options."

His head shook. He took a step away from the bed and drew another breath. It gave her a good look at his body, though this wasn't the time to be thinking about how magnificently formed it was. She was about to lose any chance she had of possessing such a spectacle. Even more amazing than his body was the heart that beat inside it.

"Don't leave, please." Her hand shot out toward him.

"I gave you options because I thought it'd be enough, but ..." He laughed, but there was no amusement in it. His head cocked into the air as though looking for answers.

"Owen." Gen stood, and he took a step back. She lifted her hand in surrender and sat, taking a more vulnerable position than when she was on her knees. "I haven't pushed men away because I've never let them get close enough to hurt me. Not even a catnap after sex. I don't do intimacy. Never have and never will."

His jaw flexed.

"Or so I thought," she added. "I care about you. And that's enough to make me bar the door and never answer my phone again, but here you are. I let you in. It might not seem like much, but it's more than I thought I had to give. You make me want things that scare the shit out of me. I want to trust you. I want to wake up next to you in the morning. I want you to stay."

"You act like intimacy is easy for people."

"It seems pretty natural for you."

"Only because I love you enough to try."

He could have shot her in the heart and hurt her less. Her hand involuntarily slapped over her mouth. It was her turn to shake her head. Tears threatened to fill her eyes. She blinked them away.

"Don't say that," she breathed.

"Why not?"

"It's too much."

"It is what it is." He shrugged. "Want me to go now?"

Gen stood once more and walked to him. He stayed where he was, his blue gaze tracking her. She stopped in front of him and pressed her lips to the skin above his heart. Once. Twice. Three times.

Owen's fingers dived into the hair at her nape and pulled her face to his. His lips were insistent and ravenous, tugging and suckling at her mouth. Gen's arms threaded around his neck and yanked him close.

This man. This aberration of the species. He was a mystery.

Her feet left the floor, and she went willingly into his embrace. The world tilted once more, and her back hit the pillowy duvet. His body followed her down, warming her front. His heavy legs pinned her to the bed. Whether intentional or not, it kept her from spreading her legs and maneuvering the heavy cock that hung between his legs where she wanted it most.

Despite the tempo his kisses set, he took his time, savoring each part of her mouth. She dragged her fingers over the carved topography of his back and shoulders, mapping him as she'd never bothered to before. Every muscle weaved its way into another, bulging and contracting under her touch. His lips moved lower, tracing her jaw and neck, before plunging lower still. He didn't drive straight to the nipples, which was where she wanted him. No, he forced her to enjoy the sweet scratches and hot kisses he used to outline her clavicles and heavy breasts.

The longer he touched and tasted, the more she undulated and sighed. Moisture slicked between her legs as though she hadn't come minutes ago.

"You've got to stop that," he groaned.

He spread her arms wide, placing his palms atop hers. His blue gaze darkened with heavy lids.

"I can't." She continued to wiggle and arch. The hair of his legs abraded her lower lips. "Owen, I can't." The weight of his muscles provided enough friction that her breath caught. She shattered under him, grabbing his hands and holding tight for dear life.

Before she put herself back together, he hooked an arm under her back and levered her up. His knees shoved her thighs apart. They perched on her bed, face to face. Her muscles still convulsed. He held her to his chest and pressed the head of his cock inside her aching body.

"Yes," Gen panted and pulled at his shoulders, needing him closer.

He withdrew and arched deeper. One of his hands grabbed her ass cheek while the other plunged into her hair. He pulled her face close and pressed his forehead to hers before spearing her to the hilt.

Her arms shook. Her legs quaked. He felt like steel and silk inside her. Never before had it felt like this.

So good. So delicious. So natural.

She froze.

Owen matched her. His gaze dropped to their joined

bodies. "Shit. I never forget." He moved to pull out, but she trapped him with her legs, holding him where he belonged.

"Me neither. Not ever," she admitted.

"I have protection." He made another move to get it. Again, she held him tight.

"I do too."

The sexy, devilish grin she'd come to know and love curved his kissed-red mouth. "You have to let me go for me to get it."

"I know. It just feels so good."

His laugh was big and nearly unhinged. "That's an understatement."

"Yeah," she agreed, rolling her hips and grinding him deeper still.

"Fucking Christ, Gen," he growled.

"This feels different."

"Yeah," he barked the reply and sucked a breath through his nose.

"Not just that." She gestured to their naked connected bodies. "All of it." Her arms tightened around him.

"Another understatement." He pulled her close and plastered a kiss on her mouth.

She kissed him again, pulled from his hot flesh to the tip, and then impaled herself on his cock.

His fingers grabbed her hips. He breathed through his nose again and let it out slowly, as though grappling for control. "We need protection. Shit, I need it. If I get you pregnant, you'll kill me."

It was her turn to laugh. Pant and moan and laugh. "I'm on the pill."

"There's always a chance."

"One I've never been willing to take." She smoothed a thumb over his severe jaw, interlocked her fingers around the back of his neck, and arched in is hold. His cock slid from her body to the full head. When he was nearly out, she deliberately lowered herself onto him, making no mistake in her intent.

"And now you are." A moan hissed through his teeth.

"And now I am." She squeezed him with her inner muscles. Her head lolled to one side, and she rolled her hips, feeling everything as though it was the first time. And in so many ways, it was.

Owen watched her work their bodies into a frenzied mess of sweat and desire. He used his grip on her hips and drove them higher, angled her deeper. His thrusts stoked every nerve ending. He shifted his grip back and filled his hands with her bottom. With each exquisite collision of their bodies, he arched into her. The muscles in his chest and neck strained. His abs rippled. The tattoos danced. His gaze locked on hers. And Gen caught fire.

Her orgasm came hard and fast, searing her skin. Melding her to Owen. She gasped and convulsed and clung to him, riding out every last jolt of pleasure. Then he was there with her. He tensed and keened. Heat filled her and spilled down her leg, proving just how foolish this wonderful man made her.

TWENTY-FOUR

SPRINGS GROANED, AND THE BED DIPPED, and Gen rolled into his embrace. It was both foreign and familiar, new and more comforting than a slice of cheese pizza and a beer.

"Morning?" she asked in a sleepy grumble.

"Afraid so."

"Damn."

His salacious lips pressed to hers, and she let him. Morning breath be damned. Maybe it'd scare him away and save her the heartache because this level of bliss was not sustainable. Like the best cup of milk, this too would curdle.

It didn't. His kiss was long and deep, and all she wanted to do was pull down the blinds and block out the day. She wanted to forget the world, the good and the bad, and focus solely on Owen for, well, ever. Her belly clenched and jerked at the thought. Forever with Owen Graham. The room spun.

"I need a shower." He rubbed his stubbly cheek against hers. "Join me?"

"Last time we showered together, I didn't get very clean."

"Me neither." His teeth nipped at her neck.

"And whose fault was that?"

"Yours. Definitely yours." He placed one more kiss on her lips and shoved from the bed. "So wanna get dirty with me?"

"Yes." She rolled to her side and watched his perfectly formed ass head for the hallway.

"But?"

"You get clean. I'll go grab coffee." There wasn't any more food in her apartment than there had been when he'd nursed her wounds the other day.

"How are you not married?" he hollered from the bathroom, mocking her.

"Stuff it."

"Already did. Several times," he reminded.

Owen hadn't been kidding when he'd said they'd be fucking off and on all night. The sun barely tinted the horizon, and they'd logged a few naps between bouts of the most intimate debauchery of her life.

"I'm not above doing it again." The shower turned on, and he continued over the rushing water. "In fact, I'd like to. Sooner than later. What are you doing tonight? Let me take you to dinner. A proper date."

Gen pushed from the bed, and blood rushed to every sensitive spot on her body. She hugged her arms around her naked skin, luxuriating in the feel. The spot above her pelvic bone was tender to the touch. Her nipples ached. Hell, the globes of her ass probably had his fingerprints. A smile curved her lips. She walked gingerly to the bathroom doorway and called through the crack in the door.

"How normal."

"Not too normal. I'll cook."

"You can cook?" She pressed her head to the door-frame. Why was he so wonderful?

"The basics. Nothing too fancy."

"What's wrong with you?" She whispered the words so he couldn't hear them. There was nothing. Oh wait, there was that one issue she'd yet to figure a course of action to maneuver. He demanded emotional intimacy, not just physical.

Gen shoved off the wall, headed to the closet, and pulled on her favorite tights, boots, and an oversized sweater. She pushed into the bathroom and mounted her wild hair atop her head with a band.

"Hey, what's a guy got to do to get breakfast with that coffee?"

Her laughter caught her completely by surprise. Just like the man did. She stared at her smiley, happy reflection in the mirror in total shock. Happiness looked good on her, better than the makeup she skipped.

"You already did it. Several times."

He gave a sexy purr. "Tell me what it was so I know for next time. I'm quite fond of breakfast."

A noise to her left caught her attention. His pants were chirping. More accurately, the phone inside his pants chirped.

"Your phone is going off."

"Ah, I have other things on my mind now."

"Oh, yeah?"

"Yeah? Eggs, bacon, dark roast."

"I'm going. Don't use all the hot water."

"I never do."

Gen always did. There'd never been anyone to save any for. She pulled the bathroom door to without latching it and went in search of her phone. The living room was dark. A chill worked its way up her spine.

"Ridiculous." She rolled her gaze toward the sky. After a lifetime of living on her own, this was hardly the time to get scared. Something caught the edge of her clunky winter boot, and she went down hard. Her knee whacked the floor. She sprawled on the hardwood, nearly catching a mouthful of rug.

"Gen?"

"I'm fine," she hollered, "just clumsy."

She rolled to her side and saw the light screen of her phone inches from her face. Hadn't she left it on the couch? She palmed it and pushed to her feet. After a few swipes and slides, the device's flashlight filled the sitting area. The files she'd left in disarray had been stacked into a neat pile, right up until she'd kicked over the box.

What the hell? Why had he done it? Was he a neat freak, or was he looking for something? When had Owen done that? They'd spent the afternoon and night in a tangle of arms and legs.

Gen killed the flashlight and saw her long list of text messages and missed calls. Sixteen was bound to be a new record. Owen was on to making his own record. His phone beeped and vibrated, dancing across the floor once more.

Had he looked at her phone sometime during the night? Maybe when he'd re-boxed her files?

And I'm the one with trust issues?

She shuffled back to the hallway, reached down, and snatched the phone from his pants. It was a record. Records, Tammy to be specific. Tammy from records had tried to hand-deliver the phone records he requested for a number she didn't recognize. He had been out, so she'd left them on his desk. Tammy hoped to catch him next time and was available any time to help with any request he might have. Smiling devil emoji.

Heat, akin to the fires of hell, engulfed Gen. Suddenly, the sweater was suffocating, and rage pounced on her temples.

Before she could think or the message could disappear, she swiped left and pressed view. She wanted to tell Tammy to go fuck a lamppost because it would show more interest than Owen. Shit! Jealousy was a potent emotion. One with which she had zero experience. And it showed. What the hell was she doing? Of course, Tammy from records wanted Owen. There wasn't a straight, blue-blooded woman who wouldn't. He was kind and hella hot.

She was about to replace the phone when the smiling devil on her shoulder jumped, making her fingers dance across the letters.

Thank you so much, Tammy. Can you grab me the records for 212-323-0087?

Owen may have packed Perry's case away, but she hadn't. She hit send. Tammy responded immediately with a bubbly, *Anything for you, Gorgeous.*

"On second thought, I have other things on my mind." Owen opened the door dripping wet, heavy-lidded, and fully erect. His hand extended toward her, but he stopped short. That steamy blue gaze dropped to the phone in her hand and then turned inquisitive.

"It was going crazy." More like she was going crazy. "I thought it might be important." Gen darkened the screen and handed it to him. "I'm gone. Coffee. Breakfast." She scooped up her purse from the kitchen counter and practically ran from her own apartment.

The trip down the street, the wait in line, the smell of coffee beans and bacon, the trip back, none of it helped the knot growing in her stomach. She shoved open the apartment door, expecting and hoping to find it empty.

Owen sat on the end of her bed dressed in the clothes she'd stripped from his body. He held the cell phone to his ear. "I understand. I'll get on it immediately." There was a pause.

Gen stepped inside and closed the door behind her. Why, of all the places he could have been, was he on the bed? It was so personal. She set the bag with his break-fast and the cup carrier on the counter inside the kitch-en. Everything inside her tingled. Fear of losing what she hadn't known she wanted forced her to grip the edge of the counter to steady herself.

"Yes, just as soon as I get in." Owen's voice was strong, steady.

She drew in a deep breath and headed to her death with her shoulders hunched like the coward she never thought she was.

He'd ended the call, and his eyes were on her, the dis-appointment fully visible in the early morning light. She stepped into the bedroom.

"Pamela and the kids weren't his only victims. Perry killed Rita Ayers when he was a teenager. His sister wit-nessed it. He scared her into silence until after his acquit-tal. She confided in me a few days ago. Then there was Tiffany and Henson Renly. They died in a hit and run with no suspects, but I can almost certainly place Perry at the scene. A dark-colored sports car was spotted speeding away from the crash. Perry's father left him a black Jaguar in his will. There's a garage at his mom's house with three old cars under tarps."

Owen stood. "You still think this is about proof, Gen." His head shook. "All you had to do was open up. Just talk to me. That was it. No matter how many or how few piec-es of the puzzle you had, I'd have given you anything you asked for." He drew a heavy breath. "Fuck, Gen, I gave you my goddamned heart."

Tears clouded her vision. His words were too true. Too perfect. And she fucked it up. So she did what she did best. She straightened and lifted her chin.

"I don't know what to do with those."

"Clearly." Owen sidestepped her and left. He didn't even bother slamming the door.

TWENTY-FIVE

SHREDDING. TEARING. SLASHING. His absence carved a void inside her chest. Pain dragged her to her knees. She clung to the duvet and pressed her heart against the edge of the bed as though the mattress could stem the sorrow flowing from her most vital organ.

A futile scream ratcheted its way up her throat. She gathered the white down to her face. The explosion should have rocked her block. It should have shaken her building by its foundation. That was what he'd done to her. He'd taken the stable footing of her life and turned it to quicksand. A sand all too happy to take her life. It pulled her down deeper than she'd ever been. Her cheek met the floor, and she sobbed into the scent of their lovemaking.

Morning turned to day.

Her phone continued to vibrate at her hip, inside the

purse she'd yet to remove. She didn't care.

The handle of her front door twisted, and then the door groaned open.

Hope, unwarranted and unearned, filled her enough that she rolled to the side and opened her swollen lids toward the doorway.

"Gen? Genevieve Holst!" Larkin's voice echoed through her home. The door slammed, and stilettos clacked across the hardwood into the living room and then the tile in the bathroom. Her friend practically ran into the bedroom before skidding to Gen's side.

"Oh, dear God!" Larkin's hands were on her face and sliding down her neck. She shoved them off.

"Who else would it be?" Gen growled.

"What?"

"Genevieve Holst." Gen glared at Larkin. "Who else lives here?"

Larkin knelt on the floor in Gen's apartment in her workday best. Her hands flitted around as though unsure of what to do. She didn't speak either, which said a lot.

"I'm alive," Gen reassured her. "I know because it hurts so much."

"What happened? Where are you hurt? Do I need to call an ambulance?"

"I fell in love like a stupid, fucking moron. It hurts everywhere. And no, an ambulance won't help."

"Oh, Gen." She'd never seen such pity pour from Larkin. Her friend leaned over and wrapped her arms around Gen. They were colder, smaller, and shorter than the ones she really wanted. Still, she hugged Larkin back. Her tears rushed back in earnest.

"Love? Gen, I'm new to this mess myself, but this isn't love."

Larkin helped her sit up. Gen wiped the streams from her cheeks. Good thing she'd foregone makeup. If she'd bothered, it would've dripped down to her chin by now or been wiped onto the covers.

"Yeah, it is. I just fucked it up." Gen bit her lip.

Sweet Larkin stared at her with wide eyes and parted lips.

"I know," she groaned. "It came as quite a shock to me too."

"Owen?"

Gen nodded and wiped her face with the sleeve of her sweatshirt.

"If it is love, like you told me, then you have to talk to him. Tell him everything you're feeling."

She rolled her eyes at her friend. Larkin wasn't deterred.

"It may not solve the problem, but you'll feel better, and he'll understand you better."

"When did you get so smart?"

"I have great friends."

Gen wrapped her arms around Larkin and held her tightly to her chest. "Me too."

Larkin rocked her back and forth.

"Thank you," Gen squeaked.

"Don't thank me yet. You're not dead, so I get to yell at you for scaring the hell out of me." Larkin squeezed her tight and then released her, stood, and extended her hand.

"I deserve it, but can it wait a couple of days?" Gen grabbed Larkin's hand and stood on shaky legs.

"As long as you learn how to answer your damn phone again." Larkin palmed her own phone and called Douglas on speaker.

"Yes?" His warm fatherly voice filtered through the device.

"She's alive. I'll be down in a few."

"Take your time. You are loved, Genevieve. Don't forget that when you go missing again. Also, don't go missing again. Not even Larkin will keep me from pulling out all the stops."

"Thank you, Douglas." She had people who cared about her. More than most, she knew how special and rare that was, and she'd taken them for granted. "I'm sorry. I won't do it again. I promise."

"Good."

Larkin ended the call and led her into the kitchen. She pulled a stool out from beneath the bar, motioned her atop it, and slipped Gen's purse from her body. Her friend presented her with her phone. "Answer it. Every time. Do we have a deal?"

"Deal," Gen agreed. She opened the screen and began cataloging each call and text. Not for a second did she dare listen to Owen's messages … from before. There were none since he'd left, since she'd screwed up so terribly.

"The detective?" Larkin grabbed one of the coffee cups from the counter, placed it in the microwave, and turned it on.

"Yes?"

"He's a nice guy."

"How do you know?"

"I haven't met him, but he and Douglas have had some back and forth. He approves, so I approve." Her sweet friend's smile was so sincere but misplaced.

"He is a nice guy. Too bad I'm not a nice girl."

"You're one of the nicest."

Gen hiked a brow. It pulled on her puffy eyelid.

"Yes, you're a bad bitch, but you're always there for your friends. You just have to let your friends be there for you." Larkin pulled the cup from the microwave, took the phone from Gen, and replaced it with the coffee.

The drink would have been better fresh and with Owen, but it knocked back the cloud of sorrow enough for her to see a few feet in front of her. She sipped and sat with someone willing to skip out on what was sure to be a day of very important business to be here for her.

"He was in the military before the police force," Gen volunteered. Not that it mattered anymore.

"Really? He doesn't strike me as the killing type."

"He wasn't. He was a Navy Corpsman. He took care of people." She pulled in a shaky breath. "He wanted to take care of me."

Larkin chuckled. "You, a woman who doesn't want to be taken care of."

"I didn't want to be until he took care of me." A stray tear slipped down her cheek.

"Did you sleep with someone else?" Her friend asked the question with no hint of judgment, just inquisition.

"No." Gen wrinkled her nose at the thought.

Two perfectly groomed brows shot high. "Oh, Genevieve, I hate to inform you, but he's the one. He's your one."

Gen's head shook.

Larkin nodded.

"I messed up."

"You clammed up. There's a difference. Talk to him. You won't regret it." Larkin patted her leg and stood.

"Like you know stuff."

"I know you." Her friend winked and disappeared left. A moment later, the whoosh of the bathtub hit her ears.

When her cup was nearing empty and the tub nearing full, Larkin reappeared and motioned her forward. What was it with the people in her life and their belief in the healing powers of a bath? Gen placed her cup on the counter next to Owen's abandoned breakfast and followed Larkin into her candlelit bathroom.

"The bath won't make you feel better, but it'll make you look a little better."

"Gee, thanks."

"Anytime." Larkin kissed her cheek. "I have to catch a meeting. I wish I could stay, but between the conference, tech meeting, and Morocco I've missed a lot of important things at the office."

"Oh, shit. Morocco." Gen was a shit friend. "How was it?"

"Don't worry about it. You've been dealing with your own mess." Larkin slipped out of the bathroom but stopped short. "Talk to him, and I'll talk to you later."

"Yes, Mom."

"Bath now." Larkin grinned and closed the door.

TWENTY-SIX

MIRACLE OF MIRACLES, the bath had helped her appearance. The puffiness around her eyes had subsided, getting her hair wet forced her to deal with it, and she'd even put on the barest of makeup as an incentive to keep her emotions in check. She pulled the door closed to her apartment, locked it, and headed for the elevator in a better head-space than she had any right to expect. Larkin was right. All she had to do was bare her soul as she never had before. If anyone in the world deserved the best of her, Owen Graham did.

A smile pulled her cheeks, surprising the hell out of her. He would forgive her because he was a great man, a man she loved without equivocation.

The phone vibrated in her briefcase.

Gen slipped it from the pocket, hoping it was Owen

and knowing it wasn't. She would have to make the first move in that game of love.

Janney's sweet and sassy picture filled her screen. As promised, Gen answered. "Good morning to the best assistant anyone could ever have." She stopped in front of the elevator and depressed the call button.

"Who the hell is this, and what have you done with my Genevieve?" Janney groused. "That broad doesn't know how to answer a phone, and she certainly doesn't know how to give a proper compliment to the woman who's kept her business rolling in her absence."

She winced. It was true. All of it. Owen had only been looking out for her; he'd only been exercising sensibility when he refused to get her those phone records or have Perry followed.

"Janney, I know I've been shit lately, and I'm so sorry."

"If you really were sorry, you'd have been here at eight a.m. for the deposition you scheduled."

"Shit," Gen hissed. She pulled the phone from her ear and looked at the time. 10:58 a.m. "I'm on my way in, and I'm back mentally and physically. I promise."

"I've heard it before. Ever since the murders."

"Now I mean it." Gen glared at the elevator. It never took this long unless someone was holding it. She scanned the corridor. It was midday. The apartment building was full of young and older professionals, which meant they were all being super responsible at their respective jobs and the freaking elevator should have been there by now.

"You better because my hands are tired of typing up extensions on all your cases."

"I'm back, Janney, and better than my pre-murders self."

"Better? How?"

"I'm in love, Janney."

"Now I know I've dialed the wrong number."

"Right." Gen headed for the narrow staircase at the end of the hallway. "I'm leaving my apartment and heading your way. I'll explain everything when I get there."

"Uh …" She'd never heard the old bat without a well-crafted comeback.

"How would you feel about a new firm?" Gen asked, taking advantage of her bafflement.

"You've worked your ass off here," Janney whispered.

"I know, and I can no longer do that for a man I don't believe in."

"Oh thank God, you're not insane."

"I wouldn't go that far." Gen chuckled.

"The man is absolutely twisted in the head and even more so since the trial. He gives me the creeps."

"Oh, Janney, why didn't you tell me?"

"I did, you little twit. You wouldn't listen."

"Fair point." Gen shoved through the door into the stairwell. "We'll get everything in order, and I'll put in my notice by Friday."

"Friday is tomorrow, crazy girl."

"I know."

"Christ, you are insane," Janney drawled.

"Just steer clear of Perry. I'll be in soon."

"Steer clear? He's not coming in today. Oh, you weren't here when he made his announcement yesterday."

The metal door slammed behind Gen. Her skin jumped off her skeleton a good foot before it snapped back into place.

"Announcement?" she wheezed.

"Yeah, he gathered everyone into the conference room yesterday afternoon and told us he was out early for the weekend because he was moving out of his Eastside home."

Gen stalled on the top step. She'd thought he'd been moving out furniture to make room for his girlfriend.

She'd been wrong. "Moving where, Janney?"

"Hell if I know. Out of that horror show set, which he should have done months ago, if you ask me."

"You don't have a clue?"

"No, child. Can you hear?"

"Just fine. I'm on my way. See if you can find some boxes."

Janney huffed. "I might have liked you better before your new self-discovery."

"Bye." Gen ended the call and shoved the phone back into the pocket of her briefcase. She gripped the railing and sucked in a deep breath. The air was stale and over-powered by a cleaner.

Perry was moving. Good. She was moving, offices at the very least. Maybe she needed a fresh start with apart-ments too. But damn, NYC real estate was a beast and her place was great. Even the stairwell was a stunning shade of white with marble-topped posts and intricate met-alwork on the banister. She took the steps one at a time, careful with her fancy stilettos. Since her usual commute had been shot to shit this morning, she'd opted to grab an Uber. She'd planned to make the request in the elevator. It wouldn't take them long to respond when she got to the lobby.

Halfway down, the pressure in the stairwell shifted as a door whispered open. Gen slowed, waiting for the rushed sound of footsteps or the whack of the door back to its frame, but neither happened. Her lungs burned. It was only then that she realized she'd been holding her breath like a scared little girl. Maybe Janney was right in calling her child.

She shoved the hair back from her shoulders, lifted her chin, and continued cautiously. Maybe the elevator was broken, and they hadn't had time to post it. When she reached the second floor, where she'd thought the door had opened, no one was in sight.

Gen shook it off and rounded the last of the levels. She had three doors from which to choose.

Small, overpriced parking garage. Mailroom. Lobby.

She turned left, away from the other two doors and hurried toward the lobby's rear entrance. Her hand reached for the latch but stalled. There it was again. The pressure change.

Gen turned in time to see meaty knuckles sailing toward her face.

TWENTY-SEVEN

THE PAIN CAME IN WAVES. **Large,** violent waves intent on drowning her jerked her left and right. They threw her deep into unconsciousness and then shoved her to the edges of a plight with which she was not yet ready to deal. For with it came the battle for her life.

A battle she was sure to lose.

Awareness slipped away for a time but hung within her reach, should she care to try, but trying only brought heartache. Nothingness was easier. She drifted in it, content, until one thought thrust her to the present.

Owen.

Her eyes shot wide, causing a stabbing sensation to rock her frontal lobe. Nausea knitted her intestines. Still, she searched. Owen was nowhere to be seen. Nothing was. Darkness swallowed her whole.

Fear froze her spine.

Where was she? What was going on?

A wretched sob threatened to ignite.

Gen mentally backpedaled in search of numbness and freedom from the horror and agony, but there was none to be had. The ground beneath her vibrated.

She blinked, and firecrackers exploded inside her skull. Her body lurched, trying desperately to escape the torment. A hard, uneven barrier connected with her shoulder. The incendiaries inside her thought it was Independence Day. They spewed off another round. Grimacing, she reached for her head only to find her arms bound behind her back.

Horror was not a movie, but life. A life she wasn't long for.

Both her arms had been folded into 90-degree angles, placing her hands at either elbow. Whatever held her together was tight and winding, starting at one elbow and working its way to the other. Even her fingers were held prisoner.

Air whooshed in and out of her lungs so quickly that what little stability she possessed slipped from her trapped grasp. Her neck relaxed, and for the first time, she really felt the ground beneath her. It was hard but hollow. Panic ebbed and observation took its place. The edge of her chin scraped across the itchy fabric. Course fibers akin to an outdoor rug caressed her. Its base rumbled and shifted slightly.

A cargo truck, maybe.

Gen lie on her side in the fetal position. If she stayed there, she'd most certainly die. Surely, there was a weapon or something she could use to free herself. First, she needed to assess her surroundings. She'd feel with her feet. She pushed out with her legs. At least she tried. They were bound at the ankles.

Do not panic. Do not panic. Do not panic.

With each silent order, Gen sucked in a deep breath and let it out slowly. As ordered, the mania hovering just in view didn't obliterate her vision. Not that she could see anything. Actually, that wasn't completely true. A small, oddly shaped T glowed only a couple of inches above her stomach.

It hit her in a rush.

She was in a trunk.

Perry put her there.

The memory of a heavy fist rushing toward her flashed. She hadn't had more than a fraction of a second to react because it'd been aimed at her face. Judging by the insistent pounding on the right side of her head, he'd missed obliterating her cheekbone, but the immense force had done the job of knocking her out.

Where was he taking her? What would he do with her when they arrived? Images of Pamela and the children's bodies floated front and center in her aching brain.

He wouldn't do that. If he did, they'd know it was him right away. Unless … What if he cut a deal with Sanchez?

Nausea hit her full force.

The car turned, and she shifted her head ever so slightly, away from the latch. No matter what Perry had planned, the end game was her death.

Death wasn't on her agenda today, and she'd do anything she could to keep it that way. She was the baddest bitch attorney in NYC. If she couldn't bargain for her life, then what good was she?

Who was she kidding? Perry was past words. He'd tried them. He'd tried wooing her with the offer of partner. He'd tried changing the course of her thoughts. He knew her too well to know she'd retreat from righting a wrong, especially one in which she'd had a hand. Which was exactly why hers were tied behind her back.

"Fuck you, Perry Carter." Her words were a mere breath, but her body rattled with rage. Rage helped keep the terror at bay. Rage got her mind churning. She used her legs and head to search the interior for anything; a sharp edge, a hook, a crowbar. Anything to get off the bindings. There was nothing. Nothing.

If she had her phone, she could call Owen. And tell him what? She could tell him that she was sorry. She could tell him to come get her. She could tell him that she loved him.

The thought of him kept her moving, thinking.

Gen rolled onto her belly and up onto her left side. She threw her elbow and her bound hand toward the emergency latch. Her elbow hit the metal trunk lip where the bottom of the lid met the car. It sent a shockwave of pain through her network of nerves already tingly from lack of circulation. She gritted her teeth and used the pinkie of her left hand, the only digit she could get free, to feel for the thin plastic T.

Only cold, unfeeling air met her efforts.

She tried again and again, but the latch was too high. Gen drove her hips and shoulder into the itchy carpet in an effort to lever her arms higher. The edge of her pinky hit something. Every muscle in her core strained. Her pinky hooked onto the curved plastic.

Elation and triumph filled her to bursting.

In one swift move, Gen strengthened her pitiful grip, released her core, and pulled with everything she had. The latch slipped out of her finger as though the latch and its cord were attached to the immovable center of the Earth.

Attempt after attempt left Gen's pinky raw. Sweat coated her skin. A mop of hair clung to her face. With each bit, she tried something new; grabbing higher, grabbing lower, grabbing with the rope. She panted on the floor of the trunk and wondered how much longer she had. New York had a ton of traffic, but it was only so big.

Gen flopped onto her belly and rolled to her right, facing the maddening latch. She wormed, insect style toward the latch for a better look. There was nothing to see but the eerie green glow of the T. It did little to illuminate anything around it. Not even the structure beyond a thin metal cord. She crunched high, opened wide, ignored the hair that slid into her mouth, grabbed one side of the T between her teeth, and pulled.

The latch didn't budge.

Could a safety feature such as this be turned off or was her bite that puny?

On the third attempt, the curve of the T slashed the inside of her cheek. It didn't stop her from trying several more times. She spit blood left, right, and center. If she didn't make it, at least there would be a trace of her to nail this fucker. Owen would look at Perry first. Whether he cared for her or not, he cared about justice most of all.

She shoved off the side of the trunk, giving herself more room to think.

The brake lights.

Using the flats of her feet, Gen searched for the corner of the batting that lined the trunk. Where the fuck were her shoes? If he was smart, he took them because they made excellent weapons. If she was lucky—and it was clear she had shit for luck—they fell off when he stuffed her into the trunk and would leave a clue to what happened to her.

When she found the corner, she used her heels and kicked downward at the liner. With only a few more kicks, the stiff fabric crunched into the bottom corner.

If only she had shoes.

Gen pulled in a full breath, levered her feet back, and fired them in the direction of the taillights. Skin was no match for metal. Something pointed and sharp sank into the meat on the ball of her right foot. A howl flailed in her throat. It gurgled and whined through her teeth. She arched and strained against her bindings. The wild inside her unleashed. Her body thrashed. Her muscles swelled and contracted. Her mind raged.

Too soon she was drained. She lie limply on the floor. The low, steady rumble of the road lulled her for a long time. They drove for too long. Minutes piled into an hour or more. Maybe less. It was hard to discern time in the dark with pain and fear as her only companions.

She needed water. She needed light. She needed a knife.

She needed to get her shit together or she'd never have any of those things ever again.

Ever so slowly, Gen lifted her feet toward the taillights or where she expected them to be. Instead of ramming, she used her toes like fingers, examining the network of metal, screws, and cords she found. Using her left foot, the one not leaking blood onto the carpet—score another one for trace evidence—she wound a clump of wires between her toes.

Drawing a steadying breath, Gen confronted the fact that she'd either unhook the taillight, she wouldn't, or she'd electrocute herself. She pulled. The wires gave in a whoosh.

Her elation lasted only a second before attempting the slog of pivoting her bound ass from one side of the trunk to the other. One dead taillight was nothing. Two just might draw someone's attention.

It was a long shot, but it was all she had.

Sabotage of the second light took far less pain and time than the first.

Gen rested on her belly for a few seconds before the car shifted from the consistent, rather straight path it'd been on for so long. It veered, then rolled to a stop. After several starts and stops, turns and revs, it slowed once more.

Then the engine died, and every cell in Gen's body went cold.

The hum of a garage door added to the chill.

Footsteps whispered across the smooth concrete. The classic tap of wing tips drew closer with every heartbeat. Oxygen turned from gas to a solid in her lungs.

Without any more warning, the latch she'd been trying to unfasten for the past hour gave way. Perry stared down at her with eyes she'd never before seen. Any trace of warmth and familiarity might have never existed. They were dark, dead.

Gen didn't bother with words. They would do nothing but end her then and there.

He leaned over, revealing long latex gloves that covered the rolled sleeves of his navy dress shirt. The top button of his collar was unfastened, and there was no tie to be seen.

Her body shivered in small, betraying jerks.

Perry rolled her to her stomach, grabbed the rope at her wrists and the one at her ankles, and lifted. Her shoulders wrenched. Her back bowed. Without a word, he pulled her from the trunk and carried her through a bare garage and into an open door of a house she'd never seen.

The house in which she'd die.

He heaved her through vacant marbled hallways, into a far bedroom, toward an open closet lined with black plastic.

Gen kicked and screamed. She pulled and twisted. The reaction wasn't logical. It was an involuntary and futile fight for life ... because his steps didn't falter.

TWENTY-EIGHT

A TRILL SOUNDED OUTSIDE THE CLOSET. The tap of his gentle-men's shoes echoed in the hallway once more, drawing closer. Gen curled into a ball in the darkness. The rage that kept her going while locked in the trunk was gone. Black plastic and unfailing bindings had fleeced her to the bone. She gritted her teeth and waited.

As it had once before, the closet door opened wide, and light seeped in. Perry stood there, obliterating the sunshine. A clump of rags hung from his right hand. Beads of sweat gleamed on his brow and neck. Wet hair clung to his forehead. His navy shirt had turned darker still with wide rings around his armpits. The color matched his empty eyes. He tossed the rags at her feet, just as he'd tossed parts of the trunk liner next to her an hour or so ago.

She was the largest scrap in his trash pile.

The realization stole her breath, just as the impact of the floor had done when he'd thrown her inside like a piece of trash. Every nerve in her body vibrated with horror.

Perry's hands rose to his shirt and unfastened the top button, and then the next, and then another.

The horror had just begun.

"No!" Gen struggled to shimmy herself anywhere, much less to the back of the closet. Once she got there, where would she go? Still, she had to try something. "No, Perry! No!"

A coy grin curved his lips. His gaze sparked the barest hint of life and narrowed. His hands continued working, unfastening the buttons at his cuffs. He pulled the shirt from his pants, slipped it off his body, and threw it at her face. The thin material blinded her. She threw her head back and flopped. Dread grew long talons and slashed wildly, releasing her greatest fear … that she would learn of her sister's heaviest burden firsthand.

The shirt fell to the side, clumping beneath her chin.

His zipper whined open.

"No! No!"

Perry toed off his shoes and kicked them at her. One hit her hip, while the other lobbed over her. He shucked his pants and silk boxers in one motion, standing before her naked and glaring.

She screamed and strained with everything she had left.

The pants flew through the air and landed atop her. His laughter was barely human. A jackal's pitched call.

"I wouldn't rape you, Genevieve. You're a slut, which is worse than a whore. At least they do it for money."

"The man who slaughtered his family wants to get high and mighty? Right." Her laughter was manic and shrill. "Did you know she was sleeping around, or did you kill her to make room for your own side piece?"

"You knew she was fucking someone else?" Perry's body didn't shift in the slightest, but the emptiness of his eyes filled to bursting with pure fury.

"Not until you got rid of her things. I went through them and found pictures." She grinned, happy to have one on him even if it was insignificant.

His eyes sparked, and his jaw worked. Whatever his thoughts, they remained locked inside.

He closed the door, leaving her once more in the dark. Moments later, the whoosh of a running shower grazed her brain. The fog of fear with which he'd left her with was hard to see through.

Gen's convulsing eased only when she heard the water turn off. Her ears pricked toward the door, intent on every noise. She tried pairing each sound with an action. Brushing teeth. Combing hair. Dressing. Walking.

She shivered in the knotted mess of his clothes.

Steps brought him past the closet and down the hallway. The trill sounded as the door opened and then closed once again. Every muscle locked up.

Was this the end? Would he come back with a knife?

Gen held her breath.

The garage door rumbled up, the car engine growled to life, the growl grew quieter, and then the garage door rumbled closed.

It was a trap. It had to be a trap.

Trap or not, this was her only chance. If she could find a phone or get out, she could save herself.

First things first.

She rolled onto her belly, wedged her chin into the plastic, and pulled her knees to her chest. Everything hurt, but none of that mattered. She levered her weight back and stretched upright for the first time in three or more hours. It took all of her balance and will to push to her feet, but push she did. The tops of her legs quivered. Sweat dripped from her chin. Knots in her back tightened, but she hopped toward the small bulge in the plastic sheeting.

Gen dragged her shoulder along the wall until she found the lump and shoved it up. Light filled the small walk-in. Her lids rebelled against the brightness. She used every second to survey the interior, making her eyes burn and water.

Black hugged the walls from the ceiling where it was taped to the door. No gaps. No hangers hanging from the rods affixed to the parameter of the wall. The plastic even extended under the door on the floor. The door. There was a small nubby catch at the top of the frame, but nothing else to secure the door from her side. She hadn't heard him slide any locking mechanisms into place when he'd slammed it shut.

Try it already!

Using her shoulder once more, she tipped her weight against the pristine white wood. When gravity took hold, the door swung wide, and she tipped forward out of the closet toward the ground. Several frantic hops kept her upright.

Her gaze skittered left and right in a panic. She expected to see him sitting on the end of the perfectly made bed with a ten-inch blade in hand. He was not. There was, however, a landline telephone on the bedside table at the far side of the large room. The old-fashioned phone had a stiff metal cradle, a sharply carved handle, and a rotary dial. A contemporary remake of old technology in a modern house.

The point of her chin was too blunt to dial the most basic number. 911. Her tongue? She wasn't willing to chance it.

Gen hopped toward the bedroom door. If she could get out of the house … The flashing light on the alarm system's pad stopped her cold. She couldn't open the knob with one pinky, much less reach and deactivate an alarm system for which she didn't know the code. Besides, she didn't know where she was. He could have brought her to a remote house in a pine forest. Even if she managed to get out, she might die of exposure trying to find help.

No. The phone was the quickest way to help. But to use it, she needed hands.

She looked wildly around the room. Her gaze snagged on the lever handle of the closet. There was no way for her to untie the knot or knots. Hell, she didn't even know how many there were or how they were connected. All she knew was they were wound tightly and were extremely secure. If she could get the end of the handle hooked around the end of the rope, then she could pull it from her bicep and over her elbow.

It was worth a try.

Streaks of red on the floor grabbed her attention with both hands. Blood. It was smeared in a small dotted semicircle on the floor. Her gaze dropped to her feet. The sight of them bound and crimson pooling between her toes elicited a wretched scream that she clamped inside her lips. Silent sobs wracked her already unsteady frame. Tears slid down her cheeks and onto the now chipped polish on her toenails.

If she made it through this, she'd never let Owen Graham out of her sight. In the deepest darkness of her misery, he was all she wanted. Action was the only thing to get her to him.

Gen hobbled to the door. Her back screamed. Her legs quaked. Her torn foot throbbed. Still, she squatted to reach the handle. Each time she attempted to wedge the rectangular edge of the grip between the rope and her skin, the door shifted, her muscles gave out, or the unforgiving metal stabbed into her tender skin. Each time she missed, a sob hiccupped from deep inside her chest. But each time, she straightened, drew a breath, changed her angle, and tried again.

Finally, after what felt like a hundred attempts, the rope caught, wedging the metal handle between her elbow and middle finger. She shimmied to the left, shifting the rope ever so slightly toward the apex of her elbow. That tiny taste of success drove her to yank harder, to shift more. She shifted so much her feet slipped on the slick floor, and she toppled forward, face first.

At the last possible moment, she turned. The floor met her shoulder, sending a shot of electricity to her brain stem. It radiated down her arms in sizzling waves. She flopped onto her belly and heaved in breaths, praying the nausea that assaulted her belly would soon pass. The rope gave, not a lot, but enough that she wiggled her uninjured shoulder.

Freedom!

She jerked and flailed with all her strength. The unforgiving loops grew slack. Her useless arms flopped to her sides. A million tiny ninjas stabbed her with a million swords. And it didn't matter. She was free.

The rumble of the garage door sliced her hope open wide.

"No."

Gen flopped onto her back and snapped her gaze toward the hallway door Perry had carried her through. It was so close.

She pushed up with numb arms onto her bottom. A knot dug into her ass cheek. There was a bedroom door, but it wouldn't hold up to Perry's size and strength. Her gaze found the phone. With her feet still bound, it was so far away.

Whether she went left or right, she had to move. Gen grabbed the rope and launched herself toward the closet.

She pressed near useless arms onto the ground and army crawled onto the black, crinkling plastic. Nausea returned. Full force. Her heartbeat thundered like a summer storm in her ears. Faster and mightier, it boomed. Just inside the relative safety of the closet, she remembered.

The blood.

Gen grabbed his navy shirt and scrambled on her belly to the center of the semicircle. In frantic waves, she wiped, but the dried blood remained, highly visible on the light floor. She spat. She spat and wiped, so near to madness, they'd embroider a straitjacket with her name on it. Or a headstone.

The *beep, beep, beep* of an alarm code being entered blasted inside her head like the detonation of several A-bombs.

Whether she'd gotten it all or not, Gen scrambled back inside the closet and closed the door behind her. She pressed the soiled shirt to her mouth to muffle her breathing. Her ears strained to hear Perry's entrance.

Again, the trill announced the devil's arrival. His shoes tapped and … was that … the unmistakable rustle of grocery bags. Not just one. It seemed that there were several. They banged into themselves or the wall or Perry, crackling like crazy. The door slammed into the frame. Her prison rattled.

The closet light!

Gen launched herself at the light switch and caught it on the first try, setting the tomb back into darkness. She scrambled to the back of the closet, gathered the trash around her, and listened. There wasn't a whisper of sound.

The rope might as well have been around her chest, cinched as tightly as it could be.

She grabbed the large loop of rope in her right hand and placed both arms behind her back. Tears fell from her eyes. Her shoulders shook as well. One turn after another, she wound the binding around her forearms and laid in a ball with her fake trappings hidden behind her.

Tears took hold, and she cried. For how long, she didn't know.

Outside the closet, all was quiet, but she didn't dare move.

Minutes later, hollow metal clacks of what sounded like pots rang in the distance. The whoosh of water accompanied it for a short time. Then the unmistakable sound of a knife being filed on steel echoed. It shot dread to her raw and broken heart.

She waited for footfalls that didn't come. Instead, the measured and consistent chop of vegetables followed.

Was he cooking?

It didn't make sense. Sounds of meal preparation, sounds she'd never made herself but had heard a thousand times in the finest of New York restaurants continued for the better part of an hour.

A last supper?

Then the footsteps came. She hunkered back, hiding her rope and his bloody shirt with her body.

Even though she'd known he was coming, when the closet door burst wide, she jumped. She didn't have to fake fear. It was as real as any she'd ever known.

Perry held a water bottle in his left hand. If he was planning to feed her and give her water, then he planned on keeping her alive for a little while. More time meant more chance to escape.

Then he pulled a pill bottle from his pocket.

"You will swallow these, one way or another. I personally hope you'll choose the hard way. It'll give me a chance to break a few of your ribs. Or there's always the chance that the water will drown you. Pick your way fast." He assessed at the Rolex on her wrist. "I'm having company in an hour."

Gen levered herself up, using her shoulder and the

wall.

Perry opened the bottle.

"What are they?"

He glared at her and took a step inside her prison. If she were brave like Larkin or skilled like Libby or big like Owen, she'd try to fight him. It was her life, after all. Genevieve Holst was none of those things.

But she was clever.

"Untie my hands, and I'll take them for you," she sniveled.

Perry grabbed her chin, pinched her mouth, and poured in half the bottle. When he placed the water to her lips, she swallowed like a good little girl, knowing these things would kill her.

TWENTY-NINE

TIGHT FABRIC TORE AT THE CORNERS OF HER MOUTH. The knot he'd tied just over her tongue tasted of cologne, chalky residue, and blood. She picked at the large tangle, wishing she had light. It wouldn't help her see what she needed to, but it'd help erase Perry's maniacal face from her mind. In the dark, she remembered the dead expression that froze his face forever in her horror as he'd said, "If you throw them up, you'll suffocate from your own vomit."

Her stomach recognized the amalgamation of toxins inside her belly for what they were. It churned and gurgled, ready to eliminate the vile mix. Panic closed in around her like a coffin. She clawed at the gag. Breaths came in weighty yet shallow heaves.

Gen opened her mouth as wide as she could and yanked the fabric down. It caught on her lower teeth. She grabbed at it near the back of her neck and jerked. The binding loosened just enough that she pulled it to her neck and rolled onto her knees. As she had some hundred times as a self-tortured teen, she shoved three fingers into the back of her throat and emptied the contents of her stomach without a sound.

Never had she thought that terrible habit would prove helpful.

She shivered head to toe for several minutes, her body revolting against the day's events. Things like this didn't happen. Only she knew that wasn't true. They happened all the time.

When her body stopped convulsing, she pushed herself to the far side of the closet and shoved onto her bottom. Gen pulled her feet close and started working on the ankle bindings. If she hadn't fought so wildly to free herself from them in the trunk, the knot wouldn't be so stubborn. It took too long. She took too long. Panic threatened to consume her whole. Owen's smug mug showed up in her mind's eye, erasing Perry. Owen's gaze was kind, warm, and loving.

Slowly, the chill fled. She focused on the feel of the rope, the intricate loops, and slowly fed one back through the first knot. Then another. Then another. Then she was finally free … ish.

Gen rubbed at the bruised skin, ushering blood flow back into her extremities until it returned. She eased to the closet door and pressed her ear to the cold wood. The confusing sounds of dinner prep filtered through the solid material. She pushed up onto her hands and knees and slowly stood for the first time in hours. How many, she didn't know. Five? Seven?

She pressed her hand to the door, held her breath, and—

A chime sounded through the door, coming from deep

in the house.

Her hand jerked from the door, and she clambered back into the corner. The tempo of her heartbeat pitched toward the heavens. It rattled in her chest. Her hands shook. Had he rigged an alarm since he'd been back? It hadn't gone off the last time she fled the prison.

Gen's gaze locked on the door, or where she knew the door to be. If he came for her, she'd fight. She didn't know how, but it was the only way to survive.

The chime rang again and then once more. It was too sporadic to be an alarm, too singsong. She exhaled a long breath and then stepped back to the door in time to hear the slide of a lock and the snick of another. The sounds came from far enough away that she went for it, pushing on the closet door.

It popped from its frame, and Gen shoved from the confines. If someone was at the door, she could signal or call for help. She closed the door behind her, making certain to walk on the heel of her cut foot, and slid along the wall toward the bedroom door.

The now familiar trill of a door being opened sounded.

"Hello, Perry." A woman's voice … no, the woman's voice—the one from the rear office elevator and the one from the phone and the one Perry admitted to having an affair with—echoed loudly through the sparsely furnished, modern house.

"Millie." Perry's voice was clipped. Cold.

Sharp heels created a tattered tap through the entryway. The front door closed.

"You're early," Gen's capturer, her would-be murderer groused.

"I've waited long enough, don't you think?"

Millie's clacking steps brought her into the kitchen, Gen judged. She held her wild hair back from her face and peeked her left eye around the jamb. The door to the garage was five yards away on the right. Just across from a closed door, another door a yard past it was open, and then the corridor opened up into what she assumed was the kitchen. A shadow appeared on the floor, and she jerked herself back into the corner.

"I suppose you have waited long enough." His voice sounded so close Gen's skin attempted to crawl from her body.

These two sounded nothing like captivated lovers. They sounded more like civil enemies.

"Great. Where is it?" Millie wasted no time making requests, though Gen had no idea what she wanted.

"Patience isn't your strong suit is it, Millie? Lucky for you, it's mine." There was a pause, then a sound of two bottles clinking, and then the trill, and another she didn't recognize. A sliding door maybe. "Please, join me."

"It's cold out there," Millie protested.

"It would be without the fire and the heat lamps. With them, it's quite nice."

"What's all this?"

"This is an accord. Since we're going to be in a lifelong relationship, it should begin the right way. Civilly. With a meal, don't you think? It's nearly finished."

"Civilly? Let's hope you're not trying to grant me the same kind of civility you showed your wife."

Despite it all, Gen expected Perry to rebuke the comment.

"Red or white?" he asked.

"Whichever is unopened."

His chuckle slipped down the corridor and down Gen's throat. The clack of heels faded. And then the sound Gen hadn't recognized lit a memory. That rolling whoosh was the ocean. She held her breath and peered around the corner once more. Sure enough, past the kitchen she caught a glimpse of a sliding glass door, a patio strung with the zig-zag of large bulb strands, and the grassy top of a dune.

The clack returned, and Gen jumped back. Perry's wing tips followed.

"Thanks for the offer, really, but I don't like scallops or pasta or you for that matter. I'll take the money and be on my way."

"Is that so?" Perry's voice dropped an octave, showing no form of emotion even if it was anger. "I don't like you much either."

"Great. Then we're on the same page. The money." Millie grew either bolder by the second or more terrified, using the added bluster to hide it.

"Dinner first," he demanded.

"It's poisoned, isn't it?" Millie charged.

"Why would I kill you?"

"Because it's cheaper than paying me."

"You're forgetting that you didn't threaten to black-mail me. I offered to pay you. Besides, it's not cheaper to kill you if it lands me in prison. You have what we call plausible deniability on your side. If you die in my pres-ence, after the trial I just survived, no jury on earth could be convinced of my innocence twice."

"You killed the children." Her whisper unsettled Gen more than Perry's laughter.

"You killed those children, Millie."

"No!"

"What did you think would happen when you black-mailed Pamela?"

"I thought she'd pay me to keep quiet." From the sound of her tapping shoes, she paced. "A few years into my marriage, after several miscarriages, Daniel and I found out that I could get pregnant, but I'd never be able to carry a baby to term. I suggested adoption, but he wouldn't consider it. I suggested a surrogate, but no. He always said it wasn't a big deal. If we couldn't have a baby naturally, then we weren't meant to. Work kept him busy. We traveled. Life was good."

"When I found out about Pamela, I was angry, hurt. Even then, I was willing to make my marriage work. He served me with divorce papers the following week. Based on our prenup, since I never bore him children to take control of his flourishing investment business, I got nothing. After twelve years of marriage, I had nothing." She growled through the sobs. "He thought I'd take it on the chin as if I'd had the affair."

Perry barked a laugh. It quickly turned into a series of belly rolls.

"No, you didn't take it on the chin. You set in motion a chain of events that shattered his legacy."

"I didn't know—"

"That I'd recognize the red in Pamela's eyes and root out the cause of her sorrow? You didn't count on me finding the pictures you sent. My wife with her lover."

"With my husband," Millie shouted.

Sniffles filled the empty space. "I never meant for …"

"Oh, you wanted me to hurt those kids, his little bastards."

THIRTY

GEN WIPED AT THE TEARS that had slid down her face while the two callously spoke about their cheating spouses and the children they produced. Everything was upside down. For the first time, it all made horrible, twisted sense.

Perry killed any woman who betrayed him. Pamela hadn't just taken a lover; she'd had another man's children and passed them off as Perry's. The ultimate betrayal.

An entire bottle of vodka was gone by the time Perry and Millie finally took their plates onto the patio and started on the wine they'd left there. The phone beckoned Gen as it had for the past hour. There had been no way to ensure they wouldn't see her cross the doorway, so she'd stayed glued to the wall. She eased her head around the doorjamb. The two sat at a small dining table facing one another, neither facing the house.

Finally, a break!

Gen dropped to her hands and knees. Her entire body screamed. Ignoring it, she crawled until she reached the nightstand. Without thinking of all the things that could go wrong, she grabbed the receiver and put it to her ear.

An obnoxious dial tone had never sounded so good. Gen pressed it to her ear in an effort to muffle the noise.

911 had been engrained in her since law school, but she found herself dialing another number she hadn't realized she'd memorized.

Why was she wasting her chance at survival on a man who probably wouldn't answer her call, especially if he knew it was her calling. This wasn't her number, which lowered the chances of him answering even more. 911 always answered, and still she wound the numbers into the circular face.

The line clicked over.

A ring.

"Graham?" He barked the most beautiful word she'd ever heard.

Emotion clogged her throat threatening to strangle her. "Hello?"

Gen slapped her hand over her mouth. She drew in a breath and shoved back the sorrow.

"Owen, it's Gen."

"Where are you?"

"I ... I'm sorry for earlier."

"Forget it, Gen. Tell me where you are?" His voice was pitched and worried. Why was he worried?

"I don't know exactly. Perry ..." She suppressed a sob. "He attacked me at my apartment. He took me."

"Genevieve, listen to me."

"Okay," she whispered.

"You've been gone for nearly eight hours. Since we figured out you were gone, Douglas and I have been pooling resources to find you. Tell me what you see, hear, smell."

"I'm in a house. It's modern, on a beach. I don't know which one, but I can hear it. He had me tied up in a ..." That didn't matter right now. "I got free. He's here with the woman, Millie. I thought she was his girlfriend, but she was the wife of Pamela's lover. She tried to blackmail Pam, but Perry found the pictures. He found out the children weren't his. Both were Pamela's and Millie's husband's."

"Why is she there?"

"Money."

"That woman knew Perry killed Pamela and the children but did nothing to out him. She's not your ally."

"I know."

"Are you injured?"

"I'm okay."

"Good. Gen, we were on route to one of three Hampton's properties Perry bought through a shell corporation. Before the trial even ended. The police have been dispatched to the others. I'm tracing your call now. If you have to leave the phone, don't hang up."

"Okay."

"Can you get out of the house?"

"I don't know. The garage is the closest door to the bedroom I'm in, but if he looks to the left just a little, he'll see me."

"What about a window?"

She looked around the room at the large paned windows on the far wall. Each of them had connection sensors near the latches. She remembered the trills when the doors opened. They probably worked similarly on the windows.

"They have sensors."

"Another door?"

"I don't know. I think they all have sensors. They make a sharp sound when they're opened."

"Fuck. What if you create a diversion? Open the door,

but instead of running out, hide inside the house. Help will be there soon."

"I'll try something."

"As much as I want you to stay on the line, you're exposed. Either get out of the house and hide in the bushes or divert and hide."

"Owen?"

"Yes, Gen?"

"I love you."

"Don't you dare say that to me right now," he growled.

She pulled the phone from her ear and stared at it.

"Gen? Gen?" His voice bellowed from the series of tiny holes. As ordered, she placed the handset on the nightstand and used the table to push to her feet.

There was no time to catalog her hurt feelings. Too many other things hurt. Too many other things took precedence. She shuffled to the corridor and peeked out. From this vantage point, she could only see the back of Perry's ego-inflated head through the sliding glass door.

She eased out of the bedroom slowly, shuffling along the wall on her heel and one good foot to the garage door. Her hand reached for the knob but stopped partway there. A deadbolt secured the door. A deadbolt that required a key to unlock it. Her gaze searched for a hook, an end table with a little bowl, the frame.

With no key in sight, Gen pressed on toward the kitchen. Maybe he'd left them on the counter. Maybe she could find the front door, and maybe it would be a levered deadbolt.

And just maybe there would be peace on earth.

Hysterical laughter bubbled in her throat.

Fear cemented it inside.

Her ankles quivered with every step. Sweat slicked her brow, yet soul deep cold made her shiver. The draft coming from the open sliding glass door didn't help. That wasn't true. It allowed her to hear the edges of their now slurring conversation, which let her know exactly where they were.

At the mouth of the kitchen and a small sitting area, Gen stopped and assessed the surroundings. A cozy fire burned in the hearth along with a massive one burning in a fire pit on the edge of the patio. A marble island split the kitchen into two sections. It offered a barrier to keep her cloaked from Perry and his unwitting victim. Another counter mirrored it against the wall that she peeked around.

Nowhere, not on any surface, did she see a set of keys, a single key, or even a briefcase.

Gen hunched low, steeled herself, and crawled into the kitchen. Slowly, staying low, she opened the top drawer of the first set she reached. It was the first drawer anyone arriving at the house through the garage would come to, so it offered the best chance of holding a key. She reached inside and slid her hand along the smooth bottom. One inch at a time, her fingers fumbled over nothing. The drawer was completely empty. She tried the next drawer, working her way down to the lowest. All of them were empty.

She shifted to the island, opened the top drawer, and plunged her hand inside. Her middle finger collided with a hard and round item. It shot from under her touch and careened away.

Her hand lurched after the object, wide and flat, desperate to catch it before it created a ruckus. Straining to stay out of sight, she pressed the crook of her stiff elbow onto the drawer's metal track. The thing stopped, wedging between her pinky and ring fingers.

A slight sigh exited her lips until she realized what she was holding. She pulled the empty pill bottle from the drawer and stared at the label.

Lorazepam

2-4mg at bedtime

2mg tablets, quantity: 100

The most upsetting part was the bold name at the top of the label.

Genevieve Holst

She clutched the bottle so tightly it bit into her flesh. Her hand shook in a steady back and forth. It wasn't possible. Sure, she'd never used the drugs prescribed to her before the start of the trial, when nothing in the world made sense no matter how her brain tried to twist it in the darkest hours of the night. This bottle was in her medicine cabinet in her apartment. She'd seen it yesterday when she'd opened the cabinet to brush her teeth before returning to bed, to Owen.

Were they there this morning?

Her emotions had been so all over the place, she couldn't be sure. She'd blindly reached for her toothbrush this morning.

The neatly stacked file flashed in her mind. Her gaze bloated. Her heart sank. Perry had stolen the full bottle from her medicine cabinet. Perry had rearranged the files, not Owen. Perry had been inside her apartment with her and Owen.

Knots bound her stomach. Icy, gooseflesh plagued her skin.

Perry hadn't emptied the bottle into her. He'd stopped with a quarter of the bottle remaining.

Gen replaced the bottle, closed the drawer, and scooted to the far end of the kitchen. She peered toward the front door. It stood thick and silver with a keyed deadbolt similar to the one on the garage door. Her gaze swung toward the sliding glass door, the open door.

Millie sat with near-perfect posture on the plush patio chair. Her legs were crossed at the ankle like a class act. A goblet of red was perfectly poised in her hand. The words exiting her mouth, though, were as misshapen as Perry's moral compass.

"I agree." Perry extended his glass across the table. "To a long and prosperous partnership."

The woman's, "Here, here," sounded more like a, "Huh, huh." Dilated pupils zeroed in on the wine Perry held. She leaned forward, reaching her glass out as though his were a moving target. Her light hip slipped off the edge of the seat, and she tumbled forward.

Perry caught her goblet and placed it on the table in a smooth motion. Millie careened toward the ground but caught the edge of the sturdy chair at the last minute.

"Whoa there, Millie." He stood and offered her his hand as though he were a gentleman. As though he were the man Gen always thought him to be. "It looks like you could use a breather."

"I ... fi ..." The words that came out of her mouth were nonsensical.

He ignored her attempt at communication, grabbed her upper arm, and hauled her to her feet. His smile was familiar. Gen had seen it right before he attempted to kill her.

"This way, Millie. The salt air will do you good." Perry ushered her to the back of the patio.

The woman tried to speak but made less and less sense.

Perry stopped at the edge, where the sand met the concrete, and pulled something out of his pocket. He set it on the concrete barrier, before adding another item, and then ushering Millie toward the roar of the ocean.

Gen stared at the open doorway, at her freedom for several heartbeats, used the counter to pull herself upright, and hobbled as fast as she could out the exit. The crackle of the fire and the whoosh of the gas lamps cocooned the intimate space in excessive warmth, given the low temperature outside. She slunk low at the patio wall.

His phone, wallet, and the keys she'd been so desperate for sat on the small pillar.

Gen strained her ears for Perry or Millie. An eerie quiet, save for the constant sway of the ocean, eroded Gen's determination to run and hide.

If she hid, Millie would die. The woman had made a deal with the devil, so it was an earned outcome. Yet she couldn't make herself flee. She'd left her sister in the clutches of evil, and in the end, it had killed her.

It wasn't her fault.

It wasn't Evangeline's.

It had been her uncle's. It had been Judge Faraday's. Two men who should have protected her and her sister, instead betrayed them in the worst ways.

If Gen hid, Millie would die. She could live with the woman's death. Millie seemed all too comfortable to live with the deaths of Pamela and the children. Gen could not live knowing she could have helped. She would not live with Perry getting to commit another murder.

THIRTY-ONE

"911. WHAT IS THE ADDRESS OF YOUR EMERGENCY?"

"I don't know. My name is Genevieve Holst. I've been abducted by Perry Carter Jr. He has another woman; first name Millie. He's taken her to the beach behind the house to kill her."

"Miss Holst, is there a—"

"Tell them to look for us on the beach." Gen set the phone back on the pillar and pushed to her feet. She shuffled to the dinner table, palmed the sharpest thing on the table—a fork— turned, and hobbled as quickly as she could toward the beach.

A slatted teak path led the way to total darkness. The uneven surface bit into her heel and slowed her already pitiful progress. Inky night, not yet tinted by the moon or even a hint of stars, crowded in.

Something caught Gen's toe, throwing off her precarious balance and pitching her forward. Her arms windmilled, and her legs sputtered beneath her. Long grass tickled her fingertips as she fell. Sand caught her, splayed wide. Air evacuated her lungs. She rolled into the fetal position and gagged.

Seconds passed. Oxygen refused to return.

From a distance, Millie's high-pitched shriek carried on the ocean's breeze. It attacked Gen's psyche as though it were an entity in itself. In it, she heard her sister's sobs. She heard Pamela's wail and her children cry. She heard her own howl for justice.

They begged her to push, begged her to fight.

Gen shoved to her hands and knees. Her fingers sifted through the sand in a frantic search for the fork. Hiccups of air anointed her lungs. Cold leathery material grazed her hand. It had a round edge and a pointed bottom. Millie's shoe. Gen must have tripped over the other one.

There wasn't time for forks or shoes. There wasn't time for regrets or hopes.

She shoved from the soft ground and ran.

Sand swallowed her feet to the ankles. The tiny granules filled the cuts on her foot. It stung. Her lungs did too. She breathed deep, churned her legs harder, and strained her gaze in search of anything discernible.

The whittled edge of Millie's protests provided her only beacon ... until she rounded the dunes. A hint of moonlight in the distance reflected off the water, giving the surface an ebony glow. It wasn't much light, but it was enough to cast a horrifying silhouette.

Millie lie on her back on the fluffy sand. Perry stood over her, shaking his fists in the air. He faced away from Gen, letting the ocean swallow his tirade. The woman's cowering was the only sign of life.

He squatted next to Millie.

Gen waited for his hands to lock around the woman's neck. They did not. He scooped her into his arms and walked slowly, methodically toward the waves. Millie's sobs met her ears, but the woman no longer fought.

Perry was scary enough to make someone welcome death. Fear threatened to turn the unstable ground to quicksand. A moment later, rage flushed Gen's cheeks. It warmed her chest and drove out all uncertainty. She ran for Evangeline. She ran for herself.

When she came within spitting distance, she leaped. She locked both legs around Perry's middle, one arm around his neck, grabbed his nose with the other, and heaved. His arms flung wide. He teetered. Gen tightened her grip to keep from falling off. Millie hit the ground with a thud.

"Run, Millie! Run!" Gen screamed the order directly into Perry's ear.

The woman scrambled to her feet, took two steps, and swiftly fell on her face.

"Run!"

Again, Millie stood, ran a few steps, and scuttled sideways.

The drugs.

"Vomit, Millie! You have to throw up now, then ru—"

A sharp pain cut off Gen's order. Perry had grabbed a handful of Gen's hair and pulled. Her eyes watered and instinct told her to move toward the agony to lessen it, but this was life and death. She grit her teeth against the hurt, shifted her fingers up from his nose to his eyes, and dug in.

Millie continued to flee in short rises and erratic falls. Only she wasn't retreating toward the house. With every jarring motion, she moved closer and closer toward a heap of jagged rocks some might call a jetty. To Gen, it was death personified, especially if you couldn't put one foot in front of the other.

Gravity shifted. Gen wasn't falling, but Perry was, hard and fast. The ground met her back, and Perry met her front in an abrupt collision.

Her breath stayed for once, but her grip gave way.

Perry's head lifted, and then quickly shifted direction. Too quickly. With her hands by her sides, she couldn't do anything to stop the sharp, jarring impact of his skull to hers.

What little vision she had in the dim night blurred.

"Fucking bitch." Perry shoved off her and stood. "I should have killed you in your apartment like I planned, you and that big bastard you were screwing."

The words hovered above her, flitting like butterflies, their wings just out of reach. Footsteps crunched away. His ghostly shape drifted off in the distance.

One by one, the words locked into place. Little by little, his form became solid.

He might have killed Owen while in her house. He was going to kill Millie on the beach.

Gen's legs refused to respond to her demands. She watched, unable to move as Perry stalked a fumbling, frantic Millie toward the rock outcropping.

Run toward the house, Millie! Toward the house!

She tried to lead the woman to safety, but her words were garbled and malformed. Her head throbbed so forcefully she'd swear she felt an ever-widening cracking of her skull just above her right eye. Next, she tried pushing up onto her side, but like the other woman, her arms flailed about, bathing her in the sand.

For every step Millie took, Perry took four. He strode past Millie as though she wasn't even there. As if he no longer cared to end her life.

For a second, Gen swore she heard sirens.

She looked over her shoulder toward the house but

saw no lights.

When she looked back, Perry was there, standing over Millie's cringing frame. His arm lifted high into the air. His hand looked larger. He clutched a rock in his grip.

"No! No!" Her voice cracked in time with Millie's skull.

Time and again, he hit her until she slumped on the sand. He threw the rock into the water and grabbed her ankle. In the slow, methodical steps she'd seen before, he dragged her lifeless body across the uneven jetty.

Perry would kill her next. He'd tried once. This time, there would be nothing peaceful about it.

Would he beat her to death?

Hell, he was halfway there. Her head hurt so much.

There had to be something she could do to save herself. She looked left and right. There was only sand and water as far as she could see. And rocks. She couldn't even make herself look in that direction.

Just sand and water.

Sand.

In her effort to move she'd nearly coated herself in the stuff.

Gen scooped armfuls of sand onto her belly and dug her legs into the powder. She pulled handfuls onto her hair, and then covered her chest. She closed her eyes and mouth, turned the injured side of her head into the sand, and covered the rest of her face. Sand crowded her eyelids. It caked around her lips. It wasn't much, but it was dark, and it was her last chance at living.

She didn't see Perry throw Millie's body into the ocean, though she knew he had. She didn't see him turn his back on the woman's body without a second thought, but she knew he had. She didn't see Perry return to the beach for her, yet she knew he would. She just had to wait him out.

Hurry, Owen.

Too soon, his feet crunched the sand within the too close distance of her muffled hearing. Closer and closer he came. The grinding of the sand overpowered the ocean. It became absolutely deafening. Like an avalanche pacing itself but promising to crush her. It overwhelmed all other sounds, all other thought.

"Genevieve!" Perry bellowed her name so loudly, she nearly jumped. In fact, she wasn't sure that she hadn't. Every muscle inside her was wound so tight. She was as brittle as a dried sand dollar. Had she jumped, she might have shattered.

"I didn't see you run to the house, so you can't be far. Show yourself, and I'll end it quickly."

She held perfectly still, only sucking in a quarter of the oxygen her body demanded. Because of the way she'd positioned her head, the sand wasn't shooting up her nose.

"Genevieve, if it makes you feel better, I'll take no pleasure in killing you. You know, I tried to save you. I really did. You're just so goddamned stubborn and kept poking your nose where it didn't belong."

Once more, she thought she heard a siren. In the sand, every sound was muffled except for Perry's ever closer steps.

"Why do you think I only used pills on you? If I'd wanted to kill you, I'd have bashed your skull in like I did to Millie or carved your heart out like I did—"

The whoop of sirens was unmistakable now.

They'd cut off Perry's tirade and seemed to funnel from every direction.

A brightness filled her lids. Light, like she hadn't seen in what seemed like days, filled her soul. They flashed and whirred.

Perry's heavy footsteps retreated one, two, three steps and more.

That's right, Perry, run.

Unable to stand the utter fear a moment more and unwilling to let a dead-eyed, cold-blooded murderer get away, Gen shook the sand from her face and turned her gaze to the house. A sea of stunning blue lights flashed at its side. Her voice would not reach them, so she had to.

Gen pushed up onto her elbows. The world shimmied around her but settled. Her entire body hurt, but it didn't matter. Help had arrived. She dug one forearm into the soft ground and pulled her legs to her chest.

A large hand clamped down on her shoulder. In her dreams, it was Owen, come to rescue her. In reality, every finger bit into her skin so hard that she knew it was Perry, and he'd come to finish the job. Another hand banded around her wrist, wrenching her from the small divot she'd created.

"No!" Gen screamed. She jerked left to right, up and down, trying to break his hold. He dragged her wild form closer and closer to the water. Vibrant lights flashed just yards away. She shrieked for help, just like Millie had. Look what good it had done her. None at all.

This called for decisive action.

She grabbed a handful of sand, called out his name, closed her eyes, and chunked the heap in the direction of his face.

His steps faltered. He sputtered and cursed. Then a sharp wing tip wedged its point between her ribs. Pain reverberated through her side. A fevered expletive exploded from her lips, followed by another.

He dragged her another few yards.

Regardless, fear fled, and her fight returned with a demonic vengeance. If she was going down, it'd be in a blaze of glory with his blood on her hands. There would be no question who'd murdered her.

Gen jerked left and sank four fingernails into the wrist pinching her shoulder. She dug in and twisted as hard as her short nails would go.

Perry released her.

Another kick assailed her ribs. This one took her breath but not her rage. He hauled her up by the neck and lifted her high. She stared into his eyes. They were as black as the night sea.

"You—"

She spat in his face. Fuck him and his words.

He turned and heaved her through the air.

Gen landed chest first on the sand. Her hands splayed wide. Frigid ocean spray misted her knuckles. A wave soaked her pant leg. She pushed up to her hands and knees. Something hard shoved her over, sending her back to meet the next wave. It soaked her spine and splashed at the back of her neck.

Perry was there. He loomed over her for a beat. The widest smile curved his lips. His hands grabbed a fist worth of her wet slacks, locked tight, and slung her once more.

Before she could orient herself, he grabbed her slacks again. She cocked her free leg back as far as she could and hammered it into his arm.

"Have it your way," he spat.

His knee dropped atop her chest, leveraging a hammer of his own. Pressure built in her abdomen. She punched at his leg. It was the only thing she could reach.

Shocking cold water rushed over her face and chest.

It nearly triggered her instinct to gasp, but the body's response to water took over, locking off her airway. The ocean rose up her breasts to her belly, and then slowly, oh, so slowly receded.

Salt water burned her nasal passages and ran up her throat. She sputtered and heaved. She gagged and gasped. She bucked and clawed.

Perry's knee pressed harder against her chest.

Another wave crashed, stealing her sight. It robbed her of her chance at breath. Her heels dug into the sand.

The moment the wave left her face, she begged for oxygen. His leg more than the ocean denied her that basic human right. He smiled down at her. It was not the last thing she wanted to see in this life.

Gen planted both feet in the grooves she made and thrust her hips toward the dark sky.

Perry pitched forward and careened over top of her. He splashed into the oncoming wave. She crawled onto her side and gulped in air. Her brain screamed retreat, but her body could only shiver and gasp.

His arms reached from the depths, latched around her middle like a sea monster's tentacles, and pulled her into the water.

She'd used it all, everything she possessed, to conquer Perry. There was nothing left. As he walked her farther into her grave, she knew true defeat. She'd pushed away her friends and Owen. She'd pursued the devil for justice, and she was about to lose. But … in the fight, she'd learned how to forgive herself. In the fight, she'd learned how to overcome the demons of her past. If only she would have gotten a chance to use them in her future.

What a future it would have been.

THIRTY-TWO

ICY COLD ENVELOPED HER COMPLETELY. Perry's harsh grip held her head under the rocking tide. Everything inside her said fight, struggle, live. There was so little oxygen in her system. The more she fought, the quicker she'd die.

Gen remained limp. If he thought she was dead before she actually was, there was a tiny chance she'd survive for a few minutes in the frigid water.

She could do this. She could survive, just to spite Perry. And see him brought to justice.

Pressure collected in her throat. It multiplied in her chest, a wholly different experience from the crush of his weight. Her lungs burned. She refused to give in to the struggle that clawed at her brain, demanding action. Action! Action!

Her skin itched. Her ears rang.

Then, like a wave, the panic washed away.

Peace filled her lungs, imbued her veins, and soothed her brain. Worry slipped away.

Like a flash of lightning to a tinder-dried forest, tranquility turned to melee.

The hands that had held her down yanked her from the water and slammed her sore shoulder into the shore. A wave crashed into her bottom, shoving her higher onto the hard sand and into the fiery air. Each gulp scalded her throat and lungs. A sickening sound accompanied each frantic breath.

The thwack of flesh meeting flesh repeated time and again.

Gen's brain connected the sound to Millie's death. She covered her head to brace from the impact of a rock only to realize nothing came.

Her gaze searched the dark horizon for Perry. What she saw didn't compute.

He lie on his back with his arms splayed at his sides. His legs shot out wide. An unnatural slack in his neck allowed his head to snap from one side to the other with every impact.

Owen straddled Perry, pounding his fist into her captor's face.

Again and again, Owen's body coiled and struck.

Fury and anguish she'd felt too intimately radiated from the man she loved. Perry's hollow eyes registered nothing. If Owen continued, they never would.

Gen dug her elbows into the sand and shoved herself from the edge of the water.

"Don't kill him!"

As much as she wanted him dead, she wanted him stripped of everything he held dear and imprisoned for the rest of his years.

As though she'd pulled out his battery, Owen stopped

and sagged over Perry's unresponsive body.

She collapsed onto the sand, wanting in the fold of Owen's arms more than she even wanted justice for Pamela and her sweet children, Perry's or not.

A swarm of officers and first responders crowded her. Their flashlights blinded what little vision she had through the sand and salt. They poked and prodded and jostled her about before scooping her off the beach and shoving her into a helicopter.

THIRTY-THREE

GEN LOOKED FROM ONE GREAT FRIEND TO THE NEXT. Larkin stood on the right side of her hospital bed with her cold little hand on Gen's forearm, dodging all the cords and tubes. Marlis hovered over Larkin's shoulder quite literally clutching her pearls. Libby glowered at the foot of her bed with her arms crossed over her chest.

"Did the three of you take turns blowing my nurse to get back here?"

"No." Mar released her pearls and slapped both hands to her hips. "He has one of those rubber wedding bands. You told me they were off-limits."

Libby's bright, wide smile bloomed under a robust laugh. Her tightly wound arms gave.

Larkin gently squeezed Gen's forearm and offered a more reserved smile.

"I never expected you to listen." Gen's voice sounded as though it'd been run through the shredder.

All three girls reached for the cup of water on the side table. Larkin reached it first and administered the life-giving liquid.

She'd only been awake for a couple of hours. Awake and alone. The fuzz had hardly lifted from her brain. Certain things were still muzzy, but the majority, the horrible things, the things she wished had vanished with the apparent brain swelling, remained in high definition.

"Earlier, I heard the nurses talking about an Irish lady threatening to castrate him if he didn't let her back here, and I knew it was Janney."

"She's a spitfire. It's a wonder you two can work together." Marlis shook her head.

"I don't understand either, but it works." Gen grinned. The cut in her mouth burned. She winced.

"No blow jobs or castrations necessary," Larkin reassured her.

"We didn't even have to threaten to buy the place and fire him." Marlis grinned. "I would have, but we had the bad broad with a badge." She hiked a thumb at Libby.

Lib nodded. "I have to catch a flight in ..." She assessed her watch. "Sixteen minutes. I promised that if I didn't get back to see you before I left, I'd accidentally on purpose place him on the sex offenders' registry."

"Can you do that?" Mar awed.

"Nope, but he doesn't know it." Libby winked.

"Where are you going?" Gen realized how long it'd been since she'd really talk to any of them.

"A remote cabin in the Blue Ridge Mountains."

Gen's heart skipped. "You found him."

"Fuck, I hope so." Libby sighed. "If not, I'll have spent a ton of federal money and resources on a dead-end and probably lose my job or, at the very least, get demoted to the internet fraud department."

"You know you found him." Larkin grinned.

"I know." Libby flashed her teeth in a sinister grin. "And I'm running point."

"I'm so happy for you." Gen reached a hand toward her friend.

"I'm so happy to see you and know you're still in there." Libby wrapped her warm hand around Gen's chilled one.

"Every sassy bone except one. That asshole cracked my orbital bone. I don't know how sassy it is right now." Gen wiggled her eye and wished she hadn't. "How bad does it look?"

"Like you went rounds with the devil himself and lived to tell about it." Libby kissed her hand and pressed her cheek to the back of it. "You know I'm here whenever you need to talk about the bad stuff. I can take it."

"I might be ready after you go get the bad guy." Gen squeezed her hand and then released her. "Now, go. You're already going to miss your flight."

"Douglas is flying me to Quantico, but I do have to go." Tears filled her friend's eyes.

"I'll be here, and Perry will be behind bars," Gen promised.

"Hell, yeah." Libby hugged the girls and left the small room.

Her exit left them in a vacuum. When Larkin and Marlis left, and they would have to leave soon, she'd be forced to deal with the aftermath of the past two days. Yes, the bad guy lost, but the not so good girl lost too. She'd lost big time.

"He called Douglas the second Janney reported you missing," Marlis said.

"He?" Gen asked because she didn't want to make any more assumptions. She'd assumed that he would have wanted to know how she felt. She'd assumed that he would have wanted to comfort her after the hell she'd been through. She'd thought he'd have forgiven the horrible way she'd acted toward him. Nope. Nope. Nope.

"You know exactly who," Larkin chided. "Douglas said he'd never seen a man more determined to find someone."

"He's a helper. It's what he does." Gen shook her head and instantly regretted it. Her brain throbbed so much that she thought it was about to force her eyes from their sockets.

"Owen might be a great police officer, but he's not going to break laws and work for, what are we at, sixty plus hours straight for just anyone." Larkin smiled. "I know from experience that only the ones who love you will do those things for you."

Where was her rule-breaking champion now? He wasn't in the room, and he was a badass with a badge.

"He's been by to check on you twice," Marlis offered.

"Am I that transparent?" Gen closed her eyes and stilled the negativity. She was alive. There was no room for negativity. How ungrateful.

Larkin eased onto the edge of the bed. "That's not a bad thing."

"Tell me about Morocco." She blinked the moisture from her sore eyes.

"I'm going to go out and see if I can trade my spot with Janney before she actually castrates the nurse." Marlis scooted around to the left side of the bed and pecked Gen's cheek.

"Thank you, Mar."

"Thank you for fighting. I don't know what we would have done without you." She kissed her again and then left the room.

"Morocco," Gen demanded.

"It was the best, craziest trip I've ever experienced."

"And you've been on a ton of great trips."

"Right." Larkin waggled her brows. "We got to Temara and spent one hot—melt your toes off—night and day in an exotic villa on the beach. Then we traveled at sunset blindfolded. Me, not him."

"What?"

The door to the small sterile room opened. Her nurse's curly blond head of hair preceded his scowl that despite its intent was the sweetest she'd seen. "Miss Holst, your friend needs to leave. Visiting hours for actual family members are over."

"Chuck, if you want her to go, and you want to maintain your clean record, I suggest you leave and let her finish her story."

"Hold that over me. Fine!" He threw his hands in the air. "I have morphine to hold over you."

"Now, Chuck." Larkin threw a small stack of puke pans at him. "Don't get mean. My friend has had quite a traumatic experience, and she needs her friends. We are her family."

"She's right." Gen shooed him out with her IV free hand.

Lucky for him, he listened.

"Back to the blindfold," Larkin huffed.

"I've never been blindfolded out of the bedroom. Was it scary?"

"No. It was pretty hot out of the bedroom, actually."

"Hmm." She pressed her sore lips together. "Something to try post-recovery."

"We arrived at some kind of makeshift headquarters in the middle of Rabat, the capital. There were men everywhere with machine guns, grenades, and knives strapped to tactical clothes. Women too. There were two of them who made me want to crawl into a corner they were so badass, but they were so nice too. Everyone was."

"Who were they?" Gen begged.

"Uh, can't say, other than Beckett is one of them, he looks too good in battle gear, and they've tried to recruit Owen for their team. Though, team is a mild word for what they are."

Gen just stared at her, shocked not to have the most interesting story in the room. She probably still had the most horrifying one. Woo, yay for her.

"They geared up, and Beckett stuffed me in the back of a Humvee with a vest and helmet. No one else needed a helmet." Larkin threw her hands up as though that was the most distressing part of the whole scenario. "Anyway, we rolled out in the dark, four military grade vehicles loaded with weapons and warriors. We got to an airstrip outside the city, and they surrounded the place."

Larkin clutched Gen's knee. "I should have been scared, but I was so excited. With Beckett, with all of them, I felt safe."

Just knowing Perry was in custody made Gen feel safer than she'd felt ever. Maybe it had something to do with the whole forgiving herself bull too. She wasn't quite ready to delve into those emotions.

"They ordered me to stay put, and then they were off, kicking in doors and lining people up on the ground with their hands behind their heads. Then Beckett brought him out with a bloody nose and tears on his cheeks."

"Bronson?"

Larkin nodded. "Bronson Beauregard." Her smile was so wide. "They extradited him to Africa where he's facing genocide charges and so much more. His accounts have been frozen as well as the family's business accounts since it was financed with corrupt money."

"Oh, my goodness." Gen grinned, despite the pain it caused.

"We've captured the bad guys." Larkin grabbed both her hands.

"Yes, we did."

"They can't hurt us or the people we love ever again."

"No, they can't." Gen squeezed her hands.

"Best of all, we get our sassy, slightly slutty—no shame—redhead back." Larkin shook a triumphant fist in the air.

Gen released her friend's other hand, placed both of hers on her lap, and let out a shuddered breath. Lord, her chest ached. "Well, Larkin, on top of the brain swelling and bruised lungs, the doctors told me I've caught a terrible disease."

"Oh God, Gen! What?"

"Monogamy."

"You little shit." Larkin's laughter filled the room.

THIRTY-FOUR

GEN WOKE REACHING FOR THE LOVELY LITTLE MORPHINE button the nurse had given her after running out Larkin and Janney and after getting the okay from her neurologist. Christ, she had a neurologist. Fuck, she was in the ICU. At least she wasn't in the morgue. Though, the simple current of blood through her veins wouldn't hurt if she were dead. She shifted farther back in search of the drip.

The unmistakable warmth of the human form cupped her from head to butt to toes. Between the irritating beeps of her monitor, the soft, long breaths of deep sleep tickled her ear. Owen's scent permeated the room, vanquishing the antiseptic stench with virile masculinity. She'd only met this man seven months ago. They'd only had sex for one amazing night, yet she'd been more intimate with him than she'd ever allowed herself to be.

It was foreign. It was terrifying. It was right.

She skipped the morphine, opting for his hand. It was warm and limp until she placed hers inside it and pulled it to her chest. His thick fingers curled around to her palm. He gently pulled her closer. She snuggled into his protective frame. Something inside her uncoiled. The thrashing in her brain eased with each passing heartbeat. As she slipped back into sleep, she realized that he provided more comfort than any illicit drug. She'd tried more than a few in her day. They'd all been easy to quit, but she knew Owen Graham wouldn't be.

When she woke again, her warmth and comfort had vanished, and a chill washed over her. Aches in places she hadn't realized existed burned with new fury. Her lids shot wide in search of her favorite drug, but he was nowhere to be found. The morphine drip was in the clutches of her death grip. She depressed it several times, releasing its allotted amount into her system, but it wasn't enough.

The small, unfeeling room seemed more vacant now than it had when she'd first come to after having been rendered chemically unconscious for the helicopter ride. They'd said she'd been frantic, trying to find someone. And here she was again, searching. There weren't many places he could hide in a hospital room.

She gave up before she started screaming for him like the maniac she was and pulled the covers over her face to block out the unyielding fluorescents. The covers smelled of him. Her eyes closed. She'd made her bed, and she had to lie in it until they discharged her. Then Owen wouldn't be able to get rid of her. Not without a court order. Judging by his presence in the night, he wouldn't go that far. It was up to her to show him how much he meant to her by opening—not her legs—but her heart and mind.

Her heart lurched, and her palms slicked with sweat.

This love business wasn't easy.

The door clicked open.

"I need to be discharged today. Oh, and the morphine has to go with me."

"If you leave, who'll play tic-tac-toe with me?"

Gen pulled the blanket from her face to see Owen shove the door closed with his foot. His boots, jeans, and T-shirt had been traded for a blue suit with pinstripes, a crisp white shirt, and sharp leather shoes. He set one of the two coffee cups he carried on the bedside table and then plopped the legal pad he'd stuffed under his arm onto it as well.

"You think you're up for it, French pressed, dark roast?" Owen teetered the cup in his hand. "After she lost our arm wrestle, the doctor said you can have one cup, but she didn't budge on outside food just yet. I think she was hungry." He shrugged. "The double breakfast I just gave her makes up for threatening to arrest her for obstruction and throw her into a holding cell with sex traffickers last night. Right?"

"I'd call it even." Gen reached for the liquid gold he offered. He placed the cup in the fold of her hands and encased them in his own grip. "Thank you."

"The doctor should start rounds as soon as she finishes, but there's no way you're leaving the ICU until tomorrow, and that's assuming all your scans come back clear."

Gen drew the cup to her lips and sipped gingerly. The hot liquid charred its way down her ragged esophagus. It hurt like the devil. At the same time, it gave her a sense of security and familiarity she needed more than she needed the pain to go away. Pain tempered with a bit of morphine let her know she was alive. For Owen, she'd live through anything.

"You good?"

"Damn near perfect." It wasn't a lie.

Owen took a step back and drew a deep breath. "We had a press conference announcing Perry's arrest for the murder of Millie Bradberry and your kidnapping, assault, and attempted murder with more charges pending. As soon as the computer tech gets finished with his and Millie's computers, we'll get him on collusion and extortion. I was executing warrants on the three properties he purchased through the shell corporation yesterday. Last night, I executed one on his home in the city, as well as his mother's home. There was a Jaguar with a crushed front end in the garage. By tomorrow or the next day, we'll have enough evidence to arrest him for the Renly double murder."

Why was he info dumping? Sure, this was all information she liked knowing, but right now, the most important thing was letting him know how she felt. "Owen."

"You're never going to believe this." He held up two hands. "We're hours away from arresting his mother on murder charges."

"What?" Gen jerked forward. Everything pulsed with agony. Her head raged. Her ribs, wrists, and ankles throbbed. Hell, even her fingernails ached. A breath hissed through her teeth.

"Easy." Owen rushed to her side. He reached out to steady her but stalled as if not knowing where to touch her. There weren't many places that didn't hurt. He grimaced.

"I'm okay. I just got carried away." Her eyes did the pleading that her throat couldn't manage while dealing with everything else.

"We found a bottle of arsenic and a recipe for a laced rum runner in Beena Carter's closet. Along with a stack of photos of Perry Carter Sr. in the naked embrace of another woman. The judge okayed the exhumation of Carter Sr. this morning, and a crew has been working since eight."

She glanced at the clock and saw that it was half past nine.

"It seems raging jealousy runs in the family."

"More like narcissism and psychopathy," she corrected.

"Smarty-pants." His thumb soothed a path over the hairline above her right eye. His jaw clenched, and his head shook.

"Looks that good, does it?"

His touch withdrew, and he stepped back. The all-too-familiar crinkle of plastic sounded a moment before he pulled a pack of peanuts from his back pocket. He ripped the top open, poured half the contents into his palm, and tossed them inside his mouth.

They had so much to talk about. Well, she had so much she wanted to talk about with him. It seemed he wasn't ready to tackle it.

He finished the package and threw the plastic into the small garbage can near the sink. The silence with him in the room was worse than being trapped in that closet all alone. His long legs stretched into a slow pace back and forth from one side of the tiny room to the other. As he walked, his thick fingers worked into two solid fists.

When he started the sixth lap, she broke.

"Owen?" Her voice sounded as though it'd been shattered and glued back together. In so many ways, it had.

"Why'd you make me stop?" His steps ceased, but he still didn't look at her. He hung his head low. "I would have killed him." Breaths heaved in and out of his chest. "I wanted to. I still do." Slowly, he approached the foot of her bed. "If I'd killed him, it would have been over. He never could have hurt you again. He could never get off on a technicality or the strength of his attorney."

"You're not a killer."

"I would have been." He nodded. His bright blue eyes

looked more vibrant and fiercer than she'd ever seen.

"And I'd never ask you to do that."

"You'd never have to ask."

"I love you, Owen." His lips parted, but she lifted her hand. "You might not want to hear it, and you might not feel the same way I do anymore, but that's okay. Because of you, I'm here. Because of you, I can face Perry in court. I can banish him to a lifetime of hell, and I will with your help."

He rounded the bed and grabbed her hand. Angry purple and black bruises stained his knuckles. Blood dried and created scabs atop two. Her heart clenched.

"You're on my team, now?"

"I'm on your team." She wanted to tell him that she was on his team and wanted to stay there forever, but that was a lot to throw at him. She'd already tossed the L-word around twice, and the first reception hadn't been great.

"For how long?" he asked.

"As long as it takes."

"For what?" His brow hiked.

"For you to love me."

He sat on her bed and pulled her other hand into his. Every one of his knuckles boasted a scrape, bruise, or cut. She squeezed his hands tight but wanted nothing more than for him to wrap his arms around her and never let go.

"I didn't want you to tell me you loved me when you were at that house."

"No kidding."

His cheeks balled, and a smile stretched his lips. At the same time, moisture gathered in his bright eyes. "I thought it meant you were accepting your fate. I thought it meant you weren't going to fight." He dropped his head into their joined hands and pressed his face into her belly. A ragged breath shook his frame.

"I'm not a fighter." She hugged his face in her hands.

"But loving you meant that I would fight as long as it took."

Owen straightened and wrapped her in his arms. Everything hurt, but he was the drug she craved like none other. "God, Genevieve, I love you more than anything or anyone ever." His lips brushed her neck, her cheek, and her lips in the sweetest kisses. He levered back and found her gaze. "Does this mean you're not on my team now?"

She grinned at the man she loved. "It means I'm on your team forever."

"Hell, yeah." Owen braced her face in his hands and made gentle love to her mouth so well that she forgot all about her pain. He levered back with a serious expression. "Except for tic-tac-toe. It's every man and woman for themselves."

It was the first of many laughs to come.

THIRTY-FIVE

A KNOCK SOUNDED ON THE DOOR. "DELIVERY." It wasn't home, but it was a regular room where her friends and lover could come and go without any threats. With all the deliveries, the room seemed even smaller than her room in the ICU. She'd already shared several with the children's unit.

"Come in." Gen turned down the television. The high tempo and even higher pitched voices pouring from the anchors of E! News was the closest thing to current events she could get without a mild panic attack. She'd face him in court, but she didn't want to hear anyone's twice chewed and regurgitated story of the events she'd survived.

The door opened, and a massive bouquet of white roses preceded a human, gender and identity to be determined. There had to be four dozen long-stemmed roses in the oversized vase.

"Wow." She slid the legal pad littered with cat games of tic-tac-toe, pen, and remnants of the delectable breakfast Owen had fetched them before he headed in to dispense more justice.

The delivery person set down the arrangement and then stepped from behind it. Roderick, Beena Carter's driver and lover, smiled down at her. Regret set off a flash fire under her skin. Owen had wanted to place an officer outside her room, but she'd dismissed the need instantly. And now she'd pay for it.

Both of the man's palms shot up. "Sorry. I'm so sorry." He dropped to both knees beside her bed. The deep voice Beena loved so much held more than a hint of emotion. "I don't mean to scare you. I just …" His smile and the tears in his eyes confused Gen further.

"What?"

"Thank you!" He clamped his hand together and shook them at her. "Thank you!"

"Why would you thank me?"

"The police arrested Beena today for murder."

Owen had said as much. He'd been optimistic, hoping the results would have come in the day of the exhumation of Perry Carter Sr. In truth, it'd been three days, and he'd been anxious to get it done. "I know, but why would you thank me?"

"Because you took down Perry, they found out about Beena, and now I get my life back."

Gen stared at him in disbelief. Her own tears surprised her. She reached for his hand and urged him up. He was a beautiful man, but he'd been a beautiful man in a beautiful prison.

"Really?" Tears flooded her cheeks.

"Yes." He nodded vehemently. "My mother cleaned for Mrs. Carter as far back as I can remember. She had emigrated illegally from Columbia and had me here, giving me the gift of citizenship. I never knew my father. She refused to speak about him, but I think now it may have been ..." His gaze hit the floor, and his shoe rubbed across the linoleum tiles.

"Perry Carter Sr," Gen gasped.

He winced and nodded.

"I never had any brothers or sisters. When my mother died, I was just a boy, so Beena and Perry took charge of my care. They paid for my education through private tutors. They fed me and gave me a place to live. I missed my mother, but I had no one else." He stared into the near distance.

"One night, when I was seven, Mr. Carter came to my room. He told me to pack a bag and keep it quiet. He'd said that after work the next day we would take a secret trip, but I couldn't tell Mrs. Carter." His hand clutched his heart. "I didn't breathe a word about it. Not until this day."

Gen squeezed his hand.

"The next night, Mr. Carter died at the dinner table. She told me I killed him. She threatened to tell the police if I didn't give myself to her. I never remembered hurting him, but I was so young. I didn't know. All I knew was she had money and power. So my tutors stopped, but my education in the ways of the rich and twisted began."

"Roderick, I ... I had no idea. None." Her head shook. Her mouth gaped.

"No one did."

"How can I help? You have no one. I can find you a place to stay, a job, whatever you need." Her heart ached for this kid, who'd had to grow up too soon with the devil as his guardian.

"Beena taught me well how to manipulate. I used it on her system of payment. I can afford college and a place to live."

She smiled at him. "Amazing."

"It's all legal," he assured. "Beena's not so much. I pointed your friend, Owen, in the right direction."

"Wow!" The wane word didn't fit too well. "If there is anything I can do to help, please don't hesitate." She released him, tore a piece of paper from the pad, and wrote her phone number next to one of her and Owen's games.

"I may ask you for an internship in a few years. I'm interested in studying law."

Gen beamed, and then her smile faltered. She couldn't work at Carter, Cleary & McMellon, not that it would be that after Perry's conviction.

"What's wrong?" Roderick asked.

"Nothing really." Her smile returned, bigger and stronger than before. She handed him the paper. "I'm going to start my own firm. It's what I should have done a while ago. It's going to take me a few years to build up a clientele, but I should be ready whenever you are."

"Perfect." Roderick bowed to her. "Thank you so very much. Thank you."

She watched him leave and quietly close the door behind him. "Thank you." She hadn't saved her sister or Millie, but she'd saved Roderick, and best of all, she'd saved herself. Her laugh was barely contained, just like the joy that filled her heart.

"Who was that, and what did he do for you?" Marlis shoved through the door with her thumb hiked toward the hallway. "You have Owen. Don't be greedy."

"Don't be ridiculous. It's nothing like that."

"Sounded like that." Mar held up the bag of seductively smelling food. She headed for the table with the oversized load of flowers but redirected to the foot of the bed.

"It's fine. You can set it there. I don't know where else we could put it." Each of her friends had taken turns tending to her. She ate up every minute of their attention.

Mar ignored her and held the bag above the bed.

"Hello?" Gen waved. "You can ..."

She noticed Mar's gaze fully fixed to the television screen. Marlis never watched TV. Not sports. Not awards shows. Not the news. Most certainly not mindless blather.

"Volume! Up!" Mar demanded.

Gen scrambled for the remote, kicked up the volume, and looked at the screen in time to see a picture of a stunningly gorgeous brunette in jeans, a black shirt, and tactical boots with FBI in bold white font across her hat. In one arm, she clutched a long rifle with one more in each hand. She exited a shipping container with hundreds and hundreds of rifles stacked against its walls and two more containers open on either side. The picture resembled Libby with the curves, the look of determination, and triumph. But this was E! News, entertainment news. Surely, it was a picture from a movie set.

"That's not Libby," she reassured Marlis.

"The latest viral photo has garnered over three million likes on Instagram. The image even caught the attention of blockbuster director Victor Juliet, who shared the photo with the caption, "I think I've found my next action star!" Could this image get the real-life FBI agent out of the field and in front of the camera? Find out more after the break."

A commercial about makeup remover filled the screen. They both gaped.

"Victor Juliet!" Mar squealed.

"No, it couldn't be ..." Gen knew it was Libby even as denial poured from her lips.

"That was Libby." Marlis dropped their lunch on Gen's toes.

"I know." She looked at Mar, ignoring the precious pantsuit she wore or the food she'd brought to share.

"She's going to be so pissed." Marlis bit her lip.

"Pissed. This photo, if it really is that popular, could ruin her career."

If you enjoyed *Who*, please consider leaving a
review on Goodreads and your
favorite book vendor.
If you enjoyed *Who*, check out *Why* …

HOW : SNEAK PEEK

HOW
STALKER SERIES NOVEL 3

A crime scene photo gone viral. A fanboy turned stalker. How far will one FBI agent go to protect the ones she loves?

FBI Special Agent Libby Irish thrives off the constant pressure of proving herself in a male-dominated workplace. After she busts a notorious weapons ring, she thinks she'll finally get the respect she deserves. When a photo of her curvy figure in front of the guns goes viral, the media frenzy that follows only makes her the laughing stock of her division. Between unwanted fan mail, a feral cat attack, and the flashing cameras, she almost doesn't notice that someone has been rearranging small items in her house.

Her first suspicions fall on her drop-dead-gorgeous neighbor who regrettably seems to be missing a few screws. But when tragedy strikes next door and her neighbor offers to help her track down the stalker, she discovers a whole new side to him she never expected. As Libby's stalker grows bolder, the pair must work together to catch him before his game of cat and mouse takes a deadly turn.

How is the third standalone book in a high-octane series of psychological suspense thrillers. If you like strong female leads, shocking twists, and a solid serving of romance, then you'll love Megan Mitcham's tale of passion and madness.

Read How to pounce on a fast-paced, fiery thriller!

BOOKS BY
MEGAN MITCHAM

ENEMY MINE

JUSTICE MINE

STRANGER MINE

WARRIOR MINE

DANGER MINE

PRISONER MINE

VERSIONS

VIRTUES

VARIATIONS

NEVER MINE

RELENTLESSLY MINE

FUIOUSLY MINE

CAPTOR MINE

BUREAU SERIES

FOR ALL TO SEE

PAINTED WALLS

STALKER SERIES

WHO

WHY

HOW

ABOUT THE AUTHOR

Megan Mitcham is a USA Today bestselling author who has penned more than 15 sizzling suspense novels. Her work is said to whisk you across the globe, wedge your heart in your throat, make your hands sweat and your skin tingle. Check out Megan's special forces heroes in the Base Branch Series. If you like the darker side of suspense, try her Bureau Series or her Stalker Series. She is a Mississippi native, living and loving it in the natural state.

Megan was born and raised among the live oaks and shrimp boats of the Mississippi Gulf Coast, where her enormous family still calls home. She attended college at the University of Southern Mississippi where she received a bachelor's degree in curriculum, instruction, and special education. For several years Megan worked as a teacher in Mississippi. She married and moved to South Carolina and began working for an international non-profit organization as an instructor and co-director. In 2009 Megan fell in love with books. Until then, books had been a source for research or the topic of tests. But one day she read Mercy by Julie Garwood. And Oh Mercy, she was hooked! For information on new releases and giveaways sign up for her

Readers' Group at **meganmitcham.com!**
Goodreads: **Megan_Mitcham**
Pinterest: **MeganMitcham5**
Website: **www.meganmitcham.com**
Facebook.com / **AuthorMeganMitcham**
Twitter.com / **MeganMMMitcham**